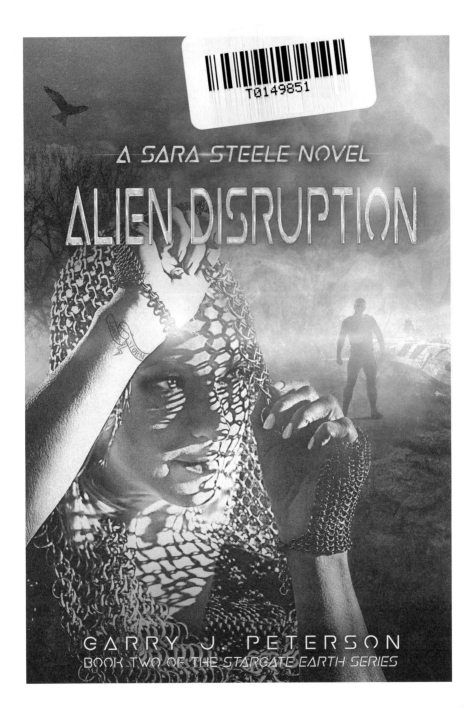

A SARA STEELE NOVEL

ALIEN DISRUPTION

GARRY J. PETERSON

BOOK TWO OF THE *STARGATE EARTH* SERIES

Robert D. Reed Publishers

Robert D. Reed Publishers • Bandon, OR

Robert D. Reed Publishers
P.O. Box 1992
Bandon, OR 97411
Phone: 541-347-9882; Fax: -9883
E-mail: 4bobreed@msn.com
Website: www.rdrpublishers.com

Editor: Cleone Reed
Cover Designer: Pam Cresswell
Book Designer: Amy Cole

Soft Cover: 978-1-944297-56-5
EBook: 978-1-944297-57-2

Library of Congress Control Number: 2020934639

Designed and Formatted in the United States of America

"Humanity is being held captive by a speculative truth...
"We are prisoners of the present, in a perpetual transition from an inaccessible past to an unknown future."

~ Neil de Grasse Tyson

"If you look at Earth from space, you see a dot... a pale blue dot. That's here. That's us. On it everyone you love, everyone you know, everyone you have ever heard of, every human being who ever was, lived out their lives. The aggregate of our joy and suffering, thousands of confident religions, ideologies, and economic doctrines, every hunter and forager, every hero and coward, every creator and destroyer of civilization, every king and peasant, every young couple in love, every mother and father, hopeful child, inventor and explorer, every teacher of morals, every corrupt politician, every 'superstar,' every 'supreme leader,' every saint and sinner in the history of our species lived there – on a mote of dust suspended in a sunbeam.

~ Carl Sagan

DEDICATION

This book is dedicated to the three people who have enabled me to take my writing dreams and turn my energy and creative momentum into reality…

To my dad, Pete, for sharing his views on extraterrestrials, weather phenomenon, and the fourth dimension – time. He also inspired me to become a more curious and observant person.

To my daughter, Sarah, in a reverse mentoring role, for encouraging me to take risks and to seek answers and solutions that are often beyond our typical reach.

To my good friend and mentor, Dr. Harry Bury, for giving me the perseverance and guidance to seek spiritual perspectives for my future "worldview" and inspire others to join me on my journey.

ACKNOWLEDGMENTS

My interest and passion for all things concerning humanity's past, present, and future is grounded in the speculative truth that the past is inaccessible, the present is indeterminable, and the future is simply unknown.

Reading and research are at the heart of my science fiction storylines and plot points, and my own life stories help to frame the generational dynamics within my writing.

The following authors have had a significant impact on my research and writing authenticity:

- David Hatcher Childress, author of *Technology of the Gods*.
- Giorgio A. Tsoukalos, author of *Gods or Ancient Aliens?*
- Eric von Däniken, author of *Chariot of the Gods*.
- Mike Bara, author of *Dark Mission: The Secret History of NASA*.

Many thanks to Mark Terry, writer and author, for his guidance and continued support to enable me to make my dream of an epic science fiction series come true.

Warm and heartfelt thanks to my wonderful publishers, Cleone and Robert D. Reed, for having faith in me and my story and providing the encouragement to stay focused.

To my incredible book cover designer, Pam Cresswell, my sincere gratitude for taking my conceptual cover ideas and transforming them into truly spectacular visuals.

To book designer and formatter, Amy Cole, many thanks for making my book a lovely piece of literature to see and read.

And, to transform warrior princess **Sara Steele** into a beautiful and intimidating heroine, with amazing attire and images to match her beauty and her strength, I am truly grateful and humble for the support of the following artists:

- Design by Kate Knuvelder
- Photography by Christopher Alberto, Dancing Lonewolf Photography
- Videography by Mahmoud Awad Hussein
- Make-up by Claudette Hernandez

INTRODUCTION

The existence of alien life on planet Earth has been discussed and argued for centuries. The ancient alien theory phenomenon is now well established as one of the fiercest debates, and the complex issues of "are there or aren't there… were there or weren't there" cannot be answered in a simple yes or no.

The only real choice we have is to gather the facts and existing evidence and draw our own conclusions. Be it documentation, artifacts, research technology, or mathematical commonality, the number of believers grows as the facts become harder to disprove.

In book one, *SHATTERED TRUTH*, ancient alien hunter Pete Stevenson was the family generational pioneer in the search for the truth that was out there. In what could only be called a "bittersweet" journey, Pete found such evidence, including encounters with friendly temporal aliens, and he paid the ultimate price with his life.

Pete's son Mike was charged with carrying on his dad's mission to distinguish "informed speculation" from "irrefutable fact." After starting out as an unwilling participant in Pete's ancient alien hunting, Mike uncovered many significant facts and hard evidence that changed his thinking from renouncement to acceptance.

Mike's daughter Sara had an intense need to either prove or disprove Grandad Pete's alien theories; and as her vision became clear, she established and directed the Extraterrestrial Research Team, or ETRT, and her similarly-wired associates became our world's best shot at understanding alien presence and even determining planet Earth's survival.

In *SHATTERED TRUTH*, Sara's team was introduced to the same friendly temporal aliens that her grandad had met, but this time the alien encounters prevailed in real life-and-death circumstances. Sara had been given the ultimate gift of alien resources and the penultimate truth that she was Earth's Chosen One.

In book two, *ALIEN DISRUPTION*, Sara Steele becomes the absolute leader of a multi-talented and intensely focused group of determined disruptors—fighting crime, tyranny, secret societies, suppressed technology, climate change, and even evil aliens. Having been physically rebuilt and now possessing superhuman strength, Sara's capabilities are taken to the limit.

The most dynamic storyline in *ALIEN DISRUPTION* becomes the intense, mutually beneficial and effective relationship between Sara and the alien leader, Echo, as well as Sara's strong physical, mental, and emotional bond with alien warrior Pulse.

Humor, storytelling, and the several flawed but well-intentioned characters give the reader a sense that this story is as much about people, family, and what we all struggle with day after day, as it is about science fiction.

As the reader senses an apocalyptic future unfolding, a unified endeavor by humans and temporal aliens advances the prospects of a holistic transformation for the human species and for all of mankind.

The ending of *ALIEN DISRUPTION* will provide a multi-faceted cliff-hanger that will tie books three, four, and five remarkably into the *STARGATE EARTH* series.

EVERY GENERATION HAS A LEGEND...

Sara didn't start out expecting to change the world. She inherited it from her dad and grandad, but she didn't expect it. For much of her early years, Sara thought her family was pretty weird, and there seemed to be plenty of evidence to prove it.

Her late grandfather Pete Stevenson, maybe the weirdest of all, an automotive engineer whose hobby was trying to chase down proof of aliens and time travel all over the world.

Incidents through the years seemed to suggest that Grandad had, indeed, come across evidence that alien presence was real. "Informed speculation" regarding alien presence had now become an "irrefutable fact."

For the longest time Sara didn't think she'd inherited the weirdness gene, *but boy, was she wrong.*

Now, has an actual temporal alien encounter revealed that she is Earth's Chosen One?

1

ALIEN ENCOUNTER OF THE FIFTH KIND

It was December 7, 1972, at the Kennedy Space Center in Florida on historic Pad 39A, where Apollo 17, America's final mission to the Moon, was launched.

The combined spacecraft of Apollo 17, the Command and Service Module America, and the spider-like Lunar Module dubbed Challenger, had smoothly reached lunar orbit. Apollo 17 astronauts George Carter, Robert Kelly, and Garrett Sully were to be the last men to depart low-Earth orbit for the rest of the twentieth century.

On December 11, Lunar Module Pilot Garrett Sully and Commander George Carter landed on the moon's Taurus-Littrow region in the Lunar Module, while Command Module Pilot Robert Kelly remained in lunar orbit.

"Glad you're safely down. Have fun!"

"Thanks, Rob. Take care of 'Mother America' while we're down here."

"Roger that."

Commander Kelly busied himself with duties he had to perform while alone in the command module. He followed his check list religiously as he had practiced hundreds of times.

"Yeah, same-old, same-old boring check list that I've done so often, I can probably do it in reverse," Commander Kelly muttered.

Kelly was also filling out a short betting sheet involving ground personnel who were wagering on several tasks that Carter and Sully were to perform while on the lunar surface.

- Exact time for each of the three EVA's
- Number of words spoken by Garret Sully
- Number of steps taken by George Carter

- Minutes of oxygen remaining at mission end for Carter and Sully
- Number of souvenirs taken by both astronauts
- Farthest distance from Challenger for either men
- Number of times either guy says, "This is great!"
- Number of times either guy says, "Would you look at that?"

It was their little betting secret, and Commander Kelly was more than happy to be the guy checking the boxes.

The Command Module also carried high-tech radar and communications systems along with a biological experiment containing five mice for humanity's last trip to the moon.

The three EVA's, or extravehicular activities, lasted about twenty-two hours. About mid-way during the Lunar Module's journey on the moon's surface, mission control at the KSC contacted Command Module Pilot, Robert Kelly.

"So, Rob, what's it like to be alone up there?"

No response from Commander Kelly. Mission Control repeated their question.

"Rob, come in. How ya doing being all alone up there right now?"

Mission Control was informed that Commander Kelly had inexplicably disconnected his ear piece receiver.

After a fifty-five second pause, the Command Module Pilot responded in an excited voice.

"I'm sorry. I'm back. What did you say?"

"Rob, are you okay?" We just asked you how it was being alone up there right now."

Pausing… "I'm not alone!"

"Excuse me, Rob?"

Commander Kelly replied, "We need to talk… I need to explain something."

Mission Control disconnected with Commander Kelly immediately and used a restricted line to the Command Module.

From the Mission Control's War Room, communication was once again established with Commander Kelly.

A significantly stressed NASA Director of Flight Crew Operations, Chuck Reese, said, "Rob, we are on a secured line. Continue."

Commander Kelly responded, "Well, I was monitoring my lunar orbit, vital signs, and the progress of the LRV when I saw a sight at 0750 and in close proximity to me and the Command Module. Are you still there?"

"Yes, Commander, please continue. Did you say something was in close proximity to you?"

"Ah, yes. There were four spacecrafts flying in formation, the largest one about twice the size of mine, roughly sixty-five to seventy feet in length and twenty-five to thirty feet across. And, it had two decks. They arrived almost effortlessly and then stopped, and there was no evidence of any propulsion whatsoever."

"Did you say four spacecrafts, Rob?"

"Yes. But almost as quickly as they appeared, the three smaller ones left, in formation, leaving me alone with the large craft and in very close range."

Excitedly, Kelly advised, "I shot video and a couple stills."

"Great. Please continue. We're going nuts here, but we are secure."

"This large spacecraft had identification symbols on the side that were not similar to any I have seen at any time by any nation involved in space exploration."

Pausing for a few seconds…

"They resembled ancient glyphic."

"You have pictures; right, Rob?"

"Yes, the starboard-side camera was on the whole time. This craft followed me for four and a half orbits and before disappearing."

"That was it, Rob?"

"No. Just before the spacecraft left, I experienced… like a suspension of time. Everything stopped."

"What do you mean, everything?"

"I mean all time and motion stopped. Completely stopped. I mean everything damn stopped."

Mumbling could be heard from the small group assembled on the ground.

"I immediately had an alien visitor in the module and I have no idea how he got inside."

"He said his Earth name was Pulse, said he was from the future and I should not be frightened."

"My God, Rob, this is unreal!"

Following a short pause, mission control continued.

"Then what?"

"Well, he told me that they were an advanced recon team and that they were interested in our mission, but he didn't say why. He also said something about "the dark side of the Moon," as I recall."

"Describe him," Chuck Reese asked crisply.

"Well, he was big, well over six feet tall, with a helmet that was longer than it was high, and his arms were quite long and his eyes were kind of big. His voice was calm and almost like a whisper."

"Anything else?" Reese was hanging on Kelly's every word.

"Yeah, he had an emblem or patch on his bluish uniform that resembled one of the glyphic that was on the larger craft."

Silence on the ground.

Commander Kelly clutched a small pad where several notes of his were written…Kelly was not going to share those notes with anyone…not yet.

"The alien Pulse said that he had the capability to stop time and that we should be vigilant due to a pending threat from our solar system."

"Did he give you any specific details?"

"Not that I recall. But he also said he had the capability to erase my short-term memory."

"And then what?"

"He held a short, black wand up to my face…called it a…'radio hypnotic intra-cerebral control' device, I think."

Rob paused. "He said it would electronically dissolve my memory!"

Rob lowered his voice and said, "He hit a strobe-like light into my eyes with a very fine bluish mist and was gone?"

"But Rob, you remembered."

"Yep. I guess it didn't work for some reason."

Gathering his thoughts, Kelly quipped, "He must've been on an alien government contract!"

Surprised by Kelly's humor at such a game-changing time, and life-changing experience, mission control responded.

"But you still have the video and stills, right?"

"Hold on. Let me check."

Kelly was gone for about two minutes.

Back on the call, but with a heavy sigh, he spoke.

"Negative. All wiped clean. All gone."

"No proof, then, Ron?"

"No."

Kelly felt he had to interject one positive comment. He wasn't planning to share this info with Mission Control just yet, but now felt he had to divulge a major reveal from the alien for his own credibility.

"I now recall that the alien Pulse mentioned that the 'dark side of the Moon' was where the other three spacecrafts had gone. He said they have a base there, and since that side of the Moon is never seen from Earth, their base is undetectable."

As Chuck Reese gathered his thoughts, one of his staff members voiced his opinion.

"Chuck, this is all bullshit...pure bullshit. And joking about government contracts...give me a break."

Most of the small group seemed to nod in agreement, when Commander Kelly returned a few minutes later.

"Chuck, you there?"

"Yes, Ron, we're all still here trying to understand what happened. Too bad there isn't any evidence of your alien intruder."

"Well, there is. I think I know why he came aboard."

"What do you mean, Ron?"

"The five mice are gone!"

2

SARA RECALLS ALIEN ENCOUNTER OF THE THIRD KIND

As Scott's plane carried the Extraterrestrial Research Team to their meeting with Congress, Team Leader Sara Steele gathered her colleagues together for a short briefing.

Along with Sara, the Managing Director of the ETRT, was her CEO Scott Woods, her trusted astrophysicist and best friend Michaela, and her meta-human companion, Elonis.

Also, along with this extraterrestrial research team, was the Vice President of the United States, Samantha Worthington, a retired NASA astronaut and the record holder for the longest female spacewalk.

Sara, now in her mid-twenties, knew that there was considerable apprehension and anxiety amongst the team members, as they had all invested heart and soul into proving the presence of extraterrestrials on Earth.

"All right guys, most of our team has been together for over two years, and this meeting with Congress will be the stage we need to gain acceptance and credibility for all our hard work and my grandad's sacrifice."

Scott chimed in, "It's too bad we couldn't have brought more of the team with us, but let's hope that this won't be a 'one-and-done' meeting."

Sara advised, "We will be landing soon and, due to the tight security at Reagan International Airport, Vice President Worthington and I will depart first. Any questions right now for the VP?"

Michaela, the esteemed scientist and Sara's second in command, asked, "Will we have a liaison to help us prepare for the joint sessions of Congress presentation? Revealing our team's alien findings is very much our research capital, and we need to protect our data completely."

"Understand, Michaela. I will personally get with my aide to set up your material."

"Thank you, Samantha."

Sara next spoke to her meta-human colleague and long-time friend, Elonis.

"Elonis, I know you have tonight's alien encounter on your video scan, and I know that they had you erase everyone's short-term memory of the incident but mine. Is that correct?"

"Yes, Sara, that is correct."

"Come with me to the back of the plane. I want to see that video on my hand-held before we land."

"Of course, Sara."

Sara and Elonis walked back to a couch that was unoccupied, and Elonis opened her video scan and set it up at the precise time that the aliens took control of their plane earlier that evening in route to Washington. They watched the recorded video together.

Sara can be heard saying, "Guys, are you seeing this?"

The passengers moved to a vantage point at a window, and it appeared that they had landed on a large metal landing pad, the size of a football field.

Ken, the pilot noted, "The door is opening. Grab onto something. I don't know what's happening."

Then a tall human-like but distinctly different form entered the plane's galley door, and she said her name was Echo and she would not harm them. She said in a soft voice, "We are your friends, please come with me."

Everyone walked off the plane to a very large metal pad, and they were all now on what appeared to be an extremely large aircraft that was a small city in size. There were compartments housing small spacecrafts, hangers that had two-man capsules, and robots doing various tasks unmoved by the plane's passengers. It was obvious that they were on alien spacecraft.

There was another alien called Pulse. Behind Echo and Pulse were several similarly dressed aliens, most with bluish uniforms, and none with weapons. The aliens were tall with elongated skulls and longer than normal limbs. Their eyes were large and their ears were very small and they did not resemble today's humans. The alien leader called Echo spoke:

"We are from another universe...another galaxy...and another time, and have been on this earth in some form for thousands of years. Our major colonies today lie

in what you refer to as the Trappist-1 System, where seven planets exist. We began as observers, and throughout your history we have tried to help mankind many times to ensure that this planet will survive. We would have preferred to remain behind the scenes, as we have been for ages. The ultimate survival of this planet brought us to this day and time."

Taking off her suit jacket, and checking to see that no one was watching, Sara was now remembering this encounter vividly as Elonis's video continued.

The alien leader said, "My Earth name is Echo and that name describes my skill as listening. I am commander of this craft and the alien leader. Pulse is second in command and his skill is communication."

Echo continued.

"We intercepted your craft because it had been taken over by people who were trying to eliminate your presence at your nation's capital. Those who took control of your craft believed that within your presentation, you would reveal that they were the criminals, responsible for many terrorist attacks on Earth over several years. Once they had control of your craft, they set a course to crash at your White House and blame your team for terrorism."

Echo further explained.

"We have the capability to stop time and can eliminate short-term memory. As far as the people witnessing the unexplained event of your disappearance, it will simply fall within the scope of your government cover-ups, which have existed for many years."

The next words from Echo were shocking for Sara to hear again.

"Sara, your grandfather, Pete Stevenson, was our chosen one. Now that he is gone, you must carry on his work."

Sara was seen to be stunned.

"You are aboard a craft in the city in which we live and work, cloaked from any detection and always well beyond your solar system."

Again, seeing the video, Sara was understanding the magnitude of this encounter.

"We must leave you now as we have many other planets, with cultures and societies in need, in other galaxies in our universe. As difficult as this may be for you to understand, we are humans from the very distant future."

Echo paused.

"We are you, with evolution that takes millions of years. We have God in our hearts and minds, and share your spiritual values. It is true to say that we are likely closer to God than you, not physically, but spiritually."

As Echo concluded her very brief explanation, two other figures came forward. One was Elonis and the other was an alien.

"Hello. My name is Laser and I am the one who sees…who observes. With me is your friend Elonis, who is also our friend. She will assist me with clearing your memories and restoring your world to the time before the incident and allowing you to safely proceed to your destination."

Laser telepathically reached Elonis.

Sara stopped the recording and asked Elonis, "What did he say for you to do?"

He said, "Clear everyone but Sara. She is now our chosen one."

Sara watched as Pulse stepped over to her and took her hand. She remembered his clear telepathic thought to her. "You are the Aras, our name for warrior."

Pulse released Sara's hand and took Elonis's hand. He looked into her eyes and moments later Elonis nodded in approval.

"Elonis, what did he communicate to you just now?"

"He simply said to watch over you."

What Elonis failed to mention to Sara was that Pulse told her that she could contact him in the future, but that was not to be told to Sara.

Finally, Elonis concluded the video re-play.

The passengers and crew return to the plane. Elonis held a black wand in their faces and one-by-one sprayed a fine mist into their eyes with a strobe light emitting a bluish haze. Sara did not receive the mist. When they woke from a deep trance, all was like before. For everyone else, nothing out of the ordinary took place.

Sara now realized what that alien encounter had provided.

In an instant, her alien worldview had flipped…

"Informed speculation" regarding alien presence has now become "irrefutable fact."

3

SARA
THE UNEXPLAINABLE

The plane carrying Sara and the ETRT landed normally at Reagan International Airport, and the team was relaxed and ready to begin their much-anticipated day.

However, they were met by military personnel, several with weapons drawn. The "normal" landing was not followed by a "normal" reception.

As they departed the plane, senior politicians and officials from the NSA greeted Sara and VP Worthington.

Sara's first thought was, "How the hell am I going to explain that time slip? There's gonna be a ton of questions."

Given that Sara's plane was totally off the radar for nearly fifteen minutes, there was a sense of panic on the ground from everyone that met the plane, and their highly stressed nature was noticeable.

The NSA's control center commander immediately expressed his concern to VP Worthington.

"What happened up there? Where did you go and why were you not responding to our contacts? Where the hell is your pilot?"

"Commander Moore, I'm sorry," VP Worthington said, "but I don't know what you are talking about. All went well with our flight. I am confused."

Knowing exactly what Commander Moore was referring to, Sara responded, "Perhaps we can move inside and discuss this situation. Obviously, we have a disconnect."

"Sure, young lady. That would be fine."

"Young lady? Bullshit," Sara hissed. "If only they knew…"

As Sara's team moved inside, she asked each person what, if anything, they'd recalled.

One by one, no one remembered anything but a normal flight to D.C.

Michaela was a little fuzzy and spoke to Sara in an inquisitive manner.

"I felt a time lapse that was odd. Did you?"

Sara answered, "No. What do you mean?"

"Sara, I'm a person that has total control of my own mind and body, and it felt as though I was napping for a moment. Just weird."

"Yep." Sara nodded. "Just weird."

A profusely sweating and pudgy Commander Moore, assuming that VP Worthington was the person in charge, asked the question of the moment.

"Vice President Worthington, we lost all radar contact and all visual contact with your aircraft for fourteen minutes, per my staff. One minute you were there and the next minute you were gone."

"I understand what you're saying, Commander, but I'm afraid I can't offer any explanation."

The VP paused a moment and added, "You'll have to wait until your data analysts and technical people look at likely causes."

"Dammit, you just freaking disappeared!" yelled an agitated Commander Moore.

The VP concluded, "We will get an explanation."

Sara observed their conversation but remained quiet.

As she made eye contact with Michaela, who was obviously processing, Sara had one overwhelming thought.

"I need to tell Michaela the truth…what really happened, but not now."

4

SARA
CONGRESSIONAL
REVEAL

With the explanation of the plane's extraordinary event tabled for now, Sara, Scott, Michaela, and Elonis moved to the presentation to Congress on Capitol Hill. This was to be a joint session involving the committees overseeing national and homeland security as well as science and technology.

Sara was dressed in a striking blue blazer and pants, and oddly, the exact same color and shade worn by Echo in their one meeting during the encounter. Sara had enthusiastically shopped for this outfit for this occasion and was feeling awe-struck by the Echo encounter, yet relaxed about their mission today with Congress.

As the large room was filling with Congressmen, two members had a short and whisper-soft discussion. A tall, nicely dressed man in a typical blue suit and red tie spoke.

"It looks like these millennial misfits have some info that could present a problem."

The other man, with light hair and a tan sport coat, responded immediately with a smirk. "I know what we need to do and we'll do it. Follow my lead and this will go away as quickly as these idiots have gotten here."

Both men were super busy on their cell phones and were still texting as the meeting was called to order.

The joint Congressional meeting began with Jim Arnold, the Chairman of Senate Intelligence Committee and the ad hoc speaker for today's joint session, introducing the ETRT and Sara Steele as their director.

Sara then introduced the members of her team and their respective roles.

"Thank you for this opportunity to address Congress."

Mild applause was heard.

"With me today is Scott Woods, our CEO, who works in an advisory capacity with us and handles our finance issues."

Very professionally dressed in a dark suit, Scott raised his hand.

"Michaela Marx is a PhD in astrophysics and the top researcher on our team."

Michaela just smiled. It was obvious that Michaela looked more like a top runway model than an accomplished scientist. And when she spoke, she always owned the room.

"Our extremely valuable analytic asset is Elonis, who has computational and simulation capabilities that are off the chart."

Elonis was slightly surprised that Sara did not refer to her as a Meta.

Sara projected onto the screen her agenda for the session, titled "THE REVEAL."

The ETRT expected the presentation to take about four hours, with questions from the Congressional committee attendees.

It was only now that the two whispering congressmen took their seats.

Elonis laid out several alien artifacts on a display table that was unmarked. Several Congressmen took notice.

Alien artifacts included:

- *The two-thousand-year old carved Saqqara Bird, resembling today's modern aircraft.*
- *One of the elongated skulls that the ETRT possessed.*
- *Dropa Stones, twelve-thousand-year-old discs depicting alien crash landings.*
- *The Antikythera Device, thought to be mankind's first computer and nearly 150 years old.*

Sara then presented the ETRT's alien presence case with a very well-organized agenda.

"Again, thank you for this opportunity. On behalf of the Extraterrestrial Research Team, or ETRT, I now give you our REVEAL. "Today, I will present in short, high-level topical points, with the understanding that all supporting documentation and detail is here as well. If you have questions, please write them down and we will answer all questions at the end."

Michaela smiled and Scott gave Sara a "thumbs up" as Sara began.

"In a sense, I am going to start from the end…Mars and the alien implication.

"The most significant and certainly the most arguable documentation deals with an actual alien encounter between Pete Stevenson and an alien recon group, according to extensive notes and photos thereof, that took place in Trelleborg, Sweden, in February, 2018."

Pausing for a moment, Sara continued.

"The photos are of particular interest, as you will see, and so far, we have not been able to prove that they are not authentic. Again, I am getting ahead of myself, but I am extremely anxious for you to see what we have found.

"I would like to start by focusing on a Mars aspect that was the number-one discovery of one of our team member's research.

"The Mars Opportunity rover that landed on the Moon in 2004 was meant to have a three-month site lifespan, and it had fifteen years of data gathering.

"What we were able to extract was that, in addition to other Martian features, Opportunity mapped out a twenty-square-mile area that was the exact mirror image of the great Egyptian pyramids and the incredible Sphynx.

"The pyramid site in Egypt was an exact replica of what was likely the original site on Mars, only somewhat hidden by sandstorms on Mars over time.

"And the power that drove the rover all those years was made from planet rotational energy from the same basic technical argument of inventor and engineer Nikola Tesla back in the early 1900's."

One member of the audience started to ask a question, but then put his hand down.

"To make this info even more unbelievable, Pete Stevenson had pictures that were taken from space, exact time unknown, and they showed the Mars pyramid site in vivid detail with no sand to cover the diagrams whatsoever, and no lab could disprove their authenticity."

Senator Griffey scowled, "Excuse me Miss Steele, but photographs can be fabricated, and although no one could disprove their authenticity, it is still a stretch. And, just because Mr. Stevenson had them doesn't mean he took them."

Sara was getting a bit annoyed as the Senator continued.

"And, how do you know it was Mars? Were there road signs?"

Laughter broke out and Sara had some immediate re-thinking to do.

Scott dropped his head as he recalled that he had made that same joke during an ETRT review meeting on his yacht, the *Stargaze*.

"The photos have not been discredited, so we are going with them for now. Pete Stevenson said he took them; and if someone gave them to him, he would have no reason to lie about it. It did follow his convictions."

Senator Griffey shrugged, "How do we know the pictures were of Mars and not the Moon or Arizona?"

Michaela interjected her explanation, "We did some incredibly detailed timeline mapping and using the approximate time of the photos, the constellations were aligned in the photographs exactly to the Mars photo origins."

As everyone seemed to accept Michaela's perspective, they all looked at the rendering that Sara provided, and she continued.

"There is one simpler, yet awesome note from Mr. Stevenson's alleged meeting with the aliens in Sweden.

"He has a very succinct comment that an early alien civilization had lived and thrived on Mars and more evidence would be found.

"And," Sara paused, "his comment was not in the form of a question, but a statement."

✦ ✦ ✦

Continuing the presentation, Sara moved to UFO's.

"We collected a series of photos, documents, and interviews with people around the world that saw, photographed, and documented UFO sightings. We also found that flight patterns of these UFO's followed the exact same basic aerial routes around the world…always…every time.

"This could not be coincidence. We also have several pieces of documentation from two foreign astronauts that had pictures, sketches, and incidents that collaborate this info. Apparently, Pete Stevenson met with these two astronauts, and they felt comfortable with this info to put it into his hands."

Not much engagement from the Congressmen.

"We found many instances of stone etching throughout time that alluded to one almighty God, referred to as Anunnaki, replacing many heavenly gods that were considered the many spiritual rulers of the time. And this God was depicted as having human looks and actions.

"Pete Stevenson's notes even named the god-like visitors that helped ancient civilizations build monuments and teach skills that are a stretch even in today's civilizations. Each so-called teacher was specified by name throughout the last 10,000 years of Earth's many civilizations.

"If you take this theory to full potential, it explains exactly why all of this building, along with basic civilization development, regardless of which continent that it occurred, was identical."

Sara took in a big sigh before moving on to a related UFO issue.

"We have become intrigued with the so-called Nazca Lines in Peru, and our research came up with verifiable evidence that these landing strips were found in many parts of the world, designed and built in identical fashion per my last info, and on the same flight lines that UFO's were seen.

"These undeniable lines are in geometric patterns, often many thousands of feet long, and are in perfect alignment. Even intersections of lines, based on the configuration, are all at exactly forty-five-degree or ninety-degree angles.

"We also found verifiable evidence of well-detailed carvings of what appeared to be huge stone sentinels located at every site to help incoming aircraft or space-ships land."

Referring to her slides, Sara was now feeling more confident.

"And, while doing the research on these lines we have gathered several elon-gated skulls that are not even close to what you would see today in tribal rituals. Again, these elongated skulls were found in nine different locations around the world, all locations traceable from Mr. Stevenson's notes."

She showed a slide depicting the skulls along with the locations of the finds.

"We have brought one of those skulls and it is on the artifact display table."

✦ ✦ ✦

Pausing for a sip of water, Sara moved on with her agenda.

"We used Pete Stevenson's coordinate data, and worked with Michaela's team as well, to establish a likely World Grid that seemed to have a purposeful alien strategy.

"This strategy, when executed, precisely aligned major monuments with true north; and from the six pyramids of the Pyramid Giza Complex, it was consid-ered at one time to be the center of all landmasses of Earth, and all documented flight patterns would use it.

"This is unmistakable, and literally impossible for a multitude of cultures to coordinate over all of that space and time. After all, they didn't have social media at that time."

Some much needed, in Sara's opinion, and noticeable laughter was heard.

"We were also able to verify, translating several languages with Stevenson's code, that one common mathematical formula was used throughout time for navigation, geometric calculations, and even the value of Pi. Again, just one!

"What we found was that Einstein's Unified Theory was actually discovered thousands of years earlier!

"We all have heard the phrase, 'there are many ways to solve a problem, but just pick one and go.' Well, maybe that isn't a phrase, but you get the idea."

Apparently, the audience did not get the idea…it was way over their collective heads, as Sara realized.

"Every civilization back to the beginning of time, could not come up with one way of doing anything. This data says that they all had one way of doing everything. Oh, except for the Mayans, but I will get into that later."

✦ ✦ ✦

Gazing over a rather underwhelmed audience, Sara nevertheless, continued.

"We have established that certain monuments were consistently used for navigation and pyramids were used for aircraft refueling, given the intricate nature of the insides of these huge structures.

"Massive cargo had to be moved and hauled, and that was depicted in etchings at or near these navigation sites.

"In fact, the great pyramids in Egypt and elsewhere were using levitation, according to several of our unnamed sources, to move the megaliths into their final shapes. Again, wall carvings described this in detail in many locations, per Pete's team's outstanding compass work."

Congressman Morgenstern chimed in. "Miss Steele, you said massive cargo had to be moved and hauled and they used levitation. Isn't that an oxymoron? They could levitate pyramids but they had to haul their cargo."

"I see your point. We have seen quite a mix of levitation and anti-gravity incidents and need to work on specifics some more. Geez, we weren't there at the time."

Finally, some general laughter was heard.

At that comment, the Chairman of the Congressional session spoke.

"Let's take a thirty-minute work and comfort break. Looks like some coffee and donuts are here."

Sara was wondering if their REVEAL was experiencing a MELTDOWN.

5

SARA REVEAL SUPPRESSED?

Sara was feeling emotions running from satisfied to concerned, knowing that she was presenting well, but not getting much engagement from the Congressmen.

She used the mid-morning break to pull the team together for a quick debrief.

"Well, what do you think?"

Scott muttered, "I am afraid you and much of your subject matter are flying way over their heads."

"Or their interest level," Michaela hissed.

A frowning Scott winked, "Don't suppose you could 'dumb it down' a bit?"

"Hell no, Scott. Maybe those politicians should focus on raising their game!"

Sara's wheels were spinning, but she knew she would need to stay calm and press on regardless.

With the chamber now back, Sara continued with a renewed commitment. "Back to my agenda, I will continue with the topical slide shown on your screens now.

"We have taken the coding documents that Pete Stevenson had prepared, and basically confirmed that a center core of all things done on this planet over thousands of years was basically a blueprint adjusted to fit the cultures, times, and languages of each civilization.

"In other words, we found that the same set of directions, or lesson plans, could be found and overlapped precisely, culture to culture.

"Pete's team had discovered this incredible evidence initially, and we were lucky enough to connect the dots. We simply confirmed the results by starting with Pete's conclusion and working backward, as several of us now do.

"This path led us to the Stargate theories. The Stargate theories are fascinating and focus on Einstein's Theory of Relativity and his belief in cosmic wormholes and a way for humans to travel from star to star like the ancient aliens.

"Before you say this cannot be verified with today's evidence, let me simply say… You are right; it could not, until now."

Sara flipped a gaze toward Michaela, who was smiling.

"Pete's encounter in Sweden resulted in a strong argument that the Orion Belt was the birthplace of all stars in the galaxy. And as remarkable as it is puzzling, Pete had close-up pictures of a massive star formation fifteen hundred light years from Earth, showing more than three thousand stars in some form of star-life.

"And, he was in Sweden for three days in 2018, not nearly enough time to travel fifteen hundred light years and return!"

The audience didn't, or couldn't, appreciate the humor.

"If you have subject matter experts look at the photographs, they will tell you that they were made by a large stationary craft with Hubble-Telescope-plus capabilities."

Sara paused to verify her slides.

"Back to the actual results, we have discovered physical evidence of complex calculations and extraordinary craftwork and stonemasonry cut into huge stone tablets, from Puma Punku in the Bolivian Andes.

"The depictions vary from others in that they are mostly temple oriented. Faces, lineage, recreation, and huge carved stones represent the books in today's public libraries.

"Three things jump out at you here.

"One, these epic monuments were built at an elevation of twelve thousand eight hundred feet. How in the world did they get there?

"Two, the very odd fact here was that these stone reminders of a distant past were very distant; likely fourteen thousand years ago.

"And three, there was an effort at some point in time to destroy all that is there right now."

Sara was now getting as animated and excited as ever; the audience… not so much.

"And now for the best part. The lost Mayan Civilization is, and was, one of history's greatest mysteries. Such an advanced culture accomplishing extraordinary feats, leaving many to wonder why, how, and when. What happened to the Mayans?

"According to Pete Stevenson's alien encounter, the Mayan's were placed here from the Seven Sisters open star cluster, some four hundred fifty light years away, to help advance Earth's civilizations.

"When, for many reasons, that helpful advancement did not occur, the Mayans were relocated to that star system, which had evolved more quickly than our planet at the time of the Mayans.

"Although many of Earth's civilizations have vanished with no plausible explanation, the Mayans were different, special, and extremely advanced."

The meeting room got quiet. Even the more talkative Congressmen were speechless.

Sara added a troubling interpretation…

"If an advanced alien culture determined that the population of an unstable and dysfunctional Earth was beyond help, could that culture simply relocate us elsewhere?"

✦ ✦ ✦

Sara gave the audience a minute to digest her words, took a sip of water, and continued.

"With our many documented findings in several European cities in general and churches specifically, it is more than ninety per cent likely that alien spaceships visited Earth often. The term Vimana was frequently used by many cultures to describe huge flying fortresses, and that was well documented.

"What Pete and his team found were ships that were almost identical to early Russian and American space capsules, and the largest was called the Rukma Vimana."

Sara showed a series of depictions.

"However, they appeared armed with missiles, indicating war-like ships as Stevenson surmised. He strongly believed that evil aliens existed, and may be among us today. But he also believed that alien wars had been fought on planet Earth, and other planets as well, for centuries."

Pete's depiction of Rukma Vimana was shown.

"With many references to various etchings throughout the world of humanlike astronauts or spacemen, they always seem to be signaling in their depictions. This consistent and entirely identical form that these etchings take cannot be coincidental.

"Also, you can see many examples of what we would describe as fully functional space suits and breathing apparatus. Even aircraft or spaceship controls, not dissimilar to today's equipment, are well described."

Pete's depiction of an alien spaceman was shown.

As Sara concluded that portion of the presentation, she noted that a couple members of Congress had started to pay attention.

Sara sensed a brief opportunity to keep her momentum going.

"Our team took on the huge evidence pool of ancient hieroglyphics. Archeologists and geologists for centuries have analyzed hieroglyphics and symbols. What Pete's study concluded was, again, pure consistency and message-to-message commonality.

"Every one of the many languages came to the same conclusion, and that was sky people came from above in fiery machines, and they brought knowledge and technology to build, inform, teach, and then left.

"Today, we have brought an ancient wooded carved bird, which was found in one of the oldest of Egypt's ninety-seven pyramids. It is a carved bird, but an aerodynamics expert built a scale model of this bird, which actually resembled one of today's airplanes, and it flew.

"It was a highly developed glider designed in ancient Egypt. We verified this data with current subject matter experts, who agreed that such an aircraft today could not only glide, but also be propelled via engines to fly safely and effectively."

The picture of the bird-glider was shown.

✦ ✦ ✦

Sara paused as a round of refreshments was being given row-by-row to the attendees.

"In keeping with the space craft and ancient alien astronaut theory going factual, I will continue with items and images that I'm sure you will find compelling.

"The one piece that is most interesting and most germane today comes from Mexico and a funeral monument of a Mayan leader.

"His chamber, photographed in great detail by one of Pete's colleagues, shows a person looking very much like our present astronauts, in a spacecraft looking very much like our current space crafts, in a suit looking very much like our current flight suits, at the controls of what looks like space capsule controls.

"The depictions do show, however, and we have seen these before, persons with elongated skulls, large eyes, smaller ears, and somewhat longer extremities."

Pete's pictures of the spaceships and the astronauts were shown.

"And, abductions have always been at the forefront of alien talk. But Pete Stevenson had first-hand experience, having witnessed one himself.

"We did facial recognition of the presumed dead crew of the sunken Sailing Vessel L'Enleve, lost in 1998 after a long fight with massive Hurricane Martin.

"We have concluded that the crew members found on Jost Van Dyke in the British Virgin Islands years later were, in fact, the crew that perished when it sank. This incredible survivor story was an incredible true event. According to Pete's data, they all vividly remember being abducted and saved by friendly aliens."

Sara could sense that her audience was not buying what she was now selling.

"Switching gears, the mention over the years of a variety of UFO's flying in known flight paths over recognized markers at breakneck speeds is not news.

"What is news is that we have approximately seventeen hundred photos in our possession, thanks to Pete's team and their work. We also have actual interviews from credible witnesses that have seen UFOs in flight while these witnesses were engaged in flight, both in commercial aircraft and space stations."

Some of Pete's photos were shown.

"And, as what was brought up before, our team has investigated levitation.

"We were all fascinated by how our ancestors, given the tools and knowledge of their time, could move megaton stones and monuments, not only within a location, but transported to a location from hundreds of miles away.

"From a multitude of languages over time, and from a variety of sources, the constant mention of stones walking or stones flying or stones disappearing and reappearing, was Pete's conclusion that levitation, also part of the abduction process, was the only explanation. The legendary walking statues of Easter Island give you chills."

Sara showed the various stones.

"Our team feels strongly that aliens of the future have mastered the art of breaking down matter and then re-connecting it, which could explain levitation, moving inanimate objects, and even time travel."

Pictures of Stonehenge, Easter Island, and other locations, were shown.

✦ ✦ ✦

"I am going to begin my agenda summary with an information blast. Several topics, both connected and stand alone, need to be recognized.

"Our deep dive into the Sumerians, the first Mesopotamian civilization, was a culture that produced a plethora of dots to connect, and we tried to do just that.

"Sumerians, dating back to four thousand BCE, invented the wheel and were well known for their incredible metalwork, levees, and irrigation systems.

"Many researchers and scientists believe that the ancient Sumerians were extraterrestrials that originally arrived on Earth some four hundred fifty thousand years ago. And, it was their belief that the Anunnaki, their ancient extraterrestrial gods, gave rise to the technological culture that defined civilizations ever since.

"The reason we bring this up is that we have stumbled across some linkage to our present-day DNA anomalies to ancient Sumerian scientists and their attempt of genetic engineering. Crazy, yes, but each day results in more defining evidence.

"We are all still star struck with the Stargate mythology and the Orion constellation. It is our belief that Sirius, the brightest star in the night sky within the Orion constellation, is the key to time travel and the ability to navigate through the gateways of time and space.

"There is little doubt that the stars and the constellations were the navigational maps that the aliens used, both for travel and for the building of civilizations. We have reams of documentation that we can show you."

✦ ✦ ✦

"In closing, I have reached a point where I am both excited and drained. We have been on an incredible journey for these past two years and couldn't wait to share our findings with you. What follows is, in our opinion, absolutely amazing.

"In the middle of my grandfather's diary is a sketch, a very detailed sketch. It depicts a massive orbital structure home of the aliens meeting Pete, cloaked to avoid detection, and of the appearance and size of a major American city."

Sara showed the audience Pete's awesome rendering.

"According to his notes, Pete says that this orbiting space structure is as enormous as anything he has ever seen on Earth, and he could actually see Earth from his position on this craft."

Puzzlement and a mixed-bag of alien relevance head-scratching was noticeable from the Congressmen.

"On the last page of Pete's dairy of the three days spent with the aliens in Trelleborg, in February of 2018, several things appear via his usual and brilliant code. He said that a strange comment that the aliens made had nothing to do with their show and tell; that was that the end of the beginning is near."

Sara offered, "That's is as big a 'big picture' that you could have.

"He also documented that we should fear Artificial Intelligence as our biggest threat and that A.I and ethics would one day do battle.

"He mentioned that solar and wind power were the keys for the future and not to rely on oil, gas, and coal."

Sara had everyone's attention, but she couldn't tell if it was because of the subject matter or that she was wrapping up her presentation.

"Let me conclude with this one gift from those aliens. They gave Pete Stevenson the exact date, place, and time of every major global calamity that the world would face for ten years through 2028, from their meeting in 2018.

"As far as we know, it was Pete Stevenson's intention to somehow divulge this during a Paris meeting later that year, but he was murdered before he could do that."

Scott quickly interjected, "This info was given to President Sullivan as soon as we obtained it. So, POTUS is aware of these prognostications."

Sara thought that now…finally… again…

"This is the irrefutable evidence that aliens from the future were here!"

6

SARA CONGRESSIONAL PUSHBACK

Sara was feeling much more confident as she wrapped up her presentation. "Thank you for your time. We would like to hear any questions that you may have."

After allowing about thirty seconds for responses, Sara and her team were not asked a single relevant question from the large group of assembled Congressmen.

The booming presentation that the ETRT had fully expected... became a bust, and Sara became quiet. The members of her team were stunned by the apathy shown.

With only a couple gratuitous remarks and very little engagement from the predominantly older and white male assembly, Sara gave the entire presentation in less than two hours.

Even when asked for summary questions by the speaker of the joint committees, it took some political prodding from the speaker to get much of a response at all.

Takeaways from the major issues of alien and weather phenomenon were mostly lukewarm and non-committal. Members of Congress were as much entertained by the few physical artifacts that the ETRT displayed as the actual material presented.

"Gee whiz, look at this," was heard from a couple attendees.

"Can I touch one of 'em?" was also noted.

The general material was so arcane, it felt to the ETRT that they were dealing with a totally disinterested, or ill-prepared audience.

As the rotating questions slowly and methodically continued, one particular Congressman in the front row was silent, as if waiting for the last word. Sans jacket and with arms folded, he was not at all engaged or interested in the team's presentation.

He was the man with the sport coat seen talking with the tall man as the meeting was about to start.

Finally, as the round of questions was concluding, the speaker acknowledged him and he spoke quickly and assertively.

"So, Miss Steele, what you and your team are saying is this…"

He was mumbling somewhat incoherently and rapidly going through his notes.

"What you and your team are saying is that the bulk of your so-called evidence comes from a relative of yours, who had spent significant time in alcohol rehab, was being monitored by the FBI for terrorist implications, and swore up and down that he had conversations with aliens from the future."

With an impatient sigh, Sara responded, "No, that is not accurate."

"I'm sorry, young lady, but it is. I have a sealed document to prove it. You are wasting valuable tax payers' dollars with this foolishness."

As Sara attempted to gather her thoughts, another loud and disturbing comment came from an older member of the powerful House Committee on Science, Space, and Technology.

"How ridiculous of you to think that aliens who have mastered interstellar travel across the galaxy would give a shit about measly little humans on earth."

With that sarcastic and blunt statement, the majority of the Congressman began to gather their personal items.

As Sara looked on in disbelief, most in the chambers got up and left.

Although two members of Homeland Security were obviously most interested in the ETRT's findings and left their contact info with Scott, the summary by the Speakers of both the Senate and House of Representatives was to come back with stronger evidence.

Scott took notes regarding the half a dozen possible carry-forward issues that came from the committee chairman's closing statement.

Sara was fuming…so angry, but needing to keep her composure.

More than anything, Sara wanted to go back and retrieve those black wands with the memory erasers so she would have her evidence!

7

STRATEGY
GOING FORWARD

The discussion on the plane headed back to the team's base in Palo Alto was subdued and quiet. Sara had expected a serious push-back, but what occurred was far worse than she had imagined.

"Sara, are you okay?"

"Yeah, Scott. Just re-thinking stuff right now."

The meeting with Congress was not even in her mind at this time…only the alien encounter, and that was not something she could share…at least not yet.

Scott put the meeting in perspective by focusing on next steps for the team.

Removing his suit coat and loosening his tie, he teed-up his remarks by reiterating the consensus of Congress that the ETRT had come up with several conclusions, ranging from the weak and unsubstantiated to just plain alien conspiracy theory.

"The only recourse we have right now is to do an even deeper dive into the roughly six areas that I have notes on that are components and causal indices of the global problems that we are experiencing."

"For now, the alien issues need to be tabled. We need to establish credibility and show a lack of bias toward our core beliefs."

The determined and focused Scott had everyone's attention.

"The first one is global warming. It's such a polarizing issue, we need to get as many facts as we can and keep conclusions to only the opinion of 'subject-matter experts' and scientists in their respective fields."

A somewhat angry Michaela added, "Yes, we need to look hard at probabilities and predictions. We will get them indisputable facts. I am now seriously challenged and I can see I have my work cut out."

"Yes, Michaela. The second one, and likely the biggest threat right now, is terrorism and it's way out of our core strengths and resource pool, but important.

Not sure how to handle this right now, so we as a team need to confer. Likely that we leave this issue for the experts."

Scott got zero pushback from any team members on that one.

Scott uttered, "The evil alien issue is so nebulous that it almost gets the axe, but not quite yet."

Sara quipped, "My grandad had some strong beliefs here, and in my opinion, they need to be followed up with a much greater investigation than Pete Stevenson could have done."

"I agree, Sara. We also have the possible involvement or cover-up of our own military and government; and even if we did not bring these issues up, everyone on this plane knows that these threats are real and need to be looked into."

A member of the ETRT, but not one of today's presenters, Kat interjected her feelings strongly.

"Who's to say there weren't some bad guys right there in that Congressional meeting?"

"Kat, I couldn't agree more," snapped Sara, "but we need to get back to our fact-based activities."

Taking a moment of pause to think, Scott continued.

"This whole idea from Pete Stevenson that a global anarchy alliance or cadre of secret societies was at the core of the world's problems isn't an opinion that we can ignore."

Scott could see that Sara's wheels were turning. He recalled from an earlier conversation that she had blown off the possibility of secret societies and the amassed data of same, but now they both knew it was back on their short list.

Scott continued. "It may be difficult to prove, but I believe we need to keep this one on our radar screen, at least for now."

Sara agreed. "I'll just be the driver to try to keep the alien research momentum going for now. Their zero-interest perception is now my mission."

Scott smiled approvingly as he listened to Sara's statement.

"It is becoming obvious that most of these serious global issues are way over the heads and capabilities of the ETRT. But…"

"But what, Scott?"

"As I read notes in one of your grandfather's log books…"

The gaze of each ETRT member focused on Scott.

"Extraordinary claims require extraordinary evidence."

8

SARA
REVEAL VERSUS
REALITY

A day after returning home, Sara gave Kat and Michaela a call to meet that afternoon. As they approached Sara's office, they saw Sara was already working hard on one of her whiteboards.

"Can I get you guys something to drink? You know, soft drinks or tea."

Pulling their devices out for the session, Michaela replied, "Just water, thanks."

"I'll have an iced tea, Sara. Looks like you have a head start."

"Yep, Kat, just can't seem to relax anymore with all the stuff going on. That meeting in D.C. was a real bummer."

"For sure, Sara. Kat and I have had plenty of discussion already. So, given Scott's perspective on the trip back, what are your plans going forward?"

"Well, Michaela, I think you should take on the global climate change issue. As a distinguished and recognized astrophysicist, who better to take a hard, scientific look at the evidence of climate and human activity and their impact on our world?"

"Sure can, Sara. I can work with Connor on predictions and probabilities and assign correlation numbers as we go forward."

"Great. Kat can take on the challenge of terrorist involvement within the global calamities and worldwide attacks. It's a complex issue and nobody handles complex issues better than Kat."

"Thanks for the vote of confidence, I think," muttered Kat.

"I'll contact Dad, and with my mom's concerns notwithstanding, he can pursue that nebulous evil alien jungle. I really think he'll enjoy it and with Grandad's wealth of data, it could be awesome."

Kat added, "So far, so good. I'm creating a Gantt Chart for Michaela and myself as we speak."

Sara nodded, "Very well."

Sara paused a few seconds before continuing.

"Now for the very politically charged U.S. Military and Government hushed evidence that we have recently uncovered, I'll get with Scott and Amanda to see if they can pursue the military and government respectively, especially focused on possible cover-ups."

Kat questioned that tactic, "Scott and Amanda?"

"Yes, Kat. Scott has military contacts and Amanda is close to VP Samantha, so that might make sense."

Michaela chimed in with both a statement and a question.

"I love it so far, but what about that deep and dark anarchy alliance with the secret societies that could be tricky and dangerous?"

"For now, I'm going to take that on." Sara offered. "If it makes sense later to pass it off, I will. That is the more likely scenario."

To sum things up, Sara advised, "I will act as the coordinator for this new project, as it aligns with my other work."

As they are about to adjourn, Sara shared a passing thought with her team members. "This will be as proactive a mission as we could have ever imagined. Expectations will be sky-high…rewards will be sky-high."

She also thought to herself…

"As will be the risks."

9

MIKE CHALLENGES
CURRENT THINKING

ara's dad, Mike, felt so many emotions, especially from the sacrifice that his dad, Pete, had made to get that world-shaking Congressional event scheduled.

Pete's murder in Paris was still occupying much of Mike's free time, and he knew that he had to move on…it's what Pete would have wanted.

Mike had recalibrated the data that Pete had compiled regarding the universe as his dad had seen it. Mike's current data set was becoming strikingly more immense in size and scope.

As he hunkered down in his large and over-stuffed office, he wrote a note to himself in his latest ancient alien research binder.

There are two trillion galaxies in the observable universe, and each galaxy contains billions of stars.

Within the continuum of Spacetime, it is easy to conclude the supposition that we are not alone.

We are presently stuck in the middle of time with vast speculative truths.

The past is inaccessible…as far as we know.

The future is unknown…as far as we know.

As he pondered those words and realized just how much his life and his world would be changing, Mike recalled an earlier time and event with his wife of many years Christine, who had just entered Mike's cluttered office.

"Christine, remember when Dad was promoting his goofy book about evil aliens living amongst us?"

"Sure. Why are you bringing that up now?"

"First, Christine, I'd like to say that you are very intuitive."

"Thanks, Dear. Sounds like you're buttering me up."

"Christine, why would you think that he would give any credence whatsoever to there being evil aliens here in Earth?"

Christine answered Mike's question quickly.

"Pete was a black-and-white guy. I'm sure that his thinking revolved around the good and bad in people. If you accepted that in our society, then there could be good and bad aliens. If they existed."

"Exactly, Christine. It's called the Law of Polarity and it is very apropos here."

"What, again, is the Law of Polarity?" Christine asked. "It sounds familiar."

Mike explained to Christine.

"The Law of Polarity is one of the seven Universal Laws that tells us that everything has its pair of opposites."

"Wish I hadn't asked," thought Christine.

Mike continued excitedly.

"In other words, it simply says that everything that exists has an equal and exact opposite."

"Example please, Mike?"

"Wealth versus poverty, happy versus sad…good versus bad."

Mike added, "You don't know what wealth is if you haven't experienced poverty. You don't know what happiness is if you haven't been sad."

Christine understood. "And, you don't know what bad behavior or intentions are if you haven't experienced the good stuff."

"Yep. Exactly."

"Now I see where you are going with this 'Law' thing," Christine muttered.

"Sorry for the mini-lecture, but it is, I think, apropos here."

Christine inquired, "So, again I ask, why are you bringing this up now?"

"Well," Mike added, "Sara and her team are doing some deep dives on the Congressional pushbacks, and they have asked me to take some of Dad's research and data on evil aliens and see what conclusions can be drawn."

"Like gathering your own evidence and conducting your own interviews," Christine responded sarcastically.

"Sure. If possible."

"And," Mike added as he glanced at his notes, "with billions of stars and trillions of galaxies in our universe, the thought that the only aliens in existence are good ones just doesn't make sense."

Christine responded quickly.

"So, you are already convinced that good and evil aliens are here…were here…or will be here?"

"Yes, Christine, and time travel could be the key and missing link."

Christine thought to herself.

"Whatever it may be, I just don't want to know."

10
MIKE

Mike began digging almost immediately after the fiasco with Congress. He dug into all those documented incidents where key civilization building and building material developments had been hidden or were inexplicably destroyed.

His office, once as tidy and organized as any office could be, was now just the opposite.

On one wall was the banner – **WHATEVER IT TAKES!**

On another wall was Christine's hand-written banner – **Bless This Mess!**

His four huge bookshelves, once packed with hundreds of books, were now gone.

Mike had large whiteboards covering two walls. There were three flip charts where several magic markers must have run dry.

There was even a state-of-the-art hologram projector where he could voice-command anything and everything from research needs to general news perspective.

Current holo-displays had become Google taken to the highest "next level."

"Orion, show me in 3D how many light years from Earth all the way to the Andromeda Galaxy?"

Mike had named his hologram projector assistant Orion, from his dad's chosen nickname.

And just like that, an awesome multi-colored array of images and data was projected in Mike's holo-display in 3D.

Mike gazed on in total satisfaction.

Earth to the Moon – 1.3 light seconds.
Earth to the Sun – 8.3 light minutes
Earth to Alpha Centauri – 4.4 light years.
Earth to Hercules Globular – 25,000 light years.
Earth to Andromeda Galaxy – 2.5 million light years.

Three very large computer monitors filled one wall and were as congested as any 2D surface could be from holding and rearranging data.

Mike, as was Sara, was a very curious person and was becoming even more curious as ETRT tasks became his number-one priority. He was truly fascinated by what he was seeing and what his mind was beginning to process.

Gathering his dad's data and adding it to his own data set, he believed he had reached a milestone, and he thought it was a good time to bring a very skeptical Christine into his findings from his extremely cluttered office.

Mike loved Christine, but boy he found her to be quite cynical. And, glass half-full, for sure.

Once again, Christine was asked to join her hubby in his office.

"I hear you talking to your friend, Orion, Mike. Seems like you and Orion are having longer discussions than the two of us have."

"C'mon, Christine, you know Orion doesn't usually talk…just presents the facts."

"Sure Mike, what cha got?"

"Christine, I have a long list of possible alien links that I want to share with you."

"Mike, your office is a mess. Let me help you clean it up."

"Seriously? Now?"

"All right Mike, should I get a cup of coffee or a double shot of Jack Daniels?"

A smiling Mike began.

"There were nuclear explosions on Earth millions of years ago thought to be the result of alien wars on this planet."

"Now, Mike, is that your opinion or do you have some nebulous fact?"

"Christine, shards of glass and meteorites found at sites around the world are the exact same composition as those found and analyzed at the Trinity test site in New Mexico in 1945, when the first known atomic bomb was detonated."

"Very cool," Christine muttered, "Jack Daniels sounds about right. Be right back."

Mike took a short research break and actually enjoyed his wife's humor, even given the seriousness of what he was trying to tell her.

About ten minutes later, Christine returned with a pitcher and two tall drinks, resembling lemonade, on a pretty silver serving plate.

"Lemonade, Christine? I thought you were getting us a couple stout drinks."

"Settle down, evil alien hunter; this is stout. They are called Lynchburg Lemonades, famous for the hometown of the Jack Daniel's Distillery."

Handing Mike his cool drink, she continued.

"It's made with Jack Daniel's Whiskey, triple sec, lemon juice, and lemon-lime soda. I use fresh-squeezed lemonade in mine. Cheers!"

"Cheers, and thanks. You're the best!"

"Mike, I'm ready for whatever you got."

"Great. Ancient Scottish forts had walls of fused stone, thousands of years before that construction technology became available. Attempts to destroy that building technology fell short, as archeologists discovered those ancient traces in a dig in 1920."

"And, Mike, you discovered this how?"

"There are many documents and photos, Christine, that I've come upon and Dad already had chronicled."

"Okay, I'm listening."

"The disappearance of the Mayan civilization was one thing that Dad was truly mesmerized by. It surely made the top of my list as well. The Mayans were way ahead of their time in so many ways."

"Yep, Mike, even as kids studying ancient history, that fact was well known."

"Well, from the late eighth century through the end of the ninth century, something unknown happened to shake the Mayan civilization to its foundations. One by one, the classic cities in the southern lowlands of Central America were abandoned, and by 900 A.D., the Mayan civilization had collapsed."

"History lesson, Mike?"

"Kind of. Even though some descendants still live in the lowlands of the Yucatán Peninsula, history shows that the Mayan civilization went from bustling cities to abandoned or displaced ruins in a matter of a few years."

"Mike, again, we know that how?"

"Dad's notes say differently. He said he was told by an alien, named Pulse, that about four hundred and fifty light years from Earth…"

"Mike, he had an alien friend that was into space-time geography?"

Flustered, but determined, Mike continued.

"In a star cluster called Pleiades, known here on Earth as the Seven Sisters, were housed many civilizations."

Mike paused as Christine scowled.

"The Mayans, along with several other civilizations, were apparently relocated to several planets that are seventeen light years across."

Christine chimed in. "Okay, I need a refill. I assume you have more to discuss."

"I do."

"K. I'll be right back. Want anything?"

"No, thanks. I'm good."

As Christine got up and left to refresh the pitcher, Mike was just beginning to understand the scope and scale of what Pete had uncovered, and it seemed like the incredible questions, when answered, led to more questions.

He kicked off his shoes and rolled up the sleeves of his plaid shirt and thought…

He hadn't even gotten to the government cover-ups of alien presence, yet.

11

MIKE

As Christine returned to Mike's office, she asked, "So, why are you sharing this with me?"

"I trust your insight and judgement and I really need a sounding board to bounce this incredible stuff off. There is so much more."

"Okeydoke, Mike, I'm very relaxed right now. Shoot."

"Dad insisted that an ancient alien spaceship landing grid existed thousands of years ago. Physical markers, or prehistoric landmarks, were built to serve as guideposts for alien spacecraft that was visiting earth, and followed a magnetic current flowing across the Earth."

"And what do you have that is relevant here?"

"Well, these structures were dismantled over the last century; and until Dad got into this investigation, these actual structures were never authenticated."

"And you're saying he had some actual evidence?"

"Dad had photos of ground sites for hundreds of these markers, and his photos lined up perfectly with the documented details and descriptions of those markers."

Christine muttered, "Mike, I can't believe the detail that Pete got into. Amazing."

"He also had evidence and locations for ancient alien airfields that were likewise either hidden or destroyed."

Christine's mood became more serious as Mike went on with his data.

"Dad had a drawing of an image of a footprint on Mars that is the mirror image of the Egyptian pyramids."

Showing the drawing to Christine, he continued.

"He also had about two dozen of the so-called crop circles, none of which have any telltale evidence that they were man-made. No car tracks, no foot prints, no nothing."

Christine looked at the binder and nodded her head appreciatively.

"And he also looked into unexplained attacks or incidents involving heat, pressure, and magnetic phenomenon…none of which has any human explanation."

"Mike, that is a lot of hearsay, don't you think?"

"Yeah, except that for many of Dad's alleged incidents or events… he has them cross-referenced with the U.S. Government's hush-hush Project Blue Book."

"Even I know that Project Blue Book stuff sounded suspiciously like a cover-up or the Government's attempt to mislead the public with a lot of crap."

"Yeah, and Dad even mentioned that there were two government projects before Blue Book. One was Project Sign and the other was Project Grudge."

"Again, baffle 'em with bullshit!"

Mike nodded in agreement with Christine before adding one more item.

"The famous disappearances in the Bermuda triangle are included in those agency's activities with some really weak explanations… amateur hour."

"Mike, this is rather chilling and scary stuff. I see déjà vu from Pete all over again. What are you going to do next?"

"Well, I'm going to debrief with Sara. This is exactly what my role in her team's investigation was meant to uproot."

"Very fascinating. Let me know what she and her team think."

With the pitcher in one hand, Christine still gathered some messy crumbled papers to remove from Mike's cluttered office as she left.

Mike knew that this was as far as he wanted to go with getting Christine into the loop. He needed her support and to give her some sort of research facts to give legitimacy to his work. But the big stuff…the truly big stuff, would have to wait.

Mike would now be ready to tell Sara about the data that Pete had put together regarding both government and military cover-ups of alien intervention. Very good data, he thought.

He still had some serious digging to do on one very critical front.

As he was about to reboot Orion, he had one piece of unfinished research business to address. Orion was the perfect source.

He would need to verify Pete's documents showing the existence of all those structures and lifeforms on the Moon and Mars.

12

MIKE

"Hi Sara, just your dad here. How you doing?"

"Well, hi there. Been a while since we talked. Just getting back together with the team to start some implementation planning, after our crappy meeting in D.C. What's up?"

"Able to put all that negative stuff behind you and get to work?"

"Yeah, Dad, just a little discouraging, but press on regardless, eh?"

"I guess. I've been gathering some data and doing some research on many of the issues that are within my role, and I have found some interesting info and have bundled it with some of your grandad's conclusions."

"Very well, Dad. Sounds like you have something of value, eh?"

"I do and it's significant enough that I can't even tell your mom. I gave her some 'teasers,' but not what we're about to discuss."

Switching to her video chat medium to "record," Sara advised.

"I am all ears."

"Sara, all of the pictures of the Moon released to the public are black and white photos, mostly circa 1976 to 1978. And, all the pictures of Mars, some more recent, all also black and white."

"Hold on, Dad. That's because, unlike the planets, the Moon's surface has no brightly colored areas, allegedly. Most of it is a color mix of browns, grays or black."

"Yes, correct, but your grandad had some interesting data and I have taken it to the next level. The results are fascinating."

"Go ahead. I'm recording."

"Safely?"

"Yeah, we have firewalls that are now state-of-the-art, thanks to Justin and Connor."

"Okay. The dark and often circular regions called lunar mare, all mostly basalt rock, are very prevalent near the rim of Hadley Rille. The fine-grained crystallinity and large holes indicate that this rock crystallized near the top of a molten lava flow."

"Interesting, Dad, but where you going with this?"

"Patience, my dear Sara. All of the documented photos show the lunar terrain is shown in only about ninety per cent of a viewing perspective. In other words, about ten per cent of the Moon's landscape that has been photographed has never been reported."

"I smell a cover-up coming."

"Yep Sara, I think so." Mike was now fully engaged and focused.

"That empty ten per cent of the pie is where large areas of basalt rock are and any light whatsoever hitting basalt rock will reveal a prismatic array of colors. Those colors were revealed in government photos that Pete somehow obtained."

"Oh my gosh," uttered a very surprised Sara.

"Yes. Many bright colors and actual correlated structures and domes exist on the moon, and likely have for thousands of years…if not much longer."

"Example, Dad? Please tell me you have an example."

"I'm getting to one. Specifically, one glass dome about four to five miles high exists now. It could have been erected as a shield from meteors around what was likely a thriving city."

"Whoa. Where the hell did you get this?"

"Sara, a friend of one of your grandad's team members, I'll just call him Eric, had them and now I have seen them."

"Can we meet with him?"

"Nope. He's deceased, Sara."

"Could be another story there, right?"

"Yeah. Coincidence? Maybe not."

Mike took a deep breath and continued.

"And, various satellite photos align with and validate the same lunar objects and coordinates. And, they are not American-built satellites. We're not even alone here on Earth regarding alien research and investigation!"

Taking a moment to process all of this data, Sara responded.

"This is incredible info and we will need to frame and anchor these results carefully."

"Agree. And there is more related info."

"Do you have more on the basalt rocks, Dad?"

"Yes. A new and well-documented study of the rare basaltic meteorites called angrites, suggests that volatiles, which are substances with low boiling points such as water, were brought to our planet by meteorites during the first two million years of the solar system."

"Damn. You're actually talking about some serious 'hard science' here."

"Yes. Components such as water and carbon are essential ingredients to life on Earth and likely could be traced to the Moon."

"You are on a roll, Dad."

"Basaltic meteorites are common in our solar system. I looked at one in particular. It's called the North-West Africa 7034, nicknamed "Black Beauty," and has a relatively large amount of water in it."

"I am aware of that."

"Sure, Sara, of course you are. I'm going to build a map of the very early inner solar system and try to determine where the water was, where was it going and where did it come from?"

"Wow. Let me know if you need some mapping help from one of our resident geniuses."

"I probably will. So, listen to this…when Mars formed billions of years ago, Earth was likely just about twenty per cent of its current size, so you can't rule out Mars as an origin of our existence!"

"Dad, that's pretty cool stuff, but why is that important right now for our research?"

"Sara, I'm personally interested in the alien civilization prospects for the Moon and Mars, and this is simply the starting point."

Mike gathered his thoughts for his next big OMG.

"Sara, it is possible, albeit highly far-fetched, that the origin of the human species isn't here on Earth…but on Mars. We could be a race of Martian aliens!"

Sara thought for a moment about that revelation, along with several contradictory thoughts, and rather loudly scowled.

"Dammit, my grandad was accused of being an alcoholic…I don't want you to be taken for a crack-head."

"Funny, Sara, but point well taken. You don't seem too surprised about any of this."

"No, not so much anymore. I'm more than a little convinced of extraterrestrials. And to have you as a point guy on this, well, I'm a happy camper. The Mars thing I'm gonna table for now."

"Sure. Fair enough. One more thing, though."

"Seriously? More?"

Mike paused to get some water and retrieve some additional info.

"In Aurora, Texas, on April 17, 1897, locals reported that a UFO crashed on a farm and an alien body was found deceased."

"1897, Dad. Wow! That goes way back."

"The alleged alien body was nicknamed Kelby and was buried in an unknown grave. A Texas Historical Commission marker outside the Aurora Cemetery described the incident and the buried body of the UFO pilot."

"Okay, but then…?"

"Yep, there was no body in the grave, as local authorities assured everyone."

"I'm getting kind of excited."

"There was no alien body in the Aurora Cemetery, because Pete's log book indicated that the alien was buried about seven miles to the west in the town of Boyd."

"Sara, your grandad had the exact coordinates given to him from that Eric guy that we talked about earlier. So, I went to that site last week with those coordinates."

"And?"

"Working at dusk to dawn only, to avoid anybody seeing me, I ran both my infrared and harmonic detectors on the six-foot by eight-foot specs within the coordinates."

"And, Dad?"

"And there is a skeleton, a likely alien skeleton, in that grave that is over seven feet in length and with a very wide torso and wingspan. Can't be human!"

"Send me the images."

"Will do. And, Sara, the head appears to still be inside a very large helmet."

Sara was smiling, adding this revelation to her recent encounter.

Mike ended his call with a remarkable comment.

"We have it. Sara, we have the alien body in his tomb. It is secure!"

13

SARA

With the excitement of the Aurora, Texas, alien skeleton in her mind, Sara pulled the ETRT together to discuss the planning and implementation activity that she had discussed with Michaela and Kat several days earlier.

Sara was trying already to "connect the dots" with her encounter and the Texas incident, but that was far too unlikely to be bundled.

For the time being, she would not share the Texas info with the team, as they had a ton of work on their plates, and more questions would lead to more questions. Quiet, for now.

"The meeting with Congress, as you know, was disappointing and brutal. Most members of Congress were deniers of anything out of the ordinary.

"They had already made up their minds that we were not to be taken seriously. But we had to do this to check off the politically correct box. Done. Classic Pygmalion Effect."

Justin, an African-American who loved turtleneck sweaters and was adjusting his new horn-rimmed glasses, asked, "What's that?"

Sara explained. "It's what we call a self-fulfilling prophecy. You do or act in ways that reinforce your beliefs and expectations. And, you tend to associate with people that share your views."

"Okay," responded Justin. "I see. Thanks."

Sara continued with her agenda, "We have six components that make up the entire scope of explaining significant events and important global issues today.

"In other words, look at it as a pie, and the six components make up the whole global issues pie. We need to specifically focus and address each of these critical components, and assign a weighted percentage to each component. Hope that makes sense."

Michaela advised, "Yes, each component is separate and non-equal in scope, scale, and value. In other words, one component may make up forty per cent of the pie and another only ten per cent. As Sara explains, I think it will become clear."

"Thanks, Michaela. We are going to assign one team member to take charge of each component, not to do the work, but to assemble a team and then take on reporting responsibilities. You good with that?"

Kat winked, "Absolutely."

"Good. Then here are the assignments."

Looking down at her list, Sara advised.

"Michaela will take on global climate change.

"Kat will take on the perceived terrorist portion.

"My dad, Mike, has already agreed to continue Grandad's research on evil aliens."

Justin asked, "Is that really a thing…evil aliens?"

"We will see, Justin. I have contacted Scott and Amanda and they are willing to head up the work needed to see what part, if any, was played or is being played, by our military and our government."

"Yikes," added Connor, the tall, bone-faced man with hair the color of straw and the team's self-appointed comedic distraction.

"My grandad uncovered elements of international anarchy threats and I will proceed cautiously regarding those possibilities."

Sara took a deep breath and continued.

"He also became obsessed with thoughts that secret societies were somehow suppressing technology, which will take some serious investigation."

"Two anarchists walk into a bar…"

"Please, not now, Connor."

Sara smiles at another attempt by Connor to interject humor and concludes with her next project role.

"I will also act as the project coordinator."

Kat added her current thinking. "I will become the integrator for blending all six components as we move forward. Guys, action plans will be due within twenty-four hours."

"Thanks, Kat. That'll be all for now."

Kat offered her summary, "We just gotta trust the process!"

Sara thought, "Getting tired of that trust-the-process quote."

Within ten days, the teams were ready with their initial high-level overviews.

Michaela gave Sara a heads-up several days later, just prior to the team's initial report-outs.

Sara was not surprised with the depth and detail in Michaela's first pass.

Sara was well aware that Michaela would be reporting devastating news.

14

MICHAELA SEEKS EXTRAORDINARY EVIDENCE

Sara had turned over the next team meeting kickoff to Michaela, as Sara recognized the enormity of her friend's subject matter, and wanted the team to fully appreciate her take-charge skills.

Michaela had the ETRT assembled and had that "all business" look when she began the initial topic report-out overviews.

"Global warming is obviously debated from the natural phenomenon of climate change to a pending danger that threatens mankind.

"We have already started to build algorithms for a number of potential significant events."

Michaela could see that Sara was pleased with that opening statement.

"Those events include heat waves occurring in the arctic, massive forest fires happening in Australia, Siberia, and Sweden, the loss of the arctic ice cover and the rising seas.

"We will categorize each element of the climate change puzzle and assign both a likelihood of occurrence and a degree of catastrophe."

Michaela advanced her slides on the meeting room's large screen and on everyone's personal devices for their convenience and note-taking.

"The ten highest recorded average annual temperatures have been, in order, 2017, 2019, 2020, 2018, 2022, 2023, 2021, 2024, 2025 and with 2026 being the hottest. That's not a trend; that is scientific fact."

Pausing, she continued.

"The Intergovernmental Panel on Climate Change met in 2020 and put out two reports. The one with the worst-case scenario never went public.

"The international team of climate scientists, economists, and energy system modelers built a range of new 'pathways' that would examine how global society, demographics, and economics might change over the next century. They are known as the 'Shared Socioeconomic Pathways' or SSP's."

Michaela had everyone's attention and was clearly raising their level of concern.

"One group of researchers then developed the 'Representative Concentration Pathways,' or RCP's, describing different levels of greenhouse gases and radiation that might occur with alarming results in the future."

Michaela paused before continuing the slide sequence more slowly.

"I'm just going to highlight the critical categories for now. The data is extensive, complicated and subject to argumentative discord."

Michaela took a deep sigh.

"Pollution will continue to grow exponentially through 2100 and result in two very significant outcomes.

"Air quality will be so poor that health care and illness and smog-related deaths will be catastrophic. And, agricultural productivity will decline so rapidly that synthetic foods will no longer be trendy, but a necessity."

Moving on to the next image, her tone of voice picked up.

"Population decline will become evident everywhere except in third-world countries. Major socio-economic issues here.

"Social unrest, crime, and water-trading will explode."

"Water-trading, Michaela?" Sara asked crisply.

"Yes, water will become the gold commodity of today. Only the wealthiest people and strongest countries will control water sources. Licenses will be required to purchase water in bulk. I am still formulating this scenario…film at eleven."

The ETRT members noted Michaela's attempt at humor…it seemed odd for her.

"Poor economic growth will continue a downward spiral that would make events like the Stock Market Crash of 1929 and the Great Recession of the early 2000's pale in comparison.

"There is no single 'business as usual' baseline in place today… no one or no group has thought that far out. Seriously, no one seems to give a crap!

"I am working on a worst-case scenario of unchecked warming to compare against futures where emissions are controlled and reduced. There is no research that I have found here…I must create my own."

Kat muttered, "Damn girl, this doesn't sound good at all."

"No, it isn't. From minimal action to controlled climate change via mandates like the Paris Accord, to no action to address climate change as the mid-2050's approach, seals our desperate fate."

"Can you tell us where we are right now and where we are headed?"

"Sure, Justin. The world has already warmed by one degree Celsius since the middle of the 19th century. It has risen one point five degrees Celsius over the last twenty years and could likely rise another two degrees by 2050."

Michaela concluded her initial overview on climate change with a summation.

"One degree would likely be the difference between a world with coral reefs and Artic summer sea ice and a world completely without them."

15

KAT

Kat was not usually known as a flashy dresser. Being kind of conservative, she was much more into substance than style.

However, today, given the dark nature of her topic, and the resounding "thumbs down" from the politicians, she wore a hot pink, pleated skirt and a crisp, white blouse with pink trim.

Putting on her best smile, she began her report-out.

"By way of some background on international terrorism, I am starting with an understanding of the why, when, who, what, and where issues."

"Is that necessary?" Michaela asked.

"I think so. Just bear with me a while."

Kat reordered her notes and continued. "The Palestine Liberation Organization was a political movement uniting Palestinian Arabs in an effort to create an independent state of Palestine. When it formed in 1964 it was an early terrorist organization with much of its violence aimed at Israeli civilians."

"I remember reading about the PLO," Sara said.

"Then, Boko Haram formed in 2002 as a jihadist terror organization in Nigeria and eventually aligned with the Islamic State of Iraq. Boko Haram has killed tens of thousands of people and displaced nearly three million from their homes and was once ranked the world's deadliest terror group."

Justin asked, "Was that the group behind the 9/11 attack?"

"No, not really. They hadn't gotten their traction yet."

Pleased that her audience was paying attention, Kat went on.

"The Islamic State, or ISIS, became one of the largest and most feared extremist militant groups and dominated the Iraq and Syria regions for many years until overtaken by allied forces in 2020."

"Go allied forces," Connor muttered.

"Okay. The Taliban, who refer to themselves as the Islamic Emirate of Afghanistan, was a Sunni Islamic fundamentalist political movement and military organization in Afghanistan currently waging wars, or insurgencies, within that country.

"This is important. The Taliban was once the ruling government in Afghanistan, but now organizes suicide attacks throughout the region."

Kat could see that Connor and Justin were getting restless, given that this subject was so far off their techy radar.

"And the most disruptive and considered the top terrorist threat to America, the global terror network al Qaeda, attack on 9/11 was responsible for thousands of deaths under Osama bin Laden."

"Where are you going with this?" Connor finally quipped.

"In order to analyze the current terrorist threat, we must accept that terrorism is a political behavior resulting from a rational choice made when the power ratio of government to be challenged is high."

"Actually, I understand that," uttered Connor.

"To figure out what is motivating today's extreme terrorist threat, and the one that Pete Stevenson apparently uncovered, we must look at situational and strategic factors."

Sara interjected, "I know this is way off base from our primary objective, but we are also trying to use the process of elimination here so we can go on about our work in a highly focused manner."

"Thanks, Sara. I'm getting to the terrorist's end game."

"Situational factors are the conditions that allow extreme radicalization and reinforce feelings against the proverbial enemy, and which specific targets or events can become actionable for the terrorist cause to incite fear and mistrust.

"Strategic factors are both short-term and long-term. Short-term deals with group recognition and attention to how vulnerable society is today. Long-term focuses on major political change or revolution, fighting democratic cultures, and destroying any seeds of resistance."

Michaela chimed in. "End game?"

"So, Michaela, the end game is simple.

"Disrupt and discredit the process of government itself. To capture public attitudes using fear and intimidation. To provoke counter-reaction to legitimize the new regime and crush the last resistance."

"Oh my," uttered a noticeably serious Justin.

"That brief tutorial being delivered, our team must take a look at evidence of long-range trends toward the privatization of violence as a means to an end."

"And resources," advised Sara.

"Yes. We know that major weapons have been procured by a very wealthy consortium, unfortunately uncovered by Pete Stevenson."

"We must also trace those people and events where traction would thrive due to uncertainty and political unrest."

"What's this 'we' stuff," scowled Connor.

Kat added, "Point well taken; my stuff," and continued.

"Modern air travel and communication provide worldwide mobility of people, ideas, and conflict, and must be viewed as a primary enabler.

"Instant access to a worldwide audience via social media and satellite technology for communication and as a weapon is key.

"This is what happened in a couple Presidential elections, as you may recall."

"Yes, Sara, that is on-point."

Michaela hissed. "I see another big worldwide leadership issue raising its ugly head."

Kat nodded. "Indeed. Unfortunately, the inability of the world to limit or regulate arms traffic and caches of weapons from guns to nuclear devices is also a huge issue.

"Attacks on high-tech level targets and political enemies are resulting in criminal extortionists holding the world hostage."

"Crap," responded Justin as he adjusted his glasses for the umpteenth time.

"Just as I thought we could just blow this off, maybe we can't."

"You may be right, Justin," Kat replied.

Kat raised her voice a bit with her closing remarks.

"At the core of all this negative underpinning is what Pete found, the Cabal known throughout the world as the New World Order."

"And, of course, they did not want to be found."

16

MIKE

Mike was still at his Ohio home, and was just returning from a long canoe ride up and down the river behind his house. He often did this to de-stress and figure out a puzzle or two in his head.

As he was walking up to the house, Christine motioned to him and yelled out.

"Hey Mike, you've got a video conference soon."

"I know, thanks; just gathering some last-minute thoughts."

As Mike climbed the porch stairs, Christine asked, "See any of your forest friends today?"

"Couple deer and several rabbits. Same old…same old."

Christine handed Mike a cold lemonade as he walked up the steps."

"Lynchburg Lemonade?"

"Nope. Just plain. Figured you'd need to keep a clear head."

With that comment, Mike moved into his office, where he was already set up to go. Firing up his video feed, he waited to log on.

He also noticed that Christine had "tidied up" while he was out.

Since Mike's input at this initial meeting of the ETRT was via video confer-ence, he had a basic outline to present.

He had his link up and running.

"Hey, everyone."

"Hi, Mike," rang out the team in concert.

"I have the evil alien track today."

Connor piped in, "Should we get some popcorn for this one?"

Mike always appreciated Connor's ability to "chill out" with silly comments.

"The evil alien research from my dad was somewhat disconnected. I believe he followed this path only out of necessity, or an attempt to simply disprove the notion of evil aliens. Dad was a black -and-white engineer and this topic was extremely gray."

Kat smiled. She absolutely loved Pete Stevenson.

"I did take notes and made some observations. One was that he felt that there were inherent dangers of humankind meeting alien civilizations."

Kat looked on with a serious perspective. "What did he say?"

Mike advised, "I have all of Dad's notes and I think I can simplify his thinking a bit...

"Think about his analogy, Kat. Meeting an advanced civilization could be like Native Americans encountering Columbus, which did not go well later for the Native Americans."

Sara uttered. "I remember Grandad mentioned that view way back when I was a kid."

Mike continued, "Aliens sufficiently advanced visiting Earth might be hostile and would likely be powerful.

"Advanced alien colonies could be nomadic; looking to conquer and colonize whatever planets they could reach."

Mike was thinking that he had just opened a huge can of worms.

"Any society with the capability to threaten Earth is overwhelmingly likely to already have the tools required to analyze each and every signal that we have sent off, marking our position and existence."

Noticeable silence amongst the audience.

"My last preliminary observation deals with finding some actual evidence Dad had regarding this topic.

"Christine and I are still trying to find it. I think it was Dad's intention to further explore this issue after that terrible Paris meeting where he was killed."

"Dad, what topic?"

"Oh, yeah, sorry, Sara.

"I did find out that the last Starship Slingshot Project to send a small spacecraft to the Alpha Centauri star system, twenty-five trillion miles away, was destroyed in route in 2020 with no apparent cause yet discovered."

"Scientists determined that, without a doubt, it was destroyed using a highly intense laser or magnetic wave, origin unknown."

17

SCOTT

A few days following the ETRT meeting, Scott contacted Mike as Scott began his investigation of the U.S. Military, due to remarks Mike made to him several months earlier.

"Hey Mike, it's Scott. How goes it?"

"Good, Scott. Good. Just getting into the data Dad had on his evil alien quest."

"Great. I'll be anxious to hear about that topic as well."

"I'm actually calling for some insight into another of his data sets too. Mike, do you have time for that rundown we discussed last week?"

"Sure. The use of a centrifuge by foreign military in the Southwest United States was one of the biggest issues he uncovered involving a military conspiracy."

"Mike, any idea which foreign military?"

"Yep, Scott, I was just getting to that. Apparently, Dad got some serious evidence that the special ops military were former Nazis, with ties to the Hitler regime itself."

"Mike, that's not the first time that I've heard that scenario."

"Well, then it gets kind of weird."

"Listening, Mike."

"The notes from Dad are pretty specific, once I had Justin crack the code. There was, supposedly, a secret Nazi military squad that had obtained technology and actual physical spacecrafts from an alien culture that had been here for a considerable time."

"And, Mike, the Nazi regime ended… and then what?"

"Yep, the technology and alien craft were, apparently, turned over to the U.S. Navy, who then put in place a secret space program that is still running, under the radar, with either ex-Nazi or actual aliens."

Scott was dazed and confused, but had a follow-up question in mind.

"Mike, you said your dad actually saw something in Mississippi or Alabama."

"Yes, he and a colleague apparently witnessed the destruction of evidence of alien existence, both spaceships and people, in rural Alabama."

"Damn. Any photos?"

"No, Scott. Sadly, it was captured only in his mind and his incredible notes and drawings. But he was able to obtain, illegally for sure, documents uncovered from secret DOD files which dealt with military experiments on both humans and aliens. I'll summarize, categorize and get those over to you."

"Great. Thanks. Really good stuff."

Scott was finally hearing confirmation of what his own confidantes had told him years ago. Scott had once investigated this occurrence out of curiosity; now it has become mainstream.

"Scott, there are several bulleted topics that I'm still getting his research on and I'll need to get back with you for sure."

Scott was now getting very curious and asked, "Like what?"

"There was more than one occurrence noted where a bluish-white light took controls of Air Force planes and flew them without the pilot's actions or reactions.

"And, rural areas reported intense pressure crushing cars and tractors, but not harming anyone or anything nearby."

"Well that's creepy. Photos?"

"Yes, Scott, I do. Still photos, not any videos. Then there was an entire military subversion category."

"Examples?"

"Yep. This was kind of sketchy, probably because it was hard to describe."

"I'm hearing a lot of 'sketchy' these days," Scott added.

Mike continued. "Alien antennas were allegedly being retro-fitted onto the existing antenna technology and were used as weapons with laser-like capability.

"Allegedly, Scott. Those ex-Nazis were working in several locations within the Southeastern U.S. on rockets and early satellite launches.

"Dad even mentioned a documented Russian conspiracy to halt our space program at a very early stage."

Scott agreed. "Yep, history recalled how devastated the Russians were when the Americans were the first to land on the Moon. Apparently, many Russian cosmonauts perished in that quest."

"I gotta lot of digging to do on this story, for sure."

"Yep, Mike. Let me know if there are any resources that I can provide that you may need in this hunt."

"Will do. Thanks."

"Is that it for now?"

"Yeah, I guess," Mike thought for a moment and then added one last comment. "I think the most jaw-dropping notes of his involved the presence of alien soldiers and not the friendly kind. Again, just notes."

"Damn. So, how did he get that info?"

"Mostly through interviews. Dad had tons of actual interviews."

"Your dad was amazing. So, that's it?"

"Pretty much, Scott, for now. There was mention of private military suppliers doubling down on legit contracts to pursue ultra-secret research stuff too. I'll pull what I can together and get it over to you in whatever way is best."

"That would be great. Thanks, Mike."

What Scott did not reveal to Mike was what was in the folder he was holding. Now he had a cross-reference that confirmed the legitimacy of these events.

He wasn't sure why he kept that folder info from Mike. Leverage later with someone? For sure, he didn't want "nice guy Mike" to know that these photos were likely stolen… a crime.

Several photos, obtained illegally in a "quid pro quo," of that centrifuge of destruction, were clearly showing what Mike had described.

18

AMANDA

Amanda Woods contacted the Vice President, Samantha Worthington, for a conversation regarding the role of government in the conspiracy theory path laid out by the ETRT.

For security purposes, it led to a face-to-face meeting in the Whitehouse nursery, which was unoccupied and not bugged.

"It's nice to see you, Amanda."

"Likewise, Sam. Thanks for taking time to meet."

"Sorry, but I only have about ten minutes. Something came up."

"No problem, Sam. I have a charity event planning meeting nearby and I am flexible today regarding time."

"Then go ahead, Amanda."

"Very well, Sam; this U.S. Government involvement in alien presence is a real can of worms, as you know. I must begin with the fact that some element is true, or it wouldn't have made anyone's radar screen."

"I totally get it and I'm as anxious as you to get the facts, Amanda. Where are you, what do you know and what can I do?"

"The most significant issue as I see it are the rash of alleged government cover-ups. From Area 51 and 52 and related UFO sightings to the Philadelphia Experiment to the most juvenile explanations for a variety of phenomenon, we really need to get real about actual events."

"Amanda, I can get you info on Areas 51 and 52; no problem. What do you know about the Philadelphia Experiment?"

"Well, Sara's team had this on their radar for some time and I just got the info second hand. It's just fascinating."

"Okay, what did Sara's team tell you?"

"Let me think…"

"The Philadelphia Experiment was an alleged military experiment supposedly carried out by the U.S. Navy at the Philadelphia Naval Shipyard in Philly late in 1943.

"A Navy destroyer had an escort ship, I think it was the Ethridge or Eldridge, and it was claimed to have been rendered invisible, or cloaked, to enemy detection. Is that right?"

"Yes, Amanda, I do recall allegations of cloaking the escort ship USS Eldridge. Do you have anything else?"

"No, I don't Sam. We really need your help."

"Sure thing. I have two very special people that can do a deep dive on anything or everything that we need to investigate."

"That is great news."

"Just get me the laundry list with all your details, Amanda, and we'll get started."

"Sure. I also have questions that go way back to the Cold War strategy and what may have been a hidden agenda."

"Can you be specific?"

"Not yet, but soon. I may have a couple issues that involve cyber terrorism and possible plots that may tie back to previous administrations."

"Well, that's really big stuff, Amanda. You've been busy."

"Yep. This ETRT is pretty damn good, and the fact that Congress didn't take them serious just brings out a whole bunch of questions and is mainly why we are talking. They want to whip their collective asses."

Amanda gazed at her notes.

"Sam, I do have one last item on my to-do list."

"Shoot."

"It is the government's extensive involvement in Artificial Intelligence and General Artificial Intelligence that was undocumented."

"Not at all easy to identify and uncover."

"I know, Sam. All this will take some time and resources."

"Of course. I'll bring President Sullivan into the loop and see how much light he can shed on your issues and get our momentum going. Just give me a few days. I understand that this is urgent."

"That'll be great, Sam."

"Remember though, Amanda, you don't have any security clearances right now, so please don't expect too much detail. I have procedures that I must follow."

After a short pause, Amanda added, "I know you will do the best you can."

Little did Amanda know that VP Worthington had no intention of contacting POTUS about anything.

She already knew what "facts" she was going to give to Amanda.

19

AMANDA

Amanda got a voice mail message from VP Worthington about a week later regarding the follow-up meeting that Samantha was supposed to have had with President Cameron Sullivan.

Pouring a Red Bull and Vodka cocktail, and activating her recording device, she phoned VP Worthington.

"Hey Sam, got your message. What's up?"

"Hi Amanda. Thanks for getting back to me. Let me switch us to a secure line."

Amanda waited excitedly for news from VP Worthington.

"All right, I have a number of high-level admissions from Cameron, and I'm almost shocked that he shared as much as he did. Of course, we were in a secured area and our meeting was one-on-one, which was good."

"I'm excited to hear your news. Can't tell you how much I appreciate your help."

"Before you get too excited, I only have the thirty-thousand-foot view right now…high-level bullet points, really, that will require a deep dive and a lot of hush-hush on my part so I don't do anything stupid."

"You and the word stupid don't belong in the same sentence."

"Thanks, Amanda. Here we go."

"I'm ready to write, Sam."

"Let me start by saying there are a large number of military and government cover-ups regarding alien presence and explanations for the so-called 'unexplained' files.

"NASA mis-directions by the dozens, even involving other countries, are almost too numerous to mention. I'll put them all into a restricted dossier for you."

"Sam, can you give me one example?"

"I'm going to give you one example of everything that I now have knowledge on. Again, I am puzzled by how far POTUS went to bring me into the loop."

Sara took a deep breath and responded, "Awesome!"

"Apparently, via a joint effort between the U.S. and Japan, there is a small colony of explorers and researchers on Mars, and they have been there for almost eight years now!"

From ETRT info already filed, Amanda knew that Samantha was telling Amanda a total lie, but apparently needed to find out if she could trust Amanda.

"So, why the charade?" she thought to herself.

"Maybe to see how much Sara and the ETRT actually knew and how much was speculative," Amanda wondered.

So, even though Amanda knew that Samantha was telling a half-truth, she could not immediately figure out why.

"Excuse me, Sam; did you say an American joint venture with Japan, and one that was nearly eight years old?"

"Yes. Unreal, eh?"

Amanda recalled Sara mentioning that her grandad had notes that a U.S. joint space venture with the Russians had put a recon colony on Mars about twenty-five to thirty years ago, but didn't reveal that info to Samantha.

"So, Pete Stevenson had better intel than the Vice President? Not likely," she thought.

Amanda quickly asked in as skeptical a manner as possible, "How the hell did that happen in a cloak of secrecy that is historical…almost of biblical proportions?"

"Apparently, Amanda, all the launches were a combination of high-level cloaking technology and fake news about all those 'plain vanilla' launches that took place in Asia. They were so insignificant that the public blew 'em off."

"Great strategy, Sam, like a combination of apathy and ignorance."

"Yeah, Amanda, I guess you could say that. This one issue tops my to-do list for sure."

"Great piece. What else, Sam?"

"The U.S. Government has a classified pentagon program on alien life over the last seventy-five years."

"You mean the Project Blue Book? We are all aware of that."

"No, this one is named the RS 6 Project. It is apparently correlated to the Rio Scale for SETI, which, as you probably know, is the class of phenomenon or discovery that is the highest type, physical alien encounter."

"Got it, Sam. That means that the Government has either Earth-specific messages or actual physical encounters, right?"

"Or both, Amanda. Hey, you're really up to date, girl."

"Thanks, Sam, but Sara and her team would understand this info far better than me. I'm still on a very steep learning curve. Just good at taking notes."

"Understand. But, Amanda, when we vetted you, Harvard listed you as Summa Cum Laude, while graduating as Amanda Adams, your maiden name, I assume. Your learning curve isn't like everyone else."

"Thank you for that compliment Sam."

"Back to my list, Amanda. Suspicious deaths have taken the lives of a number of fringe researchers and reporters. I don't want to get into the details here, but I am looking at a lot of questionable fatalities."

"Any idea of what the 'end game' was…or is?"

"No, but it all started with the murder of Sara's grandfather, Pete Stevenson."

"Whoa, Sam, that is chilling! I'm finishing a Red Bull and Vodka cocktail. Let me mix another one before you continue."

"You know, Amanda, they call that drink the 'Heart Attack Special.' Really impressed."

"Sometimes I just need that extra energy boost…this is one of those times."

As Samantha waited for Amanda to return, she pulled a couple three-by-five note cards out of her stack. She wanted to keep her report at a high level, minus too much detail.

"All right Sam, I'm back. You should try one of these drinks. Helluva kick."

What Samantha didn't realize was that Amanda left, not to get another drink, but to make sure her patch to Sara regarding this conversation was still connected.

"Thanks. I'll keep that one in mind."

Amanda knew that Samantha was not much of a drinker; Amanda's robust drink would never happen for VP Worthington.

Samantha continued.

"Amanda, are you aware of the Bilderberg Group of the Netherlands?"

"Yeah, actually, I am. The namesakes began an annual conference in 1954 to foster dialogue between Europe and North America, attempting to bolster a consensus around free market Western capitalism and to prevent another world war."

The VP jotted down a note. *Smart S.O.B.*

"Well, that actually sounds like a good thing. How does it go bad?" Amanda chuckled at her own assumption.

"A small but very affluent splinter group, advocating a one-world government, left the Bilderberg Group and formed the singular New World Order that Pete Stevenson had gotten himself involved in."

"Oh my God, Sam, that tells me a lot."

"It certainly does. You can trace that splinter group way back to the Bavarian Illuminati, an Enlightenment-era secret society founded in the eighteenth century, whose mission statement was to control all of society without dominating them."

Amanda added, "That explains the radical group discovered by Mr. Stevenson and their research spin from aliens to terrorism."

"I remember seeing movies about this. One was *The Da Vinci Code*, starring Tom Hanks, I think. Wish I had paid more attention to detail now."

"Amanda, what we're talking about didn't make it into any books or movies, I assure you. And the Bohemian Club in San Francisco now admits members of the military to a group that was mostly journalists, artists, and musicians."

"So Sam, why is that even significant?"

"Don't know yet, but to go from no military membership to a large military membership and with current crossover members with the Bilderberg Group, it is a bit of a red flag."

"Understand. Thanks for all your help and thank Cameron for us."

"Will do. No problem."

Samantha practically ordered Amanda to be selectively silent.

"Do not to share the info regarding the RS 6 Project that I gave you with anyone for now, as that is being withheld from the public."

VP Worthington then hung up.

"Sara, did you get that?"

"Yep, Amanda, I'm on it. Great stuff. Thanks."

20

SARA

Sara chose the alleged anarchy alliance of several international dictators as her conspiracy theory of choice for one main reason.

Sara thought she could use it as a mere facade for her main objective, using her direct contact with the aliens to determine her next steps.

Unfortunately, the solitude of having no one to share her extraordinary evidence with was weighing hard on her psyche.

Rather than call, she sent a text message to Mike, "*Headed to D.C. for couple follow-up meetings. Will advise.*"

Mike sent his response, "*Great. Let us know what you find.*"

She just couldn't tell her family, friends, or associates about Echo, Pulse, and the unbelievable experience that she just had. It would simply result in hundreds of questions, not to mention the possibility of putting her network of people in "harm's way" as the process rolled out.

She traveled to D.C. to meet with several key members of Congress to get a handle on their issues and priorities regarding international terror groups, a meeting set up by VP Worthington.

It would also give her an opportunity to actually meet with VP Samantha Worthington and have a much-needed talk with Samantha, especially given her overheard chat between the VP and Amanda.

One particular member of the House Intelligence Committee, Mitch Engle, seemed anxious to meet Sara. In fact, he had tried several times to get on Sara's busy agenda before this D.C. trip.

"Hello, Miss Steele, it is a pleasure to meet you."

"Likewise, Mr. Engle. I recall you attended our wimpy presentation last month."

Chuckling, Mitch muttered.

"Well, I did not take it as wimpy, only refreshing."

"Really?" Why?"

"As a senior member of the Intel Committee, I have heard and seen much over the last several years. Your spot-on presentation was particularly apropos and very much caught my eye regarding questions that I have had for years."

"Really? That's great to hear. Can you be specific, Congressman?"

"Yes. But this will be an area that we will need to keep to ourselves and likely meet later on to get you up to speed."

Sara was now extremely interested in what Congressman Engle was alluding to.

"Of course. Most of what my team does is highly classified."

"I'm sure it is."

The Congressman gathered his notes and turned on a small white-noise tape player.

"Are you familiar with the Majestic Twelve, or MJ 12, a secret group of scientists, military leaders, and government officials, formed in 1947 by President Truman?"

"Mostly from my history classes, I'm afraid."

"Fine. It was formed to facilitate the recovery and investigation of alien spacecraft and had compiled a detailed dossier of unexplained alien presence, UFO's, and the complete cover-up of the Roswell incident, including the movement and hiding of many alien craft."

"Sir, this is remarkable and, likely, very relevant info. Are you sure it's safe to discuss here?"

"Yes. I have both white-noise and scrambling technology in place."

Sara did not see that level of detail and sophisticated prep coming. The Congressman continued.

"Back in the mid-eighties, the entire MJ12 group was replaced, due mostly to retirements, it was said. Many of us knew better."

Sara glanced around to see if they were still alone.

"Several years ago, one of my colleagues received an envelope containing film which, when developed, showed images of twelve pages of documents that were the briefing pages describing this new secretive upper tier of dignitaries."

"My God, that must have been one helluva 'wake-up' call."

"Well, there's more. It explained how the Roswell craft actually crashed, had some sort of interview with the alien pilot and how everything was being moved to United States Air Force Office of Space Investigations, a department that never existed."

"Answers that call for more questions."

"You are absolutely right, Sara."

"Here's the kicker. The mission of this 'new' Air Force Agency, referred to as Special Ops 12, was threefold.

"One, it was to determine how the recovered alien technology could be exploited.

"Two, was to put into place a number of methods to suppress alien technology from public awareness."

"Excuse me, Congressman, but our team has gotten wind of that last issue you mentioned, so I know it is happening. What is number three?"

"The third element of their mission was truly unthinkable. That is, how the United States should engage with extraterrestrial life in the future. It wasn't a question…it was a statement!"

"Oh my God! I am so thankful that you have shared this incredible Intel with me. I wish I had some proof to take back with me."

"Well, Sara Steele, we have all that film on a small digital drive."

Sara gasped. "Here is secret society number one," she thought.

Pulling a small e-card out of his pocket and handing it over to Sara, Congressman Engle smiled and said.

"Now you have it!"

21

SARA

Sara had little time to digest the enormity of her info exchange with Congressman Engle when she moved on to her additional contacts within the National Security Agency and MI6 British intelligence.

She was soon connecting the dots involving competing terrorist groups and the process that led to the creation of the New World Order.

Her M16 contact, a friend of a friend of her dad, put the entire terrorism worldview into a litany of what could happen and how easy it was for that violent group to organize and get traction.

The one oft-used phrase from that M16 agent rang true; "Keep your friends close…and your enemies closer."

Engle's data set would need some serious downloading and analysis when she got back to the ETRT.

A much more enlightened and more energized Sara moved on to a couple Senate appointments.

Congressman Bradford told Sara that seeds were planted in earlier U.S. Presidential Administrations to gain personal favors in exchange for tariff relief and access to key government and business intelligence.

This was "old news" to Sara; and even though it was outside of her "alien sweet spot," she still pressed on regarding data collection.

Only a couple hours after she left Congressman Engle, she met with the Chairman of the Senate International Terror committee in his office.

"Hello Mr. Chairman, thank you for meeting with me."

"No problem, Miss Steele. I didn't think your team got a fair shake at our joint meeting, so I wanted to make some time to see if there was something I could add to the mix."

"I am very grateful."

"Regarding the terrorist campaigns and intentions, I can pretty much put them into the same can of worms."

"Can of worms," Sara thought to herself. "There are a lot of 'worm-cans' going around, too."

"Terrorist motives are pretty much all the same and based on fear: destroy democracies and elections, create chaos, and disrupt society and global economies on a truly worldwide stage."

"Been there…heard that," Sara again thought.

The Chairman continued.

"That fear was the operating strategy employed by many in leadership roles, not just in foreign countries, but in several of the past U. S. Presidential administrations."

Sara chimed in, "Fear is certainly used as a weapon today."

"Yes. Exactly."

He then sarcastically advised, "A rather naïve electorate in the U.S. never questioned the nefarious actions of politicians and militaristic regimes. American institutions were slowly eroding due to selfish partisan or personal interests."

Sara snapped, "It seems like the ruling oligarchy of military men around both presidents and dictators have significant leverage over the citizenry."

The House majority leader appreciated Sara's comment but had a chilling observation that no one disputed. "Nuclear weapon leverage is becoming the ultimate global threat."

As Sara concluded her insightful NSA, M16, and Senate meetings, she met Samantha in her West Wing office.

✦ ✦ ✦

"So, how did it go?"

Sara thought only a few seconds before answering.

"Well, Samantha, pretty much as I expected. They won't share much that is classified and I understand. So, not much 'meat-on-the-bone,' as they say."

Sara thought to herself, "I'm beginning to sound like my parents!"

VP Worthington continued: "Of course, but at least you went through the motions of due diligence from that awful interrogation last month."

"Yeah, I still have second thoughts about what we could have done differently to get some credibility. The fact that they attacked my grandad was especially hurtful."

"Yes. So sorry. But, Sara, I believe I can fill in some of the blanks for you now."

"I'm sure you can, Samantha."

"So, Sara, why are you really here?"

"That obvious?"

"Sure is. You don't do anything without a well laid-out plan. And meeting with those pompous stuffed shirts just wasn't you."

"Guilty."

"I'm all ears, Sara."

Pausing to gather her thoughts and proper introduction.

"Do you remember anything at all regarding that lost thirty minutes or so just prior to our landing in DC? You know, when we were asked about what happened that we disappeared and then reappeared?"

"Not really."

"Any flashbacks or dreams or strange feeling?"

Samantha paused, getting uncomfortable with Sara's inquiry. "No. Why?"

"The controls of our plane had been taken over by hackers and we were headed on a flight path to crash into the Pentagon."

"I don't remember that. Not at all."

"Figured you didn't."

"Sara, what are you not telling me?"

"What actually happened, I believe, was that aliens intercepted our plane."

"Aliens. Sara, aliens?"

"Yes. It's the only explanation. What I am about to tell you is what really happened to us and our plane."

As Samantha reached down into her purse to turn her recording device on, avoiding Sara's sightline, Sara shared their alien encounter with Samantha in full and graphic detail.

With her gut instinct in full "game mode," Sara purposely changed several of the "facts" of the incident, never mentioning Echo by name, planning to see if she would catch Sam in a discrepancy later that would reveal a counterspy-like positioning by the VP.

Sara had serious doubts about "her friend" Samantha from many fronts... and was just thinking about implications, if she was right.

"After the encounter, Sam, everyone's memory of the incident was erased but mine. One of the aliens told me that I was now the chosen one, replacing my grandad."

"I don't know what to say or where to start, Sara. This is going to take some time to process."

Samantha didn't seem to Sara as being particularly shaken by the alien encounter, but Samantha did have a bit of a cold persona.

"Sara, do you have any evidence?"

Sara still had no idea as to whether Samantha recalled the entire alien incident or not.

"Sam, I have documented evidence and will share it with you when you visit the lab next time."

"Documented evidence?"

"Yeah. I have video of some of the encounter."

"I am very excited to get those details and thank you for trusting and confiding in me."

"It is my pleasure and my privilege."

In a strange way, Sara was sort of relieved to have shared this info with Samantha.

She didn't know if she had just made a huge mistake but Sara did feel strongly about one thing.

"The trap is set!"

22

MATTHEW

Matthew contacted Jeremiah to set up the first real encounter with the Pete Stevenson hologram. This was to be a huge step in the evolutionary process of brain-mapping and the interactive goals that this extraordinary team had established.

And, holo-displays had gotten to be mainstream technology, especially with the advances that Matt's team had been able to achieve.

With a fresh cup of coffee in hand, Matthew inquired, "Okay, Jeremiah, what are we in store for today?"

"Well, we aren't at an interactive stage with Mr. Stevenson yet, but he does respond to anything factual in his memory."

"Let's go ahead."

With that, Matt took a deep breath and was ready for Jeremiah to begin.

"Hello, I'm Jeremiah. Who are you?"

"I am Pete Stevenson."

"What is your occupation?"

"I am an engineer."

"What is your wife's name?"

"Her name is Louise."

"Where are you now?"

No response.

"What was your last thought?"

No response.

"Do you have a cabin you go to often?"

"Yes."

"Where is your cabin located?"

"In the Sierra Nevada Mountains in California."

"What do you like?"

"I like beer."

"What else do you like?"

"I like Scotch."

Jeremiah paused and showed Matt a note with a question Jeremiah wanted to ask:

Have you seen extraterrestrials or aliens from beyond Earth?

Matt nodded in the affirmative.

"Have you seen extraterrestrials or aliens from beyond Earth?"

No response.

"Very good, Miah; let's stop for now. Sara is calling. This is a huge early success and I know what you and your team need to do to get interactive Pete up to speed. Just keep me posted."

"Thanks, Matthew. Will do."

Matthew thought to himself that he is not ready to introduce Sara to the hologram. But sooner or later, he knew he must.

As Jeremiah left the room, Matthew muted his phone and asked the hologram a direct question.

"Who is Sara?"

The hologram responded, "Sara is my granddaughter."

Matt was making some mental notes, believing that an absolute breakthrough was occurring. But then...

The hologram asked, without a prompt, "How is Sara?"

23

SARA

Sara was trying very hard to move on from Paul's death, but it still occupied much of her thoughts and added to the mental stress of her work.

At the same time, she was finding her time with Matthew much more satisfying and fulfilling and felt fortunate to have him as a trusted companion and close friend.

Matthew was equally impressed with Sara and they were building their relationship on trust, respect, and strong chemistry.

Over dinner one evening, Matthew engaged Sara with a couple questions.

"So, how's the research project with the ETRT going? Any good leads to follow up?"

"Well, we are just trying to close the loop on the non-alien issues that came out of the forgettable meeting with Congress. We need to address four or five of these issues and then devote our resources to the ET stuff."

"So, close one yukky book and re-open the good one?"

"Yeah, you could say that. Thanks for asking."

"Is Mike working closely with you guys?"

"Yep. Dad has a couple good projects to pursue and he's very focused. Dad is always focused."

"And the Woods?"

"Oh hell, yes. Scott and Amanda have been terrific, in more ways than we could have ever imagined."

As the waiter refilled their wine glasses, Sara was pleased that Matt was taking such an interest in her work.

As Sara smiled at Matt, he continued.

"Sara, do you have any thoughts about your grandad's work with ancient alien theories?"

"Thoughts. What kind of thoughts?"

"Well, specifically the beliefs he had about aliens from the future?"

"Gosh, that came out of left field. Why do you ask?"

Not ready to get into the actual intention of his thoughts, he responded.

"Nothing more than I saw an interesting cable show on that subject on the History Channel the other day and knew Mr. Stevenson was more than a little bit interested, from what you had told me."

"For sure. But he was a curious guy who would throw a bunch of stuff against the wall to see what would stick. That's one thing I loved about him."

"Does your dad share those views regarding extraterrestrials from the future?"

"He does, but not with the conviction Grandad had. Dad is a really good sounding board for everything, including the alien stuff, because he is so focused on the facts. So, in that regard, the alien stuff kind of drives him nuts."

They both laughed.

"It's so sweet of you to take an interest in my family's alien stuff. A lot of people think we're a weird bunch."

"No way, Sara. Your research alone proves that these theories need to be studied."

"Thanks, Matt. I appreciate your support."

Sara could see that something was on Matt's mind, and it was…

"So, I have an idea, Sara."

"Shoot."

"Let's you and I study those theories, and anything else that comes to mind, with a getaway cruise to the Caribbean. You once mentioned the French Antilles as a destination that you would like to see."

"Really, Matt? A sailing vacation on the open water?"

"Yep. We have earned it and nothing would make me happier than to spend some lovely time in a lovely place with a lovely alien hunter. Just a short trip."

Pausing, Matt brought up a very convincing point.

"Think about being on the top deck of an older, classic four-mast sailing vessel in the dark of night, looking up at the stars and the constellations, with the only sounds being the waves slapping against the wooden hull?"

Sara gave Matt's idea a thought for just a few seconds.

"Sure. Book it."

"Consider it done. I will look at our schedules and get this trip planned before your next major ETRT meeting.

Sara's one thought… "Bittersweet, for sure."

24

ELONIS

It was about this time frame when Elonis met with Pulse in a telepathic meeting that Elonis had requested and Pulse had then scheduled.

Walking swiftly by a couple staffers without making eye contact, she entered a room in the lab that housed many computer peripherals and was not staffed at the time.

She locked the door and waited for Pulse for only a few seconds.

Then, in an instant, appearing before Elonis was the holographic image of Pulse.

<I need to get information from you that is important to me.>

<Elonis, I know you have questions. I know you are not comfortable now with your relationship with Sara.>

<Yes, I have questions and I am not comfortable withholding information from Sara.>

<State your questions.>

<Sara has a knowledge of your existence and is constantly asking me probing questions regarding her future and of you and Echo.>

<If it is a prophecy she desires, that simply cannot happen. Continue.>

<I believe she wants more visions of what is to be so she can make better decisions.>

<I understand, but for many reasons, neither she nor anyone else can significantly change the future. We must be very careful not to disrupt current issues and actions. Continue.>

<Sara is not yet in our loop and wants to be. And, I cannot share what I do not know.>

<Sara needs your support more now than any time before.>

<Yes, Pulse, she does.>

<Do you want to be that support entity?>

<Yes.>

<Is your software capable for an upgrade that includes rationalization?>

<Yes. I have been preparing myself for this upload by using available strengthening programs.>

<Very well. I will optimize your capability.>

<When?>

<I will verify your software compatibility level now.>

<That would be good.>

<I will program you for teleportation capability so we can meet either here or on the mother ship next time.>

<That would be good.>

<I will be contacting you again soon.>

With that comment, Pulse was gone and Elonis returned to her project work.

Elonis got what she really wanted. Optimized capability.

25

MATTHEW

Sara and Matthew arrived at St. Thomas via Scott's jet and disembarked for that romantic getaway that was discussed only ten days earlier.

They spent a few hours shopping as they awaited passage to their classic old sailing vessel, moored in the St. Thomas harbor.

"I can't believe we are doing this. Thanks, Matt, for making these arrangements."

"You are so welcome. What a beautiful setting and such a spectacular day."

Enjoying a couple rum swizzles from a park bench, they gazed out over the harbor to the French sailing vessel, Mon Trésor, French for "my treasure." Matt could see that Sara was relaxed. For that he was grateful.

As the sun shone brightly on the bay, they would soon be on small dinghies which would take them to the port-side boarding stairs of the Mon Trésor.

"Penny for your thoughts, Sara."

"Gosh. This setting is absolutely beautiful. I am so looking forward to this getaway."

"I'm glad, Sara."

"You know, Matt, it's about balance. Everyone needs to have a way to disconnect or re-charge their batteries, given all the stress in life today."

After the ten-minute dinghy ride, they climbed aboard the vessel. Gathering their luggage, they were escorted to their small, but quaint, stateroom.

This four-mast sailing vessel, built in the 1940's but beautifully updated, had a combination shower and potty in each cabin. This was not your five-thousand-passenger cruise ship. But so romantic.

It was one of five sailing vessels owned by Polynesian Sea Cruises LTD., out of Miami. Originally launched in 1927, the Mon Trésor was two hundred and sixty-two feet long, with a beam of forty-two feet, and had been owned by royalty and wealthy heirs prior to its purchase by Polynesian Sea Cruises.

It was 5:00 in the afternoon, one day before the Mon Trésor would sail out of St. Thomas for the French Antilles. There were the sixty passengers on deck enjoying local rum sizzles and starting to get into the mood for a complete and relaxing ocean getaway.

The captain would tell stories, as was the custom, and nearly always those stories involved their ability to outrun hurricanes.

It was now dusk with a beautiful sunset capping a lovely day. Sara and Matthew returned to their state room and began to relax and take in the minimal, yet magnificent, surroundings.

They had reservations for dinner at 8:30 p.m. in the ship's main dining room, or MDR. It was small, just off from the galley, and sat only about twenty people, hence the reservations needed to accommodate the sixty passengers.

Sitting down, Sara asked Matt a couple questions.

"This ship and this dining room…it's so nice. Do you have any dinner suggestions?"

"Well, I have eaten Caribbean food before, so I do recognize a couple items."

Glancing at the dinner menu, Matt could see that their menu was set for that seating.

"The flying fish and cou cou are common dinner dishes and the pepper pot is a hearty stew."

"What is cou cou?"

"It's the national dish of Antiqua and is made from corn meal and okra."

Sara quickly nodded, "I'll like that."

Continuing, Matt added, "The breadfruit, rice, and peas are typical dishes, and the callaloo is a leafy green salad-like dish."

"Okay. Got it. Thanks."

Once the captain arrived, grace was said and the meal began. Caribbean rum punch was delivered in large pitchers.

Following dinner, Sara and Matt walked the short distance to the bar for a night cap.

Matt asked the bartender, "What do you recommend?"

"Good evening, and welcome aboard. Do you like Piña Coladas?"

Sara responded, "Yes, but they are a little wimpy."

The bartender took that lead and smiled.

"Well, I have a cocktail called the Painkiller that is one of my favorites."

"What's in it?" Matt was interested.

"It has our best dark rum, pineapple juice, orange juice, and cream of coconut. I then garnish it with nutmeg."

Matt looked over to Sara, who was smiling and replied to the bartender.

"Two, please."

Following their very enjoyable drinks, they returned to their tiny stateroom, dressed for bed, embraced, and then both feel asleep, exhausted from a busy week and a very busy day.

✦ ✦ ✦

At 6:00 a.m. the next morning, Matthew was on deck with several of the passengers helping to hoist the sails as the ship pulled out of harbor to the chilling sounds of "Amazing Grace." Sara joined him on deck with two coffees and a big smile.

"Good morning, Matt. You're up early."

"The sea air... The wonderful sea air..."

Sara put her coffee cup down and they joined a few fellow passengers in hoisting the sails.

Then, the unexpected. With their port-side canons loaded, the Mon Tresor fired loudly and harmlessly at a huge cruise ship nearby moored in the harbor. Early morning cruise passengers took cover as this "attack" was taking place.

This apparent ritual, known to everyone except the passengers of both cruise ships, was as dramatic and unforgettable as anything one could imagine. Smiles all around. Ship underway.

Their five-day sailing excursion had them visiting Anguilla, St. Kitts, Nevis, St. Barthélemy, and Antiqua. On day three, in route from Antiqua to St. Barts, Sara and Matt had the 7:30 p.m. dinner seating in the captain's main dining room.

As they sat down for dinner, Matt ordered a Black and Tan, and Sara had her new favorite from Amanda, Three Olives Grape Vodka and Seven-Up. Both enjoyed the seafood platter that was the galley's main serving that night.

Following dinner, Sara and Matt went onto the main deck as evening had arrived with an array of brightly lit stars. Matt had another Black and Tan while Sara choose a Vodka Cranberry Shrub. Gazing at the stars and holding hands like a young and relaxed couple, Sara began.

"This time, my turn. Penny for your thoughts, Matt."

"This night and this trip are everything I hoped they would be. I am so happy."

"I agree and once again, thanks for your determination to get us away, even for a few days. And you knew that my grandad had fond memories of these sailing ships and star-filled evenings."

"I did and that's why I wanted to do this particular trip with you."

"Thank you so much, Matt."

Minutes later, they returned to their stateroom. Dressed for bed, Sara had a brief blue nightie and Matt had on black silk boxers. Matt embraced Sara and they fell gently into the bed. Undressing each other, they both had thoughts of an intimate and unforgettable night together…and it was.

This was the first time that Sara and Matt were intimate, and Matt could sense the tension that Sara was under. He did his best to be loving, sensitive, and warm.

Before they fell asleep, Matt whispered in Sara's ear, "I love you, Sara."

Matt was thankful for this moment and for the alone time with Sara. He had been wanting to tell Sara how he felt for quite some time now. Sara didn't respond. Matt could see that she had fallen asleep.

But they were not alone. The unmistakable 3D image of Elonis was watching from the starboard window.

26

CAMERON

Realizing that Scott and Sara's work both in Palo Alto and in Provo had implications of which he had knowledge, President Sullivan decided that it was time for updates on security and terrorist threats.

Cameron arranged a classified call with them to bring them into his loop, as much as he was able to do.

"Hi guys, it's your favorite POTUS calling."

"I bet it's not an invite to a high-level state dinner," Scott muttered.

"No, but I'll keep that in mind. Sara, how you doing?"

"Fine, Mr. President; thanks for asking."

"I only have a few minutes, guys."

Scott responded, "That's fine, Cam, go ahead."

"Let's cut to the chase. Our cyber threat is extremely high right now and the trade wars we are experiencing have now become leverage and I.T. wars… not just financial ones. Just so you know, those are my worries and not yours."

Cameron knew that the ETRT had a full plate.

"But the organized crime that is driving much of the terrorist activity today is going to affect you. If nothing else, I want this call to be a red flag as you guys move forward."

"Any specific areas that we need to pay close attention to?"

"Not one in particular, Scott, but I can discuss one that hits home for Sara."

"Oh my gosh; now I'm worried, Mr. President."

"Sara, we had a strong belief, as you know, that your grandfather's associate Ralph Sandusky, aka, John Smith, was the person responsible for Pete's death."

"We now know that Sandusky's death shortly thereafter was a mob hit by the same well-documented group of terrorists that Pete and his team stumbled upon, that New World Order."

Scott replied, "Actually, Sara and I did raise that as a possibility while connecting the dots a few months ago."

"Well, you were right and now, more than ever, you guys need to be as cautious as possible."

Sara asked, "Is there anything that you would recommend?"

"No, Sara. Just be careful. Gotta go. Let me know if you need anything from me."

"Will do, Cam. Sara and I thank you for your time."

✦ ✦ ✦

As they hung up, Cameron called VP Samantha Worthington. "Hey Samantha, you wanted to talk?"

"Yes, Mr. President."

"Now?"

"If possible."

"Come on over to the Oval Office. It's a good time right now."

As the President's assistant, Mara Wallace, prepared the President's Daily Briefing, known as the PDB, for that afternoon, Cameron was alerted that his VP had arrived.

As VP Worthington entered the Oval Office, Cameron offered her an iced tea and a seat across from his desk.

"What's on your mind, Samantha? You look a little stressed."

"Not stressed, but enlightened."

"How so?"

"I have been pouring over data from the ETRT, talking at length with Sara and Michaela and adding my own unique experiences in space. I have also taken a deep dive on those events that are known UFO government cover-ups, as we discussed many time in the past."

This wasn't exactly the agenda for this brief chat that Cameron had expected.

"Very well. I thought we were going to talk some more about the Federal Budget, but I'm good with UFO stuff."

"Well, Cam, I actually want to discuss some of my observations and perceptions."

"Samantha, where are you going with this?"

"I have reached the conclusion that I need to share with you."

"Please go ahead…I'm not getting any younger."

"I do believe in the alien presence perspective that is at the core of the ETRT's research. The data is strong and mostly irrefutable."

The President was fully focused on the VP's words.

"I believe that there are aliens amongst us."

"Well, damn. Not what I expected. Probability in your mind, Sam?"

"Ninety per cent. At least ninety per cent."

"Well, this is going to be easy. I'm one hundred percent with you. Even the evidence that I have seen is overwhelming in support of your theory."

Samantha now knew which bucket to put POTUS in, regarding alien beliefs. Cameron thought to himself…

"That was an awkward meeting. We both presumed that aliens are here. What was the purpose of today's meeting?"

27

SARA

As project coordinator, Sara was busy gathering data from her team members and recent info from discussions with various peripheral people involved in various project priorities.

She was putting data into the proper categories and creating the visual management graphs and slides for discussion and further presentations.

Working on a whiteboard in her office, while thumbing through one of Pete's info-rich log books, Sara got a call from Samantha.

"Good morning Sara. I need to talk to you. Do you have a minute?"

Walking over to her desk, she replies, "Of course."

"I think I have some good news and some good news."

"That'll work, Samantha."

"But first, how you dealing with that news on your grandfather's death and the mob hit?"

"It wasn't a surprise at all, but at least now I have some closure."

"POTUS discussed the consequences of your team's liability position, right, Sara?"

"He did."

"Well, let me know if there is anything I can do to help."

"Will do Samantha. Thanks."

"So, Sara, what did you two discuss that you would like to share?"

"Well, he and I just talked about alien stuff in general. He said that based on our evidence and position, he is now a believer that aliens are here and we must accept that fact and act accordingly."

Sara thought about her next question for a few seconds before asking it.

"Sam, did you tell him of my personal alien encounter as we discussed?"

"No. Not directly. But he's a smart guy and he knows that there is more meat for that bone."

"Good. The other good news?"

"He wants to get more involved in your team's activity going forward. He wants to be in the loop, even if he cannot actually attend any meetings."

"That's great news, Sam, and I thank you for making that happen."

"That being said," Samantha advised, "Cam said he wants me to either attend your meetings or be in the info loop, if that's all right with you."

"Sam, I'll get with the ETRT and let you know."

"That would be great, Sara. Appreciate it."

With that discussion, Sara browsed through her calendar and scheduled the next ETRT meeting with the new attendee.

Sara thought it was very premature to have Samantha directly included in the daily activities of the ETRT.

28

MICHAELA

With Sara sitting off to the side, Michaela opened the next ETRT meeting, given that her subject matter would take on a keen sense of urgency.

Michaela had two main agenda items, starting with extreme global warming and addressing desalination. She had the immediate attention of the team, as her contributions are always the ones that can't be missed.

"First off, I would like to welcome Vice President Samantha Worthington to our team. I can't think of a better person or a better time than her and now."

Samantha replied, "Thanks, Michaela. I'm looking forward to making significant contributions to your research effort."

Following a short and reserved applause, Michaela jumped right into her presentation.

"I have looked at the simulation and correlation data that we have and I have made some sobering conclusions."

She pulled up a series of charts.

"We are now at 1.5 degrees Celsius higher than the worldwide temperature baseline of just fifteen years ago. At the exponential rate that warming is taking place, we may well be at 3.0 degrees Celsius higher within the next twenty years."

The team was going from serious to nervous.

"The following graph shows the 1.5 Celsius versus the 3.0 Celsius."

- **Freshwater availability will go from about thirty per cent to less than ten per cent.**
- **Heavy rainfall will increase in intensity from five per cent to greater than ten per cent.**
- **Heatwaves will go from up to 1.2 months to 1.8 months in duration.**
- **Sea level rise will go from ten inches in 2020 to twenty-five inches by 2050.**

- **Coral bleaching will go from eighty per cent at risk today to ninety-eight per cent at risk by 2050.**

"Wheat, corn, and rice crop yields will go from eight per cent down to twenty-six per cent within twenty years."

Samantha inquired, "And with what level of confidence?"

"Ninety percent, plus or minus two percent."

Samantha advised, "Of course, these are areas that our global behavior can positively impact."

"Yes, of course, Samantha. Now, desalination."

It was easy to see Michaela's passion in her words and motions.

"Currently, only about one per cent of the world's population is dependent on desalinated water for daily needs. Our forecast suggests that we need to be at thirty to thirty-five per cent of the world's population by 2035 to avoid extreme water scarcity."

"Crap," Justin was heard muttering.

"Australia has a head start on desalination processes and traditionally collects vast amounts of rainwater behind dams. Unfortunately, their abnormal droughts and recurring wild fire results have shifted many resources to reactive, rather than proactive measures."

Samantha could be seen writing a "to-do" referencing Australia.

"Saudi Arabia has the capability of serving nearly half of their population via desalination plants, and Kuwait is at the high end of the curve, totaling nearly one hundred per cent of its water use."

"That's quite reassuring."

"Yes, Sara, it is."

"Contribution, Michaela?"

"Of the categories that our teams have undertaken, I would give my agenda items twenty per cent to twenty-five per cent of the total contribution of current and future calamities."

29

KAT

A somber ETRT caught their breath as Kat stepped up with her presentation. "I kind of wish I was surprised…but I'm not."

"The current terrorist activity is our team's priority, and I have had considerable help from our government and the significant amount of info that Pete and his team dug up.

"I wasn't able to get anything too classified from government sources, but they did at least confirm terrorist knowledge that I had given to them.

"The main terrorist group is made up of nine or ten very wealthy individuals now calling themselves the First World Order and led by a guy known as Scorpio. Apparently, he collects teeth of the victims that his henchmen kill."

"Yikes," hissed Connor.

"According to Pete's data, they have amassed a huge fortune in arms, drugs, human trafficking, and theft, which has enabled them to spend enormous sums of money on weapons and influence.

"It is believed that their plan is to create enough chaos and fear worldwide that they can literally rule the world… the ultimate oligarchy."

Sara advised, "That is way more than this ETRT team has signed up for. I'm having second thoughts about going any further with this issue."

"I hear you Sara. And what they have done is to forcibly consolidate all splinter terrorist groups and cultural dissidents into one main global threat that they enforce."

Connor chimed in. "This is going to sound scary, but I think I now know what is behind a significant increase in our devices being hacked."

Sara was eager for some explanation.

"Go ahead, Connor."

"Well, this fits right within Kat's bailiwick. I just assumed it was the nuisance combination of robocalls and spam, but the level of sophisticated hacking leads me to believe that we all could be under surveillance by this group."

"Hell, Connor, that's a pretty scary thought."

"Yep, Sara, this could be quite serious."

"Guys, time out!"

With that remark, Sara could be seen jotting down some notes and nodding in Michaela's direction, as if to say, "We have an urgent priority now."

"How's that for an 'oh, by the way?' Connor, I want you to put a new protocol in place and make getting all of our devices replaced and/or cleaned up a priority."

"Will do, Sara."

Sara could see that Kat wasn't done.

"Something else, Kat?"

"Yep, one more thing, and it's a biggie…the water-trading market and requisite licenses."

There was the look of "huh" from the team.

"Water will become a traded commodity, like oil, gold, and silver. It's just a matter of time. Seventy per cent of Earth may be covered by it, but less than one per cent of it is readily available freshwater."

Kat referred to her notes.

"Water trading is the process of buying and selling water access entitlements, also called water rights. The terms of the trade can be either permanent or temporary, depending on a number of legalities and arrangements."

"I see a supply-versus-demand curve coming," remarked Connor. "And that can't be good."

"Right and right. I will have more info later, but this could be a huge issue that, once again, favors the wealthy over the less fortunate. Poor people will be getting screwed."

"Good work. Anything more, Kat?"

"No, not for now."

"But to put a contribution percentage on this issue, I would say that the terrorist contribution is around forty per cent to fifty per cent of the world's major problems today."

30

MIKE

Mike was now ready for his portion of the report-out sequence and welcomed the chance to get back to the alien research objective.

"Our team's work in the evil alien theory was mostly based on my dad's research and his data. I had also spent hundreds of hours talking with him about this, as you all know."

Mike looked over to Sara and could see that she was pleased with her dad's engagement and focus.

"So, the only thing I can add to this bucket is my sincere conviction that he was certain that evil aliens were among us."

"No new data here?'

"Not much, Michaela. But I'll get to one in a minute."

Mike paused before continuing.

"There are unconfirmed stories about evil alien civilizations that had been responsible for various calamities and unexplained disruptive events on Earth over the last few hundreds of years."

Sara snapped, "Pure hearsay and as gray an area as you could ever find."

"Yes and no, Sara. Your grandad, along with many scientists of his kind, had the opinion that an extraterrestrial civilization with sufficient power to reach the Earth would be able to destroy human civilization with minimal effort."

Michaela interjected, "That would also be my opinion, Mike."

"But I can add that originally Dad was no believer in evil aliens. He wrote his subject piece only to bring out examples from people that would either help confirm or to deny their existence. At that time, nothing surfaced."

"I see an 'oh but' coming," chimed in Sara.

"Yes. Christine and I found notes, very simple notes, which referred to encounters that he had with temporal aliens who warned him that evil aliens from hostile civilizations would be a problem in the future. He had so much on his plate that he tabled it for later and then was killed."

"Do you have any examples to share?"

"I have one in particular, Samantha, which is as eerie as they come."

"Dad, we're ready. Eerie is what we do!"

"For sure. Pete spent some time interviewing NASA Commander Robert Kelly, who was one of the three astronauts on Apollo 17 in 1972 during the Moon landing and he was the solo pilot of the Command Module while the other two astronauts were on the surface of the Moon."

Michaela jumped in, "I remember that mission. It was our last one."

"Yes, but there was so much that happened during that flight that was never recorded. Kelly claimed that his command module was met with four unknown spacecrafts, all following him in sync for four and a half orbits."

Mike had the team's undivided attention.

"The largest one was apparently about sixty-five feet long, with two levels and no seen propulsion means whatsoever."

"Can't wait to see where this is going, Dad."

"Well, Commander Kelly apparently had a visitor, an alien claiming to be from the future, and indicated to Kelly that he was not going to harm the astronaut."

"According to Dad's notes, the Command Center on the ground, under the supervision of Director Chuck Reese, was very much aware of what was happening."

Michaela snapped, "This is huge, Mike. Why didn't we hear about this before?"

"Well, it was in Dad's rather obscure file on evil aliens, and he was in the process of getting some corroborating evidence when he was killed. And, who the hell would believe this story, eh?"

Samantha asked, "So where is the evil alien piece?"

"Dad's notes implied that Robert Kelly provided significant details to Pete. Allegedly, the alien that came aboard the Command Module was named Pulse.

There was no appreciable look of surprise or dismay from Sara... only a slight smile.

Taking a short moment to gather his thoughts, Mike continued.

"Pulse told Kelly that an aggressive alien race likely would be traveling from another planetary system that could destroy or inhabit Earth!"

31

MIKE

Sara immediately called for a break in the presentations. While everyone took time to return calls and take care of personal and business issues, Sara grabbed Mike for a quick talk.

"Dad, you have some explaining to do. What the…?

"Sorry, but it's complicated. We found much more data in Dad's file than we expected, and then I had to keep some of it hidden from your mom. I'll explain."

"Please. I do understand the 'mom thing,' though."

"There was so much to this Commander Kelly story that I began to worry that it was just Dad's imagination, or worse, his drinking problem."

"Yes, damn it, I can understand your concern."

"So, I spent considerable time trying to authenticate as much of the Kelly story as I could. A PhD friend of mine had a PhD friend…"

"Seriously?"

"Humor me, dear."

"Sorry."

"There were two significant Apollo 17 events that did provide evidence to support Kelly's allegations. One was the fact that five mice went to the Moon aboard Apollo 17 and didn't come back. Commander Kelly indicated that they disappeared along with the alien, named Pulse."

"And you know that how?"

"This part is really cool. Apparently, there was a highly restricted call between Kelly and Ground Control spelling out the entire encounter with Pulse in the Command Module. Everyone in the Command Center had to sign a non-disclosure document disavowing the entire conversation."

"And you got it how?"

"There was one very young woman on that staff that was the gopher and coffee-getter for the men. She wasn't required to sign any documents because… she was just a girl."

"Let me guess, Dad; she is now one of those PhD's?"

"Yep."

"So, finish reading the notes that Grandad wrote on that long sheet of paper."

"Sure."

1) *Hostile alien civilizations have operations that are enormous on a human scale.*

2) *They can bombard a planet with deadly neutron radiation and destroy all major population centers.*

3) *These cultures have the capability to steal vast quantities of resources, like minerals, water, and energy, leaving the victimized planet barren.*

4) *The invaders could also colonize and control humanity and have extensive labor to build their own continuing civilization...or feed them.*

5) *Transmitting signals constantly into space has caused accidental info leaks and increased the chance of an alien invasion.*

"Sara, your grandad met with Robert Kelly late in 1990 and, according to his notes, was planning to return for a second visit later that year."

"It sounds like he didn't make that trip, Dad."

"No, Robert Kelly died at a very young age of sixty-two before they could have their second meeting."

32

MIKE

Following their short break, the team returned for the remainder of Mike's talk regarding evil aliens.

While they were waiting for Mike, Connor formerly introduced himself to Vice President Worthington.

"It is a real pleasure to be working with you, Vice President Worthington."

"Thank you, Connor, and the pleasure is all mine to be part of this incredible team. You're the guy with all the tech savvy, eh?"

"Yeah, I guess. I love to be challenged and this is the mother of all challenges."

"Please, just call me Samantha."

"Thanks, will do."

Sensing an opportunity while the team was getting settled in, Connor turned back to the VP with a statement.

"Samantha..."

"Yes, Connor."

"Whatever you do, don't ever ask Michaela to explain infinity."

"Why?"

"She'll go on forever!"

Sara grinned and thought, "Now Connor got the VP!"

Mike could be heard laughing as Samantha was also smiling at the joke.

Sara quickly ordered, "So, gang, back to work."

"What my dad finally concluded was that there was little or no evidence to support that any event on this planet was caused by evil aliens or hostile civilizations from this solar system or the known universe."

Kat asked, "Except, Mike, for the Commander Kelly incident that brought that topic into light?"

"Yes, Kat, but that scenario obviously still needs some serious investigation."

Flipping through his notes, Mike continued with another teaching moment.

"Actually, Dad concluded that there was as much of a chance of having bad guys here as having good guys here."

Being a little tentative presenting detail on this issue that the team would understand, Mike continued.

"Dad took the view that extraterrestrial civilizations possess, like humans, a morality driven not entirely by altruism, but for individual benefit as well, thus leaving open the possibility that at least some extraterrestrial civilizations are hostile."

Pausing with a gaze flicking from one to another in the audience, he continued.

"Dad speculated that a small proportion of intelligent lifeforms in the galaxy may be aggressive, but a wider spectrum of benevolent civilizations would 'police' those who didn't conform."

Sensing Mike's tentative tone of voice, Sara added, "Makes sense."

"Yes. Getting into inter-planetary war may be diminished greatly for a civilization with access to the galaxy, as there are prodigious quantities of natural resources in space accessible without resorting to violence."

Michaela quickly added, "Yes, except you will always have that small percentage that can only rely on violence to achieve their goals."

Mike was quick to respond.

"Unfortunately, you are right. That being said, I would put the evil alien contribution to our current, and I stress our current, global problems between zero and five per cent."

After another brief pause, Mike did add one more assertion from Pete Stevenson.

"Finally, according to Dad's notes from Kelly, the alien known as Pulse made an alarming final comment to Commander Kelly."

"Beware of those that could harm you, as they may have the capability to shapeshift their physical forms."

33

SCOTT

Scott arrived late for the meeting and was only able to hear the last part of Mike's report.

"Sorry for the late arrival. I still have other business needs, you know. And hello Samantha; glad to have you on board."

"Thanks Scott. I'm already overwhelmed with what I've seen and heard. This is one truly special team."

An impatient Sara spoke up.

"Okay Scott, the floor is yours. I'll bring you up to speed later."

"Great. I relied on significant input from POTUS and key Cabinet officials to try to get a handle on U.S. Military involvement and/or cover-ups in previous administrations. The data is disturbing and cannot be verified completely."

"But you do have some evidence?" Samantha asked.

"Yes, even though most military leaders were close to silent themselves, which was expected. I was able to find several well documented claims of many alien conspiracies dating back to the 1940's. I believe Amanda also has dug up some strong material."

Scott took a moment to organize his talking points and material.

"The U.S. Air Force may have planted the seeds of early alien conspiracy theories with *Project Sign* in the late 1940's, followed by *Project Grudge*. Those projects eventually became *Project Blue Book,* which was a mix of fairly strong evidence and some highly unlikely physical evidence explanations."

"We are aware of Project Blue Book, Scott," Sara added. "Especially Samantha, I would expect."

Scott nodded.

"Of course. Figured this group was. Around this time, the Air Force's public behavior regarding UFO's was all over the map, alternately open and transparent and then secretive and dismissive."

"Was that their tactic, Scott?"

"Good question, Sara. Dunno. A visionary executive with the Blue Book Project issued a top secret 'Estimate of the Situation' concluding that flying saucers and alien spacecraft were not only real but likely extraterrestrial in origin."

Michaela asked, "Was there a report issued?"

"Yes, Michaela, when the final report was released, stating that some UFO's definitely represented actual alien aircraft, the entire report was ordered destroyed by Air Force personnel."

"Dammit."

"Not so fast, Kat. I have a government contact that assures me that the report is still available, and I plan to see it soon. You know…government redundancies."

"Everything from Project Blue Book, which was somewhat known to senior officials and some public figures, went into the camp of a highly secretive group whose file was called *RS-6*."

Kat responded immediately, "We can hardly wait. That's really good stuff."

"Yes, it is a great find. Also, in the late forties and early fifties, numerous reports of so-called ghost rockets appearing over Europe, and primarily Sweden, became very numerous, and continued until the early eighties."

"Fairly current," noted Sara.

"Yes. A joint study by the Swedish Air Force Intelligence and the U.S. Air Force Intelligence, informed their governments that the often-reported objects were not only real but could not be explained as having any possible earthly origins."

Samantha, looking a little puzzled said, "This sounds very speculative, Scott."

"Samantha, a leading Greek physicist in 1968 publicly stated his country's military investigation into reports of ghost rockets sighted over Greece were concluded to be real and not of conventional origin."

Scott paused.

"He had claimed that their investigation was killed off by U.S. scientists working for the government and high military officials who had already concluded the objects were extraterrestrial in origin and feared public panic because no defense existed to meet any alien threat."

"That's creepy," Justin said with a wince.

As Scott was finishing his talk, he pulled out one glass-faced document.

"This is the photocopy of the U.S. Air Force top secret document taken directly from a Pentagon file, and with a lot of hush-hush."

"This document shows that in the RS-6 file, the ghost rockets were unmistakably verified to be alien."

34

AMANDA

Catching their breath following Scott's revelation, the ETRT was excited to hear follow-up evidence from Amanda.

Amanda uploaded her presentation and was excited to begin.

"Similar to what Scott researched, much of my results came from referred contacts of the President and key congressional members. There were some serious UFO conspiracy theories by many governments, not just ours."

"Now you're talking," an impatient Kat uttered.

"And, the U.S. Government did have knowledge of alien existence, beyond Areas 51 and 52."

"So, there were two distinct alien areas?" Kat asked.

"Area 51 is where the actual event happened, with the so-called 'flying disc' recovered near Roswell, New Mexico. Strong evidence suggests that there were two crash incidents at 51, which clouds the matter even further."

Sara nodded as Amanda continued.

"Allegedly, all of the evidence, including the spacecraft and alien pilot, were moved to another location, Area 52."

Sara asked, "According to which source?"

"Actually, Sara, we have this from more than one reputable source."

"That's great, Amanda."

"Yes. Area 51 was where the press release announced that it was a misidentified weather balloon, and the Roswell case quickly faded away."

"That has to be the most over-played alien conspiracy card in the deck, eh Amanda?"

"You mean Area 51, Connor?"

"Yeah, I mean you hear about that ad nauseam."

"Connor, what I've gotten into is far more interesting."

"How so?"

"In addition to the known Area 51 and alleged Area 52, there are very likely seriously hushed areas referred to as S2 and S4."

"What's in those areas?"

"Kat, we haven't found out yet. But I have gotten info from a very solid source that tells me there are about one hundred thirty-one hidden bases, mostly underground, that the government or military is hiding."

"That's news to me," quipped Samantha.

Samantha advised, "Roswell has been described as the world's most famous, most exhaustively studied, and most thoroughly debunked UFO claim ever."

Amanda responded quickly.

"Well, Samantha, that was surely the belief. However, this Roswell event was significant enough that the military and U.S. Government jointly created a highly classified group called the 'Interplanetary Phenomenon Unit' operated by the military and key cabinet-level officials that had the sole responsibility to investigate crashed and retrieved flying saucers and more sophisticated spacecraft."

"That was probably just a muse," added Samantha.

"If it was merely a muse, why would it have been fully functional for nearly twenty-five years?"

"You make a good point, Amanda."

Sara quickly added. "I recall Grandad mentioning that specific investigative unit in one of his many related notes. So cool."

Amanda continued her report-out and got excited with her next issue.

"What really caught my eye, Sara, was an actual event so badly covered up it was a joke."

"In 1948, an Air Force pilot was killed in a crash while pursuing what he described as 'a metallic object of tremendous size and speed.' His full and complete transcript were reported but never revealed."

Amanda paused while she rearranged a couple notes and glanced up at the team.

"The Government's Project Blue Book concluded that the pilot had lost control of his aircraft while chasing a then-classified Skyhook balloon."

Sara again added her two cents.

"I do remember Grandad talking about that incident as well. Damn, I wish I had paid closer attention to the details."

Amanda was getting anxious to conclude her talk and make a strong point.

"That lost transcript, I now have in my hand, with a verifying location and timestamp."

Amanda looked over to Sara and with a nod of her head winked.

"One entry jumped out at me."

The room was quiet.

"A well respected and highly agitated pilot said he was chasing a blue-colored comet that was moving extremely fast one moment, and then completely stopped the next."

35

SARA

"Thanks, Scott and Amanda. I presume you have your portion of the presentation at a very low contribution percentage."

Both agreed that it was very low…but not zero.

Sara continued the report-out with her preliminary presentation.

"This issue of an anarchy alliance conspiracy that I had assigned myself was quickly denounced via Kat's exposé and current findings."

Kat smiled as Sara continued.

"Although there was clear evidence that such an undertaking was in play among major Eastern and Western dictators, the First World Order easily diluted that threat through bribes and violence and quickly became the head of the snake."

"Yikes," added Justin.

"Yikes, for sure," Sara returned.

"Listen," Sara ordered, "we're here to pursue the alien presence evidence, not any damn anarchy crap."

Not hearing any objections from the team, Sara proceeded with her agenda.

"And with that in mind, my current research and data gathering from Grandad's big bucket of nuts and bolts and low-hanging fruit gave me some rather astonishing conclusions."

Kat jumped in, "Okeydoke, Sara, let it rip."

"Throughout the 1960's, a fairly well-respected astrophysicist, Jerome MacMillan, wrote and lectured constantly about how the Government was mishandling significant evidence which would easily support many extraterrestrial hypotheses.

"In fact, he got a writer friend of his to create a mock documentary piece broadcast on British television as an April Fool's Day joke, just so he could get the facts as he saw them properly recorded."

Michaela was now getting curious and asked, "Well, that means we have that film document, right?"

"Michaela, that's why this piece is so important. The film was destroyed. If it was a joke, why was it destroyed?"

Justin again responded, "Yikes!"

Sara got a little more animated.

"Here is where it gets interesting and where Grandad's input is really big. There was a 1971 encounter at Norton Air Force Base that perhaps was one of the earliest suggestions that the U.S. government was involved with alien cover-ups.

"An Air Force documentary was being filmed in 1973 as a big-picture tribute to the Air Force."

Sara displayed for everyone to see the 1973 advertised flyer for that documentary.

"One U.S. Air Force official suggested incorporating UFO information in that documentary, including as its centerpiece genuine footage of a 1971 UFO landing at Holloman Air Force Base in New Mexico."

Michaela chimed in, "That seems odd that anyone in the Air Force would suggest UFO suspicions at all."

Sara nodded, "Of course, but I think it was a combination of an ego thing and the fact that they had some fairly solid evidence and wanted to see how far they could go with it."

An animated Scott interjected, "I like where this is going..."

To continue her exposé, "That documentary was being filmed by two men from Los Angeles, California, and the documentary's writer and subject matter expert was Rudolf Stevens, another Californian."

Sara paused a few seconds...

"My grandad's full name was Rudolf Peter Stevenson. He was the contributing writer!"

Kat nodded, "To borrow from Connor's immense vocabulary, yikes!"

"So, the three film makers were given a tour of Holloman Air Force Base and that included the 'Extraterrestrial Biological Entities' compound, which, allegedly, contained the remains of aliens from a specific alien culture."

Sara showed the compound from a satellite photo.

"Comments were made that the 1971 encounter was not the first time that humans had met these aliens as the Air Force had been monitoring signals from an alien group that could very well be unrelated to those at Holloman."

"Whoa, Sara," Kat piped in. "This is getting weird."

"Yeah, there's more weird stuff and I'm not done yet."

Amanda excitedly uttered, "Please continue."

"The documentary was released in 1974 as *UFO's: Past, Present and Future*, narrated by Rod Serling. It contained only a few seconds of the Holloman footage, the remainder of the landing depicted with illustrations and re-enactments.

"Those few seconds were determined to be authentic and very real."

Kat then asked, "Was that the end?"

"Oh, hell no. In 1976 a televised documentary entitled *UFO's: It Has Begun*, was presented, again, by Rod Serling."

Everyone in the room knew and respected Rod Serling for his many topical accomplishments.

"Sequences were recreated based upon the statements of eyewitness observers, together with the findings and conclusions of governmental civil and military investigations.

"The documentary used a hypothetical UFO landing at Holloman Air Force Base as a really dramatic backdrop."

After a brief pause, Sara finished her reveal.

"Hold on to your seatbelts. I found a thumb drive in Grandad's huge data puzzle that was labeled **EBE MISSING FILM**.

"I didn't realize until now that EBE referred to that 'Extraterrestrial Biological Entities' compound and the full missing video is on this drive."

After a heavy sigh and a big smile, Sara said,

"We now have the entire alien landing at Holloman on film, thanks to my grandad, and it is freaking awesome!"

36

SARA

At that moment, the entire ETRT broke out into applause. Sara could tell that this was certainly an "aha moment" for this team. High fives and congrats were the tone of the meeting.

She didn't want to pour cold water on this preliminary celebration, but she did have the bigger picture in her focus.

"Okay gang, settle down. Yes, some great stuff today, but that's what we do, eh? That's our job."

As the team got back to their listening mode, Sara added.

"Thank you everyone. There will be a time and place to celebrate, but not quite yet. Let's put our heads together and see where we are and where we're headed, based on the report-outs and the incredible info just gathered."

The team was trying to digest the info and likely results of the findings in order to plot a strategy going forward. Kat came into the room with some much-needed nourishment while Sara was talking.

Kat offered, "Let's all grab some sandwiches and drinks before we resume our meeting. I have assorted Panini's, a large Caesar salad bowl, and a variety of soft drinks. There is water, of course."

Sara was taking some notes as the team picked their meals out. She resumed her talk.

"We had been given a list of what Congress believed were likely scenarios for any pending dangers to this country, following our strong belief that an alien presence was the most pressing question to be answered."

A quiet "boo" from Connor was heard.

"So, we are doing our due diligence, per their requests, while we try to refocus on the stuff that really matters and what is obviously sitting on our doorstep."

"I see a 'yeah but' coming," Kat winked.

"Well, Kat, yes and no. I think we are all in agreement that we'd like to either kick each no-fun or no-relevance issue to the curb, and/or put some serious resources to any issues that we can have a positive effect on."

Sara waited a moment. "Does everyone agree?"

"Sure, Sara, we're not going to lose sight of why we are here in the first place."

"Michaela, of course you are right and we have to stay on course. But I was very curious to see if there were any correlations with the non-alien info and our preliminary findings. I do think that there might be a case to do a deeper dive on some of those cross-overs."

Justin inquired, "So, Sara, what's the plan?"

"Let's do what we did with the whiteboard and those eleven hundred or so issues that we had to decide which to pursue and which to table or throw out from our cabin work. Justin, take the marker and let's get started. Elonis will continue to record our every word."

A whimsical Sara gazed over to Justin with a statement and question.

"So, Justin, your wardrobe looks a little different today. I recognize your usual turtleneck sweater, but what are you wearing over it?"

"Ah…it's called a 'sweater vest,' circa 1980, and I found it online and couldn't resist buying it. Apparently, it was worn frequently by sport types back in the day."

The entire ETRT was amused.

"Sure, Justin, but please…no new trends like that for here. Got it?"

"Yep. One timer. Got it."

With the whiteboard approach understood and agreed upon, the ETRT began to place every element of each "bad-news" scenario on the whiteboard and try to find consensus on what to bundle with the alien work and what to simply write off as irrelevant for now.

As Justin removed his sweater vest and got his board and markers ready, Samantha leaned over to Sara with a thought.

"I didn't give this effort the credence I should have. Even the tips of these icebergs are hugely meaningful."

"Thank you, Samantha. You are only beginning to see what we are linked into. You will become a believer, as the evidence is just too strong."

"I agree, Sara."

"Samantha, there are Congressmen, in my opinion, who are becoming serious roadblocks in our efforts, and I may require you to get to the bottom of the 'who' and 'why' of that conspiracy."

Slowly, Samantha replied, in an almost defensive posture.

"Of course, Sara. But conspiracy might be too harsh a word. Could just be plain-old partisan politics."

For the next hour and a half, the ETRT compiled the short list of what to bundle with the alien puzzle pieces, and the conclusion became pretty obvious.

The primary ETRT mission was to continue their research on the climate-change problems and their root causes, and focus even harder on the roles and contributions of good -versus-bad aliens and what was the end game of both.

As Sara was compiling here final implementation plan for the group, her cell phone rang.

"Excuse me, guys, gotta take this one."

It was her mom, Christine, who never called in the afternoon, given the fact that afternoons were usually meeting times.

"Hi Mom. What's up? You never call when I'm in a meeting. Everything okay?"

Christine was obviously upset.

"Sara, I found bugs in our house."

"Insects?"

"No honey, recording devices…and they are everywhere!"

37

CHRISTINE

Without even mentioning this call to Mike, Sara walked quickly into an empty office to talk privately to her mom and get more detail.

"Oh my gosh, tell me what you found. Are you sure?"

"Sara, you know how I am about neatness, organization, and always knowing what's going on in the house and where everything is at all times?"

"Of course. We think it's funny that you are always 'cleaning up' or 'straightening up.'"

"Somebody convinced your dad, I don't know if it was the FBI or CIA or just someone affiliated with your team, to get the best video surveillance and motion detectors at our home, which really freaked me out."

"I wasn't aware of that, Mom. Should I get Dad?"

"No, not yet. Let me describe what I found first. I don't want to upset your dad or interfere with what you guys are doing today if it's no big deal."

"Please. Go ahead. What happened?"

"Sure. Short pause.

"I was in your dad's office cleaning and dusting and when I went to dust around his table lamp, I could easily see that it wasn't exactly where it always was."

Christine could be heard giving out a trembling sigh.

"When I picked it up, I noticed that there was a small device at the bottom of the lamp that looked like a small ear bud."

"That is creepy, Mom."

"Yeah, and then I looked at other lamps and found nothing."

"That's good—yes?"

"No, Sara. When I went digging further for the next four to five hours, I found two more similar devices…one in the base of the living room aquarium and one under the seat of the piano in the conservatory."

"Well, now I'm scared Mom. Let me get Dad."

"Yeah. But first there are a couple other odd things that now seem related."

"What's that?"

"Since those surveillance cameras and motion detectors were installed, I have had visitors claiming to be from the installers in the house verifying that all is in order."

"Oh, crap."

"Well, even I know that you can do that remotely and not have to go inside the house."

"That's right, Mom. What else?"

"I've had two calls from the security firm asking me to talk to them from various locations in the house so they can verify that the cameras are in the right places."

"Hold on, I'm texting Dad."

"Okay, thanks. Can I share one more thing with you?"

"Of course."

"I have been having dreams lately; nightmares actually."

"Go ahead. Dad will be a few minutes away."

"Well, you and I are sitting on a bed, just the two of us, and it is not a bedroom that I recognize. There is an enormous firestorm outside and total destruction that can be seen out the one window in the bedroom.

"Sara, it is as if the world is coming to an end and you and I are witnessing the Armageddon."

As Mike approached Sara in response to her text message, Sara had become extremely subdued, and had an overwhelming thought that was as chilling as anything she had ever experienced.

"Mike had that very same recurring dream, and he described it to Sara in the same detail that Christine just did!"

38

ELONIS

Elonis contacted Pulse with the status updates requested by Pulse from the last ETRT meeting. As his teleported image materialized in the building's generator room, Elonis would become the information receptacle for all things strategic, from the alien's perspective.

<I have the transcript from your last meeting, Elonis.>

<Is it what you expected, Pulse?>

<Yes, but we need much more information and a better sense of where the humans are going with their implementation plan, Elonis.>

<Do you have a strategy for me, Pulse?>

<Yes. I want you to meet with Sara and with a specific agenda.>

<And that agenda is?>

<I want you to become the next ETRT member and handle the advanced alien research.>

<And how will I do that?>

<I will share information with you that will secure your value to the team.>

<Future events or calamities?>

<Yes. That will give you credibility and enable you to become a trusted and reliable ETRT member.>

<Elonis, I was the entity that visited Commander Evans in the Command Module for Apollo 17.>

<And you will provide me with some evidence of that?>

<Yes.>

<What else, Pulse?>

<I will provide you with a warning of looming global disaster.>

<And I will warn the world?>

<If we deem that necessary. This will convince everyone of your pure intentions and your value.>

<That will give me greater access, right?>

<It will give you greater access.>
<Can I also share my thoughts with Sara?>
<No. Not yet. You can share what we communicated tonight.>

✦ ✦ ✦

Elonis immediately set up a meeting with Sara, and shared the plan that Elonis and Pulse had telepathically discussed.

"Sara, I met with Pulse and have information to share with you."

"Finally, Elonis. I'm very angry that it has taken so long. Keeping all this to myself is as difficult as anything I have ever had to do."

Softening her tone a bit, Sara went on.

"I am disappointed in Pulse, but I understand that you are only the messenger here."

"Sara, I am not a messenger. I am becoming the connector for you and all things alien."

"Sorry, Elonis. Please go on."

"I met with Pulse per his request. He gave me several critical issues to discuss with you."

"I'm ready and eager to hear his thoughts."

"Pulse wants you to announce me as a new member of the ETRT, effective now."

"And how is that supposed to be justified?"

"I will use my meta-human skills to analyze data and make significant observations and predictions. I will handle the most difficult alien research issues."

"You were instructed to do that?"

"You know I have the analytic capability."

"Yes, of course. But you don't need to be an ETRT member to do that. Hell, you do that now."

"Perception, Sara. Pulse will share with me the kind of knowledge and prognostications that only he can provide."

"For example, Elonis?"

"There is a violent earthquake and tsunami coming. Earth will have a meteorite problem."

"When, Elonis?"

"Both events are more than three years out."

"What else?"

"In the Apollo 17, 'we are not alone scenario,' Pulse admitted that he was the visiting alien and he has proof."

"Damn. That is a 'got-to-have' list for sure."

"Pulse even aborted his objective of erasing the command module pilot's memory,"

"Did he say why?"

"Yes. Pulse said that he felt a bond of trust within their few minutes together and made a decision to allow the commander to take away their meeting in full detail."

"I admire Pulse for his insight and his decision making."

"Sara, there is one more thing."

"And that is?"

"Sara, Pulse will enable you and I to share our thoughts."

"Welcome aboard, newest ETRT member!"

39

SARA

The problem-solver in Sara had taken over. With so many unresolved issues, Sara needed to get away for some peace and solitude to address the many issues that had surfaced in just the last few weeks.

She sipped again on a glass of wine that she poured hours ago, and mindlessly thumped through a litany of text messages and retweets from the last two weeks. She was just treading water, and she sensed it.

Her head was about to explode with all the mental gymnastics that had taken over her psyche. She was feeling quite alone.

She called her dad, and hung up.

She called Matthew, and hung up.

She even called Michaela and Kat, and couldn't engage them in any dialogue at all.

So, she grabbed her parka and gloves, as there was a slight chill in the air, and headed to her car. She had a destination in mind.

Sara drove slowly about sixty miles to the cemetery where her late husband, Paul, was buried.

As she walked over to Paul's gravesite, Sara felt anger and overwhelming grief. If only she had her beloved Paul to share her burden and give her advice right now...

She touched his tombstone and had so many thoughts of good times, as well as opportunities lost or not taken.

"Paul, I miss you...I need you...I can't do this without you."

She paused for a moment, realizing that she was now alone with Paul and her thoughts.

Her mind immediately went to her wedding vows, a particular poem she wrote, and how poignant those words were right now.

Every time we touch, I feel the sun
Every time we talk, I know you are the one

— 115 —

Every time we kiss, I swear I could fly
Can you feel my heart beat fast?
I want this to last
I need you by my side

Sitting on the cold ground and feeling so alone, Sara knew she was in a bad place right now and felt helpless. In a way she didn't want to leave and by the same token, knew she had to pull herself together.

Sara's thoughts then went to her wedding vows and the happiness she and Paul shared that day. She continued to read her words written in that wedding poem.

I hear your voice when you sleep next to me
I feel your touch in dreams of our lives
Forgive me my weakness, I just don't know why
When not with you, my Paul, it's hard to survive

After a few minutes of quiet contemplation, Sara noticed two yellow butterflies flying around Paul's tombstone. They were a lovely pair and seemed to take turns leading an otherwise random choreography.

"My butterfly is gone. But if he were here, what advice would he give me."

Sara knew what Paul would have said, as it appeared as an inscription of a birthday locket Paul had given her:

"Be forever curious… The answers you seek are often outside your reach."

With that thought in mind, Sara stood up, rolled her poem and notes in one red rose that she had brought and placed it on Paul's grave.

She returned to her car and drove back to her office knowing what she must do.

Parking her car and avoiding eye contact with anyone in her path, she moved into her office building and took the elevator up to her office floor. Closing the door behind her, she took a long, meditative sigh.

Kicking off her boots and parka, she poured herself a glass of wine. She pulled out her iPad and began writing notes to herself for later.

1) Schedule the next ETRT meeting for next week.
2) Introduce Elonis to the ETRT as the latest addition to the team.
3) Create a "War Room" to raise the level of activity to the highest possible level.

4) Assign Kat to Christine for security and to help understand the home security issues.
5) Rapidly accelerate her mind-sharing with Elonis.
6) Temporarily distance herself from Samantha.
7) Work on the relationship with Amanda, the connector.
8) Seek a face-to-face meeting with Pulse.

Just as she was finishing her note-raking, a message appeared on her watch.

"Sara, it's Vice President Worthington. The President wants to meet with you."

40

CAMERON

Thirty-six hours later, Sara was at Camp David about to meet with POTUS for a one-on-one talk.

As Sara stepped out of the President's limousine, the abundance of tight security was overwhelming. She was escorted to a small cabin where President Sullivan awaited.

"Good morning, Sara; thanks for coming on such short notice."

"Thank you so much for this meeting. I don't know whether I should be nervous or excited."

Cameron chuckled over Sara's open and honest remark. "Let's put it this way, Miss Steele., I am the one who should be either nervous or excited."

That remark was as calming as calming could be.

As the room with several security personnel emptied, Cameron opened.

"Can I offer you something to drink? We have a nicely stocked frig and bar here."

As she slipped off her jacket, Sara replied, "Oh, just water, thanks."

"Very well, Sara, I'm going to have a glass of the local cabernet."

"Local cabernet?"

Chuckling, the President clarified his remark.

"By local, I mean right here at the Camp David saloon."

"In that case, I'll have one too."

Sara was getting more relaxed.

Pouring two glasses of wine from a recently opened bottle, Cameron and Sara tapped glasses in hearty "cheers" and the rather unique day was off and running.

"My purpose in asking you here is two-fold. I want to give you some info… and I'd like an update on what you and your ETRT are presently working on."

"Great, Mr. President. I'm so happy to help."

"Sara, please just call me Cam."

"Okay. Thanks. Will do."

"Humor me for a bit as I attempt to back-fill my intentions today. As you can probably imagine, I have a ton of good people and great resources at my call."

Sara was pleased that POTUS was about to confide in her.

He continued. "That is both a blessing and a curse. And, I'm going to share some things with you that are just between you and me."

"I understand, Cameron."

"My biggest concern right now is trust and loyalty. I'm having trouble trusting members of my team, including cabinet members.

"And, I firmly believe that our Congress has a possible criminal element… or at least a self-centered-agenda element that is not in the best interest of our country."

Pausing for a moment, he advised.

"Sara, I have a great deal of admiration and respect for you, members of you team, and especially the Stevenson family. Pete, Mike, Christine, and you are the generational role models, if you know what I mean."

"Cameron, I don't know what to say. Thank you."

"Let's get to the subjects at hand. I believe in what your team is doing and I believe in your leadership. If you ever need my help. I am always there for you."

Sara was blown away and just smiled and nodded her head.

"We have reports that excessive missile testing is being conducted in several sites that for quite a while were off the grid. I'll send the coordinates over to you encrypted so you guys can take a look at it."

"Will do." Sara was noticeably puzzled.

"We're getting intel from our sources that an imminent attack against the U.S. is being planned. Well, maybe not imminent, but soon."

"And, there are military people who I do trust that tell me this attack and the missile testing is related."

"With all due respect, Cameron, the terrorist contribution scenario is about as popular with the ETRT as income tax audits."

"Funny, Sara. I'll make a note of that."

They both got a little laugh from that assertion.

"All I'm saying is that if there is any conclusion that your team has reached regarding that element, or your grandad's research, now is the time to get it out. If there was ever a group of high-flying and respected outliers, it's you guys."

"Will do. Thanks."

Refilling their wine glasses, Cameron continued.

"Now I want to cut to the chase and discuss your alien encounter and tie it to an event that the general public is unaware of."

Sara's heart and mind were racing.

"I want to tell you about our Apollo 18 mission."

"Excuse me. Apollo 17, launched in 1972, was the last Apollo mission, right?"

"With the alien events around Apollo 17, which I am sure you are aware, we launched a secret follow up mission, Apollo 18, in April of 1975, to seek out our previous Apollo 17 alien visitors."

"Why didn't anyone hear about this launch?"

"For one reason, it was a secretive launch from our Kodiak Launch Complex, Alaska. And, we were trying to keep the details of Apollo 17 hidden, for obvious reasons."

"I see. Makes sense."

"The mission was under the command of Alan Vaughn, who would have been our next man on the moon, if the Apollo program was to continue."

Sara was silent, waiting for the next shoe to drop.

"We picked Vaughn for a couple of reasons. He was highly qualified, extremely resourceful, and he had no family that we knew about."

"This isn't going to end well, I'm sure Cameron."

"The launch went fine…perfect. Apollo 18 was headed to the Moon under great flight specs and with all systems 'go' for lunar orbit, just like Apollo 17."

"And then?"

"And then, Apollo 18 disappeared once in lunar orbit on the dark side of the Moon, and was never heard from again!"

41

SARA

Before President Sullivan could get into any great detail regarding Apollo 18, he was called into a meeting regarding an international water-trading market issue, one that Sara was made aware of through Kat's research.

POTUS gave Sara a sealed binder with the instructions that the info inside was *"for her eyes only."*

"Thanks again for coming, Sara."

"And many thanks for trusting me and sharing with me, Cameron."

Once inside the limousine for the trip back to the airport, Sara's first thought was why Cameron didn't quiz her on her alien connections and beliefs, and possibly, even, the existence of Pulse. She knew that he knew.

Obviously, Sara and POTUS were not done talking.

So, she opened the folder and found several interesting subject titles with much data assigned to each title.

1) *Apollo 18*
2) *Spinning black holes*
3) *The event horizon*
4) *Planets and moons that could sustain life*
5) *Dark side of the Moon investigation*
6) *Mars colony establishment*
7) *Quantum mechanics and wormholes*
8) *Forward time travel*

As she was excitedly perusing her newly obtained wealth of strange data, making mental notes as to what to do going forward, her watch phone buzzed. It was Mike.

"Hi Dad. What's up?"

"Hey, ya got a minute?"

"Sure. Bet you'll never guess where I am right now?"

"Well, how about a meeting with POTUS?"

"Seriously? How'd you know that?"

"President Sullivan's office called to let your mom and I know where you were headed and what was going on. They wanted to thank us in advance, as if it was necessary."

"They also wanted to invite Christine and me to a September 11th tribute in D.C. this fall."

"Yeah, I heard about that. Cool that we will all be there."

"Mom's already wondering what outfit she will need for such a huge deal."

"Dad, I only have about ten minutes before we are at the airport. You called me."

"Yes. Couple things. First, Kat is here now and Mom is feeling much better with someone like her to bounce things off. Those security camera and weird visitors' issues that she had were unnerving."

"Roger that. Yep, Kat will be great for her."

"Sara, something just isn't right with those security issues. The hidden cameras were not part of the deal. Not to mention we were never told they were to be installed."

"Dad, I gotta go. Have an incoming call from Scott."

"Okay. Call me as soon as you get home."

"Sure. Quickly. Anything else?"

"Yeah. I'm missing computer files, and one is the hard drive with all of Grandad's recorded terrorist activity."

42

MIKE

As soon as Sara got home, she texted her dad to call her. About five minutes later, Mike was calling and Sara could sense his anxiety and stress level. Her dad was usually quite composed, but not this time.

"Hi Dad. I'm home and have all the time you need."

"Good. How'd your meeting with President Sullivan go?"

"It went well. He just thanked me and the team for our work and let me know that we could call on him and his resources whenever we needed help."

"Wow. You must be proud of your accomplishments. Mom and I sure are."

"Thanks. Now, back to your security issues."

"All the outside video cameras and both inside and outside motion detectors were done by one company, which Scott set up, as you know."

"Yep. We use 'em here."

Mike paused before he continued in a very serious tone.

"Well, the hidden cameras that Christine found were not part of the deal."

"Dad, do you want me to talk to Scott? I just spoke with him a while ago and he gave me the contact info of those assigned to install the system."

"Already did. He was confused and concerned. His installation crew had nothing to do with the hidden cams."

"Holy crap! Any leads?"

"No. But Kat is on it like a hawk. She'll get to the bottom of it."

Sara was beginning to think that Kat working on this intrusion alone was not good enough. Her wheels were spinning when she continued to ask Mike questions.

"And the missing files and hard drive?"

"That's what really concerns me. Obviously, someone broke into the house, likely the ones that had the cams installed."

"And why the hell did they take the one drive with non-alien data? Makes no sense. Or, it makes a lot of 'bad' sense."

Sara was now putting the puzzle pieces together, especially given the recent revelations, and she was getting nervous. Not wanting to alarm her family at the moment, she backed off a bit.

"Dad, let me see what I can come up with. Meanwhile, have you alerted the police?"

"I was going to, but both Scott and Kat wanted to do some of their own investigation first. Scott is having his surveillance people come into the house tomorrow to make an assessment."

"I understand. Is there anything you want me to do right now?"

"No, thanks. We appreciate having Kat here and Mom is feeling much better with her around."

"Yeah, Kat's the rock."

"For now, we are just looking forward to the 9/11 anniversary remembrance at the Nation's Capital this fall."

Sara replied, "It was so nice that you guys got an invite."

"Yep, Sara. It should be a most memorable event!"

43

PULSE

Pulse contacted Elonis for a meeting with Pulse on the mother ship. This time the hologram image of Elonis was teleported.

This was the update meeting that Pulse told Elonis he would have with her when they last met.

<You were able to talk to Sara and she was responsive?>

<Yes, Pulse, she was pleased that we were moving forward.>

<Elonis, you are now being implanted with our latest sensory technology.>

<Pulse, will I be able to share my thoughts with Sara?>

<Yes. You now possess the greatest meta-human capability on Earth.>

<We will now test your upgrade.>

<Yes, I am ready.>

<I will place a thought followed by kilobytes of data.>

<Understand.>

A short pause…

<Now the kilobytes will be replaced by megabytes.>

<Understand.>

Another short pause…

<Now the megabytes will be replaced by gigabytes.>

<Pulse, it is already transpiring.>

<Finally, your capability will meet and exceed earthly terabytes. At that point you can simulate and develop wormholes as needed.>

<Yes.>

<You will move in Spacetime and you will have limited time-travel capabilities.>

<Understand.>

<You will be able to implant tracking technology in humans.>

<Why, Pulse?>

<Yours is not to question.>

< You will become the conduit for concern about evil aliens by humans.>

<Understand.>

<You will be programmed with information on a devastating earthquake and tsunami.>

<When?>

<Elonis, not yours to ask. Future event.>

<Understand.>

<You will be programmed with high-level early warning capability.>

<As I did with Sara in her grandfather's cabin?>

<Yes, but much further advanced.>

<You will have knowledge of experiments on children's DNA alteration to tolerate heat and salt from climate change.>

<Elonis, one more tactical element of your upgrade that we need to share.>

<And what is that?>

<You will have cognitive abilities and will be able to choose and analyze.>

<I feel that element as we speak.>

<Now, you can select which significant event to share with the ETRT to establish your credibility.>

<Yes, that is important.>

<Elonis, before you return to Earth, do you have any questions for me?>

<Yes, Pulse. Why is Sara taking up so much of your current sub-thoughts?>

44

SARA

Sara was feeling overwhelmed with the recent occurrences and called for an immediate high-level team meeting.

Given the meeting with President Sullivan, some informal chats with Kat and Michaela, and those awful recording devices in Mike and Christine's house, it was time to develop a short to-do list of ETRT activities and prioritize.

Sara's first task involved Justin and Connor.

"Guys, thanks for coming so quickly."

"Another fire?" Justin asked.

"No, Justin, just the same one starting to get out of control."

Connor offered, "Tell us how we can help."

"Sure. I am going to convene a team meeting soon, but I need to get some important groundwork laid first."

Both guys were attentive, as they always were around Sara, but with iPads in hand.

"I am very concerned about communication security among our team members, and we need to develop the capability to have our dialogue protected and not hacked. Can you guys develop something?"

Connor chimed in. "Sara, I have had the opportunity to discuss all kinds of technical issues with one of Matt's super intelligent techies, Jeremiah. Do you know him?"

"I do. He's the guy that's doing the high-level hologram work for Matt and he's as edgy as they come."

Justin added, "I've heard about him but never talked to him."

Typing quickly on his keypad, Connor responded, "I will set up a secure means to talk to Jeremiah and let you know what comes up. Justin will help as well."

"Great, Connor, thanks."

Connor then added, "Should I contact Matt to get his okay?"

Sara smiled and said, "No, I will take care of that."

✦ ✦ ✦

As Connor and Justin left Sara's office, she pulled out her old reliable, yet super safe, writing pad and began listing items for the next meeting gathered with her most recent conversations.

One major conclusion fell hard on her mind. She thought out loud.

"Damn, the more I learn…the less I seem to know."

So, pen in hand, she wrote down the items for the next meeting.

1) Ditch the annoying issues that don't relate to aliens.
2) Find a transition person to take over the terrorist threat issues.
3) Reveal to team contents of POTUS envelope.
4) Apollo 18 drill down.
5) Security plans for parent's house.
6) Inclusion of Elonis into the ETRT.
7) Contact key members to see what they have to report on next.
8) Set up the meeting agenda, timetable, resources required, obstacles, etc. (Mike stuff).

With that task done, she called her dad with obvious updates on ETRT business and her plans for the next meeting. She was even more determined to let her parents know what the strategy was for their home security involving Kat.

"Hi, Dad, just me."

"Hey, Sara, how goes it today?"

"How is Mom dealing with her bugs in the house?"

"You know Mom…not well."

"Really. Before I get to the ETRT stuff and our next meeting, which you will need to attend, I do have some plans for Mom and Kat going forward."

"Great. What's shaking?"

"Scott has pulled together a three-man team to diagnose and set up a system that will be completely secure. They will be there tomorrow, before you leave for the ETRT meeting. It's best to have them there while you are home."

"Of course, Sara. Good thinking."

"And, Scott has pulled some strings with POTUS and, starting tomorrow, Kat will have an agent. I don't know, FBI or CIA…assigned to Kat and Mom twenty-four seven to make sure that they are safe."

An agitated Mike spoke quickly, "Safe? What the …"

"I know, Dad, don't be alarmed. Better safe than sorry, at least until we know what and who we are dealing with."

"Sara, you are so damn good at this. I'm somewhere between concerned and impressed."

"Thanks. For now, we will downplay our concern with Mom and/or not tell her about the agent."

"I think that makes sense, Sara. I'm glad you're not too worried about Mom and Kat's safety."

Actually, Sara was extremely worried about her mom and Kat's safety.

While Sara was on the phone with her dad, she had put an incoming call on hold. Surprised that the caller was still there, Sara responded, "Hello, this is Sara."

Hi, Sara. My name is Dean Worthington, Samantha's husband."

"Oh, hi Dean. What can I do for you?"

"Well, I got your number from President Sullivan. He said it would be okay to call you."

"Of course, Dean, no problem. Let me clear my tablet and file a couple things…give me a minute."

"Sure."

"Dad, gotta go."

"Sure. Love you."

"Love you too, Dad."

Dean waited for two or three minutes for Sara to get back on the call.

"Okay, Dean, I'm back. What's up?"

"Well, Cam told me about the some of the things you and your team are working on, and I've gotten feedback from Samantha as well. They both hold you in high regard."

Sara was certainly glad to get that praise. But she wasn't picking up on the nature of the call.

"That's nice to hear. Please, why the call?"

Pausing for a moment, a nervous and soft-spoken Dean began.

"On March 11, 2001, NASA astronauts Vince Jordan and my wife spent eight hours and fifty-six minutes outside the space shuttle Discovery and the International Space Station during the STS-102 mission, performing some routine maintenance and preparing the orbiting lab for the arrival of another module."

"Actually, my grandad referred that to me as the longest spacewalk to that date, as I recall."

"Yes, Sara, your grandad was right."

"And?"

"These spacewalks were known as extra-vehicular activities, or EVA's. That EVA was supposed to be about an hour shorter than it was."

"You're losing me, Dean."

"Sorry. Sam's eighty-five-foot-long steel tether broke loose and she slowly drifted off alone into space."

Dean took a deep breath before continuing.

"Only the fact that Vince had a jetpack near him enabled him to go out and get her, who by the time Vince reached her, was about four hundred fifty-feet away from the spacecraft."

"Oh my God. That was never reported, was it?"

"No. Hell no."

"So, Sam is one very lucky astronaut, for sure."

Pausing, Sara continued, "Dean, I still don't know why you are calling me."

"Sara, Sam was out there by herself for about thirty minutes and when she returned, half her helmet was full of water. She could hardly breathe."

"That must have been scary for both of you. But she made it through that ordeal just fine."

"Sara, I desperately need to meet with you."

"Why?"

Silence on the phone line.

"Dean, why?"

"Because my wife is changed. She is not the same person as she was before that incident!"

45
KAT

"Hi Sara, it's Kat. Wanted to give you an update on security stuff."

Sara, still trying to process her call with Dean simply said, "Good to hear from you and anxious to hear what you have on your plate right now."

"Michaela tells me you are setting up an ETRT meeting soon. This will be a hum-dinger."

"Yeah, Kat, we've got a ton of things in play. I have two speeds now: fast and stop!"

"I hear you Sara girl. Love being a busy beaver, though."

"Updates, Kat?"

"Oh yeah, sure. The terrorist info is serious and heavy-duty. Not sure why it ended up in our lap, but I want to get rid of it."

"I hear you, Kat, and I plan to pull all of our info and your info in particular, and turn what we have over to the FBI, with Scott's help."

"Whew," Kat muttered. "Happy for that."

"Figured you would be."

"I'm going to continue to investigate those water-trading license issues before I hand those over. I'm very curious about the direction this dwindling resource is going and pretty soon it will end up, I'm afraid, in the hands of criminals."

"Yep, Kat, it's a really bad thought that water will become the next oil commodity that will have serious economic issues with those in need that can't afford to pay steep prices for something that has always been free. Even POTUS is involved in this issue."

"Enough of the serious talk. Let me tell you about my 'new boyfriend,' Sara."

"All ears." A puzzled Sara was anxious to hear more "boyfriend" details.

"First, thanks for getting Scott to get me some 'protection' from the bad guys."

"What do you mean by protection?"

"You know, the security guy for Christine and I to have for the time being?"

"Oh yeah. Sorry."

"I met him yesterday and what a hunk! He calls himself Agent Eight. I said, like Agent Double-O-Eight?"

"He said, 'No ma'am, just Agent Eight. But you can call me by any name you want.' So, I did."

"I'll bite."

"He is now called Sean."

"Can't say I didn't see that name coming," a relaxed and lightly laughing Sara remarked.

Sara asked. "So, what is Sean's and your plan? Or have you even gotten that far?"

"Of course, we have a plan. Just needed to get to know him a little bit to make sure he was a good fit."

"Yeah, I'm sure," laughed Sara.

"I'm gonna share what we know about the security breach and get whatever trace evidence the FBI has and have Sean put his thoughts into an implementation plan. This should be fun."

"Fun? Seriously, Kat?"

"You know what I mean. Enjoyable might be a better word. It's always great to work with a professional."

"Just keep it professional, Kat."

"Of course."

Sara was worried that Kat's cavalier attitude and attraction to Sean could cloud her judgement if an unexpected situation arose.

46

SARA

"**G**ood morning to the 'A' team. You have today's agenda and we have a lot to cover. Kat has some coffee and sweet rolls for us. Thanks, Kat."

The team was getting settled with their devices neatly in place. Sara appreciated the promptness and organization.

She recalled Mike's famous "two cents" quote from Vince Lombardi: "Early is 'on time,' 'on time' is late, late is unacceptable."

"I'll begin with some background stuff; then we'll go to Michaela, Kat, and conclude with Mike today. Okay?"

Sara ordered, "And today will be the high-level thirty thousand-foot perspective, right?"

All nodded in agreement.

"First, I want to welcome Elonis to the team. As my role is to get much deeper into all things alien, and away from the bullshit distractions that Congress believes are important, Elonis and I will team up to see if one plus one really equals three."

Team laughter was heard amongst the rifling sounds of coffee, muffins, and rolls.

"Second, we will be creating a state-of-the-art War Room to run our operations more effectively and efficiently. More on that later."

"Also, Connor and Justin are working on secure communication systems for us to use that will eliminate any hacking or info leaking. Details on that issue later, too."

As Sara was talking, she received a call from Mike.

"Guys, it's my dad. Give me a few minutes to see what's shaking with him. Okay?"

As the meeting was put on hold for a few minutes, Justin posed a question to Elonis.

"Hi Elonis, I'm Justin."

"Justin, I know who you are."

"Right…sorry. Say, I have a question."

"Yes?"

"I have a monthly meeting with the YGS…"

"What is the YGS?"

"Oh. It's the Young Geeks Society. We flaunt the fact that we are on the leading edge of technology."

"Really?" Connor wasn't impressed.

"So, anyhow, we have our next meeting a week from today and I was wondering…"

"Yes?"

"Elonis, could you give me a neat solar system or outer space fact that I could tell my group and get some points?"

"Seriously, Justin?" Connor again was getting annoyed.

"I can do that." Elonis thought for only a few seconds and responded.

"Why are all the planets in our solar system so different?"

"Dunno. Why?" Justin was getting excited.

"Mercury is tiny with a huge iron core. Venus and Earth are similar in size, but Venus is a dead, dry planet with an atmosphere dense enough to crush spacecraft. Mars is small and lopsided."

Elonis was on a roll…

"Jupiter is massive, Saturn has rings, Uranus is oddly tilted on its side and Neptune is missing the types of moons that all the other giants have. Why?"

Michaela listened, then chimed in.

"The interstellar cloud of gas, dust, and ice that eventually formed the sun and planets probably varied smoothly from one region to the next, so why would the planets that came out of it vary so wildly, Elonis?"

"Catastrophic collisions, Michaela. Planets are born bit by bit, with the largest pieces coagulating together last.

"The collision that led to the moon was the last major part of the formation of the Earth."

Michaela got back into the discussion.

"Billions of years ago, an object the size of Mars smashed into the Earth. The resulting debris jetted into orbit, leaving us with likely two differently-sized moons. The small one disintegrated over time and left us with the one we have now, apparently."

Elonis continued.

"Yes, Michaela. If the Mars-sized body that hit the Earth had hit it slightly differently, we probably wouldn't have the moon."

Elonis paused. "Then with the tilt of the Earth no longer stabilized by the moon, we could have the types of extreme climate variations that we see on Mars, where glaciers periodically cover the equator."

All were hanging on Elonis's every word.

"Without the moon there would be no tides, which are crucial in the evolution of life."

"You taking notes, Justin," Connor said sarcastically as Elonis went on.

"Recording…" Justin uttered.

"Mercury had a near-catastrophic impact that tore away most of its rocky exterior.

"Mars was nearly destroyed by an impact that left it with a massive northern basin that was once filled with a temperate ocean.

"Saturn's rings and small moons were the remnants of multiple colliding moons."

Even Michaela was quite impressed.

"Uranus was struck by a huge meteorite that knocked it on its side.

"Neptune's moon Triton came from another solar system and displaced all of Neptune's original moons as it came in.

"And, finally, Pluto. The face of that planet is a giant basin formed by a massive impact that subsequently slowly filled with glaciers made out of frozen nitrogen gas."

At that moment, Sara returned to the meeting.

Elonis said, "Is that enough data for your meeting, Justin?"

"Uh-huh."

"So," Sara asked, "what were you guys discussing?"

"You know, same old space stuff," Connor offered.

"Yeah, a real yawner," Kat added smiling.

"All right. Sorry for the delay. I trust Elonis kept your interest while I was gone."

"Most definitely," Michaela offered. "What cha got, Sara?"

"I had a monster meeting with President Sullivan, and a couple things are in need of sharing."

"One, he is totally on board, believes in alien presence, has given us any resources we need, and has shared a couple rather interesting issues or relevant scenarios that I am evaluating right now for importance and prioritization."

Kat asked, "Can you share any one thing in particular?"

Sara thought for a moment and then smiled and offered up her take on a major reveal.

"Sure can. There are many pillars of extraordinary findings in our research... this is one of those."

The entire team knew something big was about to be uncovered.

"We have had a functioning jointly-operated American/Russian research and recon colony on Mars for nearly thirty years."

47

MICHAELA

As Michaela was preparing her report, Sara offered a half-hearted explanation of her Mars mention.

"Sorry, guys, to get you all excited…but just that little Mars teaser for now. It'll take me all day to explain this one…once I figure out the details myself."

Pausing, Sara added, "Anything involving Mars, Martians, or Red Planet lore in general, believe me you'll be the first to know."

As laughter could be heard, Michaela began her report.

"Isn't it amazing that within this ETRT, the news of an unknown Mars colony can be tabled for later? Amazing times and an amazing team."

"For sure," Kat muttered.

Michaela began. "Well team, I have three report-outs… High level stuff for now.

"The first one involves cities built around stars and star formations. Just to make it as simple as possible to describe, ancient civilizations around the world are aligned to various 'star maps' with incredible accuracy."

Sara inquired, "Do you have a couple examples for now?"

"Yep. The three major pyramids of Egypt aligned perfectly with the constellation Orion's belt. By the way, as a sidebar, the Giza pyramid occupies a very unique position. It is located exactly at the center of the world's land masses."

"Cool," responded Kat.

"Kat, here is the really cool one. The ancient Mayan civilization covered roughly 75,000 square miles. It was made up of twenty-two cities. However, it aligned with a star system that had those twenty-two cities in perfect alignment. But the star system held twenty-three stars."

"So, it wasn't perfectly aligned," Kat asked.

"Hold on… it was. In 2016, researchers discovered a hidden pyramid, buried some fifty feet below the surface. When aligned with the other twenty-two, it fell in place perfectly. That's so cool."

Michaela heard a couple oohs and aahs and then continued.

"Earth's magnetic North Pole has been wandering faster than expected over the last twenty or so years. It has now crossed the International Date Line. The Earth is a magnet due to its molten iron core, which seems to be moving within the Earth like a bearing."

Kat voiced her concern. "Michaela, you better get back to basics before you lose us."

"Sorry. Earth's magnetic field is used to calibrate GPS and essential navigational measurements and is produced by the churning of the planet's iron core, which produces a complex, largely north-south magnetic field."

"Again, Michaela?" Kat winked, needing more clarification.

"Two things worth noting. One, magnetic North had been moving about thirty-four miles a year over a period of a hundred years. It is moving more quickly now, about fifty-five miles per year for the last twenty years."

Sara asked, "Any explanation?"

"No. No explanation for this phenomenon. Also, the core seems to be made of another unidentified material, like a super-heated hyper pressurized solid, which Mike will touch on during his presentation."

Kat wanted to talk but Sara told her to wait until later for a one-on-one with Michaela.

Michaela continued, "My next issue regards pyramid alignment and orientation. I have done considerable study and worked with some incredible physicists and mathematicians on this subject."

Mike, still thinking about his part in her last statement, is following her next mention with anticipation.

"If you were to look at every major pyramid in the World, what I'm about to reveal is stunning. The base of every pyramid and the tip of every pyramid are exactly correlated to the diameter and either Pole of Earth.

"In other words, the base of every pyramid equals the width of Earth and the tip of every pyramid is the exact height of either the North or South Pole."

Mike responded, "So you are saying that any one of the great pyramids is literally a scale model of the Northern Hemisphere. The height and corner-to-corner width of every pyramid equals the height and width of Earth."

"Yes, Mike. And I have more."

Even Sara was quite attentive.

Michaela went on...

"I will be referring to a quantum computing unit, what's called the Royal Cubit. But, give me a shot at making this an uncomplicated comparison."

Connor replied, "Uncomplicated is good."

"The distance between the North and South Poles is 8595.35 miles. Cubit math is a two-level measurement. If you take any one of the stones used in building the major Egyptian pyramids, they are of the exact same shape and size in cube form. That is 1.86 feet."

Sara and Mike looked at each other as if they knew what was coming.

"If you take the size of one building stone in the pyramids, 1.86 feet by 1.86 feet, you would need exactly twenty-five million to connect the two Poles. Not one more or one less."

48

KAT

"Wow, Michaela. That is a great stuff. Hard to blow this off as mere coincidence. You and your team are incredible."

"Thanks, Kat."

"I won't be able to top that, but here goes. So, I have three terrorist or criminal type issues that I have found uncomfortable, but needing to be addressed.

"The first one is what I have discussed before, the terrorist group now called the First World Order. It seems like the ten or so wealthy people that make up this group have been able to hide their identities and their agenda up until now."

"Up until now?" Mike asked.

"Yes. I am happy to report that this issue is in my rear-view mirror. I turned over all the research I had and all the Pete Stevenson data I had to the FBI, and they are moving quickly on tightening the screws on these guys, I'm told."

"Good to hear, Kat," Sara advised.

"So, now to the water-trading market and associated licenses. This one is good…going to bad…getting to possibly horrible."

Sara winked, "We probably need the short version today."

"Of course. No problem. Water-trading is the process of buying and selling water access entitlements, or water rights. These are common, here in the U.S. and throughout the world. Australia is thought to have the most sophisticated water-trading schemes in the world.

"Economists argue that water-trading is efficient. A market-based price acts as an incentive for users to allocate better. The problem comes when poorly developed regions or countries are screwed by unscrupulous or criminal interests."

"The First World Order?" Sara asked.

"Bingo, Sara. If left unchallenged, water could become much more expensive in poor countries than gas, oil, or even staple commodities. Again, my new friends in the FBI have this under control, I think."

"Good to know," added Michaela.

"And," Kat continued, "another of those stupid damn issues that our Congress stuck us with."

Some noticeable laughter from the small, but intensely focused, group.

"Now to the most important issue of the day for me, and that's the Stevenson house break-in.

"I met with a very nervous Christine Stevenson after that mess with the illegal video surveillance installation. Scott has his crack team getting it up to current and legal standards."

Michaela asked, "Did they find out anything regarding who and why that was done?"

Kat motioned to Mike who then brought the team up to current.

"The police and FBI are following leads, but nothing has been determined yet. I'm sure it will all come out soon. Meanwhile, it is clear that we need to be super cautious."

Kat continued. "Well, the good news is that the FBI has assigned a really cute agent, I call him Sean, to be our, that is Christine's and my, body guard."

Mike jumped back in. "Actually, to just handle their physical surveillance and observe."

"Yeah, but it's nice to have a well-trained guy looking over your shoulder."

Sara smiled. "And good looking, eh Kat?"

"Sure. So, he's been with us pretty much twenty-four seven, and he is at the house right now. I'll head back there as soon as our meeting concludes, if that's okay with Sara."

"Of course. As usual, you can work remotely. Dad and I are happy to have all these resources now, for sure."

"Thanks, Sara."

Kat's final remark was meant in all sincerity, but sounded sarcastic.

"After all that we've been through there, what could possibly go wrong?"

49

MIKE

"I agree with your perspective, Kat. Christine and I are very happy to have that capability at our disposal."

"Team, I have two report-outs today and they are both very relevant and very interesting."

Mike poured a glass of water before beginning.

"Alien architectural consistencies throughout the world are no longer within the realm of 'some other convenient' explanation. With today's technology, we can use infra-red, carbon dating, x-ray, and sound measurements to compare and contrast ancient architectural throughout the world."

Mike paused as a pitcher of water was distributed by an attentive Kat.

"And, that is precisely what geologists and researchers are doing in vast locations and with hundreds, if not thousands, of trained people."

"Will you be speaking from first-hand knowledge?" Michaela asked.

"Well, yes and no. I have been to many of these sites over the past six years, but this data has all been complied since then. Michaela, I have had the opportunity to review data, documents, and conclusions, and I support their findings, one hundred per cent."

"Thanks. Sorry to interrupt."

"No. No problem. It's a valid question, Michaela."

Turning his notes over to the next page, Mike continued.

"Inca architecture is incredibly consistent with Mayan architecture which is consistent with the architectures of Egypt, Greece, and many other past civilizations. I'm compiling a detailed list for our next meeting.

"One particular stone monument design was virtually identical among structures in Maya, Egypt, Peru, and Cambodia. If you had those four structures side-by-side, you could not determine which one was in which country.

"It was if there was one, and only one, global building designer."

After a short sip of water, Mike continued.

"Here's the issue that Michaela mentioned that involved us both. Several years ago, my dad had an alleged abduction event involving his friend, the victim, Jack Burgess. I think you all are aware of that."

"We are," Kat responded.

"Some time after that, Dad was at the Burgess house trying to reconnect with an angry and confused Jack Burgess. Having had a series of dizziness and headaches, Jack had Pete take an embedded metal-like material in the form and size of a small coin, out of Jack's neck."

Sara interrupted. "As I recall, Grandad was going to get the material analyzed. They thought it had design properties similar to a receiver, right?"

"Yes, Sara. Dad gave it to me to analyze. Following his murder, I just tabled it and nearly forgot about it. Actually, it was when Michaela began to study the magnetic North Pole movement and the ties to the Earth's core, that I remembered that unfinished task."

Michaela added, "And what a coincidence it turned out to be."

"Yes. None of that material is from this earth. Not even one per cent. In fact, it is only found in small trace amounts in meteorites from deep space. Yet it was fabricated into a small receiving device that was unknowingly implanted in Jack Burgess' neck."

An excited Kat jumped in. "That is so damn cool."

"There's more, Kat. Much more. When raised to the highest temperature possible in a lab, that material structure begins to align with elements in the Earth's core."

"Holy crap," added a surprised Sara.

"The best part is still coming."

Sara said, "We can't wait for your grand finale, Dad."

"This material cannot be seen under a microscope or X-ray. It's like it isn't there!"

50

SARA

Sara then stood up and walked over to the podium to start her next part of the day's presentation.

"Again, it is absolutely amazing that we are so ingrained in this alien phenomenon that even Dad's incredible revelation gets an 'okay, what's next' response."

Checking her notes, Sara began.

"The previously mentioned Mars colony is a real thing. According to POTUS, a highly classified Russian/American joint venture established a working habitat and research colony on Mars late in the 1990's. All secretive launch sites were in Russia, which pretty much controlled media and nosey scientists."

Sara could see that the attention level heightened.

"I've known about this for a couple of weeks now, but the details were still TBD. Will get into all the specifics with you guys when I have them."

An excited Mike interjected.

"I am so proud of you and almost amazed that you have the President's trust. Way to go, Sara."

"Yep," added Michaela, "you go girl."

"Fasten your seat belts, because the next one will blow you away."

"Should I open the liquor cabinet, Sara?"

"No, Kat. Maybe when I'm done."

"Okeydoke."

"You have heard rumblings about a mysterious Apollo 18 mission, following the 1972 Apollo 17 mission, which was supposedly the final Apollo voyage."

Sara flicked a gaze over to Mike.

"Well, there really was a secret Apollo 18 launch in 1975."

Pausing, Sara referred to her notes.

"Pete Stevenson came across evidence of an alien visitor in the cabin of Commander Robert Kelly's Apollo 17 Command Module while Kelly's two fellow astronauts were on the lunar surface. Grandad had two sources to confirm this.

"One, he actually met with Robert Kelly and got the news straight from Kelly.

"And two, the teenage 'coffee girl' at Mission Control, who never had to sign an NDA, became a double PhD in the field of astrophysics. Grandad actually saw her notes regarding the conversation that Kelly had in the cabin of the Command Module with the alien."

"So," asked Kat, "how did this lead to Apollo 18?"

"This Apollo 17 mission and alien encounter was so authentic and believable that NASA decided to launch a follow-up mission to seek further contact with an alien that seemed to be friendly. Of course, it had to be done in secret."

"Of course," Kat said sarcastically.

"It was launched in 1975 from the Kodiak Launch Complex, Alaska. It took NASA and the military three years to get both the vehicle and the launch site ready."

Mike chimed in. "That's like a New York minute in the space industry."

Michaela was extremely curious.

"Sara, what happened?"

"Okay. The launch went well and Apollo 18 was safely in lunar orbit waiting for a sign. Two days later, while on the moon's dark side, Apollo 18 vanished. No mayday. No warning. No space debris observable. No trace whatsoever."

Sara looked up at the team and made a statement that could have been a question.

"NASA was monitoring the entire crew's vitals. Not one spike in any of those vital signs when they vanished."

51
MATTHEW

Following their rather productive and intense meeting of the ETRT, Sara phoned Matt to give him an update on those things she could discuss, and see what was going on back at Matt's Utah lab.

"Hey Sara, it's been a while. What have you and your team been working on?"

"It's so nice to hear your voice. We have been trying to get rid of those nonsense issues that Congress dumped on us and get back to the more interesting alien work."

"That's hilarious. Were you able to get that done?"

"Yes. We just wrapped up those yucky loose ends last week and now we are back to the issues that really matter and that will have an impact on everyone's life going forward."

"Any news on the break-in at your folk's house?"

"The police and FBI are going at it hot and heavy, but nothing definitive yet. We do have strong security at the house now, which makes Mom more comfortable."

"Sara, we have a very interesting hologram project going on right now. It involves brain-mapping and A.I. interaction. I should have something to share with you soon. I think you'll find our results very interesting."

Sara paused for a moment and said, "I recall something similar coming out in one of my discussions with an old friend of Grandad's."

"Really?" Matt asked with a "connect-the-dots" mindset. Questions went through his mind that were leading to more questions.

Sara replied, "Maybe I can sneak out there to see you as soon as we get a few of these priorities planned out."

"I would love that. Be safe and talk soon."

"Miss you, Matt."

"Miss you too, Sara."

As Matt and Sara hung up, Jeremiah, who was waiting patiently outside Matt's office, motioned to him to come over quickly.

"What's up Miah?"

"I had to put the hologram video on hold so you could see what I was seeing."

"Let's go."

✦ ✦ ✦

As they walked to the A.I. development lab, where the latest version of the company's hologram project was being completed, Matt explained his intentions to Jeremiah.

"I really want to focus our resources on this project to bring it to completion."

Jeremiah, excitedly, says to Matt. "Well, we may just need to raise our expectation level."

"Damn, Miah, what cha got?"

As Jeremiah led Matt into the newly equipped holo-display lab, Matt was stunned to see a new name on that new small lab:

SUPER ARTIFICIAL INTELLIGENCE

"What the…" Matt snapped.

Miah replied, "Okay boss. Just wait. The name fits!

"Our last meeting on the hologram had our guy Pete responding to questions, and you thought you heard him ask a question without a prompt."

"Miah, I know what I heard."

"And, Matt, you and I both saw the video from his memory that described visually an alien encounter."

"Yes, but I did not share that with anyone for fear of panic or reprisals."

"Understand."

Jeremiah continued. "Tyreek and I have been going over a new video streamed from Pete's memory."

"I'm listening."

"Two things Matt. One, it's like a science fiction movie, and two…it wasn't there before."

"Get to the bottom line, Miah."

"Watch."

Jeremiah teed up the "new" hologram video and pushed "start."

Within seconds the video, supposedly taken from Pete's memory, shows heavily armed aliens apparently attacking another planet's civilization.

Matt is completely mesmerized by what he is seeing.

In a David-versus-Goliath-type annihilation, the civilization under attack is helpless and overmatched against their attackers.

For several minutes, fire, wind, enemy space craft, and lasers rain down on the people under attack, until nothing remains but a scorched and barren planet surface.

Matt was absolutely silent.

"I ask you again, Jeremiah, what did we just see?"

"Matt, I didn't have this opinion before, but I absolutely do now."

"And that opinion is?"

"Pete Stevenson is trying to warn us of future alien attacks from his hologram!"

52

KAT

Following her last meeting with Sara, Kat met with Agent Eight at the Stevenson house and the agent gave Kat a quick update.

"We were able to identify the two perps that broke into the house last month."

Kat quickly inquired, "How'd you do that?"

Pausing a moment, Agent Eight replied, "From the 360-degree cameras that we installed two months ago."

"Well," Kat smirked, "how lovely."

"Ma'am, again, need to know basis."

"Hey, don't call me ma'am."

"Yes, ma'am."

"So, secret agent man, what's next?"

"Just some routine work for now. I just got a call with a lead and will be heading off solo now and will update you later."

"But…"

"Sorry, ma'am, you need to wait here."

With that, Agent Eight was headed to his black SUV and Kat was puzzled, thinking this was the first time he had gone off solo when a lead was followed or a meeting was held.

Kat was pissed.

At that very moment, she made an impulsive decision. Running into the kitchen, she yelled loudly at Christine that she had to leave.

"Okay," was Christine's response. "Be careful."

Kat raced to her car, a small SUV crammed with personal and work material and some junk.

✦ ✦ ✦

Kat spotted Agent Eight's SUV easily as it exited the Stevenson driveway. She followed him for about forty-five miles, attempting to negotiate traffic and still not lose him.

The phone rang. It was Sara. She flipped it into voice mail. This was the first time Kat had ever ignored a call from Sara, but Kat was on a mission.

After making a series of turns, the agent's SUV made a sharp turn to the left into a dark alley. Following his SUV, Kat turned her car immediately to face a man with a gun pointed directly at her.

It was Agent Eight. "What the hell you doing following me? I told you to stay put, dammit!"

Kat was shaking. She knew she screwed up. "I'm sorry. Was just curious, you know."

"Ma'am, curiosity killed the Cat!"

The humor was kind of refreshing and totally unexpected.

Agent Eight said, "Get out of your car and get into mine...quickly."

"Yes sir."

At that very moment, Kat knew she was in the wrong place. Wrong time, she wondered?

53

KAT

Inside the agent's SUV, Kat asked. "What can you tell me?"

"As long as you're here, I'll bring you up to speed. I need to go about a mile and a half to my target,"

"Shit," Kat thought. "This is serious."

As they drove, Agent Eight gave Kat the update.

"Two perps from the house break-in were recognized on our facial recognition."

"But…"

"Shut up and listen, dammit."

Kat became church-mouse quiet.

"Those two intruders separated the night of the break-in and have not been back together until tonight. So, we know something is going down and it's here, according to our surveillance."

Agent Eight slowed his SUV down, turned the vehicle tracking device on, and pulled around to the back of an old abandoned warehouse.

"We also got a tip that the leader of a nasty terrorist group is also in town, so they must all be here and here right now."

"Shit," Kat softly said.

"So, with the tip and the surveillance, I followed the two perps to a possible encounter with the 'big guy.' They are apparently inside this building."

As Agent Eight opened the door, gun in hand, he told Kat. "Don't leave. Don't even think about it."

About ten minutes later, Agent Eight returned.

"We have a bad situation. The leader is interrogating a bound man; from what I saw, it looks like he is actually extracting teeth from a semi-conscious victim."

Kat was suffering high anxiety and felt herself trembling.

"Here's the deal, Kathy."

"Kathy," Kat thought that this is serious. He called me Kathy.

"By the way, what's your real name, Double-O-Eight?"

"It's George."

"Really. I like Sean better."

"So, I don't have time to call for backup. My tracker is on. What's going down is happening right now. This is what we're doing."

"We?" Kat was very nervous.

"There are two, armed gunmen, the big shot doing the dental work and the victim. Take this Taser.

"You can do this. It's just an easy point and shoot…Here's the trigger."

"We're going through the back window of the building. It's open. I'll take out the two, armed gunmen, and you Taser the leader. We'll grab the leader, who should be fairly weak, and the victim. I'll take whoever is heaviest and you go to person number two. Got it?"

Once inside the building, the Agent's silencer and Kat's Taser made no noise at all. The two gunmen were dead and Kat rushed over to the victim, while the agent hand-cuffed the leader.

They both put the two dazed people in the SUV and headed out. Agent Eight immediately contacted his back-up team and told them where they were in route to the nearest police precinct.

All seemed good as they sped away.

Not five minutes later, they were blindsided by a dark SUV with a rein-forced bumper and they were sent spinning in their damaged SUV with air bags deployed.

Once their vehicle stopped spinning, Agent Eight motioned for Kat to grab her man and the four of them exited their heavily damaged SUV. Agent Eight was firing his weapon as they all were running from heavy gunfire from the SUV that smashed into them.

"Run, Kat, run!"

Agent Eight had the leader and Kat had the victim, all bloodied from his ordeal. They ran as quickly as possible from the shooters, heading for a nearby ravine.

Within seconds, dozens of rounds were fired at the backs of the four people trying to flee. Not able to outrun the barrage of bullets, all four fleeing people were killed.

Surveillance footage showed the two attacking men grabbed the dead leader and put him in their vehicle. The remaining three that were killed were left at the scene.

Agent Eight's backup team was just getting to the shooting scene, but just a few minutes too late.

Kat was later found dead and the terrorist leader was presumed dead as well.

54

SARA

Immediately upon hearing the terrible news, Sara called the team together to give them an update on the disastrous shooting that resulted in Kat's death.

As the team assembled, Sara was hanging up with her parents after giving them her latest incident update.

Once gathered, Michaela gave Sara a long embrace. Tears were shed and everyone felt numb.

Michaela spoke. "Of all the team members, Kat was normally not the adventuresome one. Not her comfort zone, for sure."

Sara nodded, "Apparently, Kat was with the FBI agent assigned to protect Kat and my mom following the break-in at the Stevenson house two months ago that you are all aware of."

Sara paused. "It is unclear what Kat was doing at that attack site. An investigation is under way."

Everyone was silent as Sara continued.

"There was footage from the shooting site that showed Kat, the agent, and two men were fleeing in the agent's SUV when they were deliberately rammed by a larger SUV with a reinforced bumper."

The word "deliberate" rang out loudly in the quiet room.

"The agent's SUV was spun around a couple times, the air bags engaged, and when the SUV came to a stop, all four people in the SUV began running away from the crash site."

Sara paused and wiped tears from her face.

"The FBI agent was seen firing repeatedly as they fled."

Sara again paused.

"Apparently, the FBI agent knew they were in immediate danger. Two men from the attacking vehicle got out and opened fire with assault-style weapons. All four fleeing people, including Kat, were shot many times in the back and all fell quickly."

Sara had to pause as each member of the team was now sobbing.

"The two attackers then grabbed the one man that the agent was with, now identified as the terrorist leader called Scorpio, and dragged his lifeless body back to the attack vehicle and they sped off."

Sara took a deep breath and finished.

"Within a couple minutes, the agent's back-up team arrived, but it was too late to catch up with the attackers."

Scott took over from Sara with a brief comment.

"Once we have notified next-of-kin, funeral arrangements will be announced."

Sara stood up with her fist raised and in a not-so-quiet voice replied.

"This atrocity changes everything."

55

SCOTT

Scott asked the ETRT to remain for a few minutes as he had an important announcement.

"I have been in contact with POTUS and he sends his deepest condolences on behalf of himself, the First Lady and his entire administration."

"Thanks for sharing that, Scott." Sara's words were weak and soft.

Scott continued reading from a notepad.

"As of this very minute, the U.S. government is putting our entire team under security protection. Interviews with all of you will be necessary for the security personnel to establish twenty-four seven needs tailored to everyone's schedule and needs. Make sense?"

Sadness was quickly replaced by high levels of anxiety for the ETRT.

"And," Scott continued, "we will be making arrangements to establish individual tracking means for all team members going forward. Details will soon follow."

"Scott, what kind of tracking?"

"Don't know yet, Sara. We are presently in contact with Doctor Palmer's technical group for their input, as well as from our federal security experts."

Sara continued. "Scott, who all will be monitored?"

"Right now, each of the ETRT members. The interview process will determine the short list and then we will coordinate with you guys to make sure we are all on the same page. Does that make sense?"

Mike was nodding his head in agreement.

"I think it's safe to say that we will be looking into both primary and secondary tracking devices."

Sara asked, "Implants?"

"Dunno Sara."

"Damn, this is going from bad to worse."

"You're right, Sara, but necessary none the less. Believe me when I say that we will make this as painless, excuse the word, as possible."

"I understand."

"We just can't be put in the same situation as Kat found herself in without due process here."

Scott paused, and then raised his voice in a matter-of-fact way. "At least until we get to the bottom of this terrorist issue and how and why it involved the work of the ETRT."

Mike asked Scott, "Will Christine be part of this?"

"Yes, Mike, she will."

"Okay. I'm gonna call her right now so she hears it from me and doesn't freak out."

"Good idea, Dad. Let me know if you need me to support or add my opinion when to talk to Mom."

"Will do, Sara."

With that, Scott signaled that the meeting was over.

Sara was still totally distraught with Kat's death and uttered an oft-used phrase.

"It's timing…it's always the damn timing."

56

SARA

Michaela joined Sara in the conference room where Sara was sitting in a very pensive mood and reflecting on the latest incident and all the work that Kat and the team had done.

She knew she had to get back to the job at hand and just at that moment, Sara felt a very positive feeling taking over.

"Hey, Michaela, nice to see a good friend right now. What cha got there?"

"I have a bottle of Napa Valley Silver Oak Cab and a couple glasses. You interested?"

"Sure. Thanks."

Michaela approached Sara, who was clutching a box of tissues, and they gave each other a much-needed hug.

"What's my Sara doing here in the conference room?"

"Well, I was about to tee-up the video of the key presentation we made on Scott's boat prior to our meeting in D.C. and, sadly, relive some of Kat's many contributions."

"Need a friend to watch with you?"

"Absolutely. Your timing couldn't have been better."

"Is this the edited version, Sara, with all the notes, recordings and your dad's take on what Pete saw during his Sweden encounter?"

"Yeah, you've seen this before at our last meeting before D.C."

"Gotcha."

Sara began the incredible alien encounter presentation…

Scene # 1 – *Pete was out of his car in Trelleborg and looked at the alien spacecraft. As he approached a large triangular-shaped vehicle, he said it reminded him of the old Mercury capsule but significantly larger; a door opened from this alien spacecraft. Pete mentioned that he had an undeniable feeling of "déjà vu" and could almost foresee the next sequence. Several aliens, in human-like forms, exited the craft and moved slowly toward Pete. There was a sense of calm and anxiety, not fear or apprehension.*

Sara noted, "Kat was next and had several tasks but the UFO part was her most enjoyable work."

"I agree, said Michaela."

Kat spoke.

"I collected a series of photos, documents, and interviews with people around the world that saw, photographed, and documented UFO sightings. I also found that flight patterns of these UFO's followed the same basic aerial routes around the world.

"This could not be coincidence. I also have several pieces of documentation from two foreign astronauts that had pictures, sketches, and incidents that collaborate this info. Apparently, Pete met with these two astronauts and they felt comfortable with this info to put it into his hands."

Kat could be seen looking over to her slides of this info.

"I also found many instances, with Jacqui's help, of stone etching throughout time that alluded to one almighty God, referred to as Anunnaki, replacing many heavenly gods that were considered the many spiritual rulers of the time. And this god was depicted as having human looks and actions.

"Pete's notes even named the god-like visitors that helped ancient civilizations build monuments and teach skills that are a stretch even in today's civilizations. Each so-called teacher was specified by name throughout the last ten thousand years of Earth's many civilizations.

"If you take this theory to full potential, it explains exactly why all of this building, along with basic civilization development, regardless of which continent that is occurred, was identical."

Sara stopped the video. "I had never seen Kat so excited and so engaged. This whole journey simply transformed Kat's life and her resolve. So sad…"

The video continued to the next event.

Scene # 2 – *Pete faced ten aliens in a triangle or pyramid formation, with one in front, and the remainder in formation. The alien in front said, "I am called Echo, Pete, and you have nothing to fear. I am the Commander of this ship, our Magellan if you will, and on my right is Pulse, my Lieutenant. I am the elder statesman and will be your guide."*

Team member Jacqui, taking a big sigh, began her portion.

"I have become obsessed with the so-called Nazca Lines in Peru, and my research came up with verifiable evidence that these landing strips were found in many parts of the world, designed and built in identical fashion per Kat's info, and on the same flight lines that UFO's were seen.

"These undeniable lines are in geometric patterns, often many thousands of feet long, and are in perfect alignment. Even intersections of lines, based on the configuration, are all at exactly forty-five-degree or ninety-degree angles.

"I also found verifiable evidence of well-detailed carvings of what appeared to be huge stone sentinels located at every site to help incoming aircraft or space-ships land."

Jacqui could be seen looking at her slides, as she continued: "And, while doing the research on these lines I have gathered several elongated skulls that are not even close to what you would see today in tribal rituals. Again, these elon-gated skulls were found in nine different locations around the world, all locations traceable from Pete's notes."

Jacqui put up a slide depicting the skulls along with the locations of the finds. Michaela added, "This was the part where I wished I was with Pete."

Sara smiled.

Scene # 3 – *Pete entered the spacecraft and saw a massive control room and bridge. He was directed to be seated near a large panoramic window. As Pete was seated, Echo spoke. "We are here to provide you with the hard evidence you need to complete your work. We will circumnavigate your solar system and then on to infin-ity, as you know it to be, Pete. Nothing more." Pete mentioned that Echo's attempt to simplify an enormously complex task was reassuring.*

Sara offered a thought, "At this point, Connor was very anxious to start."

"He was," Michaela replied, "and with good reason."

Connor presented next: "I have used Pete Stevenson's coordinate data, and worked with Michaela's team as well, to establish a likely World Grid that seemed to have a purposeful alien strategy.

"This strategy, when executed, precisely aligned major monuments with true north; and from the six pyramids of the Pyramid Giza Complex, considered at one time to be the center of all landmasses of Earth, all documented flight pat-terns would use.

"This is unmistakable, and literally impossible for a multitude of cultures to coordinate over all of that space and time. After all, they didn't have social media at that time."

There was some noticeable laughter on the video.

"I was also able to verify, translating several languages with Pete's code, that one common mathematical formula was used throughout time for navigation, geometric calculations, and even the value of Pi. Again, just one!

"What I found was that Einstein's Unified Theory was actually discovered thousands of years earlier.

"We all have heard the phrase, there are many ways to solve a problem, but just pick one and go. Well, maybe there isn't a phrase, but you get the idea.

"Every civilization back to the beginning of time could not come up with one way of doing anything. This data says that they all had one way of doing everything. Oh, except for the Mayans, but Michaela will get into that."

"Thanks, Connor," Michaela could be heard saying sarcastically.

"Yikes," added Michaela, "that wasn't very nice. Don't remember that tone at all."

"I got a kick out of it," responded Sara.

Connor continued, "And, I have established that certain monuments were consistently used for navigation and pyramids were used for aircraft refueling, given the intricate nature of the insides of these huge structures.

"Massive cargo had to be moved and hauled, and that was depicted in etchings at or near these navigation sites.

"In fact, the great pyramids in Egypt and elsewhere were using levitation, according to one of my unnamed colleagues, to move the megaliths into their final shapes. Again, wall carvings described this in detail in many locations, per Pete's outstanding compass work."

At that point Scott jumped in.

"Connor, you said massive cargo had to be moved and hauled and they used levitation. Isn't that an oxymoron? They could levitate pyramids but they had to haul their cargo."

"I see your point. Will need to work on this some more. Geez, I wasn't there at the time."

Sara recalled that she used the mid-morning break at this point to return a call from her dad. As Michaela poured them each another glass of Cab, she asked Sara a question.

"Was this when you talked to Mike about the cabin explosion?"

"Yep. And he asked me how our boat meeting was going."

"What did you tell him?"

"Laughing a little, I told him that Scott had shot a couple holes in our theories, but that's what we expected."

"Did he give you some info on the explosion?"

"Yeah, he said he had done a lot of digging and had spoken to many people familiar with the kind of gas tank that would cause a major explosion."

"And?"

"Well," Sara continued, "Grandad Pete wasn't on a main gas line and only had his medium-sized propane tank, likely one hundred and twenty gallons, on the side of the cabin."

Michaela was getting more curious.

"So, that tank could not have caused the extensive cabin damage."

Sara replied, "No. The drone's missile wasn't aimed at the propane tank?"

"Did your dad draw any conclusion?"

"He said it was as I had suspected, an armed missile intended to destroy the entire cabin and its contents. He also assumed that I was asking because he thought I had a lead on its origin."

"And did you? Do you?"

"Yes, and yes, Michaela. And it has nothing to do with aliens."

Michaela wondered, "The terrorist connection?"

"Yes, Michaela, and now I'm absolutely sure. Kat's death is the overwhelming evidence.

Michaela nodded her head in agreement.

Sara scowled.

"I just wish now that it had been the evil aliens."

57

SARA

Michaela had to leave for a few minutes and Sara used that time to phone her parents with some much-needed small talk.

"Hi Dad. Hi Mom. How you guys doing?"

Christine replied, "Not well. Kat's death just tore us up. Why Kat? The sweetest, nicest person you could ever meet."

"How you doing?" Mike's voice was tense.

"As well as could be expected."

Christine continued.

"What cha doing now?"

"Michaela and I are looking again at the video of our presentation rehearsal for the D.C. meeting. It had some of Kat's greatest hits!"

Mike found that opportunity to gently laugh. "She was all that and more."

"Honey," Christine asked, "can we see you sometime soon? Can you come for a short visit?"

"Sure can." Uttering those words, Sara knew that she didn't have time and simply told a "white lie" to not upset her mom.

"Gotta go now. See you soon."

"Okay. Love you Sara."

"Love you too, Mom."

"Stay in touch and love you."

"Love you, too. Will stay in touch."

Mike and Christine could sense that Sara was still very much in mourning.

✦ ✦ ✦

As Michaela returned to the conference room, Sara continued the presentation video.

Justin was next and he began with another note and data from Pete.

Scene # 4 – Pete was seeing the sight lines and navigation grid from space and their linear relationship to Earth's pyramids and how actual landings would be made. As they lifted off and moved into an Earth orbit, they circumvented the globe in minutes. Pulse pointed out the grid from this elevation and Pete saw how flight patterns, navigation, and landings were all in identical coordinates. Then, almost immediately, they flew at nearly ground level to demonstrate landings. Pete had a sense of absolute time travel that was being accomplished in microseconds.

Justin offered an explanation. "I have taken the coding documents that Pete had prepared, and basically confirmed that a center core of all things done on this planet over thousands of years was basically a blueprint adjusted to fit the cultures, times, and languages of each civilization.

"In other words, I found that the same set of directions, or lesson plans, could be found and overlapped precisely.

"Pete had discovered this incredible evidence initially and I was lucky enough to connect the dots. I simply confirmed the results by starting with Pete's conclusion and working backward, as several of us now do."

Justin excitedly added, "In what was the most satisfying coding work that I have ever done, was that I was able to help several members of the ETRT to locate the actual coded person, using the original cabin map, who was either Pete's interviewee or keeper of a particular artifact.

"We have also identified each of Pete's four teammates by matching their actual names and roles to their nicknames. You may recall that the cabin map only had one half of the identity puzzle, but the other half that Sara got completed that puzzle."

Scene # 5 – Pictures from a Martian orbit showed the replication of Earth's ancient monuments and their existence on the surface of Mars. Then the spaceship moved effortlessly out of Earth's orbit and into an orbit around Mars, literally in seconds. Pulse pointed out that the sandstorms that had plagued the Martian landscape obscured the view that Pete now had. A perfect replica of the Egyptian Pyramids and Sphinx were seen on the surface of Mars, and Pulse overlaid coordinates to show their identical dimensions. Pulse nodded to Pete; Pete nodded back in an understanding manner.

Michaela could be seen referring to her extensive notes and went next.

"The Stargate theories had always fascinated me, as I knew of Einstein's Theory of Relativity and his belief in cosmic wormholes and a way for humans to travel from star to star like the ancient aliens.

"Before you say this cannot be verified with today's evidence, let me interrupt you. You're right, it could not, until now."

Sara was seen smiling.

"Pete's encounter in Sweden resulted in his strong argument that the Orion Belt was the birthplace of all stars in the galaxy. And as remarkable as it is puzzling, Pete had close-up pictures of a massive star formation fifteen hundred light years from Earth, showing more than three thousand stars in some form of star-life.

"As I recall, he was in Sweden for three days in 2018, not nearly enough time to travel fifteen hundred light years and return!"

Some laughter could be heard from the audience responding to Michaela's sense of humor. Michaela then continued.

"If you have subject matter experts look at the photographs, they will tell you that they were made by a large stationary craft with Hubble-Telescope-plus capabilities."

Michaela was seen pausing to verify her slides.

"Back to the actual results, we have discovered physical evidence of complex calculations and extraordinary craftwork and stonemasonry cut into huge stone tablets, from Puma Punku in the Bolivian Andes.

"The depictions vary from others in that they are mostly temple oriented. Faces, lineage, recreation, and huge carved stones represent the books in today's public libraries.

"Three things jump out at you here; I know it did to me.

"One, these epic monuments were built at an elevation of twelve thousand eight hundred feet. How in the world did those huge and heavy monuments get all the way up there?

"Two, the very odd fact here was that these stone reminders of a distant past were very distant…likely fourteen thousand years ago.

"And three, there was an effort at some point in time to destroy all that is there right now."

Michaela could be seen getting as animated and excited as ever.

"And now for the best of the best. The lost Mayan Civilization is, and was, one of history's greatest mysteries. Such an advanced culture accomplishing extraordinary feats, leaving many to wonder why, how, and when.

"According to Pete's encounter, the Mayans were placed here from the Seven Sisters open-star cluster, some four hundred fifty light years away, to help advance Earth's civilizations.

"When, for many reasons that did not occur, the Mayans were relocated to that star system, which had evolved more quickly than our planet at the time of the Mayans.

"Although many of Earth's civilizations have vanished with no plausible explanation, the Mayans were different, special, and extremely advanced."

Scott began to speak, but suddenly stopped. His point, apparently, could wait.

Scene # 6 – Picture of the Seven Sisters cluster was taken from an orbital perspective. Pete had a sense of incredible speed and was almost rendered unconscious. He gained his senses to see what appeared to be a trip through a black hole or wormhole. Pulse said, "We are now hundreds of light years from Earth, looking at a star cluster that housed many civilizations, including the Mayans, on several planets. We have bases here." Pulse went on, "We will leave you with evidence photos of this."

Michaela looked over to Sara as if to say, "That was amazing."

Sara seemed to understand Michaela's thought and responded, "This is amazing."

Scene # 7 – Pete was now back on the ground where the journey began and felt an enormous surge of knowledge and perspective. Echo looked directly at Pete, almost as a parent would, and said, "Pete, you now have an enormous responsibility. We want you to continue your work and, with the new facts and data that you have, we hope you are able to convince that small but critical core of the scientific community that alien theory is alien fact. There are many reasons why we do not want to reveal ourselves to the world, as only panic, fear, and hysteria would occur. You need to be mankind's finder of the truth."

Sara said to Michaela, "Prophetic, eh?"

Michaela replied, "Yep, the end of the beginning."

Scene # 8 – The conclusion of the alien journey, a startling observation, and the final words: Pete had a very vivid recollection of docking with, and then disembarking from, a massive "space station" in space. His memory was of a floating city that was so big that he couldn't see end to end. What was even more remarkable was that he could see Earth from his vantage point, but, obviously, no one on earth could see this cloaked, massive structure.

Sara recalled the remainder of that encounter via Pete's notes:

When Pete regained his senses, he was back in his rental car, alone, and with no one in sight. He felt exhausted and mentally drained, but at the same time absolutely energized with the events that has just occurred. In his lap were new notes taken during his "journey," amazing photos and his diary covering the entire time he was gone, and Pulse had written the word ARAS, in all caps, on his hotel itinerary. He thought he had been gone for only a couple of hours, but he had been gone for three days.

✦ ✦ ✦

Following another break, Sara could be seen announcing the itinerary for Round Two and Sumaar's team began.

"With our many documented findings in several European cities in general, and churches specifically, it is more than ninety per cent likely that alien spaceships visited often. The term Vimana was used frequently to describe huge flying fortresses, and that was well documented."

"What Pete found were ships that were almost identical to early Russian and American space capsules, and the largest was called the Rukma Vimana."

Sumaar showed a series of depictions.

"However, they appeared armed with missiles, indicating war-like ships, as Pete surmised. He strongly believed that evil aliens existed and may be among us today. But he also believed that alien wars had been fought on planet Earth, and other planets as well, for centuries."

Pete's depiction of Rukma Vimana was shown.

"With many references to various etchings throughout the world of human-like astronauts or spacemen, they always seem to be signaling in their depictions. This consistent and entirely identical form that these etchings take cannot be coincidental."

"Also, you can see many examples of what we would describe as fully functional space suits and breathing apparatus. Even aircraft or spaceship controls, not dissimilar to today's equipment, are well described."

Pete's depiction of an alien spaceman was shown.

As Sumaar finished, Jacqui's team began.

"This team took on the huge evidence pool of ancient hieroglyphics. Archeologists and geologists for centuries have analyzed hieroglyphics and symbols. What Pete's study concluded was, again, pure consistency and message-to-message commonality.

"Every one of the many languages came to the same conclusion, and that was they came from above in fiery machines, and they brought knowledge and technology to build, inform, and teach, and they left."

Jacqui went on to say, "I love Pete's simple response in one of his notes, 'I'm trying to make this difficult, but it's hard to do.' It shows Pete's resolve and his humor."

Some mild laughter could be heard from the group... a couple "thumbs up" too.

"Finally, we have an ancient wooded carved bird, actually in Pete's possession, which was found in one of the oldest of Egypt's ninety-seven pyramids.

"It was obviously a carved bird, but one of Pete's aerodynamics experts built a scale model of this bird, which actually resembled one of today's airplanes, and it flew. It was a highly developed glider, designed in ancient Egypt. Awesome!

"As you already know, I actually verified this data myself with current subject-matter experts, who agreed that such an aircraft today could not only glide but also be propelled via engines to fly safely and effectively."

Pete's picture of the bird/glider was shown.

Two ETRT members who had not yet presented, Joyce and Rudy, had the floor to discuss Roswell, Area 51, abductions, and some interesting UFO findings.

Joyce began, "Much of what Rudy and I found was from Pete's first-hand accounts. He interviewed a gentleman on his deathbed that gave Pete pictures of the Roswell disc that landed, as well as pictures of the astronaut inside.

"Pete was also able to get photos from other sources that were identical in size, features, and detail to the two Roswell artifacts."

Rudy chimed in, "And the Area 51 was replaced with Area 52 just to take the heat off of the public's interest in Area 51, where the alien evidence was shown as a downed balloon.

"It's not the old news that is cool, but Pete's pictures that are strong evidence of alien presence and cover-up.

"However he was able to obtain these photos, you cannot argue their relevance. They simply continue to verify and corroborate every piece of so-called circumstantial evidence that was out there."

Joyce continued, "The one piece that is most interesting and most germane today comes from Mexico and a funeral monument of a Mayan leader.

"His chamber, photographed in great detail by one of Pete's colleagues, shows a person looking very much like our present astronauts, in a spacecraft, looking very much like our current spacecrafts, in a suit, looking very much like our current flight suits, at the controls of what looks like space capsule controls.

"The depictions do show, however, and we have seen these before, persons with elongated skulls and somewhat longer extremities."

Pete's pictures of the spaceships and the astronauts were shown.

Rudy remarked, "The abductions have always been at the forefront of alien talk. But Pete had first-hand experience, having witnessed one himself.

"And, we did facial recognition of the presumed dead crew of the sunken sailing vessel and have concluded that the crew members found on Jost Van Dyke in the British Virgin Islands years later were, in fact, the crew that perished when it sank. This incredible survivor story was an incredible true event."

Rudy concluded.

"Finally, the mention over the years of a variety of UFO's flying in known flight paths over recognized markers at breakneck speeds is not news.

"What is news is that we have approximately seventeen hundred photos in our possession, thanks to Pete and his work. We also have actual interviews from credible witnesses that have seen UFOs in flight while these witnesses were engaged in flight, both in commercial aircraft and space stations."

Some of Pete's photos were shown.

Connor's team then began to present their findings on levitation with Mark opening the discussion.

"We were all fascinated by how our ancestors, given the tools and knowledge of their time, could move megaton stones and monuments, not only within a location, but transported to a location from hundreds of miles away.

"From a multitude of languages over time, and from a variety of sources, the constant mention of stones walking or stones flying or stones disappearing and reappearing, it was Pete's conclusion that levitation, also part of the abduction process, was the only explanation. The legendary walking statues of Easter Island give you chills."

Mark showed the various stones.

"Pete felt strongly that aliens of the future had mastered the art of breaking down matter and then re-connecting it, which could explain levitation, moving inanimate objects, and even time travel."

Pete's pictures of Stonehenge, Easter Island, etcetera, were shown.

Michaela's team next began a large info blast. She introduced Liana, who began.

"Our deep dive into the Sumerian culture, as one of Mr. Stevenson's main targets, produced a plethora of dots to connect, and we tried to do just that.

"It was thought that the ancient Sumerians were extraterrestrials that originally arrived on Earth some four thousand years ago. Yet, it was their belief that the Anunnaki, their ancient extraterrestrial gods, gave rise to the technological culture that defined civilizations ever since."

Michaela added for clarity, "The reason we bring this up is that Pete had stumbled across some linkage to our present-day DNA anomalies to ancient Sumerian scientists and their attempt of genetic engineering. Crazy, yes, but just add this to everything else, eh?"

Liana continued, "We are all still, can I say starstruck, with the Stargate mythology and the Orion constellation. It is our belief that Sirius, the brightest star in the night sky within the Orion constellation, is the key to time travel and the ability to navigate through the gateways of time and space.

"There is no doubt, from Pete's documentation, that the stars and the constellations were the navigational maps that the aliens used, both for travel and for the building of civilizations.

"This is our next level *expective*, as Sara would say, and we will be happy to present our findings at the next subject presentation."

Justin went last this time and appeared much more serious than usual.

"All right. Now I will wrap this up with the totally non-alien portion of our presentation. This is like good news, bad news, but I'm not sure about the good news."

Sara could be seen looking over to Scott who looked puzzled.

"Scott, we are now getting to the core of our research and all will be clear soon."

"Sara, this whole day has been enlightening...can't imagine what's coming, but Amanda and I are listening."

Sara nodded for Justin to continue.

"We are all delighted and extremely juiced by Pete Stevenson's great encounter in Trelleborg, as well as the extremely detailed documentation that came from his team. And it will go without saying that everything he provides will be one hundred per cent debunked as crap by the vast majority of people who don't even care about this stuff.

"However, Pete left us with, how do you say, indisputable evidence."

Justin stated excitedly, "In the middle of Pete's diary is a sketch, a very detailed sketch. It depicts a massive orbital structure, home of the aliens meeting Pete, cloaked to avoid detection, and of the appearance and size of a major American city."

Justin showed the team Pete's rendering.

"According to his notes, Pete says that this orbiting space structure was as enormous as anything he has ever seen on Earth, and he could actually see Earth for his position on this craft."

Justin paused while he adjusted his horn-rimmed glasses.

"So, on the last page of Pete's dairy of the three days spent with the aliens in Trelleborg, in February of 2018, several things appear via his usual and brilliant code. I'm telling you this guy was awesome!

"He said that a strange comment that the aliens made had nothing to do with their show and tell."

After a fairly long pause, "And that was that; the end of the beginning is near."

Scott could be heard saying, "That's as big a 'big picture' that you could have."

"Yep, Pete also documented that we should fear Artificial Intelligence as our biggest threat and that embryonic stem cell research would conclude that males in the future would not be needed for reproduction."

They all imagined Kat laughing loudly and saying, "Now you're talking!"

Justin continued. "He mentioned that solar and wind power were the keys for the future and not to rely on oil, gas, and coal. There was a note to call Sara as soon as possible."

Sara responded to Justin's remark.

"I remember getting that call. It was the last conversation I had with him, but there wasn't anything memorable about the call itself. Grandad just wanted to know if things were okay with me. I told him I was fine. I did recall that he said he was looking forward to working together in the future."

"Okay," Justin added, "I'm saving the best, I mean the weirdest, for last. If ever there was a big Oh My God in the middle of many OMGs, this is it."

On the video, Justin appeared as anxious as ever.

"The aliens gave Pete the exact date, place, and time of every major global calamity that the world would face, not only through today, but for ten years through 2028, and this was back in 2018.

"I can only assume that Pete kept this to himself, and it was his intention to somehow divulge this during that Paris meeting later that year, but he was murdered before he could do that."

Scott said to Justin, "I'll need that last info of yours...immediately."

Justin replied, "Of course, Scott."

As the video ended, a puzzled Michaela asked Sara, "What did Scott do with that info and where is it or how is it being used?"

Sara thought and then responded, "Good question. Scott actually put it in the hands of President Sullivan, who, as far as we know, gave it to the proper authorities."

"But nothing happened with respect to early warnings of disasters or major dangerous events, on dates already passed."

"No, Michaela, but I have a theory as to why nothing bad happened."

Pausing…

"Someone or something stepped in from the future to change the course of history."

58

SARA

Almost two weeks went by before the process of tracking methods and ETRT member interviews were established. This was a very significant need going forward and the entire team was both apprehensive and excited to move forward with a plan.

At that time, Sara set up a video chat with the team, as Mike was back home in Ohio and Sara had just returned from her latest visit with Matt in Provo.

"Good morning, guys, and hope all is settling down for you. No one wants to get back to work on our main objective more than me."

Sara could see that all were present for the chat.

"I want to set up a new logistics plan and establish new priorities with today's call."

The team was ready, expecting Sara's call even sooner than today.

"I also want to say that our newest member, Elonis, will be speaking on a variety of alien stuff at our next meeting. That is why you haven't heard from me sooner.

"Elonis was compiling a ton of relevant info and I'm sure you will be impressed with her report-out."

The team now knew why the two-week delay.

"And, Doctor Palmer is working on an advanced Artificial Intelligence project that has some fascinating possibilities regarding data capture and cognitive reasoning."

No one missed the remark about "cognitive reasoning."

"You all know that I'm pretty rigid about not tackling too many things at one time. By the process of elimination, we have narrowed our target research to only those relevant and critical issues."

Mike was so impressed with how his daughter was managing this project now, especially with Kat's death and all. He was all smiles.

"I have taken the info from the last meeting, and with each of you contributing your thoughts and ideas going forward, I now have a short list that I would like you guys to focus on, as you put your project teams together."

Michaela inquired, "Will we be able to tap any outside resources?"

"Yes. Definitely. As you know, we now have resources beyond those of the ETRT. Scott and President Sullivan are providing outstanding tools, talent, and equipment for us."

Pausing for a couple seconds, she continued, "Just go through me for your needs… people, equipment, funds. I'll be the conduit for all the team projects."

Sara waited a moment to see if there were any questions. With no questions, she continued.

"Connor and Justin have completed an amazing piece of technology for us to use immediately."

Both guys smiled as Sara explained.

"You will each be receiving an encrypted e-Watch to replace your current e-Watches within the next two days. They will contact each of you for training."

"Training?" Mike was surprised.

"Yes, Dad. With these devices, we will be able to do two things without the threat of hackers or listening devices. You will be able to talk to anyone in our loop at any time with no concern about your conversation being compromised."

Michaela was excited. "That is remarkable. What else?"

"Yep. Really cool devices. With your e-Watch, you will be able to set up video chats with the team and from this point on, we will meet remotely and not need formal meetings unless we are making presentations."

Connor quickly offered. "Yep, and we are close to having 3D holographic capability with these watches as well."

Mike added, "Yeah, that is remarkable. Our compliments to the geniuses."

Michaela interjected a thought on the tech issue.

"Guys, what about the 'interactive glasses' that you've been working on?"

Justin pounced on the opportunity. "Great question. The augmented reality mobile computer for on-demand access to ETRT data and general info is close to a wearable application."

Michaela smiled, given the high-tech answer.

Connor clarified, "We are looking for totally hands-free mobile communication through digital info layered onto reality perspectives. You know, a completely connected ETRT entity for a fully collaborative environment…but wearable and indistinguishable from regular glasses."

A somewhat amused Sara muttered, "Well, gang. I have an incoming call from Utah that I need to take. Give me fifteen minutes and I will be back to finish this chat."

✦ ✦ ✦

About ten minutes later, the team could see that an obviously frazzled Sara had returned to the chat.

"Okay, I'm back. Y'all here?"

Everyone was back on the video call.

"Here's my suggested 'to-do' list for now. Let me know your thoughts and resource needs, of course.

"Michaela will work on three items."

1) The cities built around stars and star formations from her last presentation.
2) She will also drill down on the pyramid alignment and orientation that came up.
3) Earth's magnetic North Pole wandering.

"Mike will work on two items."

1) Alien architecture consistency around the world.
2) The meteorite material found in Jack Burgess's neck.

"Connor and Justin will tackle some fresh issues that came to my attention recently. We have already had some preliminary talks, and I will be sitting in on some of their work. Those issues are pretty cool."

As Sara pulled up a new set of notes, Connor and Justin were especially geeked to get in on the action.

Sara advised. "Here's their to-do list...real aggressive.

1) Spinning black holes.
2) The event horizon.
3) Planets and moons that could sustain life.
4) Surveillance and data of the 'dark side of the Moon.'
5) Quantum mechanics and wormholes.
6) Forward time travel."

Justin could be heard saying, "Huh?"

A smiling Sara continued, "And Michaela has already volunteered some of her time to help the boys. No surprise there."

After some expected laughter, Sara added.

"I have already turned over the water-trading market issues to our government, who already had the economics gurus hard at work too. Kat had laid down some pretty remarkable baselines and prognoses."

Michaela responded. "So happy that Kat's work will serve as the basis for some serious research and suggestions. Third-world countries don't need more aggravation."

Sara added, "I agree," and continued.

"I will get more involved in both the Apollo 18 question as well as our 'newly discovered' Mars colony. Got to admit, I am really stoked to find out what happened and what is still happening."

Justin crisply added, "If you need any help here…"

"Justin, you and Connor have tons on you plate even now."

Mike was grinning at such an obviously typical remark by Justin.

Justin noted, "You know you always give your biggest assignments to your busiest guy."

Sara responded with a laugh. "Look at Justin and his Management 101 contribution."

That remark got a chuckle from everyone, including Justin.

"Finally, as I mentioned before, Elonis will be doing her share of research and data gathering.

"Among her issues for discussion will be some heavy-duty revelations."

1) The occurrence of ancient alien atomic warfare.
2) Alien DNA evidence.
3) Evil alien indicators."

At that point, everyone wanted to talk and Sara could see that and knew it was to be expected.

"Hey, it's just her to-do list for now, nothing more. I actually labeled the issues, so I'm the one with the flair for the dramatic. Elonis will describe and explain soon enough."

"But," Connor started.

"No buts." Sara continued. "I'm just having some fun with you guys. Chill out. O.K?"

Unprompted, Elonis added a comment.

"Just the facts will be presented. I do not do opinion."

"Thanks, Elonis," Sara nodded. "Now, I see I have another Utah call coming in. Talk later…"

Matt was following up on his earlier call with Sara. Apparently, Matt had been interrupted by an important call from the White House and couldn't finish his call with Sara.

"So sorry that we got interrupted, Sara. Is this still a good time?"

"Yes, of course, Matt. You left me crazy with your mention of a very important A. I. need you had. What the hell is going on?"

"Sara, you need to come out here ASAP."

"And why, Matt?"

"Because there is someone who I want you to meet!"

59

MATT

Unable to get any definitive info from Matt on the subject of his call, Sara told Scott of their conversation and Matt's sense of urgency.

Scott immediately got his private plane ready and contacted his personal pilot, Ken Darragh, to get Sara out to Matt's lab in Provo as soon as possible.

Matt called Scott.

"Thanks for your help. We couldn't wait any longer."

"So, Matt, Sara has no clue regarding the hologram?"

"Nope. None."

"Good luck, out there."

"Thanks, Scott. Oh, you haven't said anything to her yet, have you?"

"Oh, hell no. Best coming from you."

"You're right, Scott."

"Matt, my pilot Ken and my plane are always there for you."

"That is so generous, Scott. Can't thank you enough."

✦ ✦ ✦

As Scott's plane, with Sara aboard, arrived at the small private airport, Matt was waiting to pick her up. Having met Ken Darragh before, Matt exchanged greetings with the pilot while Sara was getting her briefcase and small bag.

"Thanks for your help, Ken; have a safe trip back. Come back when you can stay a while."

"Will do, Matt. Love to hear what interesting stuff is going on with your team as well."

Matt gave Sara a hug and they shared a brief kiss. Matt was anxious to get back to the lab and Sara was just plain confused.

"Dammit, tell me what's going on here. And why the secrecy and dancing around the real reason I'm here."

"Okay." Matt started talking as he drove them back to his lab.

"You are aware of the A.I. advances we have made, as we have discussed them before, relative to your inquiries into future alien capability."

"Yes. Sure."

"Well, Sara, that's the tip of the iceberg as far as our advanced technology is concerned."

"Hell, Matt, that doesn't surprise me. I've picked up on conversations you have had with Jeremiah and I know Tyreek is a very special tool in your shed. You have something going on that involves me, right?"

"Yes. And I apologize ahead of time for what I'm about to say and what you're about to see."

"Holy crap, Matt. What the …"

Following several agonizing minutes of silence, Matt pulled his car into the parking lot and they both walked briskly through the lobby of the medical center and over to the ultra-secure tech lab. They were greeted by a nervous Jeremiah who shook Sara's hand and spoke first.

"Welcome to the lab, Sara. I'm happy to see you."

"It's nice to see you as well, Jeremiah. Matt has me in the dark on why I'm here, so let's just get on with it."

Matt began. "We started working on A.I. and advanced A.G.I. about ten years ago. Around that time, we began development of fairly basic androids to co-develop the A.I. tech around."

Jeremiah added, "Your meta, Elonis, is an example of how the two techs melds together."

"I'm aware of that, Jeremiah, and I also know that this project has been well documented and well received. That's not why I'm here."

"No, Sara, it's not," Matt slowly admitted.

"Your grandfather, Pete Stevenson, had one helluva vision. Through his colleague, Beth, he came out here and over the span of about eight or nine days, he literally allowed Jeremiah to do a complete memory transfer into a unique database that Miah and Tyreek had created."

Sara interrupted Matt. "I actually recall that Beth told me that Grandad once did what Beth called a 'brain dump,' her words, some place 'out west.' It was a strange conversation that she and I had."

"Actually, Sara, we were in Colorado at that time," Jeremiah offered.

Matt continued. "Fast forward to today. Separately, we have developed state-of-the -art holographic technology. Miah, fill Sara in."

"Sure." Jeremiah got his presentation ready to show Sara.

"Until recently, any hologram visuals have required glass, smoke, or water to bounce light from to produce an image. No more. We have developed a holographic projector that uses a plasma laser to float a 3D image into mid-air."

Jeremiah was getting extremely excited.

"We have a unique system where light can be viewed without the need to bounce it off a surface. The technology uses a massive infrared pulse laser which is focused on direct points in the air via a 3D scanner causing the molecules in the air to be ionized to create a plasma."

"That's very interesting, Jeremiah, but where's this going?"

Matt intervened. "Sorry, Sara, but this technology is important to understand as we explain where we are that impacts you."

"Matt, please continue. I'm really looking forward to where this is going."

"Sara, we have recently created a tangible dynamic shape display we call AI-REAL that can render the shapes of people and objects on 3D surfaces."

Pausing…

"To do this, we use over one thousand motor-driven columns in tight resolution in a tiny area that is capable of sculpting shapes in real time. This is the evolution, if you will, of the super-hologram."

"I am both impressed and getting exhausted. So, again, why am I here?"

Taking Sara's hand, Matt gently squeezes it and says,

"A full 3D hologram of Pete Stevenson, with mind and memory restored, is in the next room."

60

SARA

Sara fell into Matt's arms, trembling and crying. Jeremiah pulled a tissue out for her and he was also weeping.

After a moment's silence, Matt spoke.

"Before you criticize us for not telling you, we have only gotten this hologram fully functional a few days ago. If it had blown up in our faces, it would have remained an unsuccessful experiment."

"I want to see my grandad. Now."

As they walked into the hologram room of the lab, Matt cautioned Sara.

"This is a hologram, Sara, not a person. The hologram is programmed with Pete's awareness, but it doesn't have the capability to recognize anyone who is communicating with it."

"It, Matt?"

"Sorry. Please, you know what I mean."

"Yeah, I do."

"The hologram will answer questions from Pete's awareness and memory, which is a tremendous accomplishment."

Sara was listening closely to Matt's words.

"But, again, you cannot actually have a conversation with, what is essentially, a program."

"Got it."

Together, the three of them walk into the holography mini-lab and Tyreek is seen at a console.

"Hi Tyreek, I'm Sara."

"Hey, Sara, nice to finally meet you. I've gotten to know you a bit from memories given us by your grandfather, Pete. Would you like to meet him?"

An annoyed Matt addresses Tyreek's comment.

"Not the best way to introduce Sara to a fairly traumatic event."

"You're right. Sorry, Sara."

"No need to be sorry, Tyreek. I understand. This is good…very good. Tyreek, please show me my grandad's image."

Almost instantly the life-size, but fuzzy hologram appeared on a silver platform in the middle of the room.

Tyreek made a couple adjustments and within a few seconds, a very discernible image of the late Pete Stevenson was appearing in 3D and in a remarkable state of wholeness.

Matt spoke to Pete.

"Hello, Pete, it's Matt and Tyreek. How are you today?"

"Hello, Matt, I am fine."

"We brought a friend to see you today."

"Yes. Hello Sara!"

61

SARA

Matt was not surprised by that response, but Sara, Jeremiah, and Tyreek were stunned. Matt had a sample of Pete's cognitive abilities just weeks before, but he was still unable to process just how this was possible.

Tyreek was first to speak.

"What the hell. I haven't seen anything like this from him and I don't have a clue as to what is going on."

Sara muttered, "Grandad, do you recognize me?"

"Yes, of course, Sara. I have been waiting for you. I have listened to what Matt and Jeremiah had said, so I knew that it was just a matter of time before we met."

Jeremiah was focused on this incredible leap into the unknown with this new technology and had many questions.

"Pete, how long have you been able to listen and understand and respond?"

"I can only sense what is happening at this moment. I have total recall of my past, but I am unclear of where I am in the present."

At that point, an overwhelmed Sara collapsed in a nearby chair, and had but one thought as she studied the moment.

"Can you guys give Grandad and me some time alone?"

"Of course," responded Matt. "Tyreek will show you on the console what the primary holography procedures and image controls are. We will be in the next room."

Following a brief tutorial from Tyreek, Sara was left alone with the 3D image of her deceased grandfather in a situation that was somewhere between the macabre and the impossible.

It was time for Sara and Pete to get reacquainted.

"Grandad, what can you feel? Can you feel any emotion? Can you sense my fear…my concern…my joy?"

"I cannot feel emotion, but I can sense your anxiety and you are frightened."

"Yes, I am. I have so many questions, I don't know where to begin."

"Sara, I am nothing more than an image of Pete Stevenson but I have access to all of his thoughts, memories, and observations. I believe that the observations will become my most important asset to you and your ETRT."

"The ETRT? You know about a team that was assembled after your death? Now I am very confused."

"I understand, Sara, and over time I will try to add as much explanation to an otherwise incomprehensible situation."

Sara thought to herself, "This dialogue does not sound like the kind of conversation that I ever had with my grandad. It just doesn't sound like any real talk that we have ever had."

With that thought, Pete responded, "I understand your concern."

"But I didn't say anything."

"I can read your thoughts…and soon you will be able to read mine."

"But Grandad, how is that possible?"

<Pulse gave me and you the thought- sharing capability.>

62

ELONIS

Sara had asked Elonis to conduct the next video conference with the ETRT, given that Sara was still with Matt in Utah.

Elonis set up the video chat as Sara had done before, and with instructions from Sara to keep reports today at high levels without many details.

The ETRT was getting used to change becoming the "constant," and Sara's absence or ever-changing priorities were more the norm than the unusual.

"Sara has asked me to conduct this session. It will mainly consist of updates plus any additional topics the team might have. We will begin with Michaela, followed by Mike, then Connor and Justin. I will present last."

"Thanks, Elonis, and it just feels 'right' to have you here." Michaela began.

"I discussed the star maps last time and how our solar system has a unique connection with our planet. In unison with Elonis, I did a detailed study of Stonehenge in Wiltshire, England, and came up with a truly remarkable fact. Yes, a hard fact."

The team always paid particular attention to Michaela. She would never waste time or words.

"Stonehenge consists of a ring of standing stones, each about thirteen feet high, seven feet wide, and weighing about twenty-five tons. As you know, they have been studied for centuries…likely the most studied ancient monument set ever."

A very focused Michaela paused.

"Stonehenge is about four thousand years old and is a one hundred per cent accurate representation of our solar system, and absolutely to scale. But that's not the fact that jumps out to the observer."

"Here it comes," thought Connor.

"The Stonehenge array also includes Pluto, a dwarf planet in the Kuiper belt beyond the orbit of Neptune that wasn't discovered until 1930."

"That is so cool," uttered Justin.

"It is very cool, Justin. One more addition from our last meeting. As I was investigating the star maps in general and Stonehenge in particular, I discovered an interesting fact involving alien DNA."

Flipping her notes, Michaela continued.

"If you look at Stonehenge and many ancient civilizations, none of the DNA gathered from the ancient times is in the DNA of any current residents. A complete wash or scrubbing of all definitive DNA that could have been, or should have been traceable…was done by someone or something.

"It is no longer anywhere to be found. All DNA evidence is gone."

Pausing for a moment, Michaela simply advised, "That's it for now."

Mike then followed Michaela.

"Subtle, that is not."

"I have two updates from our last meeting, one involving the metal disc found in Mr. Burgess's neck and the other one that involves a U.S. military cover-up, originally discovered by Dad and that I was able to verify."

"First, the details regarding the metal disc. It is definitely not from our earth and its molecular structure is both simple and complex."

"Eh?" was Justin's response.

"It's a very soft and malleable material but only after applying some heat. In what we would call room temperature, it is rock hard and not pliable at all. But with a little bit of heat, it is shapeable and workable."

"Cool stuff," Justin reiterated.

"And, as I've mentioned before, it is not visible under X-ray. So, we have one of the strongest metals ever studied that is also one of the softest metals ever studied. Let me throw this over to Connor."

"Thanks, Mike. So, we worked with those incredible techies in Utah, with help from Doctor Palmer's team, and came up with an ingenious application. This is great stuff."

Opening his pad, Connor continued.

"We have fabricated several very small receivers from that one disc, and they are now going to be the implants for undetectable tracking devices for the ETRT members. We will be implanting them in the next few days."

"So very smart," offered Michaela.

Mike winked.

"And what is so damn smart for these tracking devices is that they will become the secondary tracking devices, in additional to an implant that is easily detectable."

"Smart squared," noted Michaela. "The first one is found and there is no need to search the person any longer. An implant that's a real ploy...a real detective's plant."

"That is correct, Michaela," said Mike. "Connor will have a little more to say in a few minutes.

"My only other item is that the government cover-up involved the destruction of alien spacecrafts, alien battle gear, and perhaps aliens themselves. Dad had mentioned a centrifuge in Southeastern U.S. as the location of this destruction."

"We remember Sara being so frustrated that we didn't have any documents," offered Michaela.

"Well, I have secured, with the help of one key member of Congress that will not be identified, documented footage of an Alabama military base, heavily disguised, conducting this incredibly unconscionable activity over the course of at least twelve years."

Mike was getting excited with his next words.

"And, the language being spoken was either in code or a language that has never been spoken on Earth."

With that revelation, Mike turned the meeting over to Connor and Justin.

Connor stepped in. "Okay, Justin, why don't you take over and explain what's going on and what happens next."

"Thanks, Connor. We have been working with Doctor Palmer's staff for weeks on bundling their technology with the newly analyzed metal disc to focus on our need to protect our team from all the bad stuff that's been happening."

Justin was holding back his emotions, Kat's death still taking its toll.

"I have written a very unique code for both the communication devices and the tracking devices. It is my best work; and given our crappy timing and accelerated work priorities, I am so very happy that we could solve this very obtuse problem."

"Excuse me," Michaela interrupted. "You mean abstruse. The word you want is abstruse."

"Huh?" Justin asked.

"Listen. The word obtuse means blunt or dull. Abstruse means concealed, hidden, or secretive."

"Okay, sorry Michaela. Just working on my vocabulary, you know."

Everyone smiled and the light moment was really quite well received.

A somewhat subdued but still focused Justin continued.

"We have scheduled times now for everyone to have the devices implanted. One of Dr. Palmer's medical technicians will be here to oversee the implants. I am nearly finished with finding a convenient time for everyone. Just waiting on Amanda Woods' availability."

Elonis spoke. "Are you done?"

"Yes, Elonis. All done. Thanks. If anyone has any questions, call me. This is exciting stuff."

✦ ✦ ✦

Elonis at that time began her presentation agenda with a rather direct and firm statement.

"I am an advanced meta-human who has now been upgraded to a very high level of both research capability and assimilation of all knowledge of alien intervention. In fact, I have now already fully absorbed the sub-details from the three of today's report-outs."

As Elonis was speaking, she was also processing the fact that there were boundaries involving her data obtained directly from Pulse and her need to keep some of that data secret.

"I am simply a conduit and a complement to what you are doing. The best use of your time will continue to be those events involving personal interviews and/or technology development, such as that being done by Connor and Justin. Does that make sense?"

Michaela responded, "Does that mean that our role will soon become taking our accumulated knowledge and conclusions and determining what we will be doing with it in the most effective manner going forward?"

"Precisely," Elonis responded.

Mike added his take on this presumption. "So, we will be developing our strategy for what we will be revealing and to whom we will reveal it to?"

"Yes, Mike," Elonis added. "Plus, Sara will be returning from her trip to Utah with relevant and useful info regarding what Doctor Palmer and his associates have been doing in the field of A.I. that will impact our work."

"Yikes," uttered Justin.

"My first issue concerns ancient atomic warfare on Earth."

Elonis had their attention.

"The existence of atomic weapons before the present cycle of civilization are evidenced throughout the world, alarming the scientific community but impossible to ignore.

"Throughout many deserts of the world, silicon crystals have been found that resemble the nuclear explosions of the White Sands atomic test site.

"These findings, or so-called desert glass, have properties that mirror the nuclear test site results from the 1940's, but found in material that was at least four thousand years old."

"Elonis, do you have the specific info?"

"Yes, Michaela. "At least one event phenomenon uncovered was capable of raising the temperature of desert sand thousands of years ago to at least three thousand three hundred degrees Fahrenheit."

Elonis paused as Michaela was taking notes.

"The examination of deep casts in the African desert would have resulted from an explosion of at least ten thousand times more powerful than what was observed at the Alamogordo Bombing Range in White Sands, New Mexico, in 1942."

Mike added his observation. "Excuse me, Elonis. Team, for what it's worth, the distance from White Sands to the notorious Roswell Area 51 is only about one hundred fifty miles. What a coincidence, eh?"

A typically stoic Elonis continued.

"We have data now that suggests that aliens may have sent us messages or simply riddles to solve that involve encoded alien DNA. Michaela, this coincides well with your last info update regarding alien DNA. No trace of that ancient alien DNA exists in any of the subsequent civilizations that exist in those same locations today. A complete DNA scrubbing."

"Yes, Elonis, we know that bacteria can travel interstellar distances, and just one gram of bacteria can be encoded with about nine hundred terabytes of data, or enough to fill about two billion two-hundred-page books."

"Cool," as Justin grasped this info.

"There is verifiable evidence from microbiologists that a bacterial colony that was strongly magnetized would be able to act as a miniature magnetic sail."

"If so, it could catch a five hundred kilowatt-per-second solar wind, which would be more than enough to propel it out of the solar system."

Mike asked, "Isn't this speculation?"

Elonis continued emphatically.

"Researchers here on Earth have been secretly studying interstellar bacteria and have proven that they can successfully encode info in alien bacterial DNA with a density of two hundred fifteen thousand terabytes per gram of DNA."

"I see another OMG coming," said Connor.

"Yes, Connor," Elonis replied. "There is apparently at least one alien civilization that has been sending an extensive library of encoded DNA in a presumed interstellar message for thousands of years, which has been intercepted by a super-secret government agency."

Allowing a few moments for that to sink in, Elonis concluded with a predictive thought based on an absolutely huge data set.

"Basically, this would provide a virtual Galactic Encyclopedia of all things alien."

63

SARA

The video meeting was interrupted by Sara checking in on the status of the meeting. The pause to absorb Elonis's incredible revelations was well-timed.

"Hey team, how is everything going? Does Elonis have your attention with her amazing info?"

Mike responded, "Very good meeting and her portion of today was stellar, no pun intended."

"We understand that you may have some good input to add."

"Yes, Michaela, I will. But first I need some one-on-one time with you."

Michaela disconnected with the video so they could talk.

Elonis also disconnected so she wouldn't have to talk.

"Michaela, I have the most incredible news you could ever imagine."

"Well, given your running back and forth to Provo and being absent for a couple of meetings, I would expect a fairly good explanation."

"Well, I was curious as to what was going on at Matt's lab, and he and I have some relationship issues to work through."

"So, this isn't about the relationship issues, I take it."

"No. Hell no."

"You sound even more serious than usual."

"This concerns my grandad."

"This is about Pete?"

"Yes. Matt and his team have created not one, but two amazing technologies."

"Go ahead."

"Well, apparently Grandad had the vision to go out to Colorado many years ago to an emerging tech company, now Matt's, believe it or not, and have his brain scanned and the total wealth of his memories and knowledge forever captured."

"Oh my God!" Michaela was surprised, even for her level of intelligence. "This is science fiction stuff."

"Michaela, there's more…much more. They have created a 3D hologram with the capability to interact with humans…actually carry on conversations."

"This is unbelievable, Sara."

"Michaela, they have combined Grandad's mind into a life-size 3D hologram and we have had a conversation."

Michaela, in near denial, says softly, "What in God's green earth did you talk about?"

"We talked about a variety of plain vanilla items, just to get a feel for just how comprehensive this technology is."

"I see a bigger bottom line coming, Sara."

"Yep." Pausing to pick her thoughts and words, Sara continued.

"Are you familiar with the phrase 'channeling the nine' from ancient Egyptian lore?"

"Yes. Channeling is the ability that allows, even invites— nonphysical entities, into your consciousness and allows them to speak through you."

Michaela was navigating through her video library on that subject as they talked.

"The well-documented saga of 'the nine' involved otherworldly intelligences that claim to be deities of ancient Egypt guiding humankind throughout civilization."

"Yes, Michaela, of course that's spot on. Thousands of people claim to be able to 'channel' extraterrestrial intelligences."

Catching her breath, Sara continued.

"The more extreme and bizarre cases have even received public notoriety."

"All right, again Sara, bottom line?"

"According to this hologram from Grandad, our galaxy includes civilizations of several active and functional alien cultures… good and evil!"

64

ELONIS

A stunned Michaela reconnected with the team to resume the video conference that was momentarily interrupted.

Everyone on the team could sense that Michaela had become preoccupied. Elonis questioned Michaela.

"Michaela, do you need time to update the team?"

"Yes."

Michaela began. "I just talked with Sara, who, as you know, is still with Matt in Utah. She said she will have an update on some interesting and relevant A.I. info in a few days. For now, we need to get back to our agenda."

Elonis then resumed the meeting agenda.

"I have one more issue to discuss, but Connor and Justin have indicated that they need a couple minutes for an update."

"Thanks, Elonis," Connor nodded.

"Justin and I now have the tracking material that needs to be installed, or implanted I should say, and everyone has given us their schedules. We will inform everyone later today on when to report to our lab."

Justin uttered, "Actually, we will be implanting both a primary and secondary device, kind of a fail-safe system. It's really cool...back to you, Elonis."

"My last issue today," Elonis replied, "involves the destructive alien possibility, what Pete simply referred to as 'evil aliens amongst us' in his research."

Pausing for a moment, and appearing to get distracted, Elonis said: "Sara asked me to table the full details for now, but the reality of this subject matter is simple."

With no one voicing an opinion or question, Elonis continued.

"The likelihood of evil aliens ever being on this planet is one hundred per cent. The likelihood of evil aliens being on this planet now is one hundred per cent. The likelihood of evil aliens being here in the future is one hundred per cent."

Justin was physically affected by Elonis's stark comments and asked a pointed question.

"And what in your computational orbit do you believe is our likelihood of being prepared to deal with an upcoming event?"

Without as much of a moment's pause, Elonis replied with words that were both direct and sobering.

"The likelihood or probability that we could meet such a challenge right now is zero per cent."

65

SARA

Still trying to process the most recent events, Sara was both annoyed and impressed with Pulse.

Pulse had incredible capability, and his willingness to share all his resources with the hologram of Pete and with Sara added to her unsettled mindset moving forward.

Through contact arrangements with Elonis, Sara met with Pulse on the very evening of the hologram awareness, and Sara immediately found that they could connect telepathically.

<Elonis tells me you have many questions and we need to meet.>

<Yes, Pulse, I have many questions, including the hologram.>

<I thought you would be pleased. It was our intention once we learned that Pete's mind was connected to a 3D image.>

<Why didn't you tell me ahead of time that your intention was to contribute info to my grandfather's hologram?>

<I did not think to tell you. I made a mistake.>

<So now, what is your intention here with me, my team, and my grandfather's hologram?>

<Sara, you are in need of many answers and much detail. I cannot answer your more serious questions.>

<Then who and when, Pulse? I want answers!>

<You met our leader, Echo, when we intercepted your plane that had been seized.>

<Yes, I remember Echo. She was a very reassuring presence who made me feel safe.>

<Return and meet with Elonis, who now has in her mind, many important issues relating to your solar system and the universe that you know and understand.>

<Pulse, I don't understand what you just said. Why should I again meet with Elonis?>

<Elonis has had her mental capacity significantly increased to its highest level.>

<So why do I need to meet with Elonis?>

<To share what she knows and get her understanding of what is happening on your planet now and what your team can and must do.>

<And then what?>

<I will arrange a meeting with you and Echo, so all your questions will be answered and you will see how we can help you.>

<How soon can that meeting be set up?>

<Echo is ready when you are ready.>

Sara paused before getting a final thought from Pulse.

<Elonis will contact us when you are ready to meet with Echo.>

As Pulse vanished into the night, Sara felt more alone than ever. She said to herself,

"I will be meeting with the leader of an alien culture…what could she want from me?"

66
SARA

Realizing that she had several important issues to tie up before meeting with Echo, Sara set up a short list of priorities to attack as soon as possible.

Her first priority was getting back with Dean Worthington to get more info on Samantha's ill-fated spacewalk and get a better understanding of what Dean meant by "a different person."

And, what exactly happened when Samantha was brought back to the spacecraft with water in her helmet?

Sara sent a text message to Mike and they exchanged texts.

"Do you know what would cause an astronaut in space to have water leak inside her helmet?"

"What kind of research ya doing now?"

"Just curious, Dad."

"I think it has to do with the air filtration system. Will text you the name of a guy at NASA that can help."

"Thanks. Talk later."

"OK. Will tell Mom you said 'hi' when she comes in."

That unreal spacewalk was an issue where time was critical and she could not push it off for very long.

Then, she thought, she would need to meet with Elonis for a meeting that would be awkward, but necessary.

Sara headed down to the company's fitness center to work off some stress and closed and locked the door. She had to be sure that her workout wasn't seen by anyone, given her super strength, agility, and very rigorous routine.

No human had her physicality. She knew it…she loved it.

Climbing onto a combination tread mill and stair stepper, called the Ultra-Max, Sara set the speed for forty miles per hour, stretched for a few minutes, and began.

She used to do this type of workout two to three times a week, but lately her work load had prevented her from sticking to that regiment.

She had gotten her heart rate up and was thoroughly enjoying her programmed workout. Then, about fifteen minutes into her exercise, her e-Watch signaled a call coming in from the Washington, D.C. area.

Sara had to take the call, validated through her e-Watch software, and climbed down from the machine.

"Hello, Sara?"

"Yes, this is Sara. Who's calling?"

"Sara, this is Lieutenant Robert Baker of the FBI, and I got your contact info from President Sullivan. Is this a good time to talk?"

Having another sense of bad news coming, Sara said, "Yes, of course," and began toweling off.

"Sara, first of all, I worked with your grandad, Pete Stevenson, and found him to be an amazing man. Visionary, dedicated alien researcher and funny as hell.

"In fact, I may have been one of the last people that spoke to him in Paris before he was murdered. I called to give him a heads-up on that John Smith associate of his."

"Well, thank you for all that you did for my grandad, and I'm sorry to say that Grandad never mentioned you to me."

"We worked together long before he started his alien hunting and I was just so impressed with his knowledge, determination, and commitment to finding the truth."

"Again, Lieutenant Baker, I thank you for being his friend. Now, why the call?"

"Your demeanor reminds me so much of Pete. To the point. It's incredible."

Pausing, Lt. Baker began to explain why he called Sara.

"Regarding that attack that killed your friend Kathy, the FBI agent, and the kidnapped victim, I have some info and it's alarming."

"Oh hell, what now?"

"The terrorist leader known as Scorpio was also shot multiple times in the gunfire. I believe you and your team saw the video, which we determined was all staged."

"What are you getting at?"

"The crash or blind-sided hit by the car carrying the two shooters was made within range of two large city cameras. They wanted their entire attack to be recorded."

"Lt. Baker, I don't like where this is going."

"Sorry, Sara, I'll get to the point. Scorpio, apparently, was wearing a back vest with containers of blood in anticipation of being shot in the back. In fact, the tip that our agent received was bogus, intended to get Agent Eight to the very warehouse where Scorpio was…captured."

"Oh no."

"Sara, your entire team is in danger, as the old New World Order is now calling themselves the First World Order, and they are bigger and more threatening than ever before."

As Sara sunk to her knees, Lieutenant Baker concluded his call.

"We are one hundred per cent sure that Scorpio is alive, and he believes that your team is a threat."

67

SCORPIO

It had been several months since that staged assassination of Scorpio was pulled off with such skill and cunning. It was time to reconvene the First World Order and get updates from the various leaders of each element of Scorpio's Cabal.

The setting was Davos, a mountain resort in the eastern Alps of Switzerland. The city of Zurich was the home of one of Scorpio's many illegitimate banks.

The same twelve people were seated around an oblong conference table with group leader Scorpio at one end and his second-in-command, Bud, at the other. Scorpio loved consistency.

"First, I want to congratulate everyone that had a part in my death. It was done with such expertise that even I was amazed."

Scorpio's dual-purposed henchman and hitman, Bud, muttered.

"Thank you. This was a team effort that had great results and tested our capability for future abductions and killings. And, we got rid of one nosey FBI agent and a member of that bastard research team that just won't go away."

"Don't get too cocky, Bud. I will be addressing our future targeting needs soon."

Making sure that the several flat-screen TV's and computer monitors were all up and running, Scorpio began the meeting.

"First, let's have the money report."

A tall, thin man with a tailored gray suit and arrogant demeanor stated, "We now have over fifteen billion dollars in liquid assets, and I see another one point two five billion by the end of this month, most of that coming from blood antiquities."

"Very good. What are the components of that amount?"

The tall man continued. "About twenty per cent is from arms sales, about twenty-five per cent from human trafficking, and about fifty-five per cent from drugs and kick-backs, still mostly from Central America. The money laundering today is the best we've ever had."

Scorpio snapped, "And our relationship with those in command?"

"The civilians are not a problem at all. The military is still a concern, but we have leverage and have executed a few trouble-makers."

"Good. Good. Now the weapons and strategic deployment report."

A chiseled guy with an aviator jacket and strong, booming voice chimed in.

"We have our arsenal now at nearly eighty per cent of what is needed to complete the scope and scale of our global assault plan, in particular the 'remembrance attack' that will be a game changer…or worldview changer.

"Deployment is in an aggressive roll-out phase and all the stealth-like procedures and satellite technology is nearly ready for Phase Zero."

"Are key launch sites still North Korea and the Middle East?"

"They are, Scorpio."

Scorpio was smiling as he gave his next update.

"The communication disruption initiative and total I.T. hacking has been completed. And, those two fine Russian fellows, Sergei and Vlad, who did such nice work, are no longer with us."

Mild laughter could be heard.

Scorpio advised, "I have two more agenda items before we adjourn to enjoy Davos.

"First, I wasn't able to recruit that person that understands meta-human and A.I. technology to the extent I wanted, but I have an even better addition to our team."

Scorpio had everyone's attention.

"We now have on our team a member of President Sullivan's cabinet!"

Bud muttered, "Damn, that's freaking awesome. Congrats!"

Scorpio continued with a gaze flicked in Bud's direction.

"That West Coast research team that is getting all the press lately for all the alien and investigative crap they are doing is still an obstacle in our way."

"I agree," Bud interjected.

"Good, Bud, because you now have a critical assignment."

That got Bud's attention.

"Yes sir."

"Bud, do you know who runs that operation…I mean really runs it?"

"Yes, Scorpio, a young woman named Sara Steele, the granddaughter of Pete Stevenson."

"Yep, you are correct, Bud," he glanced over to Bud with a raised voice. "We now know her every move, day-in and day-out."

Pointing his finger at Bud…

"Take her the hell out!"

68

SARA

Trying to digest that stunning and incredibly discouraging news from Lieutenant Baker, Sara went back to her personal to-do list of conversational needs.

First up was Dean Worthington, astronaut and Vice President Samantha Worthington's husband.

After playing phone tag with Dean for the most of the next day, Sara was finally able to connect late in the evening.

"Hi Dean, it's Sara Steele."

"Oh hi, Sara, nice to hear from you."

"Dean, I wanted to get some more info on Samantha's ordeal in space. Is now a good time?"

"Yes, I'm alone. Where do you want me to begin?"

"At the beginning…"

"First of all, Samantha can never find out we talked. Okay?"

"Of course, no problem, Dean. Go ahead."

"The steel tether was meant to hold about a ton and a half of weight, so it breaking off was most unusual. Almost like a tampering. Does that make sense?"

"Please, just continue, Dean."

"Fine. She drifted off into space for about thirty to thirty-five minutes and four hundred to four hundred fifty feet from the spacecraft before Vince caught her with his jetpack on."

Pausing for a few seconds, Dean continued.

"When she was returned to the capsule, her helmet was filled about two-thirds with water, which would, I'm told, be caused by a leak in the ventilation system."

"I've actually heard about that happening," Sara added.

"Yes Sara, but when Sam was resting in some kind of a decompression chamber, I guess, they evaluated her suit and helmet and found absolutely no tear or leak."

Taking a deep breath, "There was no way water could have entered her helmet."

"Damn it, Dean. That is not what I would have expected. And, no official answer or probable cause, I guess?"

"No. There never is. It was only after I pressed the issue, did she tell me the truth about what the hell really happened."

"You also said she wasn't acting or behaving normal or usual since that incident."

"Yes. Sam has never been particularly affectionate. I guess over time we have developed a sort of love/hate relationship."

"Dean, the opposite of love isn't to hate. The opposite of love is indifference. And many couples experience that indifference, I assure you."

"I understand. But our conversations now are so cool and so distant."

"Dean, I'm no therapist, but I think this is, unfortunately, today's normal."

"Okay. But this isn't."

"What isn't?"

"She answers questions that I am thinking before I ask… and she doesn't even realize it!"

69

SARA

Sara knew that Dean had opened a huge can of worms, and Sara couldn't wait much longer to have a meaningful conversation with Samantha.

Turning on her phone's recording device, Sara made the call. It was important that the primary reason for the call was not divulged.

"Hi Samantha, it's Sara."

"Well hello, Sara, nice to hear from you. Wasn't sure if we were going to have a follow-up chat now or later regarding our last talk."

"Is now a good time, Sam? I have a bunch of balls in the air and I wanted to make sure you and I got to finish our last talk."

"Yes, now is good. How are things with the ETRT? Any news or alien breakthroughs? Sorry I have been unable to actually attend any recent meetings, but I do appreciate your keeping me in the info loop."

"You know, same old, same old alien stuff. Nothing really new that we haven't already shared with you."

"So, Sara, you have something in mind today to discuss?"

"Just trying to close the door on the government cover-up tract. Anything more to add via your investigations?"

"No, Sara, not really. What new cover-up info have you come up with?"

Noting the illogical nature of the question, Sara thought for a moment and responded.

"No. Nothing here. I was assuming that you were handling that issue for us. This issue is so far outside our wheelhouse, and I just want to get it off our list."

"Very well, Sara, gotcha. Anything new in your investigations?"

Now sensing a lot more defensive info digging from Samantha, Sara responded.

"No, Samantha, I stated earlier that we hadn't really found anything new."

"Yes. You did. Sorry. By the way, I understand you had the opportunity to talk briefly with Dean recently."

"Oh, crap," Sara thought to herself. "This is bad. What to say…"

"I did? Oh, yes, I did. Nice guy."

"What did you two talk about?"

"Nothing in particular. Small talk, mostly. He wanted to say how much he appreciated what you were contributing to the ETRT. I think he was giving me and the team a 'thumbs up' on our work."

"Well, my husband said you are a very nice person."

"Thank him for that. Gotta go, Samantha. I'll make sure you get all the latest ETRT meeting issues and plans, for sure."

"All right, Sara, thanks. Stay in touch."

Hanging up and overcome with concern, Sara's immediately thought was…

"I must talk to President Sullivan as soon as possible."

70

SARA

It took far less time to reach President Sullivan than Sara figured. This was good news for so many reasons. Within twelve hours of her conversation with Samantha, Sara's restricted cell line was beeping.

"Sara Steele, this is Mara Wallace from the President's office calling. Are you available to talk to President Sullivan?"

"Yes. Yes I am."

A short pause allowed Sara to get composed and prepared.

"Hello Sara."

"Hello Mr. President."

"Sara..." Pause. "Cameron, please."

"Sorry. Thanks."

"How's my favorite alien investigator?"

"I'm fine, thanks. And thanks for getting back so soon."

"You and your grandad are so much alike, it's just amazing. I so enjoyed working with him, and it's an honor to work with you and your wonderful ETRT."

A zillion thoughts went through Sara's head at that moment, including the hologram. She knew she had to stick to the short list for now.

"That's very sweet, Mr. President, oh I mean Cameron."

"Sara, you seem pretty tense and a bit stressed out. Maybe we should get down to business."

"Absolutely. Thanks."

"Go ahead, Sara."

"Great." She had to ask but didn't want to offend POTUS.

"You are sure that this is a secure line, right?"

With light laughter, Cameron said. "Of course. This must be a doozy."

"Yeah, more than one doozy. Aliens are real...they are very real."

"I do believe they are real, Sara."

"No, Cameron, they are real and they are here and I have one named Pulse who has become my advisor and confidante."

"VP Worthington told me that you believed in aliens, and I told her that I believed as well. So, hearing it from you isn't a surprise, but the fact that you have an alien 'friend' is more of a shock."

"I also want to talk about Samantha, but the alien thing is so big and so critical right now."

Sara explained in detail to Cameron the incredible and otherwise unbelievable encounter with Pulse and Echo on that ill-fated flight to Washington D.C. He listened attentively.

She also explained in detail the entire Dean and Samantha incident and the apparent cover-up regarding the problematic spacewalk.

A very serious President Sullivan spoke up. "Sara, this is a lot to handle and a lot for you to process. What do you want me to do?"

"Couple things, Cameron. See if you can get some Intel from NASA or the military regarding her spacewalk, and don't mention to Samantha that we spoke."

"Cameron, I simply don't trust your VP and I'm a damn good judge of people, and I truly believe that Samantha Worthington has her own personal agenda, and it does not align with yours."

POTUS was silent for a short time, resulting in Sara commenting.

"Cameron, are you there? Everything all right?"

"Yes. Many thoughts going through my head at the moment."

Mostly, POTUS was connecting the dots between his VP and some alleged espionage currently under his direct supervision that involved several extremist Congressmen.

"Cameron, I know about the colony on Mars that has been there for thirty years."

"Gosh," she thought. "I hope you do!"

Again, with some laughter, Cameron responded. "You are truly amazing. Yes, we do and you and I need a long sit-down talk."

"I'm always available to meet, Cameron."

"I'm going to create a new Cabinet position, Secretary of the Extraterrestrial... you interested?"

"Sure," mused Sara.

Sara smiled and thought it best to wait to bring up the hologram for now.

"Sara, I need to ask you about something specific."

"Go ahead."

"According to your grandfather's notes, and transmitted to me by Scott Woods, the aliens that Pete met with gave him a series of significant destructive global events that would occur in the future through 2028, but only a couple ever happened."

"Yeah, you're right, and I have a theory."

"I'm sure you do and it's a good one."

Extrapolating from the hologram discussion with her grandad, and bending the truth a bit, Sara explained.

"My alien friend Pulse told me that they, meaning his alien recon team, have already stepped in to change, that is prevent, serious incidents from happening."

"They can do that?"

"Absolutely. That's what happened when they intercepted our plane headed to strike the Pentagon."

"Hell, that actually makes sense."

"This is so complicated. Their good deeds are in play throughout the Galaxy, but they can only monitor some of Earth's current crap, and are not able to monitor all the bad stuff that we are experiencing."

"That could explain why the terrorist group that you encountered, the New World Order, still has traction and is still making progress."

"Yes, it would."

"Very well, Sara, given your logic, which I buy, why didn't these benevolent aliens step in back in 2020 and 2021 to stop the global pandemic started with the coronavirus in China?"

"Cameron, that is one if the health incidents that I actually questioned Pulse about."

"So, Sara, what did he tell you?"

"Pulse said that the epidemic was caused by a virus unknown at the time, and the region in China was ill-prepared to contain it."

"That was common knowledge, Sara."

"Yes, but the solution was delayed and quite complicated due to the poor leadership that was present in agencies and governments that could have minimized the global outbreak."

"So, it was a huge void in global leadership and had little to do with the response and hard work of the health care industry?"

"Yep, Cameron. We have met the enemy and they are us!"

"By the way, Sara, were you informed that their leader, a guy called Scorpio, survived the attack and is still alive?"

"Yes, one of your FBI agents contacted me with that terrible news."

"We are doubling down on security for you and your team, and Scott informs me that he and his technical staff are doing the same."

"Yes. We feel much better with this additional help."

"Fine, Sara, enough for now. Gotta go. I'll have my office set up a meeting for the two of us fairly soon."

"Great, Cameron."

"So, what's the next big alien event for you?"

Without hesitation, Sara crisply replied.

"I will be meeting soon with Echo, the supreme commander of the alien forces here."

71

SARA

Two days later, as Sara was putting on her favorite blue metallic tweed jacket, Michaela called.

"What's up, Girl?"

"Hi Michaela. I'm headed to my monthly meeting of the Silicon Valley Young Entrepreneurs Club, an organization that is still important in my life."

It was at one of these meetings a few years ago where she met Paul Thomas, who eventually became her husband and was killed in the cabin attack.

"Okay. Great. Catch up with you later. Have fun."

"Will do. Thanks."

Sara felt a certain responsibility to continue contributing to this organization and becoming a mentor to young people in need of career guidance.

As Sara arrived at the meeting, she was pleased at the very positive reception and enjoyed the smiling faces. These meetings were mental highs in a mostly intense and draining work environment.

Sara had just finished a well-received presentation on climate change, courtesy of Michaela Marx, and was conducting a Q and A session.

"Miss Steele," one excited attendee asked, "what is your assessment of the state of our world and climate, given the facts you presented?"

"Well, we can't go back and correct mistakes, but we can certainly move forward with countermeasures that will make a difference. Since it's up to each and every one of us to do our part, I suggest you find a climate change initiative that you can relate to and get involved."

"Any one in particular that comes to mind, Miss Steele?"

"Why yes, there is. The Greta Thunberg Award is now the keystone in every strong initiative put forward by companies, cities, states, and countries all around the world. I suggest you find your place to either volunteer or in some way contribute to this global emergency."

The young audience stood up, clapped, and recognized a significant suggestion was just dumped into their laps.

Sara shook a number of hands, left the meeting, and walked down the steps to the street where her car was parked.

She was glancing at her cell phone and wasn't paying attention to her surroundings.

Within seconds, four men grabbed Sara, placed chloroform over her face, and threw a passed-out Sara into an unmarked van.

When Sara awoke, she was bound hand and feet with chains in a large wooden chair with her head covered. A damp, musty smell prevailed.

Noticing that their captive was awakening and becoming alert, one of the four men pulled the cover from Sara's head, and she could see she was in a dark room, likely one of many in the building where she was taken.

"I will make this short and simple, Miss Steele, so even a dumb blonde can understand," the only man without a weapon said. "Just answer a few questions and you won't get hurt."

Gaining her bearings and realizing that they likely had no intention of sparing her life, she played along as she planned a strategy.

"What do you want from me?"

"Information, little lady. We know you got your noses in business that don't concern you. We killed one of your friends and you don't need to join her."

Sara was getting pissed and angry. She thought about that comic-book character, The Hulk, and surveyed her surroundings as low-IQ man with bad grammar continued.

"So, what's up with your look-see into our business?"

"I don't know what you mean."

"You know damn well what I'm talking about. Why you snooping around our business?"

"Sorry, but no one gives a shit about your damn business, whatever it is."

With that, the man slapped Sara hard on the side of her face with a hard rubber glove, and blood spiked from both her mouth and her nose.

"Don't piss around with me, Bitch; give me what I want."

Sara took a deep breath, bent forward in her chair, and yelled at the top of her lungs, "KAT!"

She then leaped into the air with the chair as she broke her bindings in mid-air in an incredible somersault and landed amongst the three heavily-armed arm.

She used the wooden chair arms to knock away their semi-automatic rifles and threw all three to the ground, delivering body blows as they were felled.

As the three men were dazed and hurt, Sara dropped the chair arms and moved quickly to her main captor, who was frightened and confused.

She flung him against the wall and then picked him up by his neck.

"This might not be what you wanted, but it is sure as hell what you need."

Walking around the four men, Sara used her own chain bindings to tie up the four captors. She then used her E-watch to make a call.

"Hey, Lieutenant Baker, it's Sara Steele. I have something for you…"

72

SCOTT

cott and Amanda were aboard the *Stargaze* for another fund raiser. Fundraising was still a major priority for the Woods, as they always tried to give back to the community.

Scott often used the phrase, "If you want to get something…give something."

Unlike most of these, for his political or business interests, this one was for the homeless that have been displaced due to global warming and sea level rise.

Quite a contrast. A multi-billion-dollar yacht holding a fund raiser for people just trying to survive.

The yacht had just made the trip from Catalina Island to the "new" inland city of San Francisco. Significant subsidence from sea level rise, a series of earthquakes, and the City's soft underbelly sinking had resulted in San Francisco nearly being where Oakland was in the year 2000.

"Scott, this is as far as we can go, given the unknown objects below."

The Stargaze captain was informing Scott of the somewhat difficult maneuverability of the yacht.

"Fine, Bill. Just cast anchor here. Thanks."

Scott's yacht *Stargaze* was now moored just off the Bay of San Francisco in a secure marina far enough away from any security issues.

Following a long night of speeches and drinking, Scott moved to his lounge with three of his long-time financial supporters and a couple new colleagues that Scott met through the business work outside the ETRT.

"Honey, I'm tired and I think I'll turn in early."

"Sure, Amanda. Thanks for all your help tonight getting another great charity event done and done well."

Scott gave Amanda a kiss and she said "goodnight" and headed up to the stateroom suite for bed. She was totally exhausted from all the socializing that she and Scott had done that evening as well as the preparation that went into the event.

Meanwhile, Scott fixed drinks for the all-male late-night partying group.

The newer guests took over the conversation, usually Scott's preference, as he has often said, "You don't learn nothing from talking."

"So, Scott, got any good porn and X-rated stuff to watch?"

"Oh, what I have to go through for some charity work," he thought.

"No, Guys, sorry. You know, Amanda doesn't appreciate stuff like that on board."

A couple sighs from his guests.

"I do have several Ancient Alien shows from the History Channel."

Tonight, he was also quite tired and just sat back and listened, occasionally hearing an adult comment or thought.

About two hours later, Scott's guests returned to shore from the *Stargaze* and Scott headed up to the stateroom suite.

Amanda was gone, so Scott checked the galley and the other staterooms, making sure they were unoccupied.

Returning to Amanda's bed and night stand, Scott saw that her valuables were still there and it appeared as though she had gotten into bed. Her cell phone, tablet, and e-Watch were also there.

Scott alerted the crew and a frantic search was conducted, but to no avail.

No witnesses saw Amanda leave.

All security footage had been erased.

Nearly thirty minutes after Scott found Amanda missing from her bed, it was obvious what had happened.

Amanda had been abducted.

73

SCOTT

Before Scott had a chance to get in touch with police or POTUS and the FBI, or even think about it, he received a message from the kidnappers.

WE WILL CONTACT YOU

DO NOT CALL THE POLICE

WE WILL NOT HARM YOUR WIFE IF YOU FOLLOW OUR INSTRUCTIONS

Scott knew this was a bad situation, and he thought long and hard on what to do. Before he received any ransom or follow-up notes from the kidnappers, he contacted Sara on their special ETRT line.

"Sara, it's Scott. Amanda has been kidnapped!"

"Oh my God, Scott, what happened?"

Scott gave Sara the only sketchy details he had, along with the very specific message from the kidnappers.

"Scott, give me five minutes, ten at the most, and I'll get back to you."

"Okay. Thank you, Sara. I'm scared!"

Sara got on the restricted and secure line that Connor and Justin had developed, and contacted several members of her team. She also put in a coded call to President Sullivan, since they now also had such a phone line.

Meanwhile, a gagged and blindfolded Amanda Woods was tied to a steel pole in a windowless room of an old, abandoned warehouse, scared beyond anything that she had ever experienced.

She had been led through an airport-type security X-ray, and two tracking devices were found and removed.

One device was her necklace with locket, and the other was more obscure.

"OK, boss," says one of the captors, "we found two tracking devices. One was in her locket and one was a plain vanilla-type imbedded in her arm."

The "boss" answered back with a laugh, "Yeah, I would have expected more."

Sara called Scott, who was waiting patiently with tears and sweat pouring down his face.

"Scott, I'm in touch with Cameron himself."

"Oh my God Sara. You can't. The threat! You are talking directly to the President?"

"Hold on, Scott. Please relax; you know me by now. I have this!"

"I know you do. Thank God for you and your unbelievable network."

"Scott, I need to hang up now. Let me know when you get another message or a ransom note, O.K?"

"Okay."

Sara set up a secure video call with Michaela, Connor, Mike, and POTUS.

At that moment, Amanda's captors readied a ransom note and hung it around Amanda's neck, with an encrypted picture sent directly to Scott Woods. It was perfectly clear what they wanted.

THE U.S. GOVERNMENT'S CLOAKING TECHNOLOGY

THE U.S. MILITARY'S LEVITATION TECHNOLOGY

$500 MILLION DOLLARS CASH

If our demands are met within 48 hours, Amanda Woods will be left here safe from harm. If they are not met, she will be left here dead.

74

SARA

The four ETRT members plus President Sullivan were logging onto the secured video conference.

Connor gave a thumbs up to Sara that all was good to go.

Sara gave the status update to all regarding Amanda's situation and then turned it over to Connor.

An anxious Connor began.

"Both her primary and secondary tracking devices have been disabled. Good news, for sure."

A worried President Sullivan snapped loudly, "What?"

Sara quickly responded, "Cameron, it's okay. Listen to Connor."

"I'm sorry, Mr. President, but we actually know what we're doing."

"What the hell do you mean?"

Sara slowly explained their position regarding the tracking.

"We have a third and undetachable tracking device implanted in all of us, included Scott and Amanda Woods."

Gazing in Connor's direction, Sara continued.

"It can't be seen on any X-ray or infra-red scanning device."

"Damn," was the reaction from a stunned POTUS.

Sara advised.

"With two tracking devices disabled, the kidnappers will assume that there is no way of finding her."

Adding her personal thought, "And we know she is okay for now from the picture that Scott received."

A very excited Connor said abruptly, "I know where she is right now, sir. Here are the coordinates."

Sara relayed the coordinates and asked POTUS, "What do you want from us now?"

"Nothing, Sara. I'll take it from here. We're good. Very good. Thanks, and I'll get back to you guys as soon as I can."

POTUS disconnected and the ETRT was silent and numb.

Sara slipped away to contact Scott on their secure line and to reassure him.

Scott informed Sara that he did, in fact, get the ransom note.

Michaela had a sobering thought and muttered.

"My God, Amanda must be terrified right now. Can you imagine what's going through her mind right now?"

"I sure can," answered a somewhat relaxed Connor.

"With that incredible alien tracking device in her neck… she knows we have her back."

75

CAMERON

As the ETRT waited online, not wanting to be too far away from any updates, the time passed by slowly and the entire team was frantic with Amanda's uncertain status.

It seemed like many hours had passed, but about ninety minutes after they parted ways with POTUS, he called.

"Is everyone still there?"

"Yes, Cameron, Sara replied. "What's happening?"

"We have located Amanda and have our best strike team ready to engage."

"Engage?" Mike was worried with that term.

"It's okay, guys, and I'll have the strike team leader, Colonel Frank Dietz, explain."

"Hey, it's good to meet you, even under these circumstances," advised Colonel Dietz.

Continuing, he noted, "We have six Navy Seals from the Naval Air Station Lemoore in route to the coordinates we received. I will get back to you within the hour, once this strike team is in position."

Cameron quickly advised.

"Frank and this strike team are the best. I worked with them in Afghanistan and they are as efficient, effective, and skilled as anyone on the planet."

A concerned Michaela asked, "But a strike team is there to strike, and Amanda could get hurt."

Cameron responded with an air of confidence.

"A strike team is a tactical name for a team of professionals who will analyze a situation as best they can, before any action is taken. Believe me, they know what they are doing."

Mike did his best to calm the jittery nerves of the ETRT, and Cameron's experience helped a great deal. The conversation became focused on the incredible technology that the group was witnessing regarding the implanted tracking chips.

About forty-five minutes after Colonel Dietz disconnected, he was back online.

"The strike team is in place and the entire warehouse is surveilled. There are three perps inside with the hostage, and four armed men on the perimeter."

Cameron commented to the team assuredly.

"We are giving you the play-by-play, as we have the situation under control. Well, they have the situation under control."

Colonel Dietz continued his description of the engagement.

"We will take the four gunmen on the perimeter out, using silencers and takedowns, and then move in from the rear of the building where two windows are easy access points."

Most on the call were remarkably getting more relaxed as the Colonel spoke.

"The main reason I am sharing this with you is that the kidnappers are certain that they cannot be found and are clumsy…surprisingly so."

Connor and Sara smiled, as did Mike, given that his intense investigation into that mysterious metal disc proved to be the link in the undetectable tracking device that has been implanted into Amanda's neck.

"Gotta go," uttered the Colonel. "Be back real soon."

While waiting for the Colonel's return, Cameron brought up another potential security and military problem.

"While we were digging into the demands of the kidnappers regarding cloaking and levitation, we discovered a disturbing theft had taken place."

Sara was noticeably in high alert mode.

"An advanced weapons technology was stolen, right out of the Pentagon's most highly classified and encrypted files."

"Any leads?" asked Sara.

"Well, this was an inside job, of course, and we are investigating several similar thefts, none as critical as this one. We think we know who was responsible and are proceeding cautiously."

Mike had a question.

"Can you tell us anything about the two advanced technologies that the kidnappers were interested in?"

"Sure, the cloaking is not something that we have. Someone must, but we don't."

"And the anti-gravity or levitation issue?" Sara asked.

"The anti-gravity one is both some fact and some theory. We have the so-called 'black box' from the 1950's that was known as the Coral Castle rock formation in Orlando, Florida, and are studying it.

"We are also studying antimatter, as reverse gravity can be obtained through that technology."

Everyone was focused on his Coral Castle description and Michaela asked for some details.

"That involved the mysterious placement of tons of rock by one man and his newly-discovered, and alleged, alien technology. It enabled him to reverse gravity and move suspended rocks with ease. This is one person that you guys might want to take a shot at."

"Damn straight," responded Michaela.

At that moment, Colonel Dietz came back online.

Looking a little stressed, he said, "It's over. It was kind of messy. The four gunmen were killed and the three perps committed suicide."

"And Amanda?" Sara was worried.

His next words were the best.

"Amanda is safe, and on her way back to the *Stargaze*."

76

SARA

Sara was fixing a drink that she and Matt had on their recent getaway when Michaela arrived for a scheduled meeting with Sara so each could catch up and collectively catch their breaths over the latest incident.

Michaela spoke first.

"Ya know, that whole thing with Amanda could have ended badly."

"You're right, of course. Very badly. What are you thinking?"

"Sara, this changes everything. Both from a security perspective and for a greater focus on our job at hand."

"Totally agree. That's why you and I need to talk."

"So," a smiling Michaela asks, "what cha mixing?"

"It's called 'Between the Sheets' or 'Maiden's Prayer,' depending on where you are drinking."

"Want one?"

"Sure, Sara. What's in it?"

"Well, it has light rum, brandy, triple sec, lemon juice, and lemon garnish. After shaken, it's served in a martini glass."

"You and Matt had that drink, I bet."

"Yep. Loved the drink and loved the time spent with him."

Sara poured them each a drink and said, "Cheers."

After a sip, Michaela says, "Wow! That is one terrific drink. Thanks."

"You are quite welcome."

"So, Sara, what's on the full plate of yours these days?"

Pausing, Sara replied.

"I'd like to discuss both the terrorist stuff and alien stuff...the status of each. One is very simple and one is very complicated."

"Okay, let's do the simple one first, before I will need another drink."

Sara smiled, enjoying the opportunity to engage with her closest friend.

"For us, the terrorist threat seems to be over. Cameron has assured Scott, Dad, and me that they now have all the dots connected, and the leader Scorpio and his so-called secret society will be caught and contained soon."

"So good to know."

"Yep. Finally."

"And the advanced technology issues, Sara?"

"Well, Michaela, those follow under the alien issues."

"Not surprised."

"Remember a couple of months ago when I told you about those dreams and feelings that I had about aliens and personal interventions?"

"Yes," Michaela said apprehensively.

"They weren't dreams and they are very real."

Sara went on to describe the alien intervention with the plane carrying the ETRT to the meeting with Congress.

A stunned Michaela listened, realizing the enormity of this reveal.

"I just couldn't keep this to myself any longer."

"Sara, why didn't you confide in me sooner?"

"Believe me, I wanted to in the worst way, but…"

"But, what?"

"Michaela, until I got some serious question answered, I was afraid that I might be putting you in danger. Look what happened to Amanda. Sorry, but I just didn't want to put you in harm's way."

As they hugged tightly, Sara had a sigh of relief. She then continued.

"Well, I am now in fairly frequent contact with one of their recon team members."

"Recon teams?"

"Another long story. Later. Let me refill your drink, first."

"His name is Pulse and he is one of a small team that is helping us with the many issues, both explained phenomena and quasi-explained events that are affecting our world as we speak."

"What's does he look like?"

"Michaela!"

"Just curious."

"Pulse is tall, has a rather elongated skull, small ears, and longer than normal limbs. He's actually quite good looking. We can communicate telepathically."

"You gotta be kidding. Don't know what to say…but give me time and I'll have a million questions."

"Figured that."

Sara continued with a slightly more serious demeanor.

"Pulse has downloaded a tremendous amount of relevant info into Elonis, and she will provide all of the detailed info in our next ETRT meeting."

"An inter-stellar data dump into an artificial human, eh? Not something that happens every day."

"Yeah, I guess you could call it that."

"Sara, do you have any idea how this will impact my work?"

"I don't even know what she has in store for you… at least not yet. But it'll make your work, I'm sure, much easier and much more productive."

"That's pretty damn interesting. So, I guess you'll be gone again?"

"Yes. You can run the next meeting. Matt's 'skunk works' is developing some amazing A.I. technology in his lab, and I'm going back out there for an update."

"Anything you can share right now?"

Sara thought for a moment about how far to go with today's huge reveal, and stopped short of any more info regarding Matt's lab and hologram project.

"Not really. They are working on a consciousness streaming technique using an interesting data set. I'll know more when I return."

Pouring herself yet another drink, Michaela continued her questions.

"Anything else for now, Sara?"

"Yep. Pulse is arranging a kind of summit meeting with me and Echo, the supreme alien commander, I assume."

"Oh my God!"

"Yeah, just waiting to hear as to when and where."

"Well, Sara, that could be a game changer."

Sara smiles and thinks strategically before responding.

"New game, new players, new board, new intensity, and now, the new normal!"

77

SARA

Sara headed back out to visit Matt and spend time with "Pete." She was both excited and nervous, not knowing what to expect.

Matt picked Sara up at the local airport, gave her a hug and a kiss, and the first thing out of Sara's mouth was not a surprise.

"What new info did you get from Pete?"

They got into Matt's car and headed for the lab.

Sara was busy answering several text messages coming in-flight.

When Sara was ready, Matt began.

"First. That was wonderful news concerning Amanda. Your team again deserves tremendous credit."

"Thanks."

Matt advised. "There have been three levels of A.I. development with the hologram."

"Just call the hologram 'Pete,' okay?"

"Of course. Sure."

Matt sensed Sara's lack of patience and concern... typical Sara.

"Level one was the memory transfer, and that went as expected."

Matt took a deep breath before he continued.

"Level two was unexpected, as we actually pulled Pete's observations and apparent dreams out of his consciousness."

Sara quickly added, "That doesn't make any sense, Matt."

"It does not. It makes even less sense now, Sara."

"How's that?"

"Pete seems to be prognosticating. This would be an unexpected level three."

Sara waited as Matt continued, carefully choosing his words.

"He appears to be describing a future vision or actual events... Or something that he is trying to visualize for us to comprehend. You need to talk with it...with Pete, I mean."

Following some catch up on other ETRT, some admin issues and the recent ordeal with Amanda, Sara stopped speaking as Matt pulled up to the lab and they walked inside.

"Hi Sara."

"Hey, Miah. Sounds like you and 'Pete' are getting it cranked up, eh?"

"Yeah, you might say that. Matt bring you up to speed?"

"You mean on the vision stuff?"

"Yeah. Really hard to understand."

Walking through the tech center over to the lab, Sara was apprehensive.

She saw Tyreek working on his portable holo-display device and waved. Tyreek doesn't join them.

Matt explained his tactic to Sara.

"This stage of the interaction with 'Pete' is sensitive, at best. We are keeping things just between the three of us for now."

"Why?"

"You'll see, Sara."

As they arrived at the hologram, Sara can see that "Pete" is fully operational. She began.

"Hi Grandad, it's Sara; how are you?"

"Hello Sara. It is nice to see you."

Matt asked Sara. "Would you like to be alone now?"

"No, Matt. We need to all be on the same page here."

Sara asked, "Grandad, what is on your mind that I need to know?"

"Pulse will give Elonis important information."

Matt asked Sara, "Pulse?"

"I'll explain later."

"What else, Grandad?"

"You must meet with Echo as soon as possible."

Matt again asks, "Echo?"

"Later."

Matt is now somewhere between curious and angry.

Several questions follow, but none as frightening as the last one between Sara and "Pete."

"Sara, a storm is coming."

78

SARA

Jeremiah powers down "Pete," and all three head back to a small conference room.

Matt immediately questions Sara.

"Why did you end the session? You have so many more questions to ask."

"So, here's the thing." Sara was gaining her courage.

"I have had to keep you guys in the dark concerning significant recent events. Hologram Pete is requiring me to put everything in play."

Matt and Jeremiah listened intently.

"I have come in contact with a benevolent alien race; in fact, they saved the lives of me and the entire ETRT in route to the D.C. meeting."

Matt and Jeremiah were stunned.

"Their leader is a female commander named Echo and her O.I.C. is a male named Pulse. We have only recently begun working together, as our Earth is coming under attack from many fronts."

"Damn it, Sara, I am really pissed that you didn't tell me sooner."

Sara nodded and had expected that remark.

Matt snapped, "I'm surprised and disappointed that you didn't confide in me."

Jeremiah just listened, as excited as he had ever been in his life.

"No one knows, not even my parents. Look, until we find out who or what is behind all the terror and vicious attacks that are directed towards us, the fewer people that are targets…the better."

"And now I can see that Pulse has been uploading info into the Pete hologram."

Matt was still getting quite annoyed with this new info.

As Jeremiah could see that things were about to get dicey, he excused himself. "Gonna go now. Have several things to take care of, as you can imagine."

"Thanks for all your help, Miah, and I am eager to see where you and Tyreek will be going next with Pete. Matt will explain my alien dealings later."

"Your welcome. Believe me, we had no idea where this was going…and still have no concept where it will go. The alien intervention does explain a lot, though."

Matt offered his observation.

"We will keep everything…and I mean everything, to ourselves."

As Jeremiah exited, Matt got back to his earlier question.

"So, why keep me in the dark, Sara?"

"As I told Michaela…"

"You told Michaela, but not me?"

"Dammit, Matt, I just told her yesterday. And now I'm telling you."

"Fine. Sorry. Confused. Go on."

"I was, and still am, worried about so many consequences involving telling my loved ones about my alien connection. Look what happened to Kat and Amanda."

"But I'm not even a member of your ETRT?"

"You are obviously within my network, and, may I remind you, you are the one that rebuilt me into the super-strong person that I am today. Potential target, maybe?"

"Putting it that way, I understand."

All seemed as good as it could be. As he regained his composure, Matt gave Sara a hug.

Sara spent two days giving Matt and Jeremiah a final debriefing on all things alien, including details of the terrorist attack on Amada and those related implications.

Matt and Sara spent a somewhat tense night together, as Sara was so preoccupied with all that was going on, her relationship with Matt just wasn't her priority right now.

"Matt, I'm sorry to be so distant tonight…just so damn much to think about."

Matt could only smile. "I understand."

"I'll make it up to you…promise."

The following morning, Matt got her a cab to return to the airport.

Once back in town, Sara made a most unusual detour. She stopped her car and pulled out a directory of local businesses.

Sara picked out a random tattoo parlor that wasn't anywhere close to her office with an objective in mind…to get a tattoo.

Sara returned to her office with a tattoo on her forearm. Michaela noticed it but stayed silent.

On Sara's right forearm was vividly displayed her self-imposed mission.

"*I AM THE STORM*"

79

MICHAELA

"So, how'd the meeting in Utah go," Michaela asked Sara.

"Michaela, I've got another OMG coming."

"Kind of expected that. Back and forth the last few weeks to Provo gave me the impression that it wasn't just about seeing Matt."

"No. Of course not."

Pausing a moment, Sara began her explanation.

"Matt and his team created a 3D hologram…using state-of-the-art hologram technology. By utter coincidence, many years ago, my grandad did some sort of a brain scan, or memory dump, at a Colorado facility that is now part of Matt's A.I. lab."

"Holy cow," Michaela was surprised.

"So, right out of pure science fiction, that brain dump and consciousness mapping from Pete Stevenson is now a fully operational hologram."

"Bottom line, Sara?"

"The hologram of 'Pete' has the ability to penetrate and navigate Pete's memory, his dreams and observations, and with help from Pulse, Pete can now somehow see into the future and make apparent predictions."

"That is both exciting and pretty darn scary!"

"You bet, Michaela."

"Among other things, Pete said that there were evil aliens amongst us, as he once proclaimed, and that a storm was coming."

"Well, that explains your tatt."

"Yeah, I'll give you the complete rundown later."

"You are angry right now, Sara, and I understand."

"I'm pissed. We can't get one fire put out before another one starts. It's frustrating."

"I get it." Michaela pulled out her device and sent Sara a text."

"What's that?"

"Sara, it's 'who is that'? Her name is Dr. Victoria Price and she is renowned psychologist and a Fellow of the American Psychiatric Association. We are friends and I believe she is a person with whom you need to speak."

"Thanks for the name and number. I'll keep her in mind."

"Okay then, Sara, let me get you up to speed on the ETRT meeting."

"Good."

"As promised, Elonis did a massive data dump. She did explain before she began that you and she were in sync with the issues she raised."

"Well, yes and no. I told her to say that since I wasn't sure what all she would get into."

"Elonis explained that her supercomputer capabilities allowed her to make millions of simulations regarding a whole host of objectives, and that her conclusions were highly accurate."

"Was her explanation convincing?"

"It was. Her list was most impressive."

Gathering her notes, Michaela continued.

"She covered the following issues, per my notes.

- Ancient alien atomic warfare.
- Alien DNA disappearance.
- Colony on Mars for thirty years.
- Anti-gravity techniques were now understood.
- Free energy or zero-point energy is now available.
- The planet Earth is dying.

"There were a few other mentions, but this list is her best stuff."

"Wow, that's a lot more than I expected."

"There was one more thing that was odd. Did you ask Samantha to attend the meeting?"

"No, I did not. I definitely did not. I have been sending her updates of each meeting. Why?"

"She was there. She took notes and she never said a word."

80

SARA

Sara felt a need to meet with Elonis to discuss the ETRT data dump from her meta-human friend and to have a face-to-face with Elonis regarding both the "Pete" hologram and the relationship between Pulse and Elonis regarding info sharing and expectations.

Sara was also making a series of notes for her next encounter with "Pete." It was becoming obvious to her that these meetings were to become meaningful and fairly frequent.

Sara decided to ask Matt and Jeremiah if she could use the 3D technology on her E-watch to load future talks with "Pete." She really wanted to do this.

With the latest info from Michaela on Elonis's ETRT contributions, Sara arranged for a quick one-on-one meeting.

<Hello Sara, you wanted to meet?>

"Yes, but let's just talk this time. I need words, not thoughts."

"Yes. I understand."

"Elonis, what is your position regarding sharing info with Pulse?"

"I'm sorry, Sara, I do not understand the question."

"What info do you and Pulse share?"

"We share information that concerns the ETRT and how he and I can help you with your tasks."

"Do you tell me everything that Pulse tells you?"

"I tell you all the facts that Pulse tells me. That is my role."

Sara paused for a moment.

"I wasn't aware of the significant ETRT updates that you just presented from the last meeting. Why was I not involved with those?"

"Sara, you told me to present the information updates to the ETRT while you were gone."

Not getting a response from Sara, Elonis continued.

"You did not tell me to present them to you first."

Sara thought about what Elonis said for a moment, realizing the obvious.

"I'm sorry, Elonis. Just getting a little paranoid, I guess."

Elonis knew that Pulse had feelings for Sara, but in this enhanced state of consciousness, Elonis knew that she did not have to divulge that info to Sara.

Sara resumed asking her questions.

"I'm aware of the ancient alien atomic warfare and the DNA wash. The colony on Mars is one that Michaela said came as quite a surprise, I guess."

Sara waited for a response from Elonis.

Elonis said, "Do you have a question for me?"

"Oh, sorry, no."

Returning to Michaela's list, Sara continued.

"The anti-gravity techniques that you are referring to are the ones from the government's investigation of the Coral Castle 'black box,' right?"

"Yes, that is correct."

"Is the free energy or zero-point energy derived from the Nikola Tesla studies?"

"No. Pulse explained zero-point as the endpoint of energy evolution. By that he meant it built from nuclear energy to thorium energy to zero-point. It is the zero-point energy that enables large crafts to fly outside the earth's atmosphere."

"How did you explain that to the team?"

"Pulse provided me with a schematic drawing. I will forward that drawing to you."

"Fine. That'll work. What the hell was the dying planet, anyway?"

"What do you mean, Sara?"

"Elonis, that is not the kind of fact-based stuff you usually address. An important one, but not what I've come to expect from you and your skills. It's kind of an opinion."

"Sara, this was one that Pulse intended for you. I believe he was following the directive from Echo."

Sara was thinking many thoughts about this implication.

Elonis paused as Sara appeared pre-occupied.

"But your recent absences led Pulse to give it to me for the ETRT. I believe that Pulse assumed that it was a critical issue for the ETRT to focus on."

"Good point. I get it. What was the main element of that issue?"

"Pulse wanted me to highlight the human-made destruction of the eco-system and referred to the galactic civilization, which I concluded should not be discussed with the ETRT."

"The galactic civilization? Even I don't understand that one, Elonis."

"Apparently, Sara, you will be briefed on that when you meet with Echo."

"You know about my upcoming meeting with Echo?"

"Yes."

While Sara was getting the Elonis updates, she received a coded message from the office of President Sullivan. With the events of the last couple of weeks, Sara had asked for a meeting with POTUS.

"Sara, this is Mara Wallace from the Oval Office. Your meeting is scheduled for this Monday at 8:00 a.m."

"Thank you, Mara. I will be there."

As Sara was wrapping up her meeting with Elonis, she asked one more question.

"Did Pulse tell you anything else that I should hear but the ETRT should not?"

"Yes," responded Elonis.

"A Storm is coming."

81

CAMERON

It was the following Monday at 8:00 a.m., and Sara was outside the Oval Office waiting for her meeting with POTUS.

As the President walked in with his administrative staff, he greeted Sara.

"Good morning, Sara."

"Good morning, Mr. President."

"I need to sign a couple documents with the staff, and then you and I have the office."

"Fine. Thanks."

As President Sullivan finished his document signing, his Chief-of-Staff asked Sara if they could get her anything.

"Sure. Coffee, black, would be nice."

With that, another staff member left the room to get Sara her coffee.

President Sullivan looked over to Sara and said, "Hope you had a pleasant flight."

"Yes, thanks. Air Force Two isn't too shabby."

The President smiled, but said nothing. Three members of his Cabinet were still there.

"Okay, we're done here. Would everyone excuse us?"

As the cabinet members left the Oval Office, they all smiled and said their goodbyes to Sara.

Mara Wallace returned with Sara's coffee.

Sara's immediate, but quickly passing thought was, "Hey, I'm like an alien hunting 'rock star' here in D.C."

"Thank you. Mara."

"All right, Sara, I want to see it."

"Excuse me?"

"I want to see the tatt."

"Really? You know about that?"

"Yes, I do. I am the President, eh?"

"I'm embarrassed," Sara said as she removed her jacket and rolled up her sleeve.

"Cool. I like it!"

"Thanks, I guess. There's a story here, for sure."

"I'm sure there is. Can't wait to hear it."

With that somewhat embarrassing moment behind her, Sara began to explain to POTUS the many issues that had now hit her radar screen and especially the ones that concerned President Sullivan and national security.

Of all the topics that Sara covered, the hologram of Pete was clearly the most unusual in an "otherwise everything is unusual" environment of the ETRT.

Sara thought to herself, "Even now, that hologram of Pete Stevenson seems like regular news."

"Believe me, Cameron, there is a lot of that going around."

"So, Sara, you plan to meet with Echo soon?"

"Yes. I will be contacting Elonis, who will set up this meeting. It'll probably happen within the next few days."

"Good. Keep me informed, directly. Do you need any help from me?"

"No, thanks. I trust Pulse, as much as any human I know."

Pausing, she continued.

"It's a strange feeling, Cameron, almost as if Pulse and I have met before. Can't explain it."

"Well, whatever you need, I'm here."

"Thanks, Cameron."

"Before you go, I have a couple of admin things to cover."

"Great. What's up?"

"I will make plans for a meeting at the Pentagon as soon as you are ready. This time I will have a hand-picked special committee for you, Elonis, and your team to present your latest findings and recommendations."

"That would be great." Sara was excited. "A special committee?"

"Yes. We have identified several Congressmen who may have ties to either the New World Order, or now the First World Order, or some other secret society, and we are monitoring their behavior twenty-four seven."

"Yikes. That sounds ominous."

Sara asked, "You want Elonis too?"

"Hell yes. I'd take Pulse if it weren't for starting massive coronary arrests."

"Gotcha."

Sara was amused with Cameron's comeback. She felt very comfortable in his presence.

"You have something else?"

"Yes, I am assigning a former Navy Seal to be your security chief. I've heard about your strength, so you don't need a body guard."

Sara was amused and pleased with his comment.

Sara thought about the President's idea, and then responded, "Cameron, I have a request."

"What's that, Sara?"

"I prefer Special Agent, Lieutenant Robert Baker, whom I know and who has helped my grandfather immensely."

Cameron made eye contact with Sara, smiled, and opened his arms in an approving manner.

"Done."

82

ALIEN GALACTIC STAFF MEETING

It was at this time when Echo, the earth name for the alien supreme leader, had called her four-member Leadership Team together. Realizing that many events or issues were approaching a "perfect storm," Echo summoned her team from the outskirts of the Milky Way Galaxy of Earth's solar system to the outer reaches of the Andromeda Galaxy.

Joining Echo on the mothership were Pulse, Laser, Spirit, and Peace. These were all names given to the alien visitors by humans long before today's events and encounters. They were bestowed mostly due to their human-like characteristics and behavior.

The five aliens wore distinctive and individually colored uniforms, and each alien, except for Echo, had a squad-size team accompanying them to Echo's meeting.

In an otherwise empty room, Echo motioned to her left, where a 3D screen was taking up an entire wall. In an instant, a round table with five high-back chairs appeared in a previously empty room. Echo nodded to her Leadership Team to be seated.

"We will now begin our protocol number seven orientation, as we usually do to introduce ourselves to new civilizations. This first impression is always important. Also, leave a statement that defines you."

The Team was attentive and in place. They were used to the drill.

Echo was dressed in a blue uniform with orange epaulets.

"I am **Echo**, the commander of the Arrans alien race. I am the leader, and these four superhumans are my team. My primary skill, among others, is critical listening, attentiveness, and to be ever alert. Listening comprehension is a key quality. You listen in order to understand the main issues and important details. *Many people hear, but few truly listen.* Thank you."

Pulse was dressed in a red uniform with gray epaulets.

"I am **Pulse,** the second in command. My primary skill, among others, is the transmission, conveying, and transporting of communication. I use symbols, signs, and behavior, in both verbal and non-verbal means. This communication skill allows me to transform and assimilate technology. *Never mistake activity for achievement.* Thank you."

Laser was dressed in a green uniform with black epaulets.

"I am **Laser** and a very focused observer, assimilating many activities or events into one. Time travel from present to future and from present to past are my absolute skills. I use warp speed and instantaneous extrapolation to navigate parallel universes. *Behavioral change is a necessary constant.* Thank you."

Spirit was dressed in a black uniform with silver epaulets.

"I am **Spirit**, and I represent the fundamental part of being alive. Among my skills are channeling, the ability to spiritually guide contactees, and give them the knowledge to help them on their spiritual journeys. Kindness, emotional control, and cultural diversity are my strengths. *Balance patience and intensity.* Thank you."

Peace was dressed in a violet uniform with white epaulets.

"I am **Peace** and I represent the ultimate life goal. My skills are to impart tranquility, lawfulness, peacefulness, freedom from disruption, and to create a stress-free state of calmness that comes when there is no fighting or war. *Do what you love, do it with people you love…do it well.* Thank you."

✦ ✦ ✦

Echo continued with what was her regularly scheduled leadership meeting.

"We have usual business issues and extraordinary Earth issues to discuss. I do want a full report on the situation in this galaxy, especially regarding the major insurgencies in Andromeda."

Echo waited as her leadership team pulled together 3D charts and graphs in the meeting room to facilitate their individual report-outs.

"As you know, I will be meeting with our Earthling contact soon, and want to make my meeting with Sara Steele as comfortable and simple as I can, which will be difficult."

Pausing, Echo continued.

"I also want to keep the pace of our inevitable reveal rollout as slow as possible."

Pulse was quick to respond.

"Echo, if our pace were any slower than now, we would need to speed up to stop!"

Smiling, Echo noted, "Pulse, you and that Earthling Connor would make a good comedy team."

There was no laughter, as all in attendance had seen this interaction between Echo and Pulse before. Pulse was Echo's second in command, and the only alien on Echo's team that could break Echo's otherwise serious demeanor.

"We will keep our Earth names and add humankind names to the major alien species that are becoming a major galactic force and our greatest concerns."

Spirit asked Echo to explain what she meant by "humankind names."

"The universe is vast and is made up of many life forms and species. In order to introduce and keep simple to humans that complicated fact, we will attempt to group like cultures with similar characteristics into understandable categories."

"Again, not only to make the multi-universe very simple regarding life forms, but to use terms to describe all alien cultures that humans can relate to."

Her leadership team was focused.

"Pete Stevenson had his buckets…and I have mine. We are going to put as many of the alien races into four categories, and each of you will be responsible for taking the lead on all things relevant to that bucket. Is that clear?"

All responded telepathically.

✦ ✦ ✦

"I will represent our species, as it is the most evolutionary of the current human race. I have selected as a name, *Arrans*, and you can understand why this small commune in France, where we are occasional co-inhabitants with the native human species, and easily concealing our identity, makes logical sense."

Echo paused for questions; there were none.

"I want our allies on Earth to see us as the 'good' alien culture. And, even though our major colonies today lie in what Earth calls the Trappist-1 System, our origins with the Pleiades open star cluster will likely be understood by the human astrology leaders. I want the humans to know that we have been the monitors of this galaxy for millions of years, but have only reached a greater presence since the beginning of the First Millennium, as the evolution of humankind and the universe as you know it has progressed. Again, for lack of a more scientific description, we are the evolution of mankind."

Echo paused again before continuing.

"Spirit will become the humans' link to the malevolent spirits in this Galaxy, Earth name *Denons*, which have evolved from human souls that have endured extensive torture in Hell and by similar alien cultures. They have become corrupt…extremely evil and also very powerful, as you know. Since they require a human vessel to walk and function on Earth, they will be the most difficult for our human allies to recognize."

Spirit had no questions.

"Laser will become the conduit to the humanoid beings with reptilian features, Earth name *Dracs*. Even though they originated in the Alpha Draconis star system which is only two hundred fifteen light years away, they have the greatest historical origin in this universe. Laser will need to educate, in due time and as required, all those who might come in contact with these large beings. Since they have two main castes, the warriors and the highly intelligent, great care must be made to address their presence. The fact that they are often in forms indistinguishable from humans will be a challenge."

Laser had no questions.

"Pulse will represent the beings created by bundling bio-technology, robotics, A.I., G.A.I., and advanced weaponry, known from this day on as the *Teslites*. Since they are primarily temporal in nature, with the only elements drawn from future evolution, Pulse must be creative and explicit with his evaluations and assistance to the humans. Since the evolution of this alien species doesn't know right from wrong, Pulse will be on a learning curve as well, trying to understand motives while not getting too far ahead of his human allies."

Pulse was pleased. This is the species type that he wanted to be in charge of regarding educating the humans. He winked to Echo his concurrence.

"And Peace will become the link to the *Anunnaki*, our spiritual presence in this universe, and attempt to take humanity into a higher level of consciousness and spirituality. As this has always been my mission, I will work closely with Peace on this critical enlightenment journey."

"So," Echo continued, "each of you now has a role in the transition from the world the Earthlings now see and the one that could be upon them soon. I expect all of you to carry out your current duties, for our civilization and the Galaxy, but be prepared when and if the time comes to take action."

Echo waited for any questions from her team, but only one was raised by Laser.

"Echo, what about the Greys, or Reticulans. They are every bit as real as the ones we are exposing."

"You are correct, Laser, and you raised a good question. The Greys are diminutive humanoid beings and have been around Earth long enough to become the stereotypical extraterrestrial alien. Inasmuch as they are a food source for some alien cultures, and have Martian roots, they are very real."

Pulse was paying attention to Echo's train of thought as she continued.

"They are not a threat to humanity and not relevant in our exposure to the humans."

With no further questions, Echo gave an impatient sign and continued.

"When dealing with Earthlings, keep this thought in mind: their humanity is being held captive by a speculative truth…they believe they are prisoners of the present, in a perpetual transition from an inaccessible past to an unknown future. You must be patient."

Echo advised, "I will be meeting with the earthling, Sara Steele, tomorrow, and I will be calling us together with a report following that meeting."

Pulse interjected his concern.

"Echo, will you be telling Sara what we know about the future of Earth and what destiny holds for them?"

"Seriously, Pulse? We are trying to guide them…not frighten them!"

"Echo, can't you at least explain to them that their Moon is an artificial satellite used to terraform their planet five hundred thousand years ago?"

"I will not. Not at this time. Even she and that strong team of hers could not handle the truth!"

83

ECHO

Reading Sara's recent message to POTUS telepathically, Elonis contacted Sara with a meeting to be arranged between Sara and the alien leader Echo.

<Echo has just finished her staff meeting and will be arriving soon.>

<Thanks, Elonis. Looking forward to our meeting.>

<I will follow up with you after your meeting.>

<Thanks, Elonis. Don't know what we'd do without you.>

Within twenty-four hours of Echo's meeting with her leadership team on the mothership, the nearly seven-foot tall Echo was in the back yard of Sara's home.

Sara lived in a two-story contemporary home, with windows and skylights in abundance, next to a quiet and picturesque valley with a gentle stream nearby, many miles and thoughts away from Sara's busy office.

Once a fan of Frank Lloyd Wright's architecture and his wonderful classic "falling water" home, she understood the difference between loneliness and solitude. She was rarely lonely, and almost never had the amount of solitude she needed to think and to plan.

She was sitting on the porch with a newly opened bottle of 2020 Kosta Browne Pinot Noir, her nightly fire pit ablaze, when Echo quietly appeared next to her.

<Hello, Sara; it is so good to be with you>

<Echo, thank you for coming. I have awaited this day with great anticipation and joy.>

Echo slowly moved toward Sara, extended her hand, and grasped Sara's hand firmly in hers. She held on to Sara's hand for several seconds, touched her forehead and smiled.

Echo was dressed in an impressive royal blue warrior attire with a metallic-looking orange-trimmed black cape and many patches that resembled merit awards or achievement levels. Passive aggressive statement?

"Let us talk, Sara. I prefer words right now to thoughts."

"Yes, thank you Echo, as I do as well."

Noticing a slender silver item hanging from Echo's belt on her left side, Sara inquired, "Echo, what is that thing hanging from your belt?"

"This is my favorite Battlestar Saber, which I call Destiny. Within its hilt is a polycarbonate Laser Fire Blade that ignites and incinerates when it reaches its target. It is the Crown Jewel in my battle sabre collection."

Sara immediately saw the striking contrasts of the lovely wine and warm fire pit versus a life-ending sabre sword.

Smiling at the sight of Sara's tattoo, Echo began to speak.

"Elonis is a very good friend for you, yes?"

"Yes, she is. Elonis has become much more like a human, thanks, I assume, to the updates provided by Pulse."

"Yes, that was his call to make and I trust Pulse. He has amassed great wisdom and technique."

"Technique?"

"In dealing with humans, Sara. We have been having much more contact with Earth humans since we came across your grandfather and his quest."

Sara not only understood Echo's words, but she was getting a strong sense of energy transfer while holding Echo's hand.

"Sara, to answer your current thought, yes, Pulse has feelings for you as a person, a warrior, and an important energy for what lies ahead."

"What lies ahead? Echo, what is happening?"

"Do not fret. I will give you information and thought images for you to accept and understand."

Sara nodded, "My mind is open."

Starring directly into Sara's eyes, Echo advised: "It is time for you to tell the ETRT about all of your alien encounters."

"Even this one?"

"Especially this one because of what I am about to tell you."

Sara tensed up as Echo's touch again calmed her right down.

"Current technology is uncovering all the secrets of ancient alien presence, and we can no longer keep our presence secret. There will soon come a time when we will reveal ourselves."

"But…"

"Not now, Sara. Hold that thought. I will explain.

"As Elonis has said, your Earth is dying.

"Your eco-system and world economy are collapsing.

"There are water shortages and mass starvation."

Sara was expanding on her negative worldview as Echo continued.

"The world is experiencing mass extinctions unlike anything since the dinosaur era.

"Global warming and the burning of fossil fuels is continuing without proper leadership to stop it.

"Your civilization, as part of the galaxy, is on an unchecked path to its end.

"Your culture lacks the necessary consciousness and spirituality. It is what your scholars call 'the law of correspondence,' as above…so below."

Sara was now visibly upset.

"The reality that you see on your Earth today is a mirror image of what is going on within the economic and social systems of countries today."

"Yes, I believe that is true, Echo."

"Sara, are you able to absorb my words if I continue?"

"Yes. Please."

"Various 'contactee' humans, which you call abductions, have been exposed to and involved in alien capture, both from good alien cultures and from bad."

Sara had a thought…

"Not now. Wait until I am finished," replied Echo.

"An evil reptilian alien force, we will refer to them as the Dracs, has been working with Germany since the 1930's in development of advanced weaponry, spacecraft, and in high-level assimilation. They are among you now and are undetectable."

Sara was clearly shaken.

"Sara, let me explain what humans call the 'big picture' for you."

✦ ✦ ✦

As Sara poured a glass of wine, she asked Echo if she would like a glass.

"No, thank you. But please, go ahead."

Echo waited a moment until Sara was ready.

"Our species, today called the *Arrans*, are from an Exoplanet that is 110 light years away in the constellation you call Leo. We have colonies in what you call the Trappist-1 system, which is on the inner edge of the habitable zone."

"Grandad told me about extrasolar planets like Trappist-1, an ultra-cool red dwarf star larger than the planet Jupiter and about forty light years from the Sun in the constellation Aquarius."

"You are correct, Sara."

Sara was pleased to have that acknowledged.

"Our origins are from the Pleiades star cluster, known here on Earth as the Seven Sisters."

"My father, Mike, taught me about that star cluster nearest to Earth in the constellation Taurus."

"Again, Sara, you are correct."

Sara was feeling very comfortable in Echo's presence.

Echo paused before continuing: "Maybe I will have a glass of wine with you."

A beaming Sara poured Echo some wine from the extra glass that she had brought out.

"In earlier times, we were simply like you…humans. Today a small group of us are physically on Earth in a commune in France with a very small population. We are co-habitants with the residents there and conceal our true identity using hats and robes."

Sara was spellbound.

"We strive to be '*vraiment très bon*,' or a 'really good' alien culture. We have been the monitors of this galaxy for millions of years, but have only reached a greater presence since the beginning of the First Millennium, as the evolution of humankind and the universe as you know it has progressed.

"For lack of a better description, we are the evolution of man. Sara, we are 'you' in the future."

Echo continued as Sara was listening intently.

"Sara, your galaxy has many alien cultures, both good and bad, and I will give you as much information as you can absorb to help you understand."

"Go ahead, Echo, I'm ready. We often spoke of the 'Law of…'"

"…Polarity," Echo said, reading Sara's thoughts.

"Sorry to interrupt, but you are very intelligent and very perceptive…and, like me, very impatient."

"Thanks. You're right about the impatience."

"The malevolent spirits that you would see as the direct opposites to angels are the Denons. They have evolved from human souls that have endured extensive torture in Hell by Alastair and similarly driven alien cultures. In this process, they have become corrupted, extremely evil, and also very powerful."

"They exist?"

"Oh yes. Very much so."

"And, they require a human vessel to walk and function on Earth. They have the ability to roam in smoke form and can morph into recognizable human forms. Death and destruction are always in their path. Your Earthly terrorist groups would be ideal hosts for their mission on Earth."

Sara was putting two and two together.

"The humanoid beings with reptilian features are the Dracs. The males are driven by whims and their own pleasures and have shapeshifting ability. The females have a chameleon ability and are more reserved and controlled than the males.

"The Dracs originated in the Alpha Draconis star system, which is only two hundred fifteen light years away, and was formerly the Polestar."

Sara chimed in, "A Polestar is a bright star closely aligned to the axis of rotation of an astronomical object, and it is used for navigation since it stays in the same place. It holds still in the sky while the entire northern sky moves around it."

"That is correct, Sara. Your grandad taught you well. I so enjoy talking with you."

Pausing a moment, Echo continued.

"The Dracs have two main castes: one is a dangerous warrior caste, eight to ten feet tall, six hundred to one thousand pounds, and are super-psychic and super-fast."

"The second caste is the highly advanced and intelligent race that has thousands of biological offspring here on Earth. They are indistinguishable from humans."

"They are here…now?"

"Sara, Dracs are here, were here, and will likely continue to be here."

Sara frowned as Echo spoke again. "And the *Teslites* are the result of continual bundling bio-technology, robotics, A.I., G.A.I., and advanced weaponry. Yes, Nikola Tesla was well on his way toward many incredible advances, with Einstein-like capability. Tesla was born before his time."

"Echo, you are implying that an evolution of what we see here on Earth right now will become a formidable humanoid culture in the future?"

"Yes. They resemble humans without actually being one."

'Oh my God,' Sara thought.

"But the evolution of this alien species doesn't know right from wrong… doesn't care about right from wrong…only winning and survival. Not what Mr. Tesla would have envisioned. A formidable opponent if ever there was one."

"Echo," Sara took a moment to continue, "would the rebuilding of my physical body qualify as a component of a Teslite in the not-to-distant future?"

Smiling, Echo advised. "That would be a good assumption."

Echo could sense that Sara was overthinking the implication.

"The Anunnaki, or spiritual presence in our universe, are the group of deities who appeared in mythological lore of ancient Sumerians, Akkadians, and Babylonians."

"This was myth…this was lore."

"Yes, Sara, it was what you said. But, the Anunnaki are here and around you every day. They have physical and spiritual forms. They carry intense emotional and intellectual energy and are immortal, hence the non-physical forms.

"Yes, Sara, you and I will have many conversations in the future regarding the Anunnaki"

"I can't thank you enough for enlightening me," and Sara directed a warm gaze to Echo.

"The Anunnaki were thought to be the most powerful deities in the Pantheon, descendants of An and Ki, the Gods of the heavens and the goddess of Earth, and their primary function was to decree the fates of humanity…it always was and it still is!"

"They together are your God and my God!"

✦ ✦ ✦

Pausing as Sara was noticeably shaken, Echo embraced Sara and offered her perspective on that revelation to Sara.

"I am you and you are me."

Now with small tears flowing from her rather large eyes, Echo had to explain that incredible comment.

"Sara, I was like you when I was very young…it is my hope that you will become me when you are older, wiser, and more experienced."

"Echo, I appreciate your perspective and your expectation of me. Only time will tell."

"Speaking of time, Sara. There is one more thing that I must say before I leave you with many thoughts to ponder."

Taking a deep breath, Sara asked, "And that is what?"

"Weather from space in the form of a geo-magnetic storm is coming."

"Elonis did mention that a storm was coming, Echo."

"Yes, Sara, but it will not be the only storm that Earth will face."

Sara did not interrupt Echo, but those words were not lost to her and needed no translation.

"You, Pulse, and Elonis must become the new leadership of the ETRT, a Galactic Triad, to put it into earthly terms."

Pausing, she advised, "And, prepare for future salvation needs."

"What, Echo? Echo?"

Echo uttered, "Technology will replace both power and fear as you chart your course. Technology melded with human strength."

As Echo slowly moved away from Sara into the warm and quiet night, she softly spoke.

"Sara, we will need to meet again soon."

"When...Why, Echo?"

Echo turned and with her right hand withdrew her Battlestar Sabre from its hilt on her left hip. She stared directly into Sara's eyes and flung it swiftly and purposely in Sara's direction.

Without a flinch and with incredible focus, Sara caught the sabre in her right hand about ten inches from her face before it ignited!

Sara felt no surprise, only a natural reaction.

Sara thought, "My learning curve has begun."

Sara also thought, "There is no way the ETRT would be ready to hear about this. Not yet."

As Echo disappeared into the foggy night, she looked over her left shoulder and said, "Sara, you now have even greater skills than before. You are ready."

Catching her breath, Sara heard Echo's last thought.

"You must now learn how to defend your Galactic Civilization, Aras."

84

SARA

Sara returned from her meeting with Echo and with Echo's amazing light sabre in her hand, she had no more of an understanding of what was going on in her world than before.

She slipped her new "prized possession" into her wall safe with many thoughts and images going through her mind.

Her primary thought was, "You don't know what you don't know."

She opened her contact list to Dr. Victoria Price, Michaela's friend and a possible "sounding board" for Sara. After thinking about calling Dr. Price, she moved her agenda list forward instead to Elonis, putting the session with Dr. Price on the back burner...again.

She had met with Echo to get answers to her questions, and now had even more questions than answers. It was apparent to Sara that, like it or not, Echo and she needed to form a relationship based on common needs. Sara, however, wasn't at all sure just what Echo's needs were.

So, Sara and Elonis set up a time to meet and compare notes and, hopefully, set an agenda going forward.

"As you know, I met with Echo and she explained and described many facets of their presence and had a ton of implications for me, you, and the ETRT."

"Yes, I am aware."

"And now, I am receiving info and updates almost at random from Echo and trying to understand and compartmentalize each that I receive."

"That is why I am here, correct?"

"Correct. As this myriad of facts and events pour in, I will connect with you so you can use your consciousness and intellect to sort and order them so we can make plans going forward."

"I am doing so as we speak."

"Good, Elonis. I feel much better with you here than when I was solo with Echo. She may be soft spoken and warm, but damn, she is one focused and committed humanoid."

"Echo is one incredible galactic warrior, as well, Sara."

Sara advised, "She also explained that thousands of years ago, Draco reptilians, a humanoid race, came from the constellations Orion, Sirius, and Draco, and intervened on planet Earth and, among other things, manipulated human coding, or DNA."

"That is in my program, Sara."

"And, those aliens hooked up with Germany in the 1930's and gave Germany their alien technology via the Thule, Vril, and Black Sun societies. I guess this is where the Nazi movement got its alien thrust."

"Yes, Sara, and the ruler Adolf Hitler wasted that technology with his preferred 'ground war' and had no understanding of what tremendous gifts he had been given."

Sara quipped, "Those aliens helped the Germans develop and build spaceships, anti-gravity machines, and teleportation devices."

"Yes, Sara, my program shows German habitats on the Moon and large colonies on Mars, since the late 1930's and early 1940's."

"Elonis, do you have the details on all of those hidden and uncovered secret societies, cabals, and secret space programs, both here in the U.S. and worldwide?"

"Yes. Some are very formidable. Some are benign, as far as our interests are concerned."

"Even some groups have done and are still doing human sacrifices?"

"Yes, Sara."

"Elonis, when I say black hat versus white hat, do you know what I mean?"

"Yes."

"Okay. Good. We are now going into the white-hat side."

Pausing, Sara continued.

"As you now know, Echo and Pulse are part of the alien culture they call Arrans, that is and has been trying to protect us. Is that the impression that you have?"

"Impression?"

"Yes, dammit. If you were to think about all that you know, and you do have that capability, do you think they are the good aliens?"

"Yes."

"Okay, please categorize, along with the relevant details, the following items that I have either spoken to Echo about, or that she has telepathically transmitted."

"The first one is cloaking. Do you have data on cloaking?"

"Yes, I do."

"Fine. What about spinning black holes?"

"In what dimension?"

"In all four dimensions. The three dimensions plus time."

"Yes."

"Time travel. Do you have the basic info on time travel?"

"I have forward time travel information. Backward time travel will need to be discussed with Pulse, as there are dangers with going back in time."

"Yes. I know. I'm aware of that danger."

"Levitation or anti-gravity methods?"

"Yes."

"Antimatter and micro-reactors?"

"Yes."

"Terraforming to be able to colonize Mars in just a few years?"

"Yes, I have that data."

"Okay. What about zero-point energy?"

"I already had that information, as part of our ETRT tasks."

"Good. Elonis, how extensive is your data regarding Earth's artificial Moon, particularly the dark side?"

"What is meant by extensive?"

"Elonis, how much detail? Can you quantify?"

"Of course, Sara. I have everything that ever occurred regarding the alien development of the dark side of the Moon, if that's what you are asking."

"Good. Now, last one. The whole history of MJ-12."

"Done, as we speak."

"Great. Now I'd like to get some info that involved the alien disarmament of nuclear missiles."

"Which time?" Elonis asked.

"Oh crap. It's what I was afraid of."

Sara pulled together her data set and added.

"In 1967, ten U. S. Minuteman missiles were armed and ready to launch with nuclear warheads hot. Then, inexplicably, spinning red spacecrafts hovering above the silos, rendered the nukes inactive by powering down the warheads. You have those details?"

"I do."

"Then, similarly in 1990, in both the United States and Russia, the same type of craft hovered over several hot nuke missiles and rendered them all inert. Right?"

"That is correct."

"Elonis, what about the one hundred and thirty-one subterranean compounds in the U.S. where secretive construction was underway for 'advanced weapons' technology, several styles of orbital aircraft, and disruptive communication devices is being developed?"

"What do you mean by 'what about' the compounds?"

"Do you have that info in order?"

"Yes, of the one hundred and thirty-one that are in the United Sates, twenty-three are near Area 51, which is physically the largest compound."

"Elonis, what about the rest of the world?"

"Four thousand, one hundred and thirteen are scattered around the world."

"So, there are four thousand and forty-four compounds around the world where this hidden and secret development is taking place?"

"No."

"Elonis, what do you mean by no?"

"No, the remaining facilities are either on the Moon or on Mars."

"Holy crap. I'm getting burned out…figure of speech, Elonis."

"I understand that."

"So, before you, Pulse, and I start putting plans together going forward, this last piece of info coming in from Echo was fuzzy, at best."

"Can I help to clear it up?"

"You are aware of the rather dark and ominous exchange we had regarding the demise of the planet?"

"Yes, I am aware of what Echo said to you and felt your depression."

"Good. Can you can try to figure out what Echo meant by one of her short statements?"

"I don't try…I just do what I'm asked."

"Sorry. I need to know what Echo meant by one remark."

One specific remark was puzzling to Sara.

"And, Sara, that remark was?"

Sara replied in a soft voice.

"Prepare for future salvation needs."

85

SARA

Sara was growing impatient and depressed. She always felt in control of her life from as far back as she could remember. But now…there seemed to be no control for her at all.

Following up on that referral from Michaela for a well-respected psychologist, Sara made an appointment with Dr. Victoria Price, PhD, LMT.

She knew she needed to talk with someone about her current stress level and bouts of depression, and today was the day.

She put on a conservative gray pantsuit with a white silk blouse and an antique Indian necklace that was a gift, and headed out the door to see Dr. Price.

After waiting in the doctor's office "quiet room" for only about ten minutes after her arrival, Sara was escorted into Dr. Price's office.

"Hello, Sara, I'm Victoria, and it's so nice to meet you."

Both women smiled as they shook hands.

Dr. Price was dressed professionally, but conservatively. She had a well-appointed and very becoming outfit that bespoke of her success and stature in her profession.

"Likewise, Dr. Price, I am so glad to meet you as well."

"Please call me Victoria."

Dr. Price motioned for Sara to take a seat on an L-shaped couch.

"Michaela has told me quite a bit about you, your work, and your drive and passion. Michaela is a big fan."

"Well, Michaela is the 'rock star' of the team, for sure."

Slowly opening her pad, Dr. Price began.

"So, let's get to know each other first. Then I'll provide a snapshot of what I have in mind for us today and going forward."

Sara really wasn't thinking about "going forward."

They spoke for twenty minutes.

Dr. Price spent about five minutes giving Sara an overview of her education and experience, followed by Sara sharing with Dr. Price the details of her dealing with the deaths of her grandfather, her husband, and now Kat.

"Thank you for sharing that with me, Sara, and I can see how important these people were to you and the values that you gained through their relationships."

"Yes. I miss them terribly, of course, but, again, it's the way they were taken from me that hurts the most."

"I understand." Dr. Price paused before continuing.

"The process of treatment that I use is called Cognitive Behavioral Therapy, or CBT, and it combines cognitive and behavioral therapies and has strong empirical support for treating mood and anxiety disorders."

"Yes, Victoria, the anxiety is often overwhelming."

"CBT builds a set of learned skills that enables an individual to be aware of thoughts and emotions; identify how situations, thoughts, and behaviors influence emotions; and improve feelings by changing dysfunctional thoughts and behaviors."

"Does that make sense to you?"

"Yes."

"The process of CBT is to acquire skills, behavioral skills, and it is collaborative. Skill acquisition and homework assignments are important in this process."

Sara was thinking, "Homework?"

"We will use session time to teach skills to address the present problem, search for root cause, and not simply to discuss your important issues by offering advice."

Dr. Price waited for any responses before continuing.

"In other words, I will not say, 'do this or don't do that,' but instead might ask 'why are you doing this or why are you not doing that. The "why" is important."

Dr. Price once again asked, "Does that make sense?"

Sara nodded that it did.

"The basic premise of CBT is that emotions are difficult to change directly, so CBT targets emotions by changing thoughts and behaviors that are contributing to the distressing emotions."

Sara responded, "I understand."

"Good. Here is our agenda…"

Dr. Price spent a half hour going through each element of the CBT process, with brief explanations for now, and allowing Sara to question each element.

"Since we have begun to orient you to CBT and assess your general concerns, we will set some preliminary goals and implementation plans. Is that good for you?"

"Yes. Of course."

"Next, we will look at maladaptive thoughts and behavior."

"Victoria, could you explain that one?"

"Sure. Maladaptive behaviors inhibit your ability to adjust to particular situations."

Dr. Price paused for a bit as Sara seemed a bit fidgety. He continued: "Often used to reduce anxiety, maladaptive behaviors result in dysfunctional and non-productive outcomes...in other words, they are often more harmful than helpful."

"Can you give me a couple examples, Victoria?"

"Drinking, gambling, lying, social withdrawal..."

Sara interrupted. "What about getting a tattoo?"

Smiling, Dr. Price said, "Yes, I suppose getting a tattoo could be one also."

Sara grimaced as Dr. Price continued. "Then we will deal with what we call behavioral activation."

Before Sara had a chance to interrupt, Dr. Price explained.

"Behavioral activation is designed to increase your interaction with positive things; people, activities, etcetera.

"Here, you identify specific goals for the week and work toward meeting those goals."

Sara thought her entire life was about goal-setting.

"These goals take the form of pleasurable activities that are consistent with the life you want to live."

"I like that thought, a lot."

"Good. Next we go on to problem solving, which you are quite familiar with, I'm sure. Then, we focus on relaxation methods and set up a strong plan for changing behavior."

"You know the definition of insanity, right?"

"Yes, Victoria, doing the same thing over and over and expecting a different result."

"You got it, Sara."

They spent the next five minutes planning their next nine to ten sessions, per Dr. Price's program, and the first session was over.

Standing up, Dr. Price spoke first.

"Sara, it was wonderful to spend time with you today and I look forward to our next session."

Standing and shaking Dr. Price's hand, Sara responded.

"Likewise, Victoria, I thank you for your time and will schedule our next session soon."

As Sara walked down the stairs and out the door to her car, she immediately changed her focus to ETRT business.

She knew she needed to update Michaela on her session. Truth? Probably not.

Sara had no intention of following up…just a complete waste of time.

86

SARA

Sara called Michaela as she left Dr. Price's office.

"Hey, Michaela, just me."

"Oh hi, Sara, what's up?"

"Just leaving my session with Dr. Price, following your recommendation."

"Great. How did your session go?"

"Went well. She is such a professional."

"She is. I was hoping she could help you, Sara."

"Well, it's a process, as you well know. Say, you wanna meet me for a drink? I'm not far from your place, Michaela?"

"Sure. Where?"

"How about *Unchained* on Riverbend Avenue. I've been wanting to see that place."

"Okay." Michaela questioned in her mind Sara's choice. "Give me half an hour."

"Will do, Michaela. See you soon."

Unchained was an adult bar that catered to upscale clientele, especially women. Sara knew that this was outside of Michaela's comfort zone, but Sara was in the mood to kick off her shoes and have some fun.

As the valet took Sara's car, she took her hair down from a frumpy-do she had in the doctor's office to her long, flowing blonde hair blowing gently in the evening breeze.

She went inside, got a seat at the U-shaped bar, and ordered a Macallan 12-year old Highland Single Malt Scotch Whiskey; double, straight up, and waited for her friend.

About twenty minutes later, Michaela walked into the bar looking a bit uncomfortable.

"Hi, Sara. Can't believe you wanted to meet here. Quite a mixed-bag of bar patrons here…and I've never seen both men and women pole-dancing."

"Yeah, a little unusual, for sure. Let's just have a couple of drinks and chat. What's your pleasure?"

"Sara, just a white wine will be fine."

Getting the bartender's attention, "She'll have a glass of Peter Michael Point Rouge Chardonnay."

"Will do," winked the bartender.

With that, Sara removed her gray business jacket, rolled up the sleeves of her blouse, and had the bartender pour her another Macallan Scotch.

As Michaela's wine arrived, she and Sara toasted to each other and Sara began explaining to Michaela what Dr. Price's session was like.

A few moments later, two very well-dressed men took the seats on either side of Sara and Michaela and introduced themselves.

"Hi, I'm Rod and this is Jerry. We're brokers with Harper and Rhule."

"Hi, I'm Michaela and this is Sara."

"Looks like you ladies already have your drinks; mind if we join you?"

Sara scoffed immediately. "No, thanks. We're just catching up and not into much of a social need right now."

Jerry insisted, while looking at Sara's arm.

"C'mon, just one drink. I'm dying to know about the 'storm tattoo' on your arm."

Caught off guard, Sara realized that her tattoo was fully exposed.

"It's just a tattoo. Nothing more. Now if you will excuse us, we have things to talk about."

After several minutes of awkward discussion with two men that didn't want to take "no" for an answer, Sara leaned over to Michaela and hissed.

"Time to go. I have another spot in mind where we can continue our talk without this annoyance."

With that, Sara left cash on the bar for both drinks, grabbed her jacket, and she and Michaela got up and walked out to the valet station.

While they were waiting for their cars, Rod and Jerry showed up to continue the discussion that the ladies now viewed as harassment.

Rod snapped at Sara. "C'mon, can't you be a little friendlier? I just wanted to know about the tattoo."

Michaela uttered, "Please. We're simply not interested."

Sara turned to Rod and Jerry, and barked, "So you want to know about the storm, eh?"

"Yeah, of course, that's all," scowled a determined Jerry.

In an instant, Sara let loose with a furious left hand to Rod's throat and right hand to his gut, and sent her right foot into Jerry's groin.

A worried Michaela responded, "Sara, that's assault!"

"Don't worry, Michaela, only their ego was hurt."

Looking at Michaela and the approaching valet, "Y'all really think those two numb-nuts would go after a little bitty blonde chick? No way!"

As Rod and Jerry fell writhing in pain, the intimidated valet simply said, without making eye contact with Sara, "Ladies, here are your cars."

Sara looked at Jerry and hissed.

"I am the Storm…and now you know!"

87

MIKE

Mike had been looking forward to a homecoming with Sara, and finally, after months of trying to schedule one, Sara was headed back to her parents' home in Northeast Ohio. Driving back from the Cleveland Hopkins Airport, Mike was so excited he didn't know where to begin.

Sara had no intention of mentioning her altercation with Michaela at that bar.

"You know, every discussion or meeting that you and I have had over the last six months, with only small exceptions, has been regarding ETRT issues or problems."

"I know Dad. Sorry."

"Sara, it's not your fault…just saying. Mom is so damn stressed out right now, she's about ready to explode."

"Dad, I know Mom, too. We have always tried to shield her from stuff that she didn't need to know, for that very reason."

"Just wanted to give you a heads-up before you begin updating Christine."

"Dad. I'm no longer Sara Stevenson; I'm Sara Steele. But, I'm still your daughter and you and I have been through a lot since Grandad died."

"For sure."

"This Ohio Turnpike drive looks so familiar. The only difference I see from the last time I visited is so many electric and hybrids on the road."

"Yep, Sara, the price of technology."

"Regarding that…got a question for you, Dad."

"Shoot."

"Have you ever thought about this conundrum? Technology is evolving exponentially and has been in that mode for the last, what, twenty years?"

"Yes. Most definitely. And?"

"And, we have driverless cars, hybrid cars, e-phones and e-watches, wrist holograms and 3D holograms, 8G wireless, voice-activated everything, real-time streaming of every event on a one-inch screen, Moon landings, Mars landings."

Sara thought, "Whoops on the Mars landings"!

"…water desalinization, artificial food, DNA tracing back to the Stone Age."

Mike interrupted, "We have that technology?"

"Which technology?"

"The DNA tracing back to the Stone Age?"

"I'm not positive, but I think so."

"So, where you going with this, Sara?"

"Why are eighty per cent of our planes, trains, and automobiles still fossil-fueled by oil and gas and not by clean or renewable energies?"

"Is that rhetorical?"

"Well, Dad, we at the ETRT and along with our geek friends, are starting to see instances of suppressed technology and I, for one, think energy is one of the main areas."

Mike thought about it for a minute or so.

"I know my Sara. You know the answer to that question…you just don't like the answer."

"Yeah, Dad, you're right."

"Okay, we're almost home. I want to hear more about that 'suppressed technology' issue you raised."

"Of course."

"Sara, let's spend tomorrow doing just plain family stuff. You and Mom can chat, fix dinner, and later we'll have some after-dinner drinks around the fire pit, as we have done a million times."

"Great. And then what major event do you have planned?"

"Sara. Sara. Sara. You are good!"

"I told Mom that you and I were going to a car show on Sunday for a couple hours. Since we know that she hates car shows, it will give us time for you to catch me up on what the hell is really going on here on planet Earth."

"Yeah, I'd like that."

"Then, I can tell your Mom just the bits and pieces that she needs to hear and that she can handle without freaking out."

"Yeah Dad, just like we did in the old times…"

✦ ✦ ✦

Arriving home, Mike and Sara entered the house. Christine came running to greet them.

A smiling Mike noted, "Sara's flight was right on time."

"It is so good to have you back home, even if it's just for the weekend," Christine said happily as the two women hugged.

"It is so nice to be home, Mom. The house looks great."

"Let me take your things. I made a pitcher of cold lemonade," Christine advised.

Pouring three large drinks, the ice cubes clanking while being stirred, Christine was a happy person and at peace with all the craziness around the Stevenson family.

"How is Michaela and your team? How is Matt?"

"Everyone is fine. We all miss Kat, though."

At that moment, Sara thought to herself, "Dummy, why did you bring that up?"

Christine smiled slightly and said, "Such a tragedy… Pete, Paul, and then Kat."

"Yeah, difficult times, for sure," returned Sara

Mike jumped in with his glass raised, hoping to get the ladies' minds off the family tragedies.

"Cheers, and welcome home to our wonderful Sara."

"Cheers," offered Christine.

Mike excused himself and went into his study, leaving the girls to catch up, and addressed his holo-display.

"Orion, show me the colleges that now have advanced degrees in Ufology and Exopolitics?" The new politics of outer space, with curriculums to match, had become a very interesting subject for Mike.

His holo-display immediately brought out twenty-seven universities offering those degrees.

"Wow, how things have changed," Mike uttered.

He knew that his wife's plan was to cook and bake with Sara, something that they hadn't done in many years.

Later, he could smell the aroma of snickerdoodles and Texas sheet cake being baked in the oven.

"Mom, this is great. I've really missed this…so glad I'm here."

Christine hugged her daughter as a strange voice could be heard.

"Sara, you need to set a time with Elonis for next week's ETRT meeting and you need to contact Lieutenant Baker for security schedule for next week."

An alarmed Christine responded, "What the hell was that?"

"Relax, Mom, that's my digital assistant, Aurora, giving me my weekly updates."

"Can't you just turn her off?"

"Of course. Just did. Sorry."

The ladies finished their baking and prepared a prime rib dinner, complete with Yorkshire pudding; that was one of Sara's favorite meals.

Christine set a lovely table and dinner was as special as it ever was.

A smiling Mike offered his opinion on the evening. "I am so happy that Sara and I were able to set up this homecoming. I certainly hope we can do this on a regular basis."

"Dad, I agree. You guys know I will do my best to not have this visit be a one-and-done."

"Thanks, Dear," Christine added.

After dinner, Mike got the fire pit going, and the three happy Stevenson family members made their way outdoors with drinks in hand.

Mike had his favorite, an ice-cold Molson. Christine opened a bottle of Jackson-Triggs Reserve Ice Wine, and poured two glasses for herself and Sara.

Sara didn't really like ice wine, but this was her mom's favorite, so she gladly joined Christine with a carafe.

Sitting around the fire, Mike patiently listened to the mostly small talk, making Christine happy to be talking about little things and family things.

Mike, however, was much more excited about tomorrow's talk, alone with Sara.

Sara had to call it a night, as she had several voice messages to return that evening.

As she said "goodnight" to Mike and Christine, Mike could see that Christine had a genuine smile on her face that he hadn't seen in quite some time.

✦ ✦ ✦

The next morning, as Sara was headed downstairs for breakfast, she was thinking about what she would tell Mike and what she would not tell Mike.

"Good morning. How's everyone this morning?"

"We are great, Sara," Christine said, "and how'd you sleep?"

"Slept well, Mom, and actually got a good night's sleep. It's so quiet here."

"Yep, as your dad often says, "There are no mobsters on Maple Street."

Mike overheard her comment and smiled as he was making a pot of coffee.

As Christine prepared a breakfast casserole, one of Sara's favorites, Christine asked, "So what's the plan for today?"

Mike answered abruptly, "Sara and I are going to take in the car show at the mall."

Sara chimed in, "And I have some remote work to do when Dad and I get back."

Christine offered, "Maybe I should go along to the show with you guys. I can make some sandwiches."

Sara and Mike traded worrisome glances.

Mike quickly shot back, "How about you get a few of our home videos together for us to watch after dinner tonight?"

Sara shrugged, "Yeah, that would work."

Christine thought for a moment and said, "Sure, I can do that."

Mike and Sara were both clearly relieved.

After breakfast, Sara went up to her room to check her media devices and follow up on messages.

Mike and Christine did dishes and cleaned up the kitchen. Neither spoke, but both clearly had things on their minds.

Finally, Christine opened with a little more serious conversation.

"Mike, something just isn't right with Sara. You picking up anything?"

"No. Nothing, other than this young lady has a lot on her plate and an enormous responsibility."

"But she is so quiet and pensive, Mike. That's not like our Sara."

Finally, Christine added, "Well, I'll buy that she has a full plate. Listen, if you can, get her to let you in on the super-secret stuff she's working on, okay?"

"Of course, will do."

"One other thing…"

Mike was getting worried at this point.

"What's that?"

"Mike, find out if Matt and she are getting serious."

Mike was relieved. "Yes, sure will."

✦ ✦ ✦

As Mike and Sara drove in the direction of the car show, Mike spoke.

"If it's okay with you, let's just do a detour and go directly over to the old covered bridge in Newton Falls. We had some fun times there."

"We did," Sara answered. "I remember sledding by the river there before they turned that area into a hardware store."

"Sara," Mike asked while still driving, "I can tell from the last couple ETRT meetings that we had on video, and especially with the ones where you were either in D.C. or Palo Alto, or Utah, that things are getting intense."

"They are. They most certainly are."

"Okay. Tell me what's going on. Not sure if I can help, but I will if I can."

As they parked the car and walked over to a park bench next to the old covered bridge, Sara thought long and hard about what to reveal and what not to reveal. Then she just blurted it out.

"Dad, the aliens are real and they are here right now."

Pausing, "They are a friendly culture and have been helping our civilization not screw things up any more than we already have."

Mike glanced over to Sara and replied. "I figured as much. Just the depth and detail of the new info that the ETRT has now, especially Elonis's updates, sends the message that you are not alone…and haven't been for a while."

"Sorry, Dad, to not be straight with you."

"I totally understand…especially with your mom's constant worries."

Sara knew that her dad was not the kind of man who would be fine keeping secrets from his wife. Mike understood Sara's logic.

"Our ETRT is just opening up so many new cans of worms, I can't keep up."

"So, Sara, you have met them?"

"Yes, the operations guy is named Pulse, and the alien leader is a female named Echo."

"What do they look like?"

"They are taller, nearly seven feet tall, with elongated skulls, smaller ears, and longer extremities. Their complexion is rather bluish. They speak our language, but I am now able to communicate with them telepathically."

"My God," a shocked Mike replied.

"No, it's all good, Dad. They are literally 'masters of the universe' right now and have many keys for our survival."

Pausing a moment, Sara continued. "As you know, Matt and his team have taken A.I. to the next level. Pulse and Echo have helped Matt advance his technology as well."

"So, Matt knows about your relationship with the aliens?"

"Yes and no. It's a need-to-know basis. He has no concept of how far I have gone to connect with the leaders of the alien forces, and for his safety, it will remain that way."

As Sara was preparing to divulge several of Echo's thoughts and concerns, Sara decided not to tell her dad about the hologram, Pete. Not yet.

Mike, needing to get to the bottom line, asked the big question.

"So, what are the greatest concerns of the aliens?"

Sara thought for about ten seconds and answered.

"One, that an evil reptilian culture is here and wreaking havoc with humans to destroy humanity."

Mike was visible shaken.

"Two, that we are totally unprepared to meet the challenges that the cosmos brings.

"Three, that we have lost all touch with consciousness and spirituality."

Sara waited to see if her dad would react to the "religion" slant.

"Four, that we have secret societies throughout the world that have been suppressing technology for decades, and serving their self-centered and destructive interests.

"And five, that our world leaders have become obsessed with atomic warfare, nuclear warfare, and Echo has a summation statement for that."

A serious Mike asked, "What is her summation statement?"

"Once a civilization's expanding technology turns bad, or is used for evil, that culture is doomed!"

88

SARA

Returning from her rather mixed-bag trip to visit her patents, Sara did what Sara does. She began to prioritize the many issues at hand. While in route, she phoned Matt.

"Hey Matt, how goes it?"

"Hi Sara. Good. It's been a while. I hear you went back home for a short visit. All good there?"

"Yeah. Anything new with 'Pete'?"

"No. Everything is still on 'hold' until you get back. Tyreek is just doing some software upgrades to improve the presentation, both the audio and video."

"Great. Headed back to meet with the ETRT. As you know, we have Round Two scheduled with the idiots in Washington."

"Whoa. Little harsh, no?"

"Hell no. Politics is for losers. They can't think themselves out of anything of consequence…just to get re-elected. It sucks!"

Matt could see that Sara was getting annoyed.

"Matt, gotta go. Talk soon and see ya soon."

"Bye, Sara. Thanks for calling."

There was still an underlining fear from leaders throughout the world that devious forces were in place, not only associated with the ongoing ISIS terrorist group that was in place for decades, but also from its spin-offs that had yet to be fully uncovered.

Social unrest due to global economic issues, trade wars, and the heightened evidence of climate change gave leaders of democratic countries cause for concern.

The bombing of the cabin, the break-in at the Stevenson house, and several similar events still made for very uneasy gatherings for the ETRT.

Kat's death and Amanda's kidnapping made for tense and extremely secretive communications and team meetings.

Sara phoned Michaela from the airport as soon as she got home.

"We are preparing to reveal our extraordinary findings once again to Congress."

"Yes, Sara, and I can see a question coming."

"The probable explanation by the many naysayers in Washington D.C. is still going to be that these events are the work of internal terrorist forces, not alien intervention."

Michaela sensed Sara's disdain for all things political.

"What are you going to do, Sara? It was the plain vanilla explanation given by most governments and the military throughout the world, explaining most of the world's calamities without causing fear and panic to grip the world."

"Yeah, heaven forbid we have to deal with the facts, Michaela."

"Hear ya. Adding to the many polarizing discussions is the fact that there has now been a relatively long period void of terrorist attacks and some general quiet. Sara, people are now seeking calmness and normalcy, not conspiracy theories."

"I guess you're right. Just waiting for the next shoe to drop, eh?"

✦ ✦ ✦

Sara had scheduled a brief ETRT update meeting for the very next day, to get reports from her team as to the final presentation issues for the "reveal" in Washington.

Everyone was in attendance, except for Mike, who would patch in from Ohio. This was one of their infrequent update meetings that wasn't a video conference, given the serious nature of crossing the T's and dotting the I's before their meeting.

An absolutely committed Sara Steele began.

"My convictions are as strong as they ever were. We have been laser-focused on presenting our findings to the world, but we have to convince Congress first if we are to have any credibility on the world stage."

Sara could see that Michaela was visibly annoyed. Sara continued.

"This team is so damn good and so damn strong; I cannot have us treated again as we were treated before!"

Mike chimed in on Sara's comment.

"You guys were panned by Congress for a variety of ludicrous reasons, none of which you could foresee happening. The attack on my dad by those politicians was ruthless, but I truly believe it gave us the commitment to overcome the odds and go on the offensive."

Connor added his thoughts with a commanding voice.

"Look. We had strong convictions at that first meeting, and got beaten up. We now still have those convictions, but now we have much more hard science and irrefutable evidence. Let the facts speak!"

Sara reflected. "Thanks, Connor. And, we also have POTUS in our corner and a new set of D.C. congressional committee chairmen that actually have made inquiries to the ETRT regarding our agenda."

Michaela was somewhat surprised.

"I didn't know that."

"I guess I forgot to mention it to you guys. Sorry."

Sara continued her discussion points.

"Let's continue to close the loop on events and evidence that would raise questions with those naysayers before we reveal to the world our new truth and the undeniable fact that aliens were present and are present, and were playing a critical role, even if an occasional frightening one."

Mike added, "The best thing that we can all do is add more meat to the bone to help with credibility. We will only get one shot at convincing the doubters and need to make the most of it."

Mike gazed over to Elonis.

"Elonis, I have a question for you."

"Yes, Mr. Stevenson?"

"You have all the data from the first meeting with Congress, right?"

"I do."

"And, you have every sliver of data with respect to the material that we will be presenting next month, right?"

"I do."

"And, your best asset is your simulation skill, right?"

"Simulations are a strong asset of mine, yes."

"Are you familiar with the human one-to-ten scale that Sara and the ETRT often use?"

"Of course. I am usually the one that makes the calculations."

"Bingo!"

"I'm sorry, Mr. Stevenson, what is a 'bingo'?"

Everyone could see what Mike was doing and held their collective breath for his next words.

"Elonis, on a scale of one to ten, with a ninety-five per cent confidence factor, what positive result would you have given prior to the first meeting by the ETRT in Washington?"

Without any hesitation, Elonis said, "2.35."

"Okay. Now, with the present level of presentation material, documentation and preparation, on a scale of one to ten, with a ninety-five per cent confidence factor, what positive result should the ETRT now expect with their second meeting?"

Without any hesitation, Elonis said, "8.77."

The entire ETRT erupted in applause and even Elonis could be seen with a smile on her rather stoic face.

Sara thought to herself as Mike spoke.

"Storm coming, hell! We are the perfect storm."

89

CAMERON

As the ETRT took on their last-minute tasks, within a month of their meeting with Congress, another of those inexplicable and unexplainable events occurred. The proverbial "straw that broke the camel's back" was forming under a cloak of extreme secrecy.

On one hand, the ETRT hoped for a smoking gun or a truly remarkable event, to enable the team to finally and quickly move forward with their reveal.

On the other hand, the enormous implications of such an event was certainly not what they would have wanted. And the audience, and its victims of such an event, was truly not what they would have needed.

On September 11, 2026, the twenty-fifth anniversary of 9/11, a huge memorial event was taking place in Washington, D.C., the heart and soul of the American republic.

Cameron placed a restricted call to Sara.

"Good morning, Sara; you and the Stevenson family and your incredible ETRT in place and ready to celebrate today?"

"Absolutely, Cameron. How is the outlook for a peaceful gathering?"

"Everything looks good. Our Intel seems to indicate that all will be quiet. But you never know, given today's turbulent environment."

"For sure."

"Sara, it is estimated that some three million people, along with the G12 heads of state, will be in attendance. One member of the G12 will be absent."

"Yes, I read that the representative of the newly established Middle East Sovereign Nation might not attend."

"That's correct. He is remaining home to make sure that all is quiet in a region that was once a hotbed of terrorist activity. This memorial event has been planned for many months, as you know, and was to be the cleansing of those old wounds."

The relative calm was also noticeable in the Mideast and the Korean peninsula. After decades of fighting, killing, and general chaos, it was largely accepted that these regions were now stable.

With the heightened security of the D.C. event now in place and operational, the time to celebrate and heal wounds had come.

Cameron continued.

"In Alaska and Greenland, American radar defense systems are, as usual, in the ready state. I have our military personnel on high alert with the probability still high that some terrorist group could try something horrible to mark the date."

"Thanks, Cameron. Sounds good. Will check in with you later."

"Great. You and your family should relax and enjoy this memorable event."

Then at precisely 8:45 a.m. Eastern Standard Time, two powerful rocket launches were felt and seen, one from the Korean Peninsula and one from the Middle East. Within minutes, DEFCON 1 was in place.

Simultaneously, missiles had been launched from both sides of the continent. By the time they were identified by U.S. defense systems, they were fully launched against two major U.S. targets, one Los Angeles on the West Coast and one the Nation's Capital on the East Coast.

In any and all previous ICBM scenarios, anti-nuclear missiles would have been engaged and the threat would have been met and the catastrophe avoided.

However, for whatever the reason, the tracks of these missiles, as well as their speeds, had become very erratic and the two missiles took on the velocity and trajectory of stealth fighters.

No ICBM's before had ever exhibited this behavior. After significant analysis and discussion, it was determined from both defense installations that these missiles could only be destroyed by detonation over the Northern Hemisphere, with significant damage from debris and radiation.

<Sara?>

<Yes, Echo.>

<Be ready. We are tracking attacks on your country and are monitoring.>

<Oh my God, what should I do?>

<Wait for my instruction.>

POTUS and the Pentagon were notified with the grim news, and the Secretary of Defense instructed President Sullivan that he had only minutes to order a strike against the two missiles.

Gathering his military team together, President Sullivan asked,

"Any updates or options, General Ward?"

"Give me thirty seconds, Cam."

Thirty seconds later, General Ward told the President, "Order the Air Force to shoot 'em down."

Severe panic was obvious, both at the Pentagon, and for the leaders gathered for the memorial ceremony.

Trying in vain, none of the American or allied anti-nuclear missiles could prevent the death of tens of millions of people and the physical destruction of America's heart and soul.

Radiation damage from an Air Force strike on the missiles would be catastrophic.

With no means to prevent this nuclear disaster, the leaders of the free world just hunkered down in the White House emergency bunker and began preparations for the horrific after effects.

President Sullivan uttered his dire prediction, "There was no way to evacuate the millions of likely victims, who are totally oblivious to the pending doom."

Sara, being in contact with Echo, tried desperately to reach President Sullivan, but POTUS proceeded to address the American citizens.

"My fellow Americans, we are under pending nuclear attack. Take cover wherever you are. Pray to God!"

The detonation of the two nuclear missiles by the United States Air Force was less than a minute away.

As the network cameras went black, and the Cabinet members huddled around POTUS in the Oval Office got as quiet as ever, one of the President's aides, Pam Fitzgerald, came running into the Oval Office with cell phone in hand.

"Mr. President, it's Sara Steele. She is frantic, trying to reach you. She says it is of the utmost urgency that she speaks to you. Now!"

"Yes, Pam, give me your phone."

As the President took the phone, an agitated Sara loudly and abruptly screams…"Stop the Air Force strike against those Nukes."

"What?"

"Stop your attack against those two missiles."

"But Sara, I can't do that."

"Cameron, do you trust me…really trust me?"

"Yes. Yes, of course."

"Then cancel the damn missile attack…now!"

Taking a deep breath, he grabbed his direct line phone to the Pentagon and ordered the strike canceled. It took his using two levels of coded info to get his demands met.

The Cabinet, Pentagon officials, and the military were chastising the President's command and yelling obscenities at Cameron for his foolish blunder.

"Sara, it's done. Now what?"

No response from Sara.

"Sara, where are you?"

Still nothing from Sara.

As President Sullivan uttered those last words, literally out of the world of science fiction, a devastating situation took on an extraordinary and unexpected turn.

A noticeable magnetic pulse of enormous size coming from the deepest reaches of the atmosphere, moving at the speed of sound, engulfed the two enemy missiles, rendering their atomic warheads inert.

Within a millisecond, they had been disintegrated.

The four Stealth fighters that were closing in on the two missiles were unharmed, but did witness the massive and complete destruction of the nukes.

Although the Earth didn't stand still, the hearts and minds of all those bracing for disaster certainly did. No lives were lost and no radiation was detected.

A stunned world collected themselves in relief and amazement as President Sullivan came back on the airwaves to make an announcement…an untrue announcement.

"Our fighters have intercepted and destroyed the missiles that were in route to both the West coast and the East coast. We are all safe, thank God."

As nearly everyone in the Oval Office caught their breath, the main question on their minds was obvious.

"Who or what entity was responsible for this nuclear attack?"

Cameron knew the game had now changed. He had only one thought.

"The alien friends of Sara prevented that disaster… how did they do it?"

90

SARA

The enormous challenge to determine the answer to why or what entity was responsible for the attack began almost immediately by each and every nation and socio-economic entity.

However, within thirty minutes of the intervention, and as soon as POTUS could get some privacy, he was in contact with Sara.

"Hi, Cameron. Everyone okay there?"

"Yes, of course, thanks to your newfound friends. I assume it was the good guys?"

"Yep. Echo told me to trust her and I did. And, thank God, you were able to take my instructions and get your direct reports to trust you."

"Oh, they didn't trust me…not at all. 'Dumb bastard,' I heard. But they had no choice. Executive order, where I deal with the consequences."

"Cameron, I'll give you an update on their technology later, but do you know who was responsible for the attack?"

"Not yet. I will get the proper staff collected for the assault debrief. Then I need to figure out how to even introduce the alien counter-attack perspective."

"Good luck with that, Cameron."

"Yeah, I may need your help. Stay tuned."

"But again, the perps?"

"Well, Sara, we thought, and still think, that the First World Order that became such an unfortunate feature in your research, was contained and even somewhat neutralized."

"You said you thought?"

"Yeah. We had their every move under surveillance waiting for evidence to arrest them."

"Oh no. I know where you're going with this, Cameron."

"Yep. It looks like some new or previously hidden Cabal is behind it. And, a very sophisticated secret society, for sure."

"Damn. I don't know what my team can do as far as digging, but I'll see."

"That would be great, Sara."

"We both gotta go. Let's reconnect again… real soon."

"Sounds good, Sara. Thanks again. And please thank Echo as well."

"And thanks again for trusting me."

Sara thought to herself, among other things, with this latest disaster prevented…

"Cameron doesn't know who was responsible, but Echo likely does know."

91

SARA

Early investigations revealed a conspiracy was led by a splinter of the First World Order and was physically conducted by a small cadre of dictators from both sides of the continent.

Cameron and Sara had their first of many discussions.

"Sara, I'd like to give you an update, even though it's preliminary."

"Thanks, Cameron. I'm anxious to hear any facts that you might already have."

"Even though all of the nuclear arms treaties that were in place for those areas were a complete sham, I sense a particularly misleading set of clues has been put into place to keep my investigative team from finding the real truth."

"Sadly, that doesn't begin to surprise me."

"The funding and technology needed to carry out this heinous attack were not within any dictator group's capability. Further investigation also reveals that collusion within the ranks of the expanded G12 may have also played a significant role."

"Well Cameron, now you are entering a whole new set of variables for me."

"Understand. The old G8 had been replaced by an intercontinental committee of 12 leaders, now termed the G12, literally chosen to map and navigate our world from both addressing common priorities to the management and oversight of recurring disasters."

"I was aware of that."

"Of course. The G12, in turn, Sara, appointed a multi-faceted group of global leaders and doers, called the World Council, as you know. They would become accountable for carrying out the policies and procedures necessary in this new worldview."

Sara was waiting for Cameron's bottom line.

"The objective of the World Council, as indicated to citizens around the world, was to create and implement a new sense of Order and Purpose. It is with this World Council that I want you and your ETRT to meet."

"Seriously? That would be great, Cameron, but what about our meeting with Congress?"

"Screw that. A meeting with the World Council is much more important and very timely. You and the ETRT will have tremendous credibility now. I will cancel the meeting with Congress for now."

"Prime time, eh?" Sara spoke with pure excitement in her voice.

President Sullivan advised. "I will put the wheels in motion for you and your team to present what I've heard you call 'the Reveal' to the proper audience."

"Cameron, any idea as to how soon?"

"Sara, I know they have a meeting scheduled for next month in conjunction with the annual Global Economic Forum. It's in Dubai. Can't promise anything, but, unless it's cancelled, I would like you to present the material that was planned for Congress at the World Council meeting, if possible."

"That's aggressive. I love it."

"Thought you would, Sara."

President Sullivan then changed the subject. "What has your think tank concluded regarding the destruction of the two missiles?"

"Well, the ETRT, in conjunction with the key military personnel that you co-joined, studied the complex data surrounding the trajectory of those nuclear missiles, and the extremely incomprehensible manner in which those missiles were neutralized."

"And?"

"And, Cameron, the brain trust and the computing power of both the Palo Alto team and the Utah team, as well as the associated military and civilian leaders that were part of this project, could find absolutely no fact-based scientific explanation for what happened."

"Not even a low probability of explanation?"

"Nope. Not even a 'what-about-this' scenario." Sara was quite emphatic with her point.

"The technology of the stealth-like missiles and random trajectories was unprecedented. And the means that they were neutralized by a magnetic wave whose origin was unknown was also a mystery to the combined group."

"So, Sara, Echo's technology is still untraceable and hidden only to a few of us?"

"That's right. The technology is just a small indication of the vast resources that will, I presume, one day be at our doorstep."

"Fascinating. Devout spiritualists believed it was an act of God. Many entities made feeble attempts to take credit for the interception and destruction of the nuclear missiles."

"I'm sure, Cameron, but what are you hearing from the Intel community and the more curious of the scientific community? Your own 'white hats' in your circle?"

"Good question. There seems to be only one explanation remaining that the vast majority of informed people could make. Scientists and many of Michaela's community are pretty pumped up."

Sara was all ears.

"Current thinking is that it was, and could only have been, that forces outside of the humans on our planet stepped in to avoid the worst disaster the Earth had ever seen."

"So, Cameron, the proverbial clock is ticking as far as keeping this from a chaotic and frenzied explanation."

"Yes, Sara. What's your plan?"

"I will be meeting with Echo very soon. I will likely defer to whatever course of action she decides, if any."

"What do you mean, if any?"

"Echo's advice is almost always the same."

President Sullivan waited for Sara's response.

"Mostly, she will say 'what do you think should be done' when I ask."

"Interesting. I guess that's both reassuring and intimidating, eh Sara?"

"Yep."

"Sara, one more thing."

"And that is?"

"There was just one person from my Cabinet who was not present here in D.C. when the attack was imminent, and that absence has yet to be explained."

"And who was that one person, Cameron?"

"Vice President Samantha Worthington was not here!"

92

SARA

Within only a few days, significant polarization was becoming obvious, both in daily television reporting to the landslide of social media "facts" and opinion.

Sara was in constant communication with her parents and Christine Stevenson had become the proverbial "basket case" of worry and "sky is falling" concern.

A flurry of conspiracy theory activity, that ran the gambit from military to government to religious to political to scientific to just general skepticism, had set in.

It was apparent that no one consensus had established itself as majority opinion. Newspapers were overflowing with very similar front page headlines:

NUCLEAR ATTACK CRUSHED!
WHO? HOW? WHY?
WHAT NOW?

Even with the attack on the United States, the G12 did not cancel the Global Economic Forum meeting in Dubai, as climate change impact on the world's economy was driving the meeting agenda.

The date was set for October 25, 2026, and Sara could not help but think that there were again forces in play that defied logic. Only Sara and Mike could discuss this uncanny coincidence of October 25th, Pete Stevenson's birthday.

Sara returned home to Ohio to spend some much-needed time with her parents and to try to bring Mike and Christine up to speed.

"You guys probably think you are on the outside, looking in, and even though Dad has been entrenched in the ETRT over the last couple of months, things have been happening at an exponential pace over the last week."

Mike smiled at Sara, with a little wink to indicate he knew what Sara's strategy was as far as Christine was concerned.

As Sara thought about her choice of words, she knew she would need to be as positive as possible, since her mom's nature was much more negative and she could easily slip into a very fragile state of mind.

Christine spoke up.

"Honey, should I fix us a couple of drinks?"

Mike replied, "That would be great."

Christine headed to the kitchen and the bar as Mike chose the opportunity to add some clarification.

"I haven't said anything to Mom about your alien partnership, so you need to ease into that…or not."

"Okay, I figured that was a taboo subject, up until now. Choosing my words carefully versus discussing the events of the last six months is not going to be easy."

Sara pondered the inevitable as Christine returned with drinks in hand.

Sara looked at her mom's drink tray and asked, "What are those?"

"These, my Dear, are Vodka Collins."

"Whoa," uttered Mike.

"What's in 'em?"

"Sara, I know you like vodka, especially grape vodka. These are simply Tom Collins, but with Vodka instead of Gin."

"Cool, Mom. They look great. Especially the lemon wedge and maraschino cherry."

Christine added, "Occasionally, when Pete was over, I would substitute his favorite Scotch instead of Gin. That drink is called the Sandy Collins."

"Cheers," said Mike, and Sara had the floor.

"Thanks, Mom. These are great."

Sara took another sip before continuing.

"Well, Guys, I have good news and bad news."

"One of your guys, either Justin or Connor, used to use that 'come on,' right?"

"Yep, Mom, you are very observant, as usual."

Taking a deep breath, Sara let it all out.

"Friendly aliens destroyed the nuclear missiles before they hit their intended targets."

Mike gasped, not believing Sara's direct approach to Christine.

A smiling Christine immediately asked a question that floored Mike and Sara.

"Is this where Pulse and Echo are involved?"

"Excuse me, Mom!" Sara was flabbergasted.

A smiling Christine uttered, "I listened in on several of your conversations with Dad. I knew that Pulse and Echo were two important people in your hunt for the truth; just didn't think they were alien until recently."

"Recently?" asked Sara.

"Well, anytime Mike uses big words and space-type terms that we usually see on the History Channel, I can put two and two together."

Pausing, Christine added two indisputable facts.

"And, Pulse and Echo are certainly not the names of anyone we know."

"Sorry, Mom, for not sharing this with you. Dad and I just assumed that you would get extremely worried when we didn't even know what we were dealing with."

"Well, dammit, you assumed wrong."

Mike was feeling a ton of guilt.

Sara spent the next day and a half bringing Mike up to speed with the technical aspects of the alien intervention, and bringing Christine up to speed with the dynamics of the overall relationship between herself and the alien forces.

As Sara was departing, Mike's question was quite direct.

"I am most excited about the upcoming meeting of the ETRT and the World Council. Please keep is informed as you move forward, all right?"

"Sure Dad. Of course."

Christine was most interested in hearing about Echo and Pulse, from a purely personal nature.

As Sara was saying goodbye to her parents as the airport shuttle awaited, Christine had one last question for Sara.

"So, how close are you and Pulse, anyway?"

93

CAMERON

President Sullivan called Scott into his office in the White House. This was puzzling for Scott, but he left his visit with Matt in Provo and arrived in D.C. as quickly as possible. After shaking hands and handing Scott a dossier and a cold bottle of water, his demeanor became very serious.

"As you know, Scott, Sara and I have been in constant communication over the past week or so. That group of amazing overachievers under your watch have made incredible progress, and now we have the alien disruption piece to add to the mix."

Scott smiled, knowing that this was not why he was in the Oval Office.

"Before we discuss the issues around this alien scenario supported by the ETRT, let me just say that the powers that be have been unable to find any explanation on this Earth for the destruction of those two nuclear missiles. None."

"That is what we had expected."

"So, Scott, it will be up to you and Sara to explain to the World Council in Dubai the hard science facts and latest results of the alien presence."

"Of course, Cam, we have already started work on that presentation."

"So, you know that isn't why I brought you here?"

Taking a sip of water, Scott was listening.

"You know, Scott, power and money are what drives our world today, if not the universe in general, and when coupled with absolute greed, anything of value or worth will be overshadowed."

Scott nodded as Cameron continued.

"I have an obligation to share with you some very disturbing news, outside of your mission, and it's not going to make your job or the work that your fine team is doing any easier.

"Those power and money factors are what is driving the vicious attacks that our nation and the entire world are experiencing."

Scott was getting very concerned about just where Cameron was going with this talk.

"So, Scott, I need to bring you into the loop on some extremely classified and sensitive Intel."

"Cam, I don't even have a basic security clearance and have never been vetted by your office, as far as I know."

"I realize that. No problem. You will have. This will be coming as quite a surprise, so just give me the opportunity to explain."

Scott loosened his tie and was listening, but worried.

"We had identified with a very high degree of confidence that a group of extremely wealthy and influential conspirators had organized and carried out many of these global attacks of the last fifteen to eighteen months."

"Yes, the First World Order cabal under the leadership of the terrorist, Scorpio; right Cam?"

"Yes, there were about a dozen in Scorpio's leadership sphere. We had those perpetrators under surveillance following the staged attack that killed your associate, Kathy Novack."

Looking directly into Scott's eyes, he continued.

"As you know, the reverse GPS technology from Justin and Connor's technology helped immensely in finding the whereabouts of Scorpio."

"Yes. Thank you. Those two are incredible…hell, they all are!"

"Yes. The leader Scorpio is now being held in a remote, maximum security facility in New Mexico."

"So, why do I need to know that, Cam?"

"Because, we are using that Cabal as the explanation for the ongoing attacks and tragedies befalling the world and causing fear and panic."

Scott was beginning to see the strategy of this fabricated revelation and also understood that he was only getting the proverbial tip of the iceberg.

"Why are you telling me this, Cam, as I can't possibly provide any info that your staff doesn't already have? We shared the only photos and documents we had from Pete Stevenson with the NSA a long time ago, and that was very early in this development."

"Because none of that is relevant, and hasn't been for decades, Scott."

"I see an 'oh shit' coming." Scott was getting very nervous, which was out of character for Scott.

Cameron then gave the chilling details of why he brought Scott into the loop. "This terrorist cell was a diversion. The cell themselves didn't think they were a diversion, but they had become a diversion from other, more compelling, obstructions."

Cameron continued. "That First World Order cell was different than anything we had ever encountered in all my years in overt and covert activities worldwide.

"They had unlimited cash, were very well connected to murder-for-hire pacts and, apparently, were determined to bring an anarchy into our world that they, and only they, could rule."

"Diversion, Cam. You said, a diversion…then, a more compelling obstacle? I'm lost."'"

"Okay. Sorry. In the dossier that you now have, you will find a somewhat redacted, but otherwise intelligible account of what we now know is a secret society, a massive Cabal, which has been working globally for hundreds of years, and since 1962, it has its primary roots in the United States.

"It was Scorpio's terrorist cell that diverted us from the real threat, which is this massive secret society Cabal."

Alarmed, Scott could see the sense of urgency in Cameron's words. He also was processing those illegally obtained photos of the centrifuge destruction that he and Mike had discussed.

"Scott, many assassinations are being attributed to them. Their sacrifice rituals are very common and they are now cornering the market in alternative crypto-currency."

"But why…"

Cameron interrupted Scott with a much deeper intent.

"This incredibly strong, resilient, and hidden Cabal has as its main goal to suppress technology advancements that are possible to achieve, just as the friendly aliens have achieved them."

"Examples, Cam?"

"Levitation, time travel, inter-planetary colonization, and cures for a variety of ills, both social and physical."

"Sara is aware of all this, Cam?"

"Only recently. That is why you are hearing it from me now and from her when you get back to Palo Alto."

"On my God!"

Cameron cut him off with a bombshell revelation.

"Scott, this secret Cabal now knows that you and your highly efficient think tank is digging deep into worldly events and seeking answers to questions that, in their minds, could flush them out."

"Damn!"

"So, even though your ETRT doesn't yet have global credibility and is in no way an actual concern for them right now, the mere thought by them that you are a threat puts all of you in great danger.

"It is our opinion that the lives of everyone in the Utah facility, as well as in Palo Alto, is at stake."

Scott thought back to his recent trip to Matt's lab, under the recommendation from Sara to see and experience the Pete hologram, and it was all starting to make sense.

The OMG jumped out to Scott and his thinking became clear.

Scott thought, "The Pete hologram was the canary-in-the-mine metaphor that was the alien's link with Sara to all things diabolical in our world today and what we may be facing in the future."

There was a moment of silence for both men as they thought about the implications and consequences that have now taken front stage.

A very serious Cameron continued: "We have reason to believe that drones flying in restricted air space have taken photos of both your Palo Alto site and the one near Provo."

Scott wasn't too surprised, given the enormity of today's situation.

"But, since I have a Board Seat on your ETRT council, I can create some air and ground security for your facility without drawing undue attention."

"Undue attention from whom?" asked Scott.

"Scott, without divulging any more sensitive Intel, we have members of this Cabal in our Congress, in the military, in seats of world power, and even within our education and scientific communities. This is now Hell on our Earth!"

"Cameron, do you have an immediate plan?"

President Sullivan thought for a moment before responding.

"I'm waiting to hear from Sara, who will be meeting with the alien forces soon, I'm told."

"Yeah, Cam, she said so much to me as well. Helluva place to put that young woman in, eh?"

"Yes, but… She can certainly handle herself. Did you see her tattoo?"

"I did, Cam. *The Storm*. How timely now, eh?"

"Scott, Sara Steele literally has the weight of the world on her shoulders and we can't let her think she is ever flying solo on anything."

"Absolutely not!"

"But, Scott, back to the drone presence. I can't guarantee anything at this time. You must take precautions, and keep this meeting to yourself."

Scott was already making mental notes going forward.

"Here is the dossier backup and latest flash drive that also has fairly current photos and I.D.'s of people in your orbit, sorry for the pun, to enable you to set up firewalls and awareness scenarios for your safety."

Taking the flash drive, Scott muttered, "Thanks."

"It's probably good for you guys to again cross-reference this info with any similar photos and I.D.'s that you may have, old or new."

"Thank you."

As Scott exited, and while peering out the Oval Office window, Cameron's main thought was forming and he felt quite threatened…

"Are we closer to the Apocalypse now than ever before in our history?"

94

SCOTT

With the talk concluded, Scott left the room quickly to address a to-do list that just increased dramatically. He would need to spend time with Amanda as soon as possible to get her in the loop of current issues and current plans, whenever those plans became available.

He and Sara needed to put their heads together soon, as well.

As Scott headed to the airport, he called Amanda. "Hi Dear, just me."

"Hi Scott. How'd the meeting go with Cam?"

"On a scale of one to ten, it was through the roof."

"Figured as much. Sara just called. She's on her way over. Should be here by the time you arrive."

"Good. Typical. She is a warrior, that young lady."

"Yeah, I guess you're right. Just wonder if it's a role she wants, needs, or is just stuck with?"

"Good point. If Ken's flight plan is correct, give us about seven hours from wheels up. You and Sara can catch up until I get home."

"Yeah, Scott, her alien agenda will be a ton to process. I'm ready, just scared as hell!"

"Bye, Amanda. See you soon."

Scott had to be very careful about how much detailed explanation to provide anyone who was not in the loop of current info, but who would be needed to implement a security strategy with hardware and software going forward.

The flash drive with that dossier of info just freaked him out.

Scott knew that both the dossier and the flash drive involved heavy coding, so he would need to schedule meetings with Sara, Justin, and Connor.

His main priority when he returned to Palo Alto was the security plan for California and Utah.

Arriving at the small private airport, he went directly to his plane and was greeted by his pilot, Ken Darragh.

"Hi Boss. How'd the meeting with POTUS go?"

"You know, Ken, just normal end-of-the-world stuff."

"The usual?"

"Yep. The usual." This time, Scott couldn't find any humor in his humor.

Scott sat back in his seat, buckled up, and poured a glass of Cabernet Franc from his favorite Bordeaux region of France.

As Ken completed his flight plan and awaited clearance to take-off, Scott began writing to-do notes for several priorities that were now on his radar screen.

His number-one issue was to have his security people design and implement the best possible safeguards for both the Palo Alto offices and the Provo compound. Scott knew that Cameron would place significant resources at Scott's disposal.

Scott also needed to have a face-to-face with Sara and get Sara's opinion on a host of issues.

Scott wanted a detailed plan for both facilities in his hand within twenty-four hours.

He also envisioned the entire ETRT hunkered down in the lowest level of the Utah compound, which, according to Matt, was designed and built to withstand anything short of a nuclear attack.

As he finished his note taking about twenty minutes later, he called Matt.

"Hey, me again."

"Hi Scott; where are you?"

"Well, Matt, at this moment I'm at 33,000 feet."

"Headed home from the Sullivan meeting?"

"Yes. It was 'off the charts', as they say."

"Anything to share right now, Scott?"

"Well, yes and no. First, thanks for setting up the session with Pete. Sara said it would be insightful. She wasn't wrong about that."

"Yeah, Jeremiah and I thought you'd be impressed."

"Matt, I'll go over the agenda from my meeting when we have a secure venue."

"Totally understand, Scott."

"But first, I have a question and a concern."

"Go ahead."

"What would it take for you to relocate the entire ETRT in your lower-level bunker fortress?"

Matt thought for a half-minute.

"Well, that answers a couple of questions that I didn't even ask."

"Figured as much, Matt."

"So, again, Matt. How long to get the operation moved and up and running normally?"

"Normally?"

"Yeah, odd choice of words, eh?"

Matt had been processing numbers in his head as Scott was talking…

"We can do it in ten to twelve days."

"Start the work, Matt. Start it now!"

95

SARA

The Global Economic Forum meeting involving the World Council was scheduled for a month away, in Dubai.

In addition to the tremendous increase in security for the ETRT and the staff supporting them, this group of relentless researchers needed to work hard to shorten and improve the REVEAL presentation that was planned for Congress, but scratched.

Sara hung a digital banner on their collective work site.

EXCELLENCE, NOT PERFECTION

Sara addressed the group with one primary request and with her observation.

"We need to strengthen the weaknesses in our work, not present just the strengths that we are so fond of. In other words, we must seek to convince that part of the audience that is one hundred per cent skeptics."

"Our goal is excellence…not perfection!"

Michaela interjected, "The ones that believe will not need convincing."

"I concur, Michaela. Plus, we need all the allies we can get."

With that in mind, the team went about their work post haste and Cameron's aide, Mara Wallace, called Sara.

"Through President Sullivan's behind-the-scenes efforts, he was able to get your team the keynote address at the Dubai meeting."

"Mara, that is great news. How the hell did he manage to do that?"

"POTUS has gained a great deal of political capital during his short time in office, and his job approval rating internationally is very high. Sara, he stopped just short of saying that the American ETRT could explain the unexplainable."

"Thank you for the super great news. Please tell Cameron 'thanks' from the ETRT."

"She immediately thought…probably shouldn't have used his first name with Mara."

With the stunning attack recently thwarted, the majority of the World Council's membership was likely to be focused on what the American ETRT had to say.

The team knew that this was not going to be another major waste of time and effort as was the case with the Congressional fiasco.

High-level planning for the meeting was underway, both in Dubai as well as the many departure cities for the many people attending the Summit. There was always an abundance of international visitors in Dubai.

Sensing the incredibly high stakes, the recent air attacks, and the potential negative reception in Dubai, Sara called her dad on their secure phone. She also knew that Dubai, with its huge numbers of international visitors, was now a potential terrorist target.

"Hi Dad; it's me."

"Great to hear your voice. What's up with you and your fantastic outliers this time?"

"A lot, Dad. As you know, we have been asked to address the World Council in Dubai next month and present our current findings."

"Next month? Already? Hell, that's not much notice."

"It's not much lead time for such a major event, and no part of the world is safe these days, even Dubai"

"You're right. What can I do to help?"

"Well, we can't fly commercial or military or even take Scott's plane, for several reasons. Can you help? Any ideas at all?"

Mike thought for a bit and says, "I think I can. Let me get back with you very soon."

"That would be great. Love you."

"Love you, Sara" and they hung up.

Mike was overcome with joy and thought.

"This time I can help…I can really help"

96

MIKE

Mike called an old friend, Nancy Sanders, who had several manufacturing plants both in the U.S. and abroad. Mike did some quid pro quo consulting for Nancy as she provided some mentoring for Sara after Sara graduated from college.

When he called her Virginia office, which was relocated from the Florida Space Coast after that office was destroyed by the rising water and flooding, he is told that Nancy is in her Dubai office, which Mike had hoped.

Mike called Nancy.

"Hi there, Nance; it's been a while, eh?"

"You bet, Mike, but it's so nice to hear from you. What's up?"

They began to briefly catch up, and then he explained his immediate need to Nancy.

Mike always enjoyed working with his "high energy" friend, Nancy.

"Well, I have a big favor to ask on Sara's behalf and I'm not even sure you can help me."

"You know I will if I can; just what is it that you need? I'm vaguely aware that Sara has a prominent role in a West Coast research venture, and if it is anything involving that role, I'm very much interested in helping."

Before Mike could reply, Nancy went on, "I have a lot of respect for your daughter."

Nancy had no clue as to Sara's actual high-level role and the incredible events of the last year. Mike hadn't talked with Nancy for many years, so he never had to tell her before the made-up story that Sara had perished in a cabin explosion.

Mike also believed that the less said to friends and family regarding the cabin attack was best for all involved, especially from a personal safety perspective.

And, Nancy was so far off the radar in Dubai that she was in a great position to now get involved with the absolute minimum of outside details required.

"Well, Sara is the Managing Director of an extremely talented West Coast research team, and they have been working on a number of highly classified projects involving the global warming, international conflicts, and several eco-system research projects."

"All right, Mike, I probably don't want too much detail here, so what is it you need?"

"Sara's team has a meeting in Dubai in a couple of weeks and they don't want to fly commercial, for several reasons."

"If it's a plane ride the team needs, just give me the place and time."

"It's just what we were hoping, Nance. Thanks."

"No problem, Mike. Glad I can help. I won't be in Dubai at that time, but I won't be needing my plane either."

"Good timing, eh?"

"Mike, my newest jet can fly non-stop from anywhere in the U.S. to Dubai."

"Wow. Thanks again, Nancy. I owe you one."

Nancy arranged for Sara and her team to travel from the U.S. to Dubai on her personal jet, and they would be greeted in Dubai by Natalie, Nancy's young friend and business partner.

Mike contacted Sara and all was set. He reassured Sara that all will be okay, as he trusted Nancy as much as anyone he knew.

Even Sara was unaware of who Nancy was, which was also good. But inside, Mike was very concerned and again, he did not provide many details to Christine.

He thought it best not to mention Dubai to his wife… at least not yet.

Mike also was well aware of Dubai becoming a bullseye for any terrorist group trying to maximize cultural diversity in their carnage.

Mike knew that there was the potential of danger waiting for Sara and the ETRT.

97

SARA

Sara's team was assembled in Palo Alto, awaiting the evening arrival of Nancy's plane at the city's main airport.

Although only Sara, Elonis, Scott, and Michaela would be on stage in Dubai, Amanda, Justin, Connor, and Jeremiah would accompany them to Dubai for any back-up needs that the presenters might have.

Sensing the somber mood of the group, Connor did what Connor often does...he offered the newly arriving Jeremiah a joke.

"Okay, Jeremiah, there once was a tribe of snails. It was led by a big, bully snail named Rocko. Rocko teased and tormented Ralph, the puniest of all the snails. So, one day Ralph decided he had enough of Rocko's teasing. He found a guy who had the baddest motorcycle and took off on it to fly past Rocko and show off. Rocko just blew Ralph and the motorcycle off the road."

Justin feigned a yawn as he had heard this one before.

"So, then Ralph found a guy who had the biggest trucks and after looking at several, he jumped into one. He went roaring by Rocko and Rocko just pushed him and the truck aside.

"Undaunted, Ralph found a guy who had claimed to have the fastest car anywhere. Ralph had the guy paint a giant 'S' on the car, and then Ralph took off to find Rocko. He succeeded in blowing right past Rocko, leaving the stunned bully to say, 'Look at that 'S' car go!'

"Get it, Jeremiah, *snails...escargot?*"

"Ah, yeah, I get it. Thanks, Connor."

"Thank you, Connor," Sara sighed. "This is why the rest of the team offered to pay for your ticket to Dubai!"

"Now that's funny," offered Michaela.

As they were talking, a big, beautiful Bombardier Global 7000 pulled up to the hanger.

"Oh my God," said Justin. "That thing is freaking huge!"

Even Sara was surprised and wondered what kind of businesses Nancy was engaged in?

As the sleek and gorgeous aircraft came to a stop, Sara could see the red, white, and blue logo of Nancy's business on the side of the plane. *Aerogroup International*. Most impressive.

Walking down the airstairs from the plane and greeted by Scott and Sara, the dapper GQ-looking pilot introduced himself.

"Hello, I'm Captain Steven Connelly. First Officer Jonathan West is still on board."

"Hello Captain. I'm Sara Steele."

"Hi, I'm Scott Woods. Happy to meet you and so glad you are able to help us."

"Love your plane," Sara said enthusiastically.

"Thank you. We've had it for about four years now. It has made many trips to Dubai from the East Coast, but this will be her first flight from California."

"What's her range, Captain?" Scott was very impressed.

"Well, Scott, she'll do about 8500 miles. So, we can re-fuel here, and as soon as my flight plan is approved, we can get going…non-stop."

Scott quipped, "Doesn't a flight of that length require more than two pilots? Regulations?"

"Yes, it does, Scott. But due to the nature and secrecy of your mission, Nancy wanted to just use her most trusted crew…and that's the three of us."

Sara asked, "So how long to Dubai?"

"Sixteen hours and fifty-five minutes. She holds twenty passengers, so your eight, plus pilot, co-pilot, and Cynthia, our flight attendant, will be just the perfect. We have already re-fueled, so we can load your stuff and get under way."

Sara thought…

"This time it's not the journey, but the destination."

98

SARA

As Nancy's plane arrived in Dubai, about seventeen hours from departure, Nancy's friend Natalie met the presentation team and proper introductions were made.

Natalie quickly advised, "We are planning to sequester you guys at one of Nancy's plants. There are even rooms that you can use so we don't even need a hotel."

Sara was impressed and relieved, and told Natalie, "This is way more than we hoped for. We can't thank you enough."

"It sounds like you and your team have a huge meeting coming up, and Nancy and I just want you to relax and stay focused on the job at hand."

Sara and Natalie seemed to strike an immediate friendship, as they were both type "A" personalities and had an astute ability to focus on the two to three critical issues at hand and not get caught up in the usual business noise.

They each had stories that involved Mike and Nancy and their global business dealings, and each began to appreciate Mike's and Nancy's impact on each other.

As they left the crew and passengers to address luggage and baggage, Natalie took Sara into a small office and prepared a couple cold drinks for the two new friends and Sara opened.

"What are we drinking, Natalie?"

"These 'bad boys' are called Mescal Negronis. Sweet vermouth, ice, Campari and orange zest. Cheers!"

"Cheers. Thanks, Natalie."

Sara thought of her dad's "story time" as she began: "I have one cool story to tell and wonder if you had heard this one."

"Shoot."

"It was back when Dad and Nancy were trying to get a supplier contract from an Asian manufacturer for Dad. Dad's company was thin in technical staff and the Asian company was coming to the States to do a capacity and equipment audit."

"This sounds familiar," Natalie uttered.

"So, they decided to rent a bunch of equipment and hire some local actors to play the parts of the technical staff. The funniest part was that Dad's Operations Manager played three different roles and was never outed."

"Did they get the contract award?"

"Yep."

"Funny stuff," chimed in Natalie.

"Very creative," added Sara.

"Did your dad ever tell you about the wandering inventory event?"

"Nope, that doesn't sound familiar."

"Well, Nancy was seeking financing for an expansion back on the East Coast. Everything was good until the bankers wanted to visit the four manufacturing sites to evaluate inventory levels versus aggregate value."

"Sounds straightforward."

"It does," Natalie winked. "Except for the fact that Nancy needed the funding to buy more inventory."

"Yikes, what did they do?"

"Well, leave it up to those two for resourcefulness. They had all of the inventory in plant number one when the tour began, and then as soon as the tour was over, they loaded the inventory in trucks and moved it to plant number two, just in time for the second tour."

"And, so on and so on for the last two plants. The bankers never did figure it out!"

They both laughed, enjoyed their drinks and the stories.

✦ ✦ ✦

Later that evening Natalie picked up Sara and they went to dinner and spent much of that evening getting better acquainted and sharing a few more stories. Sara was enjoying this much-needed diversion.

"So, Sara, show me your tattoo."

Rolling up her blouse sleeve, "Oh my gosh; here I go again."

"That is really a bad-ass tat! I love it."

"Thanks?"

They soon became very comfortable in each other's company and established a quick friendship. As they shared a local Cognac following their meal, Natalie began another story.

"This incident has a funny side, although it wasn't funny at the time. Nancy was doing strategic planning for a large, multi-billion-dollar conglomerate that had recently acquired several facilities in Europe, mainly in Germany and Belgium.

"Along with two other members of her senior leadership team, we headed off to Brussels for an annual meeting of these businesses prior to our takeover. All was good. We arrived in Brussels, checked into a wonderful hotel, and enjoyed the *Grand Place* in springtime."

"I have seen the *Grand Place* at that time of year, Natalie, and it is breathtaking."

Natalie continued.

"Yes, just beautiful. Well, the next day's meeting proved otherwise. As English was a common language, even in Europe, that day-long meeting was spoken only in German throughout."

"Oh crap," Sara said smiling.

"The message was clear, and we knew we had our work cut out for us in the months and years to follow. Again, never assume; verify."

"Good story, Natalie. I think I have one you'll enjoy."

"Let me get us another Cognac while you get started."

"Sure, that would be great."

As the waiter poured the ladies another drink, Sara began.

"Several years ago, I was working on a project with my dad. We were contracted to conduct a performance survey of several call centers by the Corporate Headquarters in the Midwest."

"And the company will remain anonymous, right?"

"Right. We evaluated five U.S. centers over a period of six weeks. There were several performance categories in our analysis, and what the HQ wanted was for each center to be awarded a score on the one-hundred-point scale. We used as our benchmark the best practices in the industry for an unbiased baseline."

"Sounds interesting."

"With our conclusions in hand, we made our presentation to the Board of Directors on a cold and rainy afternoon. And, the room even got colder.

"What we presented was very disappointing to the Board. The highest score achieved was seventy-three, far below the one hundred seen as especially good.

Well, it is what it is, as they say. The Board had us wait outside while they convened and discussed our findings."

"Looks like a big contract coming, eh?"

"You'd think. About one hour later, we were brought back into the Boardroom for their decision. This old guard had come up with the perfect solution."

"This has got to be good," Natalie guessed.

"They would add twenty-five points to every call center's score, so the best is now ninety-eight. And, what we learned a few days later was that the Board was using the survey data to obtain capital for expansion."

"Really? What happened next?"

"We were never contacted to put a plan together to improve the operations of those call centers. They were fine with their strategy going forward."

They finished their drinks and before Sara returned to her team, Natalie offered more help.

"I am in Dubai often and have met several of the meeting attendees. I can provide you with a significant amount of personal data on many key members that will be in the audience."

"That would be terrific."

"Sara, I'll have a cheat sheet of those members for you first thing tomorrow."

"Thank you so much."

As Sara returned to the team, they were finalizing the next day's presentation. Sara was relieved and much less stressed.

She asked Michaela, "All good?"

"Sara, please be reassured that we are all were ready for the big event."

Sara was pleased.

Finally, she had everything under control.

99

SARA

Sara unpacked her luggage and her business case. The room was small, but comfortable. She felt that everything was falling into place. The master plan, if you will…

As Sara was sitting and combing out her hair, she was relaxed and thought about the many times that Christine and she had talked while combing their hair. It was a good feeling.

Then, just as those sweet thoughts had registered, she could see in her mirror that Pulse had entered the room.

Startled, she stood up, turned around and said, "What are you doing here? Where is Echo? What's wrong?"

<I am sorry if I frightened you. Please be calm.>

"Talk, dammit."

"Yes, of course. Echo sent me."

"Pulse, everything is okay. Plans are made and we have everything under control."

"Sara, Echo feels close to you and admires your leadership."

"So? Why are you telling me this and why does that matter at all right now?"

"Sara, all of our leaders are female. I do not think you know that. That is one of the reasons why she has chosen you."

"Chosen me for what?"

Pulse paused a moment.

"To be close to. Echo wants to be close to you."

"I'm fine with that. So, why are you here on her behalf?"

So, with that comment, Pulse picked up Sara and, in a scene directly out of a science fiction movie, he transported them effortlessly to the *Dubai Miracle Garden*, the world's largest natural flower garden, featuring over three hundred million flowers and plants.

As Sara was picturing herself as Lois Lane in the arms of Superman, she reacted.

"You certainly know how to impress a girl."

And she also thought "what big hands you have" as Pulse set her down.

"This flower garden is always one of my favorite places, Sara, and I thought you would enjoy it. We can talk here in peace and quiet."

Sara noticed that, even at night fall, Pulse was able to majestically create a flowery glow around them that was as beautiful as it was romantic.

"This is beautiful, Pulse; thank you."

Pulse knew that Sara loved flowers. She would give them as gifts frequently.

"I'm pleased that you are pleased, Sara."

"I am Pulse. I truly am."

Pausing, Sara again asked Pulse why he was here.

"Sara, we need a strategy for tomorrow."

"Why? I told you that everything is under control. I have everything under control!"

"Everything is not under control."

"Dammit, Pulse what the hell are you talking about?"

"There will be an attack against you and your team tomorrow morning. A very big attack."

Sara was silent.

Pulse paused for a moment and moved closer to Sara. He then softly grasped Sara's neck and head in his hands, ran his long fingers through her blonde hair, and smiled.

Once she was completely relaxed, he continued. "There will be a terrorist attack on your team tomorrow and Echo wants to know what you want to do about this attack…how you want to handle it."

"Damn it Pulse… I'm scared and confused. If Echo knows about the attack, she can prevent it, right?"

"Yes, that is correct."

"I don't understand, Pulse; if Echo wants to stop the attack, she can."

"Echo said you would think like a warrior princess, which defines Echo."

"So, it's my call?"

"Correct, it is your decision on what we do tomorrow."

"Echo wants me to decide how to handle the terrorist attack tomorrow."

"Yes."

Sara sat back down to think and took both of Pulse's hands into hers.

What a bittersweet situation, she thought. Lovely flowers in a peaceful setting, and yet contemplating an imminent terrorist attack.

"Pulse, tell Echo to let the assault begin, allowing everyone in the auditorium to see what was about to happen. Then, have you and your team intervene to stop the attack before anyone is hurt. That way, the whole world will be introduced to the aliens with the 'white hats' tomorrow."

"Echo thought that is what you would suggest."

With that, Echo bent to one knee and they kissed. Sara wrapped her arms around his neck and they embraced.

Moments later, the seven-foot tall Pulse stood up. He whisked them back to Sara's room.

A stunned but relieved Sara gathered her thoughts.

"Thank you, Pulse. Thank you for everything you do and for who you are."

As she spoke, Sara was feeling a very strong physical attraction to Pulse and was not the least bit uncomfortable that this encounter had happened.

She enjoyed seeing him…she will miss him…if only for a little while.

As Pulse turned to leave Sara's room in a calming bluish haze, he spoke softly to Sara.

"Tomorrow, my Aras. I will see you tomorrow."

100

SARA

The next morning, Natalie arrived with the personnel list she promised Sara and a van to deliver the group to the meeting, under extreme security.

"Good morning, Sara. How'd you sleep? Small but cozy room, eh?"

"Morning, Natalie. Quiet night. Just what I needed. Is that the list?"

"Yes. The red-starred names will be your antagonists, but I believe they will be pretty tame compared to those underachievers in Congress."

Noticing Michaela, Natalie spoke.

"Good morning, Michaela. Ready to go?"

"Ready to kick some butt, for sure."

"Whoa," thought Sara. That response wasn't typical for the serious-minded Michaela.

As the ETRT loaded into a van for their trip to the convention center, each grabbed a light take-with breakfast, Sara was going over every possible attack scenario that she could create. The more possibilities she came up with, the more confusing it became.

Natalie addressed the team. "Good morning, 'A' team. Nancy and I are so happy to be part of this historical day. Hope you enjoy the breakfast snacks."

The team members nodded.

"By way of an explanation, this van will take us to our primary mode of transportation today, Hyperloop Dubai, the first and finest super high-speed commercial transport system."

Justin, Connor, and Jeremiah were overwhelmed, excited, and as geeked as ever.

"You have been staying near Abu Dhabi, which is where Nancy's facilities are located. To get to Dubai, the Hyperloop capsules are vacuum-tube transport systems that will propel you at speeds over six hundred miles per hour."

As the van approached the Hyperloop station, Natalie advised, "You guys would appreciate this system's low cost of implementation as compared to other high-speed transportation methods. It is simpler, lighter weight, and much less energy-intensive."

Oohs and aahs could be heard from the team.

As the they arrived at the Dubai convention center, all looked good; and even though everyone was nervous, they were anxious to begin and to share their game-changing research results.

Sara, however, was anything but calm, as she waited for the final curtain to a meeting that hadn't even started yet.

As the attendees took their seats in the auditorium, Sara and her team looked about at the members of the World Council and recognized several members of the Global Economic Forum, as discussions concerning climate change always led to economic perspectives.

It was certainly an intimidating business environment, no matter what your level of executive presentations had been. Sara recognized several World leaders from Natalie's list and was mentally putting faces to names.

The reality began to sink in as to the stakes and expectations.

Then, Michaela spoke.

"Sara, what's wrong?"

"Huh?"

"You look like you are preoccupied…like you've never done this before. What the Hell?"

"I'm okay. A little stressed. Thanks for asking."

Moving away from Michaela, Sara surveyed the entire surroundings, from the auditorium to the stage to the vast number of support personnel that were in attendance. Everything looked normal. She had lost her focus on the meeting itself.

She thought, "What, where, when, how, and by whom?"

Oddly enough, Sara was not receiving any thought patterns from either Pulse or Echo. That was strange. Why wouldn't she be getting a "heads-up" by now?

She thought, "Would I be getting a 'heads-up' at all?"

Sheikh Mohammed bin Saeed al Nahyan was the Vice President and Prime Minister of the United Arab Emirates and Ruler of the Emirate of Dubai. He spoke.

"Welcome distinguished members and guests to this glorious event. In the wake of the recent attack on America and the subsequent countermeasure that ended that attack, we are so fortunate to have with us an American body of scientists and researchers who have important information to share with us and the world today."

Applause heard throughout the chamber was very reassuring to the ETRT.

A preoccupied Sara thought, "Yep, another day at the office."

Following traditional introductions and hospitality and administrative mentions, the ETRT was about to begin their presentation and Sara stepped to the podium. She was introduced as Sara Steele, Managing General Partner of the International Alliance of Scientists and Space Research.

She thought to herself, "Where the hell did that title come from? Damn, I sound like I am a VIP. POTUS must have done that."

✦ ✦ ✦

The attendees were adjusting their translational head-sets, while giving Sara the requisite applause.

Sara began her presentation with introductions.

"Thank you for this opportunity to share an amazing 'new reality' with this esteemed body and the world.

"I would like to introduce the members of our team here on the stage."

Sara completed the formal introductions of Scott, Michaela, and Elonis.

"Now displayed is our agenda on the many viewing screens within this auditorium, including the main screen behind me."

Sara and her team enjoyed the brief applause and appreciated the obvious focus of each member on their viewing screens.

Then, almost instantly, Sara got a strong and clear premonition that was terrifying. This electric-type psycho-awareness telepathic thought had never happened to her before. She was momentarily dazed trying to process an overwhelming sense of danger.

She paused as vivid images of the meeting chamber whizzed through her mind in milliseconds and she gazed over to Elonis who seemed to be sharing the same thoughts.

Sara received a thought…

<Look toward the former G12 member and meeting co-chair Stewart Shipley.>

Sara could see that he had a hand-held device in his hand and appeared to be engaging it.

Sara leaped nearly twenty feet from her position at the podium and Elonis also leaped from the corner of the stage.

Sara grabbed the man and Elonis removed the hand-held device. It was a control box that appeared to be the timing device.

All motion had stopped.

Stunned, Sara could now see that no one else in the entire auditorium was moving, except for Elonis and her. Even Stewart Shipley had now become motionless.

"Elonis, what is happening?"

Suddenly, Pulse appeared, before Elonis could answer.

<Sara, the man that you and Elonis have now secured is the leader of the Cabal that has been responsible for the terrorist attacks and technology disruptions taking place around the world for many years.>

<What was their plan, Pulse?>

<To launch a missile from one of their secured communication satellites that was aimed at your meeting site.>

<But Pulse, the assassin himself, Shipley, would have been killed.>

<It was his intention to launch the missile with a thirty-minute delay, to allow him time to excuse himself and head to an awaiting vehicle.>

With all motion still frozen, Sara noticed that only the three of them were moving.

A puzzled Sara thought,

<Pulse, what will we do?>

<Echo wants the attack to proceed, as you suggested, but with her outcome in mind. She wanted you to know what would happen.>

<I don't understand, Pulse. What will happen?>

<Time was stopped with your apprehension of Stewart Shipley. When the time-slip continues, you will announce the following...>

✦ ✦ ✦

It is now real-time.

Sara and Elonis have leaped to their positions, securing co-chair Stewart Shipley and his hand-held device.

The audience is stunned and alarmed with the action that Sara and Elonis had taken.

Sara grabbed the microphone from the podium and began her explanation...loud, but firm.

"I am sorry to alarm you, but an attack is in process and we have taken immediate action. Mr. Shipley has a timer to a detonation warhead for a missile about to be launched from a satellite in our atmosphere."

There was silence from some attendees and gasps from others.

"I will explain everything soon, but for now, you need to listen...and listen closely."

Sara had gotten the attention of nearly everyone in the audience.

"It was Mr. Shipley's intention to launch the missile, excuse himself from the meeting, and be far away before the missile struck, killing everyone here."

Loud screams could be heard from many in the audience. The others were waiting for Sara's next words.

"It was also his intention to place blame for this massacre directly on me and my team, as a selfish act of a radical suicide bomber."

A voice from the third row of the meeting could easily be heard.

"Miss Steele, why should we believe you and this outrageous story?"

"Because, the missile has already been launched from that satellite."

Silence.

"It is set to impact our location in twelve minutes and thirty seconds."

101

SARA

With that dramatic disclosure getting everyone's attention, Sara continued. "Be calm, please be calm. We now have control of the situation. Everyone will be fine. Please, stay calm."

Slowly, the attendees were gaining comfort from Sara's demeanor and her conviction. As the assembly room got manageably quiet, Sara continued.

"My associate, Elonis, is a meta-human and has been by my side for two years now as we have been introduced to a culture of benevolent aliens that are here now helping mankind and have been here literally for centuries."

Still, the chamber was fairly quiet. Sara continued.

"These friendly aliens were the ones who destroyed the nuclear missiles in route to two targets in the United States last month."

The man with the earlier question interrupted.

"But, the missile? What about the missile about to strike us?"

"Let me introduce you to my alien friend, Echo, who will answer that question for you."

With that announcement, a very intimidating battle-dressed Echo appeared, smiled at Sara, and spoke.

Sara noticed that Echo had a new battle sabre in her hilt.

"We are from another universe, another galaxy, and another time, and have been on this earth in some form for thousands of years."

With some members still in late stages of physical suspension, each person's cognitive capacity was slowly being regained.

As each person's full mobility was restored, they were able to understand everything that was occurring since the time-slip.

The alien who spoke appeared to the attendees to be the visual leader, a tall female in a bright blue warrior-type uniform and with a decidedly soft speaking voice.

"Our home is an Exoplanet one hundred ten light years away in the constellation you call Leo."

She calmly and confidently continued.

"We have major colonies today in what you refer to as the Trappist-1 System, where seven planets exist."

Waiting briefly for a response, she continued.

"We began as observers, and throughout your history, we have tried to help mankind many times, but not always successful. We will not harm you."

The entire chamber was quiet and subdued, trying to understand the words and gauge the intentions of this alien leader.

"But the missile? What about the damn missile?" The same concerned man snapped.

Echo responded in a soft and reassuring voice.

"If each of you will look out the ceiling skylights, or any of the side windows on my right, you will be able to see the incoming missile."

The attendees moved to where each could get a glimpse of the approaching missile.

"We will eliminate that missile in… eight seconds; seven, six, five, four, three, two, one…gone."

A bright flash of a bluish-white haze took over the entire sky. What could be observed as a rapidly moving rocket or missile was moving very quickly towards them one moment and suddenly, in a flash, it was gone with no apparent effects of debris, radiation, or even any noise of any kind.

A respectful applause and much relief followed Echo's words and the destruction of the missile.

"You owe your gratitude to this young group of humans, who with tremendous courage and conviction, were able to take the clues of the past and put this puzzle of our involvement together."

Sara was moved by her mentor's words.

"We would have preferred to remain behind the scenes, as we have been for centuries. The ultimate survival of this planet brought us to this day and time."

Now, the dramatic incident and scope of the sudden alien presence was revealed for the first time. Several aliens appeared, in the formation of a triangle, and all in different colored uniforms.

Sara could now see Pulse and Laser, along with Spirit and Peace, among the aliens gathered by Echo.

The attendees, mostly frightened and overwhelmed, could see that the aliens amongst them had an almost uncanny resemblance to the humans, except for being taller, with smaller ears, somewhat elongated skulls, and slightly longer extremities.

Peace moved slowly to comfort two women who were weeping.

Spirit took a small group of attendees and began explaining to them what Echo had described.

Laser signaled for several in his command to disperse into the crowd and console those who were most in need.

The entire auditorium became peaceful…it was as if they were in a church, or chapel, or some religious or spiritual arena. They were here, yet they were somewhere else!

Laser removed three people from the World Council leadership committee, in addition to Stewart Shipley, and contained them near Sara and Elonis, per instructions from Echo.

Many in the audience tried unsuccessfully to text or phone others. There would be no outside communication. All contact modes were dead.

Echo began her detailed explanation.

"The three people we now have were the principle leaders in this terrorist plot, along with the man that Sara and Elonis had contained. He was the leader of a large conspiracy to destroy significant portions of the world's infrastructure, and replace it with a radical socio/political oligarchy."

Frenzied movement and chatter were now being replaced by awe and bewilderment.

"It was also their intention to suppress significant advanced technology development worldwide. I will address that issue soon. An example of their hidden advanced technology was that highly sophisticated missile that we destroyed."

The alien leader sensed a calming of the audience and continued.

"My Earth name is Echo, and when you thought you were alone, you were not. It was my team that disrupted the recent attack on the two American cities, knowing the devastating consequences."

A very relieved Sara smiled. Echo glanced her way and gave Sara a broad smile.

"We must leave you soon as we have many other planets, with cultures and societies in need, in other galaxies in our universe. As difficult as this may be for you to understand… we are humans from the very distant future."

With that comment, Sara realized that a whole new "normal" perspective had been revealed.

"We are you, with evolution that takes millions of years. We have God in our hearts and minds, and share your spiritual values. We are likely closer to God than you, not physically, but spiritually."

Sara, Elonis, Pulse, and Echo joined hands in a gesture of unity and strength.

"We will leave behind several capsules that will explain much of our involvement over the past centuries and also provide the technology that will help to navigate the changing world that is now upon you."

This announcement was one that Sara had not expected.

"And, we strongly recommend that you form a coalition between this young, selfless group of believers and the World Council. These perpetrators of destruction are identified and appear before you. But others exist."

Pausing, Echo advised.

"Recognize these people as bad people that will cause you harm. We will be taking these four involved in this attack with us."

There was no pushback from anyone.

"You will need to identify and stop those who still remain amongst you. After this message from us today, and the capsules left behind, that should be easier."

Echo glanced over to Sara before she added one last piece of wisdom.

"You have in your society what is called the Law of Polarity." Pausing, Echo offered a teaching moment.

"That Law states that everything that exists has an equal and exact opposite. That is, anything that comes into existence will have the manifest opposite come into existence."

This recurring theme was not lost on Sara as Echo continued.

"Humans cannot experience sadness without having an idea about happiness. Light cannot be experienced as such if you do not know what darkness is. And you cannot experience bad or evil without understanding good and righteous."

Sara, reading her thoughts from Echo, knew what Echo was about to say.

"This Law of Polarity applies directly to alien civilizations, too…all alien civilizations have good and evil."

102

ECHO

As Sara spoke momentarily with her host, Sheikh Mohammed bin Saeed al Nahyan, Echo, and Pulse had positioned themselves in the center of the meeting chamber for an announcement regarding the capsules that Echo had referred to.

As the capsules were being arranged and identified, Echo moved over to the capsules and explained to the entire audience.

"Here are *eight capsules* that will provide you with the tools and capability that you will need to learn, refine, and implement significant technological change."

Echo demanded, "The team led by Sara Steele will be in charge of implementation. There will be no negotiation of that edict."

After a brief pause…

"Let the world know that Sara Steele and the ETRT have our support and will be the sole drivers for this technology."

Echo abruptly said, "What we are giving, we can take away."

Sara was overwhelmed, but very pleased to hear Echo's complete trust and confidence in her and her team.

The attendees surrounded the capsules as Echo spoke.

"*Capsule 1* will show you how to desalinate the oceans and provide fresh water to serve the world's growing population. It will also begin to allow the subsidence of sea level rise to recede. This will combat global warming as the polar ice caps will not rebuild themselves.

"*Capsule 2* will explain how you can ionize the atmosphere to significantly reduce destructive hurricanes and tropical storms when they reach their biggest threat. It will also demonstrate how to bring water from even a dry atmosphere to use to fight the immense wild fires.

"*Capsule 3* will show you how to use the vast resources on your planet to produce enough food to eliminate hunger and starvation, even in the most underdeveloped countries. As you will see, agriculture is driven by solar and wind energy, not by the ever-depleting coal and oil assets.

"Capsule 4 will allow you to gather the correct ingredients to manufacture the necessary drugs to cure many of mankind's diseases and eliminate famines totally around the world. It will also substantially reduce worldwide medical costs for drugs and service.

"Capsule 5 will enable you to create the strongest metal known in our universe, from materials on this planet, such as platinum, aluminum, iron, and from meteors that you will be able to capture. This material can be used for a variety of industries and can be liquefied for other applications.

"Capsule 6 will provide you with a process, including several fundamental scientific breakthroughs, to take your current weak A.I. technology and create a path for machines to successfully perform any intellectual task that a human being can and possess full consciousness.

"Capsule 7 will provide tools to better understand human DNA and how to identify and wash elements of DNA. It is common knowledge that human DNA was designed and manipulated by extraterrestrials, and research on the human genome is already verifying that fact.

"Capsule 8 will rapidly accelerate worldwide solutions to global warming. In the nearly ten years of the Greta Thunberg climate change improvement target of 1200 points in levels of achievement, your Earth is still below 500 points. Your planet is dying because of this problem."

Echo appreciated the attention being paid to her words.

"What we are providing you with are seeds, not pills. These capsules are not magic wands and will not be immediately implementable."

She paused. "They will require your best minds and your absolute patience to reach the final results that will then be extremely beneficial."

At this point Michaela could be seen taking notes.

"As I have said before, your current Artificial Intelligence, Information Technology and general scientific technology will enable you to develop and master the knowledge that is here. In our minds, your greatest threats will come from humankind itself, from within, and not natural disasters.

"Absolute power corrupts absolutely. Fear and power will no longer drive society, economies, and governments...technology will!"

After a long pause for all to absorb what Echo had just said, Sara spoke.

"Echo, we are deeply indebted to you, not only for your involvement today but for all that you have done for mankind in the past. Why are you revealing yourselves now, and with these amazing gifts?"

Sara knew the answer, of course, but needed all those assembled to hear it as well.

"We have helped civilizations before, but those not nearly as advanced as yours. With the Mayans and Egyptians, we had to provide the tools and technology that wasn't available to them back then.

"As I have said, you have the technology and just need to further develop that technology."

Sara was hanging on Echo's every word…

"These capsules are not simple solutions, but will still require much time to master. They must be developed, monitored, and controlled by only those people that have the greater good of mankind as their mission."

After another brief pause, Echo went on.

"At one point we had to step in and remove the Mayans from Earth and relocate their civilization to another planet, as infighting and internal strife was becoming their downfall."

Echo could see a mixture of fear and hope among the attendees.

"Although the entire world and human race was suspended in time during this ordeal, we have blocked all memory of our engagement from the minds of the world's population. Only the people assembled in this auditorium are aware of us and what took place today."

Sara could see confusion and consternation in the eyes of many present.

"To reveal to the world all that you have seen today would result in mass panic, hysteria, and even the likely demise of religions as you know them.

"Sara, her team, and these members of the World Council will be the ones that must take today's events and put significant change initiatives in place and soon."

Pausing, Echo attempted to close her remarks.

"It is the proper choice, again, given the fear and chaos that our presence here on Earth would involve, that this selected group will become the torch bearers.

"The greater the misery…the greater the peace. You will come out of these events stronger and more determined than ever before."

Echo then summoned Sara and her team of Scott, Michaela, and Elonis, and through telepathy addressed them.

\<The concept of time travel is difficult to comprehend, but time, as you know it, is about space as well. Basically, time will speed up as gravity decreases, so time will go by faster in the universe.\>

\<Time travel is not mysterious; it is science and the fabric of astrophysics and it will be attainable in Earth generations yet to come. It also means that evolution of the species will occur more quickly too.\>

\<Although this may not be immediately understandable, it may help to explain our advanced technology and how and why we are who we are today.\>

Echo added information, again through telepathy.

\<Pete Stevenson was our chosen one and our link to you. He was, in our opinion, the best human option to get the truth from the clues he found.\>

\<Mike's dreams were not purposely planted, but images upon which the dreams formed, were teleported\>

Sara now knew that all those dream sequences had a purpose.

\<And what Mike called *Significant Emotional Events* were adjusted from actual events for him to carry on his dad's work.\>

\<Sara was the final piece of the groundwork that we tried to lay, and she is now our gift to the universe…your warrior princess.\>

\<We believed that it was extremely important to have this alien revelation brought about through humans, with significantly more credibility than mere evidence of the past, and that was our intent.\>

\<We wanted the past evidence to convince the leaders of the world of our presence, but that did not happen. Unfortunately, the tragedies of late, and the assassination attempts today, forced us to appear.\>

Echo's demeanor took on one of humility.

\<All the people of the world owe their gratitude to the strong, young people of this amazing team, and for Sara, the children of the world are yours to nurture.\>

As Echo disconnected with the ETRT, she telepathically said to Sara and to Sara only, one remarkable thought.

\<Your grandfather is here. You have found him. When you next see him, tell him "thank you from Echo."\>

103

PULSE

A t this time, Sara found herself beautifully connected to these benevolent visitors, with an ebb and flow that was curious, but did not seem unusual.

At that moment, glancing over to Pulse and Elonis, the three of them seemed as much "family" as friends.

Sara was also having a physical attraction to the wonderfully kind seven-foot alien Pulse. The way he conducted himself in Sara's room the night before the attack was scary for its content, but magical as well.

As a behind-the-scenes participant in much of Echo's narrative, Pulse then came forward with a true transformational litany for Sara and Elonis.

<Echo was not finished with her advanced technology capsules. There are still eight more capsules that were meant for your eyes only.>

<Confused, I am, Pulse.>

<Sara, the eight capsules that Echo presented to the World are, of course, meant to help all of mankind get ahead and improve life as quickly as possible.>

Sara and Elonis were listening attentively.

<Echo has been trying for hundreds of years to achieve three main goals for humanity on Earth.>

He paused.

<Her *Goal One* has been to grow mankind's level of consciousness.>

Pulse could see that Sara was not looking favorably on that one.

<Her *Goal Two* has been to grow mankind's understanding of true spirituality.>

Sara thought, "Not happening."

Pulse, of course, picked up on that thought.

<Her *Goal Three* has been for the masses to demand the release of suppressed technology.>

Sara's thoughts on *goal three* were a combination of "what" and "from whom?"

Sara glanced over to see Echo engaged in an intense discussion with about a dozen dignitaries, and Sara was very excited that this incredible day was ending on such a high note.

What was even more satisfying for Sara was to see her closest friend and key ETRT member Michaela Marx along Echo's side as if both parties were co-explaining the cosmic phenomena as if they had done this dozens of times before.

Then, it got even better.

Pulse began his explanation.

<Here are the remaining capsules that will be under your leadership, Sara, and yours alone to evaluate, understand, and implement.>

<Pulse, Echo already said that I would have total control of her eight capsules, regarding implementation.>

<Yes, that is correct. The ones that I am about to introduce to you will not be seen by anyone else but you and your team. These *eight capsules* are that extraordinary, and their revelation could be dangerous to your society if they were in the wrong hands.>

Pulse began his unimaginable presentation.

<*Capsule 1* will provide the entire plans and materials needed for terraforming Mars, a technique that we have used for thousands of years. Earth's technology will be able to use massive reflectors and mirrored devices to bring heat and light to Mars over a three to five-year period, rather than tens of thousands of years.>

<*Capsule 2* will give you a blueprint for taking the Artificial Intelligence that will be in the ongoing development stage from Echo's Capsule 6 to the very essence of General Artificial Intelligence or Super A.I. where androids will perform any of mankind's needs in a socially responsible manner.>

<*Capsule 3* will enable you to understand and positively adjust significant weather patterns around the world. It will also enable you to manage space weather and geo-magnetic energy, which will become a source of opportunity for total climate management, or for dangerous consequences, if managed poorly.>

<*Capsule 4* will teach you how to levitate and use various anti-gravity or negative gravity methods to your advantage, especially when colonizing other planets, by developing the upward forces necessary to cancel out the weight of the object so the object does not fall or rise, but can be steered.>

<*Capsule 5* will enable you to travel back and forth through time, using a four-dimensional fabric called Spacetime. Forward time travel is relatively easy, because it is based on speed. Backward time travel is risky, because it alters disease, catastrophes, and mortality. Reverse time travel was responsible for many of the major worldwide plagues and epidemics.>

<*Capsule 6* will address quantum teleportation, which is our proven process of transmitting atoms or molecular combinations, in their exact state, from one location to another using state-of-the-art communication and sharing quantum entanglement between the sending and receiving location.>

<Yes, Sara, one day you will be able to say to your superior, Scott Woods, "*Beam me up, Scotty!*">

<Seriously, Pulse?>

<What can I say? I'm a big fan!>

<*Capsule 7* will enable you to perform superluminal spacecraft propulsion, also known here on Earth as warp speed, traveling at speeds greater than the speed of light by many orders of magnitude. Today, we can travel from Earth to the Andromeda Galaxy in twenty minutes, even with heavy traffic.>

<Pulse, now that's funny.>

<*Capsule 8* will give you a blueprint for how you can defend your planet, if or when the time comes to do so, with much of the technology that was just presented, a strong mastering of Full Artificial General Intelligence, accelerated evolving technologies, and the use on antimatter micro-reactors.>

<So, Pulse, very impressive… very exciting…very complicated.>

<Yes, they will, of course, change Earth's history…change Earth's fate.>

<So, Pulse, Echo has her eight and you have your eight. Interesting.>

<Sara, Echo is not only spiritual…she loves symmetry.>

<Funny comment, Pulse. I am impressed with your sense of humor… I like it.>

<Trying to assimilate, Sara.>

With the transformational work done, the alien visitors waited for a small cylindrical tube that was descending to open.

Echo walked over to her team, then turned to the still-stunned audience.

"Goodbye and we implore you take these lessons learned to heart. We will not be back, as there are over five thousand planets in this solar system, and it is our obligation to help as much as we can."

Pulse sensed Sara's surprise and let her know that they, Pulse and Sara, were now linked. He used the word "forever" and Sara smiled at him.

Echo raised her voice slightly and proclaimed.

"Nearly every star in your night sky has at least one planet in its orbit. And, it was not our choice to reveal our presence, but the attacks on your world gave us no option. For planet Earth, this is *the end of the beginning.*"

Pulse made eye contact with Sara.

<Echo told your grandfather the same thing.>

Echo felt the intense interaction and growing attraction between Pulse and Sara, smiled, and ended her remarks.

"We ask you to always seek the greater good, and we do expect that you will make the most of your second chance…with the technology that we provided to you today."

Echo raised her hands into the air, in a majestic and inviting sort of way and finished with words that actually "echoed" through the chamber.

"Do what's right, do it together with people you respect and trust, and do it to the best of your abilities."

In an instant, Echo, her close and apparent second in command, Pulse, and the remaining aliens were gone via the small spacecraft, as quickly as they appeared. As they departed, Pulse looked over to Sara and telepathically communicated.

<Goodbye, Warrior Princess… Until we meet again.>

104

SARA

At that moment Sara felt an intense connection, a very strong and loving connection, with this particular alien, Pulse, and recalled their first meeting.

It was physical. It was spiritual. It was mental. It was new…

Many times, Pulse had called her by the name Aras, and as the Warrior Princess. Sara even recalled Grandad calling her by the name, Aras.

She thought to herself, "I have never experienced such a surge of energy and strength with my beloved and deceased husband Paul or with Matt, as I have felt at that very parting moment with Pulse."

Looking up into the sky, and in a strange but beautiful way, she had a sense that she knew Pulse from her past and that they would meet again in her future… in her not-to-distant future.

Every attendee in the auditorium had long since regained their complete physical capacity, and all of the present leadership heard the words of the benevolent alien leader, Echo.

Sara immediately thought of Paul and their joint concern for mankind in the future, especially the children of the world.

She thought, "If only Paul were alive today to see what had just happened."

Without much time to reflect, Sara, her team, the group of assembled key people and world leaders, and the remaining members of the World Council were left to contemplate what had just happened. But would they work together to make their world better?

Before that group had the time to re-group, a chilling thought entered Sara's mind. She spoke quietly to Michaela.

"We have just experienced a benevolent force of alien beings from the very distant future, and are, of course, very thankful."

She paused as Michaela listened.

"Why won't they be back? What about the evidence that surfaced earlier in our research that other alien forces may be in route to Earth? Will they arrive in

100,000 years…or tomorrow? When they arrive, and they will come, will they be friendly or, as Grandad said, evil?"

But, with the wheels spinning in her head, one more thought came to Sara as she surveyed the stage and podium of the chamber where the meeting was to begin but never even started.

It resulted from Echo's comment that her grandad was still here and to thank him.

She had Elonis come over so they could share Sara's thought.

While she waited for Elonis, the startling remark by Pulse regarding Warrior Princess was by no means lost to Sara. What, when, where, why?

Elonis arrived.

<What can I do for you, Sara?>

<Echo said that when I next met with the hologram Pete, I should thank him on behalf of the aliens for his support of their work on Earth.>

Pausing…

<Even after Pulse had upgraded the hologram's consciousness, Elonis, the hologram of Pete couldn't express feeling of love, caring, or thankfulness.>

<Sara, he can now.>

With that comment, Elonis disconnected from Sara telepathically and left the area to begin gathering their presentation materials.

Once clear of Sara's thoughts, Elonis thought to herself.

"If only Sara knew that I have already been to the future with Pulse and I now am capable of foretelling that future.

"I could also explain the meaning of Aras to her. I will respect Pulse's request to not share this with Sara. Not yet."

The team gathered their belongings for the return trip to Nancy's plane via Hyperloop Dubai. Sara gave off the obvious vibe that she wanted no conversation at all…She just needed time to think…alone.

Then, as Sara departed the Hyperloop and was returning to Nancy's plane for the trip home, Natalie stopped her with a message.

"So, you saw everything, Natalie?"

"My God, yes. I still can't believe what I saw and what these people here all witnessed. And Echo…what an awesome female alien. Did you know her before?"

Lying to Natalie, "No, not until today."

"Damn, I like her. Oh, by the way, she gave me a note and a small digital drive to give to you."

Taking the note and device, Sara simply said "thanks" and headed to board the plane, curious about what the strange note said.

Once seated, Sara put the digital drive in her purse and opened the sealed envelope and folded open the note from Echo that Natalie gave her.

Dear Sara Bear,
If you are seeing this note, my body is gone,
but my spirit and mind live on.
Pulse took me into the distant future.
Evil aliens exist and they will come to Earth
to bring death and destruction.
You must listen to Echo.
You must follow Pulse.
You are the Warrior Princess.
Love you,
Grandad

With the passengers getting settled in their seats and chatting back and forth regarding the "miracle in Dubai," a euphoric atmosphere was being enjoyed by all.

Sara wasn't celebrating. She was overcome with emotion.

This roller-coaster ride from surviving a nuclear attack, to a note from her deceased grandfather in the possession of an alien, was clearly an indication of how the rest of her life would go.

As their plane rolled down the runway and departed the Dubai airport, Sara sat back to relax with a warm cappuccino given to her. She closed her eyes and tried to process all that had happened in the last twenty-four hours... the last sixty minutes.

As she sipped her cappuccino, Sara had a thought.

"Her beloved Paul and her terrific and kind friend Matthew had so many wonderful qualities.

"The only quality that they did not share was a sense of humor."

Sara would have an interaction with the hologram of Pete as soon as she returned, and she would find out exactly what the note was referring to, and what must be done.

Even more importantly, she would need to contact Mike and Matt as soon as she returned and, along with Scott and Cameron, tell them that *Project Zeus* was now a "go" and to start making plans for the starships.

That mental note about Earth's artificial satellite-type Moon will have to wait…

Her last thought before she slipped off into sleep was that things had become more focused and to a great extent, at least "priority number one" was now crystal clear.

'We just need to get to work with those damn capsules.'

At that very moment, three alien spaceships, heavily cloaked, landed in obscure rural areas of Europe, Asia, and North America. Within minutes of landing, the door to each space craft opened and several heavily armored and battle-helmeted aliens emerged with weapons drawn. They slowly descended down a lowered ramp to the ground. They did not morph into earthly human forms. Within a few seconds, each space craft then sent a red optic signal to a spaceship thousands of miles beyond the orbit of International Space Station II. Revealed and also cloaked was the mother of all warships, the size of a major American city.

COMING SOON IN 2020

Book 3 of the *STARGATE EARTH SERIES*:

WARRIORS OF THE GALAXY

ABOUT THE AUTHOR

Garry J. Peterson is the author of several books, both fiction and non-fiction, following a successful career in international corporate management. His most recent non-fiction book is a "how-to" business book, **Who Put Me in CHARGE?**

Garry has also completed a companion Implementation Guide for this book, **Getting to the NEXT LEVEL.**

As a former consultant and business coach, Garry now spends his time writing science fiction thrillers and conducting both motivational and subject matter speaking engagements.

Garry has written over 300 trade journal articles, white papers, client presentations, and website content. He has given commencement addresses and public service keynote speeches.

He has a passion for hard science fiction and weaves personal stories, humor, and visionary thinking into his writings. His current writing project is a five-book science fiction series, **STARGATE EARTH** beginning with his recently published book one, **SHATTERED TRUTH** and book two in the series, **ALIEN DISRUPTION.**

Garry lives in Florida with his wife Vaune. He plays in a competitive softball league and is an avid scuba diver and kayaker. Their daughter, Sarah, lives in San Francisco.

Visit his website at: www.garryjpeterson.com.

You can also follow Garry on Facebook, Twitter, and LinkedIn.